The Dowry Bride

The Dowry Bride

SHOBHAN BANTWAL

KENSINGTON BOOKS

http://www.kensingtonbooks.com

KENSINGTON BOOKS are published by

Kensington Publishing Corp.
850 Third Avenue
New York, NY 10022

ISBN-13: 978-0-7582-2031-8
ISBN-10: 0-7582-2031-6

First Kensington Trade Paperback Printing: September 2007
10 9 8 7 6 5 4 3

Printed in the United States of America

Acknowledgments

No project of mine can begin without offering a prayer to Ganesh, the god who removes obstacles and grants wishes. So, my initial salute of thanksgiving goes to Him.

I want to thank my daughter, Maya, my most ardent champion. I couldn't have done it without you.

My sincere appreciation goes to my agents, Stephanie Lehmann and Elaine Koster. Thank you for putting your faith in me and patiently guiding me through this exciting yet bewildering process.

My heartfelt thanks go to my warm and supportive editor and publisher respectively, Audrey LaFehr and Laurie Parkin, for taking a chance on a new author. To the two other lovely ladies, who are so enthusiastic about my book and working hard on my behalf, Magee King and Joan Schulhafer, a special thank-you. The editorial, production, marketing and sales staff at Kensington Publishing richly deserve my gratitude and praise for a job well done.

Dorothy Garlock and Anjali Banerjee, I cannot even begin to thank you both for your generosity. Despite your bestselling author status and hectic schedules, you gave me such prompt and thoughtful cover blurbs that I will always think of you fondly.

I am forever indebted to my critique partners, Teri Bozowski and Linda Aldrich, for their incisive and thoughtful feedback.

To my son-in-law, Sameet, I love you for your constant support. And for my long line of friends, family and well-wishers, too many to list, a big hug of appreciation.

Last but not least, to the love of my life, husband, partner and best friend, Prakash. I am deeply grateful to the fates that brought you into my life. We are in this together, as always.

Author's Note

Dear Reader,

India has a rich and diversified culture filled with colorful folklore, gracious people, a delightful profusion of regional cuisines and breathtaking natural wonders. And yet, as shocking as it may seem to the more advanced cultures of the world, the archaic system of dowry is alive and thriving in contemporary India.

Dowry is a gift of cash, valuables and household items presented by the bride's family to the groom at the time of marriage. It is considered a contribution toward the household expenses of the groom's family. Although a dowry is not universal among all Indian castes and classes, there are some that practice it very strictly. To this day, it plays a significant role in many of India's arranged marriages.

Despite a highly educated middle class, the glitzy Bollywood movie and fashion industries, the high-tech and call-center boom that is touted as India's pride and joy, there is a shameful secret that casts a dark shadow on all those brilliant accomplishments. In spite of a federal law, the Dowry Prohibition Act of 1961, and its amendments in the 1980s, the dowry has continued to proliferate and become more entrenched.

India's dowry system is a corrupt and decadent tradition, and yet, its advocates argue that it is merely a method of ensuring equitable distribution of a parent's estate among daughters and sons. But when one analyzes the crude and inhuman way it is sometimes practiced, it can be viewed as a form of extortion.

As if that were not enough to qualify as a misdeed, if and when a bride's family fails to produce the expected dowry or falls short of the promised amount, the bride is often abused or tortured or killed by her husband's family—and, indeed, may suffer all three, in that order.

Statistics on bride abuse and bride killings are highly skewed because of a large number of cases that go unreported or undocumented. They are often brushed aside as accidents. Corrupt police officials that condone the perpetration by looking the other way serve to add to the travesty of an already distorted legal system. Allegedly, anywhere from 5,000 to 25,000 dowry brides are killed and maimed each year. There is no way to gauge the validity of any of the available statistical data.

Although *The Dowry Bride* is entirely fictional, some of its elements are based on facts surrounding the dowry system. In narrating the story of my young protagonist, Megha Ramnath, I often placed myself in her shoes, and as a result I experienced her fears, concerns, joys and tribulations. Notwithstanding the drama, adventure and action essential to a work of fiction, I have tried to paint a realistic portrait of a culture that is simple yet complex in many ways, abundant yet lacking in some areas, progressive yet shockingly primitive.

I sincerely hope you enjoy reading and sharing with others *The Dowry Bride* as much as I have enjoyed writing it.

Best wishes,

Shobhan Bantwal

Chapter 1

Her parents named her Megha, which means "cloud" in Sanskrit, perhaps because she cast a gray shadow over their lives at a time when they didn't expect overcast skies. She was an unexpected, unpleasant surprise—rather late in their lives. Her father was in his forties, her mother in her thirties. When they were desperately hoping it would at least turn out to be a boy after having had two girls, now ages thirteen and eleven, she came along—another screaming infant girl—with all the wants and needs and tribulations of a female, all the burdens of a Hindu Brahmin woman.

Her father never recovered from the disappointment. Her mother quietly accepted it as her destiny. Together they began to contemplate how they would ever manage to put aside enough money to pay three *varadakhshinas*. Dowries.

Some Hindus believe that if you give your child a depressing name, you can keep evil away from it. They often apply a dot of kohl on a baby's face to mar its perfection, as no one will be tempted to put a hex on a flawed child. Megha was told she was an unusually beautiful baby, bright and full of energy. She often wondered if the name Megha was her spot of kohl, guaranteed to deflect the evil eye. When asked about it, her mother said the only reason they called her Megha was because they happened to like the name.

Then there was the astrologer, a man known for his accuracy, who had cast her *janam-patrika*. Horoscope. He had apparently predicted a dark, threatening period in Megha's life, when a large cloud would settle over her head, and *Yama*, the god of death, would pay her a visit. He wasn't able to foretell exactly when . . . but the menace would come, he'd warned.

It would come. It was bound to come—sooner or later.

Chapter 2

At the age of twenty-one, Megha Ramnath was not only married for a year but was about to be executed. In the damp, foggy darkness of the night, she stood outside the wood-shed, her brows drawn in puzzlement, the loose end of her plain blue cotton sari tightly drawn around her slim shoulders. Had she heard correctly, or was her mind playing strange tricks on her?

Standing on her toes, she peeped into the shed's window, secretly listening to her would-be murderers whispering, hatching their sinister plan to finish her off.

There was no light anywhere except for the ominous, dull yellow glow coming from the *kandeel*. Lantern. It barely illuminated the woodpile leaning against the wall in the corner and the two tins of kerosene standing nearby. The concrete floor, reduced to a blotchy gray from decades of sawdust, oil stains, and dirt, looked grungier than ever.

Icy fingers crept down the nape of her neck, telling her something was not quite right. What was it she sensed? What unexplained electric charge sent chills up and down her spine? Megha strained to listen, trying to make sense of the conversation going on inside the shed.

Kuppu, the fat old calico cat, sat huddled at her feet, shuddering, sending tremors up Megha's legs. Was it experiencing the same eerie feeling she was? Cats could sense danger better than humans. The leaves rustled in the nearby guava tree, making her jump. She looked up, afraid to breathe, but realized it was only some night creature stirring—perhaps a bird disturbed by Kuppu's presence. Just then Kuppu's back lifted in an arch—a definite sign of fear. And Megha's breathing turned ragged.

Then it dawned on her. Her large dark eyes opened wide with alarm. She was going to be killed! Realization struck her like a punch in the stomach. Terror replaced numbing shock, sending her heartbeat soaring.

Oh, God! Could this really be happening to her? And why? She was an ordinary housewife with a boring life; she had no enemies. She was considered pretty, but it couldn't possibly be a reason for anyone to kill her. She had no particular talents and posed no threat to anyone. Although her life meant little to anybody but herself, her death would mean even less.

And yet, she was going to be murdered!

The most puzzling part of the mystery was that her executioners were none other than her husband, Suresh Ramnath, and his ferocious mother, Chandramma Ramnath. The children in the family called her Amma. In their native *Kannada* language, Amma meant mother, but since she was also the eldest female in the family, she was Amma to all the kids, including nieces and nephews. Even the male servant who came in daily to wash the clothes and mop the floors addressed her as Amma-bai. *Bai* was the respectful Indian equivalent of the English term *madam*.

Despite what was going on in the woodshed, the surrounding scene looked perfectly normal. The nondescript Ramnath home, with its sooty windows and aged concrete frame, was like many other homes in Cantonment *Galli* or Street—single-storied, with three bedrooms and a small backyard. The houses were dark, boxy squares rising out of the fog.

The neighborhood was middle-class, where most of the women stayed home and cooked and raised the children while the men held office jobs or owned small businesses. Most every family had a servant come in daily for an hour or two to perform the menial tasks—not a luxury but a necessity. Very rarely did this class of folks travel for pleasure. They ate at a restaurant or went to the cinema perhaps once a month. Money was usually tight and every rupee had to be saved for the children's futures.

At this late hour, the rural town of Palgaum was asleep. Even the most vigilant watchdogs dozed in languorous abandon in the sultry humidity of the tropical October night. The last show at the movie theaters had let out and the crowds had gone home to their beds. Except for a handful of individuals who had business staying awake, like night-shift guards and policemen, nurses minding hushed hospital wards, industrious prostitutes, and the occasional nocturnal youth or drunk loitering on a darkened street, the place was tranquil. A fine, damp mist had wound its way from the river and spread like a ghostly shroud, while a silent quarter-moon watched over the slumbering town.

After long hours of slogging in the kitchen to keep her husband and in-laws well-fed and content, Megha usually slept like the dead. It was her sole escape from a life she had slowly come to abhor—her only relief for those aching feet, back, and arms that resulted from shopping for endless lists of rations and hauling them home on foot, grinding spices, coconut and various kinds of batters on the heavy grinding stone, serving meals, and handling heavy pots of steaming food and buckets of bath water. One of the advantages of being so young was the ability to sink into oblivion once her head settled on the pillow each night.

And yet, a little earlier, startled by an odd sound, her eyelids had flown open in an instant. It was different from the normal nightly cacophony of snores coming from her in-laws' room. She could only hear her father-in-law, Vinayak Ramnath, or Appaji as the kids called him, snoring in the master bedroom, and her teenaged sister-in-law, Shanti, breathing like a muffled whistle in her room across the passageway.

But what about Amma, her mother-in-law, the Amazon witch? The older woman's notorious snoring was ominously absent. It was generally riotous enough to disturb anyone within a hundred meters. Was that corpulent mass of a woman, Chandramma, lying awake? Was she hatching another one of her twisted plans to make Megha's life even more difficult?

After a minute, Megha recognized the peculiar sound. It was the door to the small storage shed that sat at a little distance from the rear of the house and contained their monthly supply of wood and kerosene. The hinges on the door were rusty and squeaked every time it was opened or shut. It was a familiar echo from her daily trips to the shed to haul in the wood for the kitchen and bathroom hearths. The Ramnaths were too stingy for a gas stove, and the daily bath water was heated in a big brass cauldron because electricity was both expensive and unreliable.

Megha's breath caught on the possibility that she might have forgotten to lock the shed before retiring for the night. Amma would surely take her to task for such carelessness. Her fierce and tyrannical mother-in-law would never tolerate incompetence on Megha's part. A young daughter-in-law could not afford to make even trivial mistakes. A bride had to earn her keep and the right to be called a good Brahmin wife.

Megha turned around in bed, wondering if her husband, Suresh, had heard the noise. She was mystified to find him missing. Generally he'd be huddled under the sheet beside her, his bony buttocks sticking out at a strange angle, his wide-lipped mouth hanging open in deep, childlike slumber.

Frowning, she glanced at the bedside clock. The neon-red digital display read 12:23 AM. The bedroom door was ajar. Where could Suresh be? It was a warm night and she'd wondered if he'd gone for a glass of water. She herself had awakened perspiring. Her thick, long plait lay limply against her moist back. Her sari clung to her hips and legs.

Sleeping in a sari, which was six long yards of fabric, was terribly uncomfortable and impractical, but in an old-fashioned family such as this, she was not allowed to wear nightgowns or *kaftans*. There were established rules of etiquette and attire for ladies. Amma had made them clear right from the beginning. "Those silly gowns and frocks that show the legs and bosoms are not allowed in our house, okay? Ladies in our house only wear saris."

Assuming Suresh was probably in the kitchen or bathroom, Megha called out to him. She received no reply.

That was when the first faint ripple of fear crossed her mind. Could a burglar have broken into their shed? Thefts were not uncommon around this neighborhood, and wood and kerosene were expensive commodities.

Her next thought made her sit up in stark alarm. *Oh my God! Someone is stealing our firewood and Suresh is trying to confront them—all one hundred and five pounds of him. They'll crush him to a pulp!* Her heartbeat had leapt in panic. *He needs my help.*

She shot out of bed like an arrow, her long, slim legs moving rapidly despite the bulky folds of the sari and the petticoat swirling around them. She rushed through the old-fashioned kitchen, nearly stumbling over the round grinding stone before reaching the rear door leading to the covered veranda. Kuppu, the family cat, hearing Megha's footsteps, bounced off the window sill and followed close on her heels.

Standing on the veranda steps, she puzzled some more over her husband's absence. The fog made it difficult to see much, but a faint sliver of light was visible underneath the door of the woodshed. She visualized images of Suresh lying in a pool of blood, his skinny body motionless. As far as she had determined, Suresh was incapable of defending himself against even the weakest of attacks. Suresh needed her. But what should she do?

Well, defend him, of course! Steely determination goaded her into action. Being the youngest of three girls, she had learned to wrestle with her older sisters for everything including space in their small, cramped house, their parents' attention, clothes and toys. So now she'd put those acquired defensive moves to good use.

Megha wasn't about to let some petty thugs make her a widow at twenty-one. She'd fight them with everything she had—if necessary, even give her own life to save her husband's.

It was her duty as an ideal wife. But she had to come up with a strategy. Barging into the shed like a crazed woman wouldn't do her any good, nor Suresh for that matter. First she had to determine the gravity of the situation.

She was afraid of the dark, always had been, but something in the shed seemed to beckon her with a force that both frightened and excited her. She stepped down from the veranda.

Nearing the shed, Megha heard hushed voices, barely audible. Talking burglars? Or was it Suresh, her naïve, impractical husband, actually trying to strike a compromise with the thieves? There was only one way to find out. Despite the misgivings nipping at her brain, she tiptoed barefoot across the dirt-covered yard toward the shed.

She'd been so preoccupied she nearly walked right into the big *tulsi* pot. Somehow she managed to break her fall by grabbing it with both hands. But she grazed her knees and nearly banged her head on its edge in the process.

The holy *tulsi* plant was a tropical variety of basil, held sacred by Hindus. In most conservative households it was planted in a clay pot or urn anchored to the ground in the center of the courtyard—an honored place. The urn was usually painted in bright colors and the plant well-tended. It was customary for women to pray daily to the *tulsi* for blessings.

Despite the clammy heat of the night, Megha felt goose bumps pop up along her arms, her stomach instinctively tighten. For a fleeting second she was tempted to run back to bed, pull the covers over her head and let this weird, eerie night go on without her. She wanted to be a little girl again; she didn't want to know about dark nights and the fearsome things that stalked them.

But she was not a little girl anymore; she was a grown woman with responsibilities, and she couldn't afford to shirk them. Besides, the mysterious force in the shed seemed to draw her closer. Was Suresh still alive?

Taking care to avoid the narrow band of light under the door, she edged along the side wall as noiselessly as possible and positioned herself to peer through the open window. Puzzled lines formed on her brow. There was no sign of strangers and certainly no burglars. Only Amma and Suresh were inside the shed.

A stench suddenly assailed her nostrils. Kerosene! That potent, unexpected odor made her stomach revolt.

What in heaven's name were her husband and mother-in-law doing in there at this hour? Why did the place reek of kerosene? Bewildered, Megha continued to observe them in silence. This was entirely out of character. The obese and sluggish Amma should have been deep in sleep and so should Suresh. They were both heavy sleepers. And yet, here they were, in the dead of night, murmuring to each other in the dusty, rat-infested woodshed of all places.

Amma wore a deep purple sari and stood with her tree-stump legs apart, in her usual militant posture, fat hands planted on her hips. Even in the pale light cast by the lantern her face was plainly visible. Perspiration glistened on her dark-coffee skin as she stared at a crude bed fashioned out of crisscrossed logs of firewood lying on the floor. "Suresh, make sure the kerosene is soaked into the wood, boy. It has to catch fire quickly and burn for a long time," she instructed.

Burn valuable wood in the middle of the night? For what purpose?

Tiny beads of sweat showed on Suresh's wide forehead as he crouched on the floor beside the logs, still wearing the sky-blue pajamas he'd worn to bed. He appeared shaky, anxious, as he looked up at his mother. But then, he was always like that around his mother. "Amma, are you sure about this? What if the neighbors suspect something?"

"Don't be silly," snorted Amma. "They're all fast asleep."

"What if they inform the police?"

"Stop worrying over nothing, boy."

"We'll all end up in jail, Amma." His voice sounded feeble and pleading.

Jail? Megha's heart missed a solid beat. What kind of illegal business was her husband getting himself into? And his own mother was leading him into it? How come Suresh had said nothing to Megha, his wife? She would have talked him out of it in a minute. But then, he was always Amma's little boy, hanging on her every word—too stupid to think for himself.

Amma slapped Suresh's shoulder, making him lurch forward and nearly fall on his face. "Don't be an idiot, Suresh. Do you see a single light on in any of the neighbors' homes?"

"That does not mean someone is not awake, Amma," he argued weakly.

"Nonsense! Besides, we don't socialize with any of those low-caste people. They don't even know us."

"But, Amma, this is still illegal. You understand that?"

"There is nothing illegal about what is right, Suresh."

Suresh merely stared at his mother, too much of a coward to stand up to her.

"Don't you understand that she is worthless?" Amma rolled her eyes, seemingly frustrated with her son's lack of intelligence. "Her father is never going to come up with the dowry. *His* actions are what I call *illegal*."

"But nothing was in writing . . ." Suresh's voice trailed off.

"Humph," Amma fumed, "a spoken agreement is still a contract. When he doesn't pay up, he is breaking that contract, no? It has been almost one year and she is not even pregnant yet. She must be barren also. We can easily get double or triple the dowry from some other girl's father. Do you want to give that up?"

Dowry? Barren? As the truth began to sink in, Megha's stomach plunged. They were talking about *her*! What she'd stumbled upon wasn't some mildly dishonest mother-son project. They were plotting against her. The ominous words coming out of Amma's mouth meant only one thing: Death!

Suresh shook his head and poured more kerosene on the wood as his mother demanded, spreading more noxious fumes into the surrounding air. His lips quivered. "But Amma, can't . . . can't we just send her back to her father's house? Divorce is legal now, you see."

"No! In our family there is no *dye-vorrce*," Amma hissed. "Do you know how long it takes? Two years? Three? Besides, divorced men are treated like donkey dung, but a widowed man is looked at with sympathy, especially one whose wife dies a tragic death. Divorce brings dishonor upon the family, Suresh. This is a much better way; nobody will know. They will think it was an accident."

"How t-to explain . . ." Suresh stuttered, the perspiration on his forehead beginning to run.

"How? She was here to pick up firewood with a lantern in hand; she knocked down the kerosene tin and the lantern set her sari on fire."

"But, Amma—"

"Just do as I say and leave the rest to me, Suresh. I know all about these things. Two months from now, girls will be lining up to marry you. You are our only son and an officer in a big bank. You will be in much demand, no?"

Megha sucked in a horrified breath. They were planning to burn her alive! They were going to tie her to a bed of kerosene-soaked wood, and set fire to her. She had read about such atrocities. But those had been merely sensational stories in newspapers and magazines—they always happened to someone else—mostly in the rural northern sections of India, not here in the southwest, where the culture was different, more liberal, more enlightened. Bride-burnings occurred among uneducated folks, rarely affecting the modern middle class.

How could something so vile and contemptible as dowry death come to touch *her* life? This had to be a nightmare. Nothing like this could happen to ordinary people. And yet, here she was, at the center of a plot to do away with her.

So, this was what the three evil women, Amma and her two sisters-in-law, Kamala and Devayani, had been planning behind closed doors earlier that night: kill Megha off in the most brutal manner and find another wife for Suresh. Suresh's uncles and their respective wives and children had been invited to dinner, and Amma had been behaving more strangely than usual in the presence of their guests. Amma had conveniently gotten rid of the men in the family by sending them off for a walk, dispatched the young women to the kitchen, and then huddled with Kamala and Devayani for a long, secret meeting.

Amma had probably been plotting this for days, perhaps months. No wonder she'd looked smug during the past week. The old witch was planning a major event: Murder.

As Megha faced the fact that she was literally at death's door, a feeble hand went to her mouth to stifle the sob that rose in her throat. She was about to die!

And along with the dismay came pain—like a hot poker thrust into her belly. Suresh, her husband, was going along with the scheme, even though he sounded reluctant. Was this the extent of his love for her? If not love, at least some sense of loyalty? How could she have trusted him? How could she have rushed out here to save him from danger, and perhaps give up her own life in the process?

A wave of nausea made her gag. She swallowed hard to block the surge of bile and looked again at her husband's gaunt face. This was the man who had tied the *mangalsutra*, the black and gold beaded necklace symbolizing holy marriage, around her neck only a year ago. He had given her his name; he had made love to her, or rather used her body for his pleasure; he had accepted her as his wife and life-partner. Megha had tried hard to be a loving and considerate wife to him despite his unattractive appearance, his selfish and ill-mannered ways, and his total lack of emotion.

Now she realized Suresh was much more perverse than she had imagined. He was disgusting, worse than a primitive animal. In fact, most animals treated their mates with a certain amount of care and respect. How could she have felt anything in her heart for such a loathsome creature? The warm feelings of fondness she had worked hard to cultivate over the past months turned to bitter revulsion. How could she not have recognized that side of him?

Her husband was a potential murderer!

Get out of here, Megha, her inner voice commanded. *Don't let them take your life.* But her legs refused to move. They seemed to be frozen. It felt as if her feet were rooted to the spot, mired in solid concrete.

The feeling of impending doom intensified. *Run! Now!* In

desperation Megha looked around in the misty shadows. What was she to do? Where could she go? She could not remain there any longer.

As she heard Suresh and Amma stirring from the shed she knew without a doubt they were headed back to the house to drag her out of bed and to her death. She didn't want to die. She was too young to die. And too scared to perish in such a horrific way.

She had to escape. Somewhere! Anywhere!

Chapter 3

Galvanized by terror, Megha finally managed to uproot her-self and move. She made a mad dash through the back-yard—away from the woodshed, away from the house.

They were killers—and they were coming after her.

At first her steps faltered; she wondered if she'd been foolish, perhaps misunderstood Amma and Suresh's intent. Having woken up slightly disoriented from a deep sleep, had she some-how overreacted to something that had nothing to do with her? Why would anyone want to kill a young and innocent member of the family? It didn't make sense.

But there was no mistake. She had heard every word clearly—Amma's remarks to Suresh couldn't have been any plainer. Their objective was nothing short of execution.

As Megha began to comprehend the grave peril she was in, she gained momentum. She forged ahead blindly in the cloud of fog, with no particular direction in mind, stark fear giving wings to her feet. Every instinct prompted her to keep running, put distance between herself and the Ramnaths and their evil house.

Move! Keep running. Don't let them find you. Run, woman, her adrenaline-crazed brain repeated furiously. She knew she was trespassing on people's private properties but she didn't care. Wet grass, sharp stones, root clumps, fractured cement and thorns grated on her feet. Twice she ran into prickly bushes and trees, tripped and fell, and got her arms and face scratched. But she managed to get up and find her way around them.

Dogs growled at her from the shadows here and there, but fortunately none had pursued her so far. That was all she needed to make this wretched night an absolute curse: a crazed dog taking a bite out of her. Fatigue started to set in after a while but she kept on going.

Time was running out.

Megha stepped on something sharp. It felt like a hot blade slicing into her flesh, sending a stab of pain all the way up her leg and into her groin. She was sure she'd suffered a deep cut, but she didn't stop to investigate. Shards of broken glass were always a menace on the streets. She couldn't afford the luxury of stopping to examine her injuries.

Suresh was probably out there, chasing after her. Distance between the Ramnaths and herself—that was all she cared about at the moment. She didn't dare slow down. She was running for her life. Death was not an option and neither was giving in to weakness.

After negotiating innumerable private yards, she abruptly emerged into a street, gasping for air. Blinking, she skidded to a stop and wiped the sweat out of her eyes.

Streetlights illuminated the houses on either side. In her confusion it barely registered that it was nearly *Diwali*, the annual festival of lights, and many of the homes had the traditional terra-cotta oil lamps adorning their front steps and their verandas. At least the lights allowed her to see her surroundings instead of running blindly in utter darkness.

Some of the homes on this street had elaborate lighted *akash-deeps,* the colorful paper lanterns of *Diwali*, hanging above their stoops. But in Megha's mind they were objects of no importance.

She didn't know what street she was on. The homes were larger and more opulent than the ones in her neighborhood, with neatly laid-out gardens and fences and gates. Well-lit streets meant danger—she would be visible, the perfect prey. But, as long as she could feel the pavement under her feet, she would keep moving—until she ran out of steam.

Exhausted and out of breath, she stopped for a brief moment, panting, gulping mouthfuls of air. In the isolation of the dead of night she felt totally disoriented. The nausea hit once again with ferocious intensity. No amount of swallowing the saliva helped to keep the bile down. This time it rose like boiling lava in her throat. Bending over someone's bushes, she held her head in her hands as her stomach emptied itself out in a single, violent motion. Then she straightened up and stood still for a minute until she felt it settle. Despite the bitter taste in her mouth and the burning in her throat, the sense of relief was enormous.

Her breath became less labored. Wiping her mouth with the edge of her sari, she shifted her throbbing foot and looked down. There was a small cut with blood oozing. But what was a minor wound when her life was at stake?

She picked up the pace again and soon reached an intersection she recognized. She knew the commercial area well. She shopped there often for food and other essentials. It looked different now with the stores dark and shuttered. There was an eerie look about it—a neighborhood she generally associated with dense crowds—the mingling smells, colors and sounds of people moving about in a mad rush, buying, selling, haggling, and arguing. The stray cow that usually ambled up and down the street and survived on fruit and vegetables tossed out by the merchants was missing, too. The lame mongrel that scavenged for food was nowhere in sight either.

She caught her reflection in one of the store windows and stopped short. The sight was so unexpected and alarming, she nearly gasped. It was like discovering a ghost. Her own ghost! Staring back at her was a narrow oval face with huge, dazed eyes, full lips trembling, a bloody scratch on the chin, and a smudge of dirt on the nose. Locks of hair had come loose from her normally neat plait and hung about her sweaty face. Her cheeks looked almost hollow in the murky light, her eye sockets dark and deep. In the tinted glass her faded blue sari appeared gray and rumpled.

What was happening to her? She could hardly recognize herself.

Good grooming had come naturally to her, and despite her

meager wardrobe and lack of fancy cosmetics, she had always taken pride in her appearance. She was used to receiving compliments about her looks and dress sense, and yet now she looked like a homeless teenager, combing the streets late at night looking for scraps. A young woman from a dignified family and a decent home had no right to look like she did right now. In less than an hour she had gone from being a bride with a future to a homeless woman. How could that be? It was inconceivable.

Without her wristwatch Megha had no way of telling how long she'd been running, but by now Amma and Suresh had to know she was missing. They would surely set the police after her. Then she'd be arrested and dragged back to her in-laws. That, too, was unimaginable, and yet, it was likely to happen sooner or later. It was the only outcome she could foresee.

She went rigid at the sound of an approaching automobile. The police! Desperately looking for a place to hide, she did the only thing she could: she fell to the ground and crawled behind a discarded cardboard box lying on the footpath. The box smelled of rotting fruit and God knew what else. It was hardly large enough to cover her, but it kept her somewhat concealed from the streetlight. Her dark sari would have to do the rest.

The vehicle, a compact light-colored car, came closer. Her heart thudding like mad, she rolled her body into a tight ball, hoping she remained invisible. God, what if the driver saw her? What if it was a policeman? Or could it be one of Amma's brothers, combing the town for her?

When the car didn't slow down and kept going at a steady pace, she let her breath out. Only after the car turned the corner and disappeared did she realize it was merely a passing vehicle and not a direct threat. She rose to her feet. How long could she keep herself hidden?

There was no time to think. She had to run some more. But where exactly could she go? Surely not to her parents—they would send her right back to Suresh. "A married woman belongs in her husband's home, no matter how he treats her," her father, Lakshman Shastry, would remind her in that annoyingly righteous way of his, his dark eyes turning to ice. "It is a wife's duty to remain loyal to her family at any cost." He'd then escort her to the Ramnath household and abandon her on their doorstep once more like a bag of rubbish. "Now be a good wife to your husband. Behave yourself!" he'd order her, his gnarled arthritic index finger raised like a whip. He wasn't above using his twisted hand to swat her bottom if necessary.

If she was condemned to die in an inferno, would he even care? With his burden gone he wouldn't have to worry about producing that wretched dowry. Maybe he'd even welcome the news of his youngest daughter's demise.

Megha's mother, Mangala, although a caring woman, was the quintessential Brahmin wife: conventional, obedient, and compliant to a fault. She would support her husband in all matters, even to the extent of letting her child die a gruesome death.

So, what were Megha's options? She had no living grandparents on either side. Her mother's two older brothers lived around Chennai—too far for her to travel. And they hardly ever kept in touch with the family. If she showed up at their homes, they wouldn't even recognize her. The last time they'd seen her was when she was about nine years old. Her father had no living siblings. His two sisters and one brother had died young, and their children were scattered throughout India. Longevity didn't seem to exist on her father's side of the family. No wonder Appa talked about dying all the time.

If she went to her best friend, Harini Nayak's house, the police would easily track her down there. Amma knew Harini was Megha's closest friend. Besides, she couldn't show up at Harini's door at this time of night. Perhaps she could go to her older sister Hema's house in Hubli? But there would be no bus leaving for Hubli until the morning, and in any case, she had no money for the bus fare. Other than the clothes she was wearing she had nothing. Besides, the bus depot and the train station would be places the police were most likely to monitor.

Without money and support, Amma would have her back in a minute. Amma had made up her mind that her precious son was to become a widower. That way he'd be guaranteed another bride immediately, without the stigma of divorce. And that meant Amma would hunt Megha down and kill her with her own two hands to get what she wanted.

That left Megha with no place to go and no one to turn to. She was alone in the world—completely alone. She had no home and no family to speak of anymore. All at once, desolation struck her. Blind to the dust and debris around her, she sank to the footpath for the second time and buried her face in her hands. What was she going to do?

Hard, painful sobs racked her body as she surrendered to the hopelessness that engulfed her.

Her father would never be able to come up with the dowry. So why had he promised the Ramnaths a dowry he couldn't afford? How could her parents do this to her? She would have been better off remaining a spinster. Was marriage so important in a woman's life that cruelty and even death wouldn't be considered too great a sacrifice? Why did people like her parents insist on having children they could ill afford in the first place? Just so they could give them away in marriage to murderers? Didn't a precious human life mean anything anymore?

In that instant, she hated her parents with a passion she never knew she was capable of. In fact, she loathed them even more than she loathed Suresh and her in-laws. She could never forgive her father for this. He was a monster for selling her to the lowest bidder.

But she despised herself more than anyone. Why hadn't she had the guts to stand up to her father and refuse to marry that ass named Suresh? Why hadn't she lashed out at Amma and her meanness? After hearing about the murder plans why hadn't she marched over to the neighbors' house and summoned the police? Because she was afraid.

Once the cathartic weeping fit was over, Megha wiped her eyes and began to think hard and take stock of her situation. Most important, she was still alive. And her chief priority was to stay alive. She had to get out of the immediate vicinity first— find a relatively safe place to hide. Ignoring the small puddle of blood her injured foot had left behind and the throbbing pain, she looked around, trying to figure out which direction to take. And she froze.

A man sitting huddled under a sheet was watching her from several feet away. Where had he come from? Had he been there all along, observing her while she had taken cover behind the box and then cried like a baby? Why had she not noticed him all this time?

When she glanced at him again, he rose to his feet, dropped his sheet and stretched to his full height. He was looking directly at her. Something about the tense stillness of his body told her he was going to make a move on her any second. He had the look of a predator, crouching, silently poised to pounce on its prey. He started to walk toward her. His white teeth flashed at her in the muted light—a sinister smirk that terrified her to the very marrow of her bones.

Dear God, he probably thought she was a prostitute, ripe for the taking! She had never been out on the streets alone at this time of night. She had no idea what kinds of peril stalked the town after midnight. Purely on instinct she shot to her feet. Sprinting across the street, she lost herself in the shadows of a dark alley. The fog seemed thicker there, making it hard to see anything, but she ran on.

She heard the man's footsteps behind her. He was now running to catch up with her. Since he had probably not expected her to take off so abruptly, he might have been taken by surprise, and that fact alone had allowed her a few precious moments to get a head start. But she was still in serious danger. His feet were pounding the alley's surface.

Her breathing began to deteriorate into desperate huffing. Nothing could have been more terrible a few minutes ago, she'd thought. She was wrong. Things had just gone from bad to worse, to much, much worse! Just as she was running to save her life from a fiery death, a derelict man had discovered her—was chasing her. *I can't allow him to get me! He will not rape me . . . I won't let him,* she vowed in silence, staying in motion with difficulty. But how long could she elude him?

Ahead she noticed a large wall looming to her right. A stone wall encompassing someone's property, she guessed. Sliding to a stop for one breathless moment, she quickly studied the wall. Surrounded by darkness, it was impossible to tell whether there was a gate in it. There was only one thing she could do: climb over the damned wall and take her chances with a vicious guard dog. If she kept running she'd soon be out of strength and eventually collapse. Her hunter would catch up with her. He had looked big and muscular—a man accustomed to the hard, violent life on the streets.

She eyed the wall again. Could she scale it? The man was gaining ground behind her. She could feel his presence closing in. It was now or never. Clenching her teeth hard with the effort, she gripped the top edge of the wall, pulled herself up with one strong thrust and vaulted over it.

With a dull thud she fell into a garden of some kind, wincing as her bottom hit the hard ground and her arms and legs got scratched some more by low-lying plants. Swallowing against the sharp sting, she gave herself a moment to recover then tried to rise to her feet. She couldn't—her legs were paralyzed rubber. Could she have broken a bone somewhere?

Setting all thoughts of injury aside for a second, she cocked her ears to listen for sounds. The hastening steps were unmistakable. He was coming! She'd made it over the edge not a moment too soon. Her pursuer had reached the spot where she'd been standing mere seconds ago, and come to a stop. She could hear his labored breathing clearly on the other side. Even the combined stench of his stale-liquor breath and body odor was wafting up and over the barrier.

Paralysis worked to her advantage, however, since she seemed to have frozen on the spot, although she hoped her own hard wheezing wasn't too loud. Even the beat of her heart sounded like drumbeats. With any luck, the miserable bastard was too intoxicated to be able to hear well.

For what seemed like endless minutes, Megha heard the man inhale deeply. Did he know she was on the other side? Is that why he stood there, waiting for her to reappear?

She glanced about in panic, looking for an alternate escape route in case the man decided to scale the wall and come after her. A large house stood in the background, shrouded in dark silence. If there was a way around the house, she couldn't see it. Thank God there was no sign of guard dogs. Maybe there was a garden tool or a piece of wood or something she could use to defend herself. But it was too damned dark to see anything. The fog was proving to be one hell of a nuisance.

"Kidhar gayi salee?" she heard the drunkard murmur in Hindi. Where did the whore go?

So he didn't know where she was! Megha exhaled a deep but quiet sigh. *Thank you, God!* The bum hadn't seen her leap over the wall after all. Good thing she was wearing a dark sari. And the fog, which she had considered a curse a second ago, was proving to be a blessing in some ways.

She seemed safe for the time being. But she didn't slump in relief or budge from her spot despite her temporary sense of reprieve. The man was still very much there. She could hear the profanities he kept grinding out and his cough, a deep, guttural, phlegm-packed sound typical of people who smoked *beedis*: tobacco leaves hand-rolled into tubes that resembled thin cigarettes. A *beedi* was the poor man's cigarette.

After a minute, Megha's brain thawed a little and her numb limbs seemed to come semi-alive. She flexed her hands, wondering if she would be able to climb back over the wall. What if that wretched beast decided to camp out right there for the night?

Another round of panic shot through her when something soft skittered past her feet. Snake? She was terrified of reptiles. Or was it a rat? She hated rats, too. Could it be the blood oozing from her injured foot that was attracting some kind of blood-sucking creatures? She sat still, hoping to play dead. Maybe they'd sniff and go away.

God, what had she plunged into—from the proverbial frying pan into the fire? Only, in her case, it was more like the fire to the frying pan. And how much longer could she hide out in some stranger's garden? Daylight was only a few hours away.

Time was running out.

She listened, praying the vagrant would give up on her and leave, praying the night creature wouldn't return with some of its friends to feast on her wounded foot, praying she hadn't broken any bones and had the strength left to scale the wall once again, praying she could find a place to hide.

Finally, after what seemed like ages, the man started to stir. She waited till his footsteps began to fade away. He kept murmuring expletives under his breath and coughing, which in a way was to her advantage. It told her he was on his way back to the filthy hole he had emerged from. Only then did she crumple in relief for a few moments to think and plan her next move.

Now that the immediate danger had passed, it was hard to concentrate on rational matters. Exhaustion and pain were warring for attention in her body. Her eyelids began to droop from weariness. The thought of running aimlessly through the streets with an injured foot was becoming more and more repugnant. It was tempting to curl up in that bed of dirt, ignore the night creatures and drift into sleep—at least for a brief hour or two. But she fought the urge to rest. She couldn't give in to weakness now, not after she'd come all this way. She had to concentrate, force herself to focus on what was imperative: saving herself. *Think, Megha. Think hard!*

Gradually the cobwebs in her mind began to clear. An idea started to take shape as she squatted in the dirt: Kiran. He was Suresh's cousin—Amma's brother's son. Maybe she could go to him for help. Although he was probably one of the most unlikely and unsuitable sources of assistance at a time like this, he was still a decent man, or he seemed to be. He had always been sympathetic and friendly toward her. He would surely not turn her away? Maybe she could borrow a little money from him. A few hundred rupees would be pocket change for a wealthy man like him. She would use the money to get on a bus to Hema's house and then look for a job there. Afterwards, she'd find a way to return Kiran's money.

Her mind made up, she carefully pulled herself to her feet, and sighed with relief when she realized her legs and back felt normal, except for a general soreness and the burning pain in her foot. No broken bones. She brushed the mud and rotting garden debris off her sari and with the same motion she had employed earlier, hoisted herself up and jumped over the wall. Once again she was back in the alley.

She stood still and glanced around her to make sure the man wasn't holding vigil in a corner somewhere. Who knew what kinds of cat-and-mouse games the street bum was capable of? She stood still for a few seconds, her eyes and ears alert. Thankfully nothing happened. He was truly gone.

She started to run once again.

Chapter 4

Kiran Rao drummed his long fingers on his car's steering wheel while he grimly mulled over the night's bizarre events. No matter how he examined the pieces of the puzzle before him, they continued to baffle the hell out of him.

He rubbed his eyes with the heels of his palms to get the grittiness out. It was two hours past midnight and he'd had no sleep. He knew he looked unkempt in the slacks and T-shirt he had hurriedly pulled on, and a day's growth of beard roughening his face.

Kiran had woken up at five o'clock the previous morning to prepare for an early conference call at the office and put in a long day at work after that. Fatigue was beginning to set in, but he was too keyed up to go home to his bed. Besides, he needed to find out the facts surrounding the mystery and his nagging sense of dread. He had to do what he'd come here to do. Until he found out the truth for himself, there would be no rest for him.

Although his car was parked some distance from his aunt, Chandramma Ramnath's house, he could clearly hear the uproar inside the home. The two police constables who had arrived on bicycles were still in there, questioning the Ramnath family and taking notes, building a case against young Megha Ramnath, his cousin Suresh's bride of one year, for spousal abandonment.

Megha had allegedly disappeared, deserting her husband and in-laws.

The front door of the house remained ajar, and a few curious neighbors, obviously disturbed and intrigued by the commotion so late at night, sat on their stoops, listening attentively. Before the sun came up in the morning, the gossip mill would be grinding out all the shameful facts of the Ramnaths' story along with the embellishments: the pretty young bride had run away from her ugly husband and vicious mother-in-law. They'd probably shake their heads and wonder why such a lovely and refined girl had married into such a hideous and unsophisticated family in the first place.

Wasn't that the question a lot of people asked? Kiran often speculated about it himself. As far as he knew, her father had fallen on bad times and couldn't afford a dowry; therefore he had settled for the first man belonging to the right caste who'd take his youngest daughter off his hands.

Kiran couldn't really blame Megha's father for trying to do the right thing, but did the old man really have to do something that desperate without giving any thought to his daughter's future? Had he even made an effort to look any further than the Ramnaths when he'd set out to find a suitable boy for Megha? There were surely other, more eligible young men who'd jump at the chance of marrying a girl like Megha. Instead, she'd been thrust into a dull marriage by her parents.

Somehow Kiran was convinced that Megha had been coerced into the marriage. She would never have voluntarily agreed to marry Suresh Ramnath of all people. Though Kiran held a certain amount of family loyalty for his cousin Suresh, he doubted if Suresh would ever qualify as the ideal husband. Suresh and he had practically grown up together and he knew him like a brother. Suresh was always an impassive, introverted man with no interest in anything but looking after himself. He had nothing to offer a wife emotionally, financially, or intellectually, especially not a wife like Megha. What a bloody awful situation for poor Megha!

Voices floated out the door once again, this time a bit louder.

His aunt was always loud enough to be heard two streets away. Besides, Kiran had just come out of that house himself. He'd had more than enough of the emotionally charged scene, so he'd made a quick escape.

At the moment though, Kiran's mind was on Megha. Where was she? It was hard to imagine she was gone. Sweet, beautiful Megha was nowhere to be found. It was so uncharacteristic of the bright, lively young woman he'd come to know in the last few months that he was still in doubt about her deliberately abandoning her family. Even supposing she had, a young and naïve bride with no money couldn't have gone too far.

Her parents, who lived only a couple of kilometers away, had been contacted by the police, and apparently they were as stunned as everyone else. They hadn't seen her or heard from her.

Fear gnawed at Kiran as he speculated about Megha. Could she have been abducted? With her youth and movie-star looks she was a prime candidate for being kidnapped and sold into prostitution. What if right now she was being transported to some hellish brothel in town? Or worse yet, out of town? His hands gripped the wheel in frustration. What could he do to find her with no clues of any kind? The police were already doing their part, but they weren't particularly bright or efficient or even dedicated to their task.

The DSP, district superintendent of police, was a close friend of the family, and Kiran was tempted to request him to start a more comprehensive investigation instead of depending on those two clowns in there. But that would make people wonder why Kiran was so interested in the case. He couldn't afford to have anyone suspect why he wanted to be so involved in the matter of Megha's disappearance. So he'd decided to say nothing—at least for the moment.

He shut his eyes and a picture of Megha rose in his mind: big, dark, trusting eyes surrounded by long lashes, a perfect nose, a smooth, fair complexion, a rosebud mouth, thick, wavy hair woven into a braid that fell to her waist, and the most heart-wrenchingly attractive smile.

An intelligent girl with a keen interest in literature, sports, world events and politics, Megha could hold her own in any intellectual conversation. Her eyes lit up with excitement whenever the topic turned to books and politics. She seemed to know so much about literature and the latest political scandals. Her life's ambition was to become a journalist. With her natural curiosity and flair for words, she probably would make a first-rate journalist. If only she had a chance.

Megha was a tall woman but a bit thin. There were fascinating curves in the right places, though. Even in simple and inexpensive saris she managed to look neat and elegant. For some reason he always pictured her in an urbane setting. She had an aura of refinement and had never seemed to fit in with the Ramnaths. God, she was uncommonly lovely! And so incredibly cheerful.

She always had a kind word for everyone, even Kiran's snobbish cousin, Kala, who never missed an opportunity to make snide remarks about Megha's lack of expensive clothes or sophisticated accessories. Amma, who could put terror into people's hearts and probably made Megha's life a living hell, was treated with quiet respect by Megha. And that good-for-nothing, gutless Suresh somehow managed to earn affectionate glances from her. But how did she do it? How did she keep her spirit intact in the face of such gloom and tedium?

He was positive Megha was not the type who'd pick up and run from her family. Something terrible had happened to drive her away, or else she'd been taken against her will.

Kiran had been smitten with Megha since the day he'd laid eyes on her. It was on her wedding day. Like a fool he'd fallen in love with the girl who'd just become someone else's wife—that someone else being his own cousin. At the wedding, Kiran had shaken hands and congratulated her and Suresh—pretended to wish them a long and happy marriage while envy for Suresh and lust for his gorgeous bride had plagued him all evening. Wow, what a girl! What an enchanting bride Suresh had bagged.

After the wedding, Kiran had tried hard to convince himself that what he felt for Suresh's new wife was only infatuation, but every time he'd seen Megha she'd seemed more appealing. And every time his reaction had been the same: heartbeat rising, a tight feeling in his chest and abdomen. And the obsessive need to see her, spend time with her, perhaps touch her. As weeks turned into months, he was forced to admit that his feelings were beyond temporary fascination. His was no adolescent attraction; it was full-blown love with all its excess baggage.

And then there was anger, because Megha didn't deserve to be married to a weak, spineless loser like Suresh—didn't deserve to be treated like a personal slave by Amma. Talk about life being unfair! Thoughts of a rare illness striking and killing off Suresh had crossed his mind a few times, thoughts Kiran had quickly suppressed. How could he think such awful things about his cousin, the man he had played childhood games with, the boy he had looked up to when he himself was no more than a toddler?

It had bordered on hero worship then, because Suresh was four years older. Suresh could read sentences when Kiran could hardly master the alphabet. Suresh could do multiplication when Kiran could barely add and subtract. At some point, Kiran couldn't say precisely when, he had surpassed Suresh academically and physically, and then continued to grow and run. That was when Kiran had recognized Suresh for what he really was: a weak, selfish and shallow man with little respect for others. He even suspected Suresh had some sort of mild mental affliction that made him so apathetic. Kiran wasn't sure what he felt for Suresh—respect, brotherly affection, contempt, anger, pity? Lately, the negative sentiments had overshadowed the positive.

A plaintive wail coming from the direction of the house nudged Kiran back to the present. And with it came the worry and serious concern over Megha's whereabouts once again. Was she gagged and bound? Was she in pain? Was she sobbing her eyes out in a dark hole somewhere? And the most frightening speculation of all: had she been molested and perhaps even killed? The questions and images that filled Kiran's mind were deeply disturbing.

Amma claimed that her thoughtless daughter-in-law had run away from home for no apparent reason. Putting on her best distraught mother-in-law act for the policemen, Amma was bawling with all her might. "My husband and I love Megha like our own daughter," she claimed, her wide face crumpling in what appeared to be genuine pain. "How could she run away from us? We want her to come home. Please find her," she'd pleaded. Amma was currently continuing the farce with remarkable aplomb. She'd even managed to redden those fearsome eyes to make her grief seem authentic.

But Kiran knew better. Amma wasn't capable of love, at least not the kind she claimed she held for her daughter-in-law. No doubt Amma had a deep capacity for affection and loyalty to her own flesh and blood. She was generous and kind when it came to her brothers and their families.

Kiran was Amma's only nephew and the object of her fondness and adoration. In her eyes he could do no wrong. He was bright, handsome, wealthy, and just about the most eligible young man in the state, if Amma were to be believed. She often compared her own puny and pasty-faced son to Kiran in the most crude manner. It left Kiran embarrassed and, despite his mild disdain for Suresh, feeling sorry for him. Poor Suresh's ego was put through the shredder again and again, and no man deserved that, not even Suresh. But despite Amma's pounding, Suresh had managed to survive in that strange household.

Survive was the key word for anyone who had to live with Amma. Was it survival that had forced Megha to vanish? Had she been abused by the Ramnaths and couldn't tolerate it anymore? The thought of what she might have suffered at Amma's hands made Kiran wince. What about how Suresh may have treated her? As the popular proverb went, still waters could run very deep. Megha had always smiled a lot, showing the rest of them a happy and contented bride's face. Had that been a façade?

Only minutes ago, Kiran had noticed Suresh sitting silently in a corner, dressed in disheveled blue pajamas, eyes downcast, clasping and unclasping his hands while his mother talked to the police. He had spoken haltingly when questioned by the men. Claiming he had woken up to find his wife missing, and searched for her everywhere in vain, he had gone back to staring at the floor.

Amma's husband, Vinayak, on the other hand, looked genuinely distraught. He hadn't said much, other than to mention that he'd been asleep until Amma had awakened him with the grim news that Megha's bed was empty and neither she nor Suresh could find her anywhere. Uncle was a decent man, but he was henpecked, and keeping his mouth shut was his way of dealing with his aggressive and bossy wife. Amma had her husband tucked firmly under her thumb.

Cousin Shanti, Suresh's younger sister, blinked, as always, through her thick glasses and serenely answered the policemen's questions. Very little seemed to affect Shanti, the poor, simple soul. She lived in her fantasy world of poets, playwrights and authors—the world of English literature, her first and only love. Only names like Shakespeare or Chaucer or Whitman seemed to stir her to life. Neither Megha's presence nor her absence would mean much to Shanti. In fact, due to Shanti's detachment from reality, she seemed to be the only one who didn't cower under Amma's intimidating gaze.

Going back in his mind to earlier that evening, Kiran tried to recreate the scene in the Ramnaths' home. He and his parents and his other uncle, together with his wife and two daughters, had been invited to dinner at the Ramnaths'. It had been for no special reason other than to socialize as the close-knit family often did, or so it had seemed in the beginning. His folks were extremely family-oriented.

Had there been any signs in Megha's behavior to indicate this mysterious disappearance? He attempted to analyze her actions minute by minute except for the time she'd been alone in the kitchen. Nothing had seemed extraordinary. She'd been her usual cordial self.

The only thing unusual he'd noticed was that Megha had looked thinner and there were faint shadows around her eyes. In fact, he'd wondered what was wrong, whether she'd been ill. He could tell she had been working hard—her hands, with their narrow, tapering fingers, had looked a bit rough and red.

He'd also observed that she had hardly eaten any dinner. She had cooked a delicious meal and fed them well, but since Kiran was always so finely tuned to her actions and reactions, he'd noted that she'd practically skipped the meal herself.

Then his mind wandered to that odd episode after dinner. Amma had dispatched the men, namely, Kiran's father, his two uncles, Suresh, and himself on a long walk. "You men should go take a nice walk and digest the rich meal, you know. And Suresh needs the exercise to build some muscle." When the older men had put up some resistance, she'd firmly pointed out, "Walking is good for the prostate also, no? And the three of you are getting old. Go, go walk!"

Kiran had flatly refused to go with the other men because he'd become suspicious. Amma was up to something. He'd sensed an undercurrent of excitement in her all evening. She had been more animated than usual, more talkative, more manipulative.

After she'd disposed of the men, she had shepherded Kiran's mother, Kamala, and his aunt, Devayani, into the drawing room and shut the door, making it obvious that something of great importance was about to be discussed. Megha and his three female cousins, Kala, Mala and Shanti, had been told to amuse themselves by playing card games in the kitchen.

Pretending to relax in the master bedroom with a newspaper, Kiran had found a spot where he could put his ear to the wall separating the drawing room, so he could eavesdrop. Somewhere deep inside he knew this secret conference among the ladies had to do with Megha.

What he heard over the next few minutes was disturbing. The walls in that home were rather thin, and thank God for that.

"Megha's father has still not paid you any of the dowry money or what?" Devayani asked in her nasal drone. His Aunt Devayani was a small woman with an overbite and perpetual allergies that left her with a congested nose and a voice that sounded like a broken guitar.

"Not one *paisa* yet. And I don't see any chance of it coming soon. That's why I'm thinking about this," replied Amma.

Kiran had wondered what *this* meant. Exactly what was the old bat planning?

Then he heard his mother's voice say, "Chandramma, it's only one year since the wedding. Why not wait a bit?" Kamala was generally the voice of reason amongst the three women.

"One year is more than enough if you ask me," Devayani sniffed. Amma had mentored Devayani since the time she'd married Amma's youngest brother, Rama Rao, and since then Devayani had become Amma's staunchest supporter and friend.

"I have been very patient," Amma confirmed. "They promised us the money. This is clearly a breach of contract, no? Also, there is the matter of infertility to consider."

Kiran frowned. *Breach of contract? Infertility?* Where had his aunt learned such terms? She had obviously been educating herself on these matters.

"A healthy young girl can't get pregnant in one year or what?" Devayani wanted to know. "Then she must be barren also."

"Wait a minute," Kamala interrupted. "The girl gets along well with the family. And she is beautiful and bright, Chandramma. That was the main reason you chose her for Suresh, remember? You always wanted someone just like her for a daughter-in-law."

"I have considered all those things, Kamala; I'm not a fool." Amma sounded irritated at Kamala's words of caution.

"And pregnancy takes time," Kamala argued, somewhat impatient herself. "It took me many years before Kiran was conceived."

"That may be, but don't forget you had miscarriages before and after Kiran."

Miscarriages before and after his birth? Taken by surprise, Kiran contemplated the matter for a minute. Nobody had told him that and he'd never really questioned why he was an only child. It was something to which he'd never given any thought, always assuming his parents had ended up with a single child because fate had determined it. And well . . . it had.

No wonder his parents doted on him and the rest of the family treated him like a precious commodity. As the son of the oldest Rao brother, Kiran's was a special position to begin with. On top of that, his father's brother had two daughters and no son. As the only male in the Rao clan, it was up to Kiran to carry on the family name. It was small wonder that they thought he was handsome and bright although he considered himself ordinary. Their adoring attention bordered on smothering at times.

Kiran had forced his attention back to the drawing room and its occupants.

"That girl is getting too clever for her own good. She has started to question my actions," Amma fumed.

"What exactly has Megha questioned?" inquired Kamala.

"Do you know what she did last week? She openly defied me by going next door to that Muslim family's house when I told her not to go."

"Oh dear!" Devayani seemed to agree with Amma's cause for indignation.

But Kamala asked, "Why did she go there?"

"She said she went to help that woman because she had an appendicitis attack."

"What was Megha doing there if the woman had appendicitis? She needed a doctor, not a housewife," Devayani, in her infinite wisdom, added.

"But Megha claims she stayed with the woman until her husband came home. She said their three-year-old daughter was crying and she had to do this to help out. I suspect she stayed there to laze, to get out of doing her own work here. When I asked why she disobeyed my orders, she called me selfish and thoughtless."

There was a moment of silence as the two other women apparently absorbed this interesting piece of information, while Kiran silently cheered for Megha.

"Then she comes back home as if nothing happened. She polluted our Brahmin home by stepping into a Muslim house. That is total disregard for our religion, no?" Amma's tone was one of righteous indignation.

Kiran nearly laughed out loud. So Megha had helped a neighbor in distress and for that she was branded a villain. Amma's sense of right and wrong was twisted beyond imagination.

Unfortunately, too intent on eavesdropping to pay attention to his surroundings, Kiran's elbow had accidentally struck a hairbrush on the dressing table and sent it crashing to the floor. Damn! After that, probably realizing that Kiran was able to hear them, the rest of the conversation in the other room had turned to whispers and gone on for several minutes. Kiran hadn't been able to catch any of it. That was the part he needed to hear the most, and clearly, it was also the most damaging part of the meeting. And he hadn't a clue as to what it was.

The only portion he'd managed to overhear at the end was his mother saying with an ominous sense of finality, "Chandramma, please, I beg you, don't do it, at least for the sake of family honor. Imagine the scandal."

A sense of dread had engulfed Kiran. The men had returned from their walk shortly after that. On the drive home, his mother had been strangely quiet and contemplative. He'd been tempted to ask her about it, but he knew she'd never reveal a family secret, especially when it involved her older sister-in-law. In old-fashioned Hindu households, one did not betray family, and especially not an elder.

After he'd dropped his parents off at their large, affluent home, Kiran had driven back to his flat. He hadn't been able to relax or sleep. Something had nagged at him for hours, especially his mother's last remark: *Don't do it, at least for the sake of family honor. Imagine the scandal.*

What could be that scandalous? Was Amma planning to force Suresh to divorce Megha? If that was the case, then it would be a good thing—for Kiran. Megha would be free, and perhaps Kiran would have a chance to offer her marriage in the future. Of course, it was all conjecture at that point. And his parents would never condone his marrying a divorcee, especially one who had been previously married to his cousin.

But somehow he'd sensed that divorce was not what Amma had in mind. If not divorce, then what? He had no idea what she was contemplating, but the ominous feeling in his gut only escalated. Then there was that mysterious bit of information he had accidentally found in Amma's bag recently. That, too, was something that kept bothering him. But would his aunt stoop to something that evil? It was hard to say.

Megha was in some sort of trouble. He was sure of it.

After considerable private debating, he had pulled on some clothes, hopped into his car and driven to the Ramnath home. It was well after one-thirty at night then and the town quite dead. In all the chaos no one had questioned his unexpected arrival at such a late hour and he was grateful for that.

The scene confronting him at the Ramnath's made his stomach lurch: lights on; the door open; and two policemen in the house. And his aunt weeping! His immediate thought was that something had happened to Megha—either accident or illness. Or worse?

But after listening to what his aunt and uncle had to say, one thing was clear to Kiran. His instincts had been right. He'd sensed all night that something was wrong. And it was.

Megha was gone.

Chapter 5

Megha knew that Kiran Rao lived alone in a flat, and vaguely remembered the address: Gandhi Road. It was some distance from the center of town, a high-class suburb of Palgaum. Amma made a point of mentioning the address to her middle-class friends quite often—her wealthy and peerless nephew's home. As far as Megha could recall, there was only one building on that street with multiple flats. The rest were plush, sprawling individual homes.

Without giving much thought to what time it was, she raced towards Kiran's house. Her foot continued to throb, her head hurt, and her stomach kept churning, but she couldn't stop. It was too risky. The police were probably combing the streets for her. According to the Hindu edict she was a runaway wife now, a common criminal escaping from the law. The thought pushed her forward. Besides, who knew how many other drunkards were lurking around, waiting to pounce on hapless women?

Despite having to run and hide every time she heard a vehicle or unusual sounds, it didn't take her very long to find Kiran's residence—a modern, three-story building sitting amidst a walled and landscaped compound. It had a parking area on the ground floor.

The compound wall was a couple of inches taller than she, so she stood on her toes and surveyed the complex. There was no sign of people. The parking lot was almost full, indicating that the residents were all home and likely asleep in their beds. Every one of the windows facing her was darkened. All she could hear were the typical night sounds: insects twittering and the very distant drone of trucks on a highway somewhere.

The bad part was that the compound was brightly lit and nearly every part of it was clearly visible. Tiny moths fluttered around the brass pole-lamps standing like sentries at attention around the building. Not a single dark corner was available in case someone were to see her. For the residents it was probably an asset, but to her it was a major problem.

Afraid that she might be spotted by a passerby, she hunched down and crawled along the length of the wall to the black steel gates, which fortunately stood open. Once again she made a careful survey of the surroundings. She wasn't sure if there were security cameras or any of those fancy surveillance systems they repeatedly advertised in newspapers and on television. Who knew what kinds of advanced gadgets these types of neighborhoods used to keep the riffraff out?

What if there was a security guard for the building? She hadn't thought of that when she'd come running here. Expensive buildings usually had one or more guards or *gurkhas*. Given her present condition, there was no way a guard would let her in. She crept up to the glass windows of the lobby and, positioning herself behind a croton bush, looked in. From where she stood she had a wide view of the entire lobby. It was bright and spacious—tan marble floors, recessed lights in the high ceiling, and a modern wall-hanging on the largest wall. But there was no sign of a *gurkha* anywhere.

She waited a few minutes to see if a *gurkha* would appear. When there was still no sign of anyone, she tried the heavy front door and miraculously it opened with no effort. Where was all the security she had expected? She entered the lobby cautiously and sighed with relief to find it empty. Then, for a few moments she froze, wondering if some sort of alarm would go off. It made sense that an electronic sensor or something would be on guard, if not a human being. But several seconds passed and nothing unusual happened—no whistles, bells, or buzzers.

Well, she'd made it so far. What next?

The marble floor felt cool and smooth under her feet—a relief after the hard, rough surfaces she'd been traveling. Looking around she spied the red sign marked *Stairs* and made her way towards it. She dashed up the staircase. Amazingly, in her heightened state of mind, she even remembered that Kiran lived on the second floor. She was panting again by the time she reached the landing. Holding on to the handrail, she bent over to inhale some much needed air and calm her elevated heartbeat.

There were only two flats there, one to the right and the other left, with a long, wrought-iron balcony running the length of the landing. It looked down on part of the concrete and landscaped area below and a portion of the street was visible. She turned to the flat on the right, anxious eyes scanning the nameplate on the glossy polished door. It was a name she didn't recognize. Her heart slumped in disappointment. She ran to the second door and almost cried in relief. It read K. K. Rao. This had to be Kiran's flat. *Please God, please let it be Kiran's flat.*

She raised a hesitant hand to ring the doorbell. Although during the last several minutes it had made perfect sense, all of a sudden it felt strange to be standing here in the middle of the night. Earlier that evening, Kiran had said very little to Megha other than to compliment her on her cooking. Conservative Hindu families frowned on a young woman socializing freely with any men other than her husband. There had been lots of general chatter and noise around them, but there had been no interaction between Kiran and her. Now she was standing on his doorstep, desperately looking for help. How odd was that?

Overcome by doubts, she withdrew her hand from the doorbell. Although she'd had frequent contact with Kiran, she didn't really know him well enough.

Under the bright overhead lights Megha looked down at herself and the slovenly picture she made. She knew she looked like a destitute woman. Her sari was crushed and muddied; her hands and feet were scratched and filthy from having traveled miles over dusty streets. Her injured foot was bleeding on the gleaming gray tiles.

With her sari she wiped her face to remove the dripping perspiration and any traces of dirt. Then she tucked the stray tendrils of hair behind her ears and smoothed down the rest. There was nothing she could do about her ruined sari. Despite her efforts to improve her appearance she knew everything about her said *beggar*.

Coming to Kiran's flat was a ludicrous idea. How could she have dreamt up something this witless, even in her wildest dreams? Although Kiran was a compassionate man, his loyalties would surely lie with his own flesh and blood. Why would he want to help her? Just because he'd acted as her champion on a few difficult occasions it didn't mean he was going to be disloyal to his family in times of crises. Aiding a truant wife was probably against the law, and Kiran didn't appear to be the sort to resort to anything illegal.

After giving herself another minute to regain a little of her composure, Megha decided she would hide out somewhere for a day or two. Maybe Harini would take her in for a brief period. Harini was loyal to a fault.

Sometimes, when doing homework together as little girls, Megha had been mean to Harini, beyond mean, especially when Harini couldn't figure out the answer to a problem. Megha had deliberately given her the wrong answer and watched her getting humiliated in Mother Doreen's arithmetic class. Then the guilt would set in after Mother Doreen yelled at Harini or hit her over the knuckles with the sharp edge of the ruler. Megha would resort to apologetic hugs and regretful tears, promise Harini and herself she'd never do it again. But she'd do it again . . . and again. After all that, Harini had forgiven her. How could one not love a person like that dearly? It wasn't until the girls had become teenagers that Megha had recognized her own malicious ways and stopped herself from mistreating such a wonderful friend. After that their friendship had become stronger.

So, how could Megha put her best friend through such deceit now, especially when the friend happened to be pregnant? Besides, Harini and her husband lived with the husband's family. What would Harini's in-laws say? She couldn't throw Harini's life in turmoil. So that option was out.

There was the women's shelter in town, but someone had told Megha it was a smelly, grubby building filled with prostitutes and abused women battered beyond recognition. Even if she did go to that hellhole, the police were certain to look for her there.

She needed a plan right away. But no matter how many times and how many ways she examined the different options, she came back to a single solution: ask Kiran for a loan and then get out of town as quickly as she could. Kiran was her only hope. But would *he* be willing to help *her*? Well, she'd never know if she didn't try.

With her mind finally made up, Megha rang the doorbell. There was no answer. Of course, Kiran had to be in bed at this hour. She repeatedly pressed the bell with no more luck than the first attempt. She wondered what was keeping him from answering the door.

Naturally Kiran would be astonished to see her. He might even ask her politely to go home to Suresh. If she refused, he'd probably threaten to turn her over to the police. Quickly she made a mental note of what she would say and how she would say it convincingly. She had to make him see reason. Being a practical and intelligent man, he'd be likely to listen to logic.

Just then a dark car drove up the street. She couldn't recognize the exact color or the make from where she stood beside the metal railing of the landing, but she anxiously watched it come through the gates and enter the garage below. It disappeared from sight as it moved further inside and then came to a stop. The engine went silent.

A few seconds later she heard footsteps coming up the staircase—firm, heavy, masculine steps. Gripped by panic, she huddled close to the door. Her eyes darted about, making a quick survey of the landing for a place to hide. Unfortunately, there was none. This building probably had more lights than *Rashtrapati Bhavan*, the President of India's official residence.

The person climbing the stairs would be sure to mistake her for a thief trying to break into Kiran's flat. Total disaster! The police, neighbors, relatives—they would all converge upon her. And, the deadliest of horrors: Amma!

Taking a deep breath, Megha braced herself to make a run for it. Her only hope for escape would be to dart quickly past the unsuspecting stranger, fly down the stairs at lightening speed and disappear into the night before he knew what hit him. She'd have to count on the element of surprise to help her along. With any luck the person would be too stunned to react instantly. Clenching her fists, she readied herself for escape.

A split second later, instead of bewildering the man as she'd planned, it was she who became immobilized.

Kiran came into view as he reached the landing. Megha held her breath in. Their eyes collided and held for a stunned second. Her body tensed instinctively. Like a wild animal caught in the headlights, she stood poised to take flight in an instant. She had come all the way here to talk to Kiran, and yet, now that he stood before her, she'd lost her nerve. All she wanted to do was run.

The expression on Kiran's face was wide-eyed astonishment. "Megha! What are you doing here?"

At a complete loss for words, Megha merely continued to stare at him, her heartbeat slamming inside her chest.

Kiran seemed to recover quickly. He made the first move. Stepping forward, he held his hand out to her. "Thank God you're okay!"

Still dazed, but astounded at Kiran's unexpected greeting, Megha took a step backwards, her eyes wary and unblinking. Something was odd about this scenario. Had he said thank God? He was supposed to be furious with her, wasn't he? He should have turned her away or threatened to call the police. Instead he looked relieved and almost glad to see her on his doorstep. Was her traumatized mind playing tricks on her? She eyed him suspiciously, and took another step back.

But his expression still looked relieved and his hand remained extended. Something was wrong here. Very wrong. Megha couldn't trust her own eyes or ears. Was Kiran playing a prank on her, only to trap her later? A flutter of fear went through her.

He stepped closer and took her clammy hands in his. "Megha, I went looking for you at your house, but Amma told me you were gone. The police have been summoned. It's chaos over there. They're frantically searching for you."

So the hunt for her was already under way. And Kiran knew about it. Surely now he'd turn her over to the police. He had a clever way of getting her to trust him, too, pretending to be all concerned and sympathetic. She should have known. It was a stupid move on her part, coming to him for help.

Trembling, she withdrew her hands from his and held them behind her, backing into the corner until there was no place to go. The cool iron railing pressed against her side. Her lower lip started to quiver uncontrollably. Kiran stood only a couple of feet from her and she was trapped between him and the railing. He was a big, strong man. She'd never be able to escape, unless she arched her back and somersaulted over the balcony. And even that wouldn't guarantee death from this height.

She was terrified of heights—they made her dizzy, but then what did it matter when she was hurtling down to meet her death? However, with her miserable streak of bad luck she'd probably end up with a broken neck and paralyzed for life. And wouldn't Amma just love that?

No, she resolved in that instant, she wouldn't let Kiran take her back to that slaughterhouse. She would make him see sense. She'd try that logical approach she'd been practicing during the last few minutes. She'd make it sound nice and rational, even fall at his feet and beg if necessary. If all else failed, only then would she throw herself over the balcony. It would surely be less painful than death by incineration.

However, instead of sound argument her voice erupted in a high-pitched torrent of desperate appeal. "I d-don't want to go b-back, Kiran! Please, please, don't make me go back. I can't—"

"Shhh," he interrupted. "It's okay, Megha."

"It's not okay! They want to burn me to death because my father can't give them a dowry. Kiran, don't tell them you saw me here . . . please . . ." Her voice trailed away and her brain froze once again. Kiran was one of them. It was no use wasting her breath pleading.

"Burn you to death!" His jaws clenched visibly. "Are you sure?"

"Of course I'm sure! Do you think I made the whole thing up?" Her heart sank even lower. He couldn't even bring himself to believe her. Why would he bother to help her?

"But . . . killing in cold blood? My aunt and my cousin?"

She nearly punched him in the stomach for the look of disbelief on his face. "Do you think I imagined Suresh in the woodshed, preparing the wooden bed and pouring kerosene over it? Their talk about how Amma would explain my death—that I was supposedly picking up wood and the lantern tipped over and set me on fire?" A sob caught in her throat, making her voice come out raspy. "How dare you think I fabricated it, Kiran!" Angry tears came rolling down her cheeks and she brushed them away. "What else does burning Megha and finding a new wife with a big dowry for Suresh mean, damn it?"

Comprehension slowly replaced the shock on Kiran's face. "Dear God! I didn't think that horrid woman would sink to . . . murder!" He pulled the mobile phone out of his pocket. "That's it! I'm calling the police superintendent right now."

"No!" Megha yelled. "Y-you can't do that! It will be Amma's word against mine."

"But you can easily explain what happened, Megha. We're talking premeditated murder here, for God's sake!"

"Who will the police believe—your aunt or me? She's a very clever woman, a pillar of the community who can lie with a straight face. All I know is what I saw and heard; I have no proof of any kind."

Kiran studied Megha thoughtfully for a second, then thrust the phone back into his pocket. "You're probably right. Come here." His thick, black brows settled in a scowl before he gently disengaged her hands from behind her back and held one of them in his own. He reached inside his pocket with his other hand to pull out his keys. "Let's discuss this." Unlocking the door to his flat, he ushered her inside.

With some reluctance she went in. At this point, what did she have to lose? Foolishly she had come here expecting the impossible. Within the hour she'd be shipped back to Amma's house of horrors. And from there straight to hell, unless . . . she could . . . still jump off that balcony? Going up the stairs to the roof of the building would improve her chances of quick death. Anything would be better than perishing in a fire.

They stood in a small entrance hall. Megha's anxious eyes fell on the interior of the flat. A night light glowed in the drawing room and she could see the outlines of a modern, comfortable-looking sofa, two matching chairs, and an oblong wood-and-glass coffee table.

Kiran shut the door behind them, pocketed the keys, and led her to the sofa. He turned on a floor lamp, flooding the seating area with light. She looked at the expensive upholstery and hesitated. "I better not sit. My sari is very dirty and I . . . uh . . . well, your sofa will be ruined."

"Sit down, Megha," he said firmly. So she did, conscious of the dirt on her clothes and wondered if she smelled as bad as she looked. Heaven knew what kind of filth from the streets and the private properties she'd traveled through had attached itself to her sari. When she trembled he sat down beside her and patted her arm. "Calm down, Megha."

She shifted away from him. "I must smell awful, Kiran."

"You don't. You probably feel that way because you've been walking through some rough neighborhoods to get here." He must have seen how she sat warily on the edge of the couch or perhaps noticed the apprehension in her eyes because he said, "Relax, Megha, and sit comfortably. You're safe here and you don't have to go back."

"You won't let them kill me?" Despite his smooth assurances Megha was still suspicious.

He nodded and smiled a little, offering her a glimmer of encouragement. "I promise. I knew they were planning something. I heard them discussing it earlier. When you and my cousins were playing cards in the kitchen I was in the master bedroom at your house. I was pretending to read the newspaper while the rest of the men went for their forced walk." He stopped then, seemingly trying to gather his thoughts.

"I had a hunch Amma was up to something. She made it sound harmless enough while she discussed it with my mother and my aunt, but this defies reality." He still seemed dismayed. "I didn't think it was this bad. I thought it involved packing you off to your parents and then getting Suresh to divorce you. I even heard Amma mention big words like breach of contract and infertility."

"I thought she might have been considering divorce, too," said Megha, "especially after I disobeyed her and helped our Muslim neighbors."

"Although I should have—" As he stopped in mid-sentence Megha's head bobbed up instantly, her eyes posing a mute question. Kiran raked a thoughtful hand through his hair. "Damn, I should have guessed!"

She stared at him. "Guessed what?"

"Several weeks ago, I found some literature on bride-burning in Amma's bag," Kiran said.

"Amma's bag!"

"She forgot her shopping bag at my parents' house and I was asked to return it to her. Curiosity made me look in the bag. It had all kinds of articles on national and regional statistics and about how no arrests are ever made because of lack of evidence and how the police usually look the other way when offered substantial bribes. It even had information on the unique ways people dispose of the bodies so no one can guess what happened to the brides who disappear mysteriously."

"You didn't think it was strange that Amma was reading such bizarre things?"

"It was very puzzling, but I didn't understand the purpose at the time, so I dismissed it from my mind. The articles were printouts from the Internet."

Megha frowned. "But there's no computer at home."

"She probably went to a cyber café or some such place to do her research. I should have suspected something then, but I didn't put two and two together, never thought my aunt could be that evil." His expression was bitter. "Even a little while ago, I thought of every possible thing that could have happened to you, but I never wanted to believe my aunt and cousin could have tried to kill you. I guess I was wrong."

At hearing his chilling words Megha shivered once again. "We were both wrong."

"I'm sorry I didn't rescue you from them earlier, Megha."

Something in Kiran's expression let loose the emotions within her. Despite her efforts to rein them in, she couldn't help bursting into tears. Kiran offered her a handkerchief then sat quietly, letting her cry as long as she wanted. All he did was pat her hand occasionally and say, "I'm sorry." When the sobs finally turned to mere sniffles, he looked at her. "You must be exhausted and hungry. Would you like something to drink or eat?"

She shook her head. How could he think about food at a time like this? Didn't he understand the gravity of her situation? "I would have been dead by now, Kiran. They were going to tie me down to a bed of wood and burn me to death." The dread in her voice had lessened after the weeping fit, she realized. Now it sounded hollow, devoid of emotion, her gaze dispassionate, as if she were looking on the scene of her own execution and yet completely removed from it, like watching it happen to a stranger.

Though hovering on the brink of a furious outburst, Kiran kept his rage under control. Megha needed him, needed his strength and sympathy. She had come here looking for protection and support. Giving in to the urge to go on a ferocious tirade against his aunt and cousin would do nothing to dispel Megha's fears and misery. So he held his own emotions tightly restrained.

As he pictured the gruesome scene in his mind, Kiran shuddered inwardly. Thousands of young brides perished each year in India because of dowry, or the lack of it—heartlessly killed—some crushed to death, some thrown out of high buildings, others strangled or poisoned, many burned like so much refuse. How could one human being do that to another? In this day and age, in a middle-class, educated family no less? How could his aunt and cousin dream of doing that to a sweet, innocent daughter of the house? And all that, for money. How sickening!

Well, he wouldn't let those monsters succeed. Never! He glanced at Megha, suddenly feeling possessive and custodial of her. "Shh, try not to think about it."

She raised her gaze to him, her exquisite eyes still damp and rimmed with red. "Kiran, why are you being so supportive of me?"

Kiran asked himself the same question. Though he knew the answer, of course—he was in love with her. Was this a good time to be honest about that with Megha? Probably not. She was too distraught and fragile to handle that kind of confession from him at the moment. On the other hand, he couldn't altogether lie to her either. "Because I care . . . you're family, Megha," he said finally, making it sound harmless without being dishonest.

"But I'm the outsider. The Ramnaths are your family."

"That's not the issue here. This is a matter of life and death— your life. In fact, I was hoping Amma was planning on getting Suresh to divorce you."

"You were?" She stared at him as if he'd suddenly grown an extra pair of ears. "Why would you want to see your cousin divorced?"

"Because I . . . uh . . . realized you were being mistreated in that house."

Her expression looked uncertain. "How did you guess that?"

Kiran chided himself privately for his outburst. It had only served to make her suspicious of him. But part of the truth had slipped out and there was nothing he could do to take it back. At least he'd had enough sense not to confess his deeper, more personal feelings for her. It was time for some damage control. "It didn't take much to guess, Megha," he said. "I've watched you wither away under Amma's thumb and Suresh's weakness."

"How? You were only a visitor."

"I'm not blind. I noticed the way Amma treated you and how Suresh never lifted a finger to defend you. Despite the smile on your face at all times, you've lost weight and there are dark shadows around your eyes—you weren't like this when you first got married. I could tell you were unhappy with the Ramnaths. I came to the conclusion that divorce would be your only way out of there."

"Hmm." She continued to look skeptical.

"You could have done a hell of a lot better than having Suresh for a husband. I can't imagine why your father turned you over to him."

"I think the Ramnaths lied to my parents about a lot of things. My father was told Suresh earned a high salary and the family was cultured and well-off."

"Is there no end to Amma's deceit?" Kiran groaned. "I'm convinced you should get a divorce, Megha. I'll help you in any way I can."

She turned to him again, her expression hopeless. "But you can't really help me all that much, Kiran. Suresh and Amma can force me back. You won't be able to stop them."

"I won't let them harm you, Megha," he assured her. "I went there to save you tonight. After I returned home from dinner at your house earlier, I just couldn't relax. At first I tried to tell myself that my imagination was running wild. Since I thought it was divorce that Amma was planning, I decided I'd let it take its course, because it would be the best thing for everyone, especially you. But then, those printouts I had seen in her bag kept bothering me. The possibilities were ghastly. I couldn't let them come true, so I came to look for you."

"Even if it meant antagonizing your family?" When Kiran nodded, she said, "But I still don't understand. You're one of them, Kiran."

"Being one of them doesn't mean I support them in everything. I happen to believe in things like decency and integrity, you know."

"Oh." Megha looked away, apparently not quite convinced.

"Listen, Megha, I just thought of something. Part of my future plans is to quit my job and move to Mumbai to take over my father's branch office. I've already purchased a flat there in preparation for my move. Maybe you can stay in the flat for a while?"

"I can't stay—"

"You'll be safe there. Mumbai's a huge city and it's easy to remain anonymous there. When the police give up their hunt, Suresh and Amma will file for divorce on grounds of desertion. They're desperate to find Suresh another wife. I believe they'll welcome this opportunity."

She shook her head, still looking troubled. "You can't do this. What about your parents?"

"In time we'll let them know—when things settle down—when your divorce is under way."

"No, Kiran. The idea of a runaway wife, their nephew's wife, seeking shelter in your home will destroy them. Divorce in itself is enough to upset them."

Kiran snorted with typical male indifference to convention. "This is the twenty-first century, Megha. Look around you. Divorce is not all that rare these days."

A wry smile touched the edge of Megha's mouth. "That may be true, but the injured party's cousin sheltering the offending party is unheard of. You and I still live in Palgaum. We were born in an orthodox Brahmin caste and culture mired in a swamp that goes back a thousand years. The world goes around, but our traditions remain static. Don't you see that? Besides, it's not my divorce I'm worried about. It's *your* reputation that concerns me more."

"You have a way with words, you know that?" Kiran said, trying to help ease her anguish. "I've noticed it—the way you express yourself is so colorful, interesting. And you can quote poetry learned in high school as if you read it only hours ago."

"That's what my English professor often told me." Her answering smile was wistful. "I've always loved writing and reading."

"I'm not surprised. Some day you'll have to show me what you write. But right now you need to get some rest. You've had a traumatic night."

He noticed the doubts cloud her face once again and realized all this was too much for her to absorb at present. She was still in shock. After some rest she would be able to think rationally. Tomorrow he'd explain his plans to her in detail and then she'd see some sense, recognize the logic in his thinking.

But first she needed to get cleaned up. She was clearly embarrassed about her appearance. He noticed how she was trying to hide the dirt on her sari and tuck her hands and feet out of sight. And those scratches on her arms and face combined with her heartbreaking tears were tempting him to rush over to Amma's house and strangle the fat old bitch with his bare hands. He had never been particularly fond of his aunt, but now he detested her. He wasn't a violent man by nature, nor was he vindictive, but if Amma and Suresh had succeeded in their evil plans for Megha, he would have made sure those two paid the price for the rest of their lives.

Thank God it hadn't come to that!

Megha was suffering and there was not much he could do for her right now other than to offer her a safe place for the night, a chance to have a hot bath and rest for a while. After that she was likely to feel better, maybe even fit enough to start thinking of a viable plan for her immediate future.

He rose and motioned her to follow him. She stood up without any arguments. He showed her to the bathroom. Before she went in he stopped her. "Wait, I'll be back in a minute." After rummaging through his bedroom he came back with a T-shirt and a pair of shorts along with a fresh towel and a new toothbrush still in its cellophane wrap. "Not much, but it's the best I can do. At least they're clean and the shorts have a drawstring, so they won't slide down."

She took the clothes but glanced at them with a mild frown. "But how can I. . . ?" She seemed to change her mind about whatever she was about to say and nodded instead.

"There's running hot water twenty-four hours. Take your time—have a nice hot shower if you want."

"Thank you," she whispered with a grateful half-smile and stepped into the bathroom.

Then the doorbell rang.

Chapter 6

Shaking with terror all over again, Megha huddled in the bathroom. Someone was at the front door. *Oh God, oh God!* They had found her. How had they located her so quickly?

Holding the door partly open, she strained her ears to listen to the two male voices in the foyer. Kiran's was a bit clearer than that of the other man. It was neither Suresh's nor Appaji's voice. The police? Kiran's father or uncle? By this time the entire family would have rallied to Amma's side and started their own search.

She closed her eyes in defeat. Her time had run out after all.

The sound of the front door shutting with a slight squeak reached her. Kiran must have let the person in! She listened to the approaching footsteps. Her life was about to end. All that running was for nothing. She should not have come here. Stupid, stupid decision!

She shut the bathroom door quickly and turned the lock. Unfortunately, there was no window in this bathroom to even contemplate an escape. Despite the thud-thud of her heartbeat in her ears, Megha clearly heard a set of steps approaching—but only one set. Was the policeman or whoever the man was, waiting in the drawing room then?

A knock sounded on the bathroom door. "Megha."

She didn't answer. *Think, think. . . .* Looking around for something heavy to wedge against the door, she realized there was nothing, so she pitched all her weight against it. Maybe she could plead for her life with Kiran one more time. But if a policeman was here, what could Kiran do? Promise the man a bribe . . . perhaps? Weren't the police always looking for rewards?

None of those options seemed viable, so she pressed harder against the door.

"Megha, are you okay?" When she remained silent, Kiran rapped harder. "Megha, answer me!"

The silence on Megha's part continued.

"I know you heard the doorbell, and I know you're scared. I want you to know it was only my downstairs neighbor."

Neighbor? Likely story! As if she was going to fall for that. "What did the . . . uh, neighbor want?" she managed, her voice barely coming out as a murmur.

"He heard our footsteps and voices on the landing earlier."

"Is that so unusual?" Her heartbeat continued its frantic beat.

She heard Kiran hesitate on the other side of the door. "Yes, it is. Because it's so late at night and my lights are still on, he wondered if there was some emergency and whether I needed help."

"What did you tell him?" Even now Megha wasn't sure Kiran was being entirely honest. If this was his way of getting her to open the door and come out so the police could cart her away, she was wise to him. If he thought she was that naïve, he was not as bright as she'd imagined.

"I told him it was an office problem and someone on my staff delivered an emergency report."

"I don't believe you, Kiran. I know there's a policeman in your drawing room." She might as well be direct in her accusations. Even if she was helpless, at least he wouldn't mistake her for a fool. She'd never tolerate being labeled dimwitted.

"Damn it, Megha! There is no policeman."

"Then prove it!"

"Quit acting like a brat, will you?" He sounded thoroughly annoyed. "You'll just have to trust me."

Standing there in the bathroom, Megha speculated. If he wasn't telling the truth, he'd have been nice and persuasive instead of angry, now wouldn't he, at least in the interests of gaining her trust? She gingerly unlocked the door and opened it a crack. "Kiran, if you're lying to me, I swear I'll get even with you."

"Fair enough."

"I won't forgive you for pretending to be my friend and then turning me in."

Kiran nodded gravely. "I understand. Now come out and see for yourself."

Very slowly, she opened the door all the way and stepped out. "I'll tolerate open hostility any day, but I will not put up with back-stabbing, Kiran." She pointed a finger in his face and glared at him for a moment. "I detest two-timers."

Kiran stood aside and motioned her to go out and look for herself. After making sure the flat was empty save for the two of them, Megha returned to the alcove outside the bathroom where Kiran still stood, with his arms folded across his chest. "Satisfied?" he asked. He didn't seem so irritated anymore.

She nodded grudgingly. "I'm sorry I didn't trust you." He hadn't been lying after all. She felt foolish and didn't know whether to laugh or cry from relief. She couldn't blame him for being cross with her. She had behaved like an ungrateful little brat.

To her surprise, Kiran chuckled, his eyes glinting with amusement. "Suspicious young lady, aren't you?" When she shot him a quelling look, his chuckle turned to a hearty laugh. "Can't blame you, I suppose. If I were in your place, I wouldn't trust anyone either."

"Glad to hear that."

He gestured toward the bathroom, looking even more amused. "Now that you're somewhat convinced that I'm not a two-timing back-stabber, you may want to go ahead and wash up."

With her head held high despite feeling embarrassed about acting so churlish, she swept into the bathroom and shut the door with a decisive click. Well, he could laugh all he wanted! She wasn't ready to trust him completely yet.

A nice long shower was exactly what Megha indulged in.

Accustomed to a more austere lifestyle, she had never used a shower before and it took her a couple of minutes to figure out how it worked. Once she got it started, the spray of warm water felt like heaven. Hot water without having to heat it on a wood fire in a big brass cauldron? How wonderful was that! And then not to have to scoop it out of a bucket with a mug and pour it over one's head? That was pure luxury.

Putting every other thought aside for now, she lifted her face, closed her eyes and delighted in the water raining over her and flowing down her body.

The soap was deliciously fragrant. The sheer lavishness of the modern tile-and-marble bathroom made Megha feel weepy again. So foolish—to cry over a simple bathing routine—but her nerves were frayed and the tears came easily. After a while she washed the cut on her foot, which stung from the soapsuds and continued to bleed a little. Her scratches and bruises burned under the hot water.

But otherwise the shower was marvelously soothing. Even better was getting that awful grime and stench off herself. She used large quantities of Kiran's shampoo to wash her hair and spent a long time in the bathroom trying to speculate and strategize. But for the life of her she couldn't think of a plan of action. Right now, all she wanted to do was lie down somewhere and sleep. It was as if her mind had shut down completely. Having made it this far, to a state of relative safety, a strange kind of numbness seemed to have set in.

While Megha was in the bathroom, Kiran heated a mug of milk in the microwave oven and stirred some Ovaltine into it. After hunting around in the kitchen cabinets he found a packet of chocolate cream biscuits and put a few of those on a plate.

He then made a cup of instant coffee for himself, pulled out a chair at the dining table, and sat down to think.

What was he going to do with Megha? This late at night there was nowhere she could go. He could probably afford to keep her with him for one night, maybe two, but after that? His mind drew a complete blank. She might have a few uncles and aunts and cousins somewhere, but relatives and friends could not be told of her whereabouts. Hotels were not particularly safe for a lone young woman, and anyway the police would be sure to look for her in every hotel within a twenty-mile radius.

His own Mumbai flat was large enough and completely furnished in anticipation of his impending move. But though he had mentioned the idea to her, he now realized Megha was too young and inexperienced to live alone in a big city. Her petrified reaction earlier to the imaginary policeman in his living room had shown him that.

All Kiran knew for sure was that she was in danger and had to be protected. But if she remained so close to him, under his roof, the threat to his sanity was equally troubling. He was a man infatuated, with all the needs and instincts of a healthy male. At the moment, with her in the next room, naked and bathing, his nerves were already tied in knots.

However, where else but in his home could she remain safe? He was the only one who really cared about her, and he was also the least likely to be suspected of harboring her. The police and his family would target all of Megha's family and friends, but nobody would think of asking *him* regarding her whereabouts. That more or less clinched the matter. She would have to stay with him indefinitely. He'd have to keep his baser needs and his emotions under strict control. Perhaps in a day or two they could review her situation and come up with some practical answers. There had to be some way to resolve this.

When Megha came out of the bathroom he noticed the edge of the T-shirt fell all the way down to mid-thigh level on her, but despite its looseness it didn't hide her feminine shape. The absence of a brassiere was obvious from the way her breasts strained against the soft cotton of the shirt. It took all of Kiran's self-control to tear his eyes away from that particular spot. A wave of longing to feel her crushed against his own hard chest washed over him for a second before he ordered himself to stop behaving like a hormone-crazed juvenile.

The shirt's sleeves covered her elbows, and the shorts hung well below her knees. Her face had a clean pink glow. Her hair fell in damp waves over her shoulders and down her back. The enormous dark eyes were less red now. She smelled of his soap and shampoo, and something else . . . essentially female. She smelled sweet.

Looking like an incredibly beautiful teenager, she seemed so unspoiled and innocent. And, with that sense, an all-male desire to defend and protect once again replaced the need to touch and possess her.

The bright red dot on her forehead had been washed away, too. The *mangalsutra* was tucked inside the shirt. For some reason it gave him deep satisfaction to see her dressed in his clothes and the dot gone. That dot had meant she was still married to Suresh. Kiran wanted Megha to belong to himself. He'd make sure that would happen soon. Knowing what the divorce laws were like, it could be at least two or three years in the future, but Kiran considered himself a patient man.

He'd wait as long as he needed to. Megha was worth waiting for.

Megha stood awkwardly in the kitchen, embarrassed at wearing Kiran's clothes. She hadn't exposed her legs in years. She felt naked. When she saw that Kiran wasn't laughing at the odd picture she made, she took a step forward, feeling more confident. Encouraged by the kindness in his expression instead of the ridicule she'd expected, she moved closer to the dining table.

"Feeling better?" Kiran asked.

She nodded. Eyeing the steaming milk in the mug, she smiled at him. "Sorry, I didn't mean to put you to so much trouble."

"No trouble at all." He rose and pulled out a chair for her—one of four matching chairs surrounding a round, smoked-glass dining table. "Come, sit down and drink some Ovaltine."

She sat down with some hesitation and studied the table. It felt strange to be waited on by someone, especially a man.

"Eat some biscuits," Kiran encouraged. "Unfortunately, mine is a bachelor's home. I don't have anything more substantial than this."

"Ovaltine is fine. It smells wonderful." She gratefully picked up the mug with both hands, hoping to savor the aroma and the heat from the cup seeping into her palms. Instead she winced and put the cup down with a thud, the scalding liquid sloshing over the rim.

"Too hot, Megha?" Kiran half rose from his chair.

"It's my hands. I bruised them earlier."

"Did you fall down?" His eyes traveled to her arms and chin, probably wondering about the scratches, too.

She nodded reluctantly. "I was running in the dark—it was hard to see where I was going. And then . . . I had to climb over a rough-surfaced stone wall."

"Why?"

"Some disgusting drunkard was chasing me." She avoided meeting Kiran's eyes. Her story was beginning to sound like something out of the movies. Such bizarre things didn't happen in real life.

"Did he hurt you?" Kiran sounded angry, as he'd sounded earlier.

"I'd rather not talk about it." Suddenly she felt very exposed, talking about a near molestation to a man she didn't know all that well.

"Can you at least tell me if you're all right? You don't need a doctor?" He was still scowling.

"Uh . . . no. I'm okay, thank you. "

"You've been through hell tonight, haven't you?" Kiran's expression softened. "Here, hold this around the cup," he said, handing her a cotton napkin. Then with a sponge he carefully cleaned up the spilt Ovaltine.

She did as he suggested and it felt better, the warmth from the mug comforting. She realized she was ravenous as she sipped the Ovaltine. It tasted delicious.

Kiran drank his own coffee and pushed the plate before her. "Eat."

She gratefully accepted some biscuits.

Feeling refreshed after a few swallows of the nourishing liquid and the food, Megha took stock of her surroundings. Earlier she had been too distressed to notice the flat. This was her first real glimpse of Kiran's home. It was not a very large place, but still spacious and airy compared to both the cramped homes she had lived in.

The contemporary domed light fixture above the dining area was made of etched glass. The sofa and chairs in the drawing room were covered with tan damask and accented with forest green pillows. Curtains in the same shade of green covered the window directly behind the sofa. There was a hand-woven area rug in shades of tan, white and green. Two matching brass floor lamps sat next to a pair of end tables on either side of the sofa. A large bronze sculpture of the god Ganesh rested on an oblong table against one wall that had no other furniture. The Ganesh looked like an antique. On the wall above the sculpture hung a set of four miniature Rajasthani paintings mounted on ivory silk mats in intricate gold frames.

Kiran's flat had the look of understated elegance. So this was how rich bachelors lived. He worked for some corporation at the moment, and had family wealth, as well. His father was the sole owner of a flourishing petroleum and chemical products distribution business. Megha could see the discerning taste of his mother, Kamala Rao, in the décor around his home.

"Nice place you have here," she said, turning to Kiran. Talking about the flat gave her mind something else besides her misery to think about. It also helped to alleviate the awkwardness of sitting there in *his* dining room, dressed in *his* clothes and drinking *his* Ovaltine.

"Thanks. Not very spacious, but it's a place to call home."

"Pretty impressive kitchen, too," she added, noting the tall, gleaming wood cabinets, the modern appliances, including a microwave oven, and the cream granite countertops.

Kiran chuckled. "Fully equipped kitchen, but I never cook. My parents invite me to eat with them at least twice a week. The rest of the days I eat out or reheat something that my mother insists on packing for me."

"No servants?" she asked, surprised. Wealthy people always had servants. Megha knew Kiran's parents had several. Even Amma and Appaji had a servant.

"I have one man who comes in on Sundays to clean the flat and wash my clothes and linens." He grinned sheepishly. "I'm a typical spoiled Indian male. I don't know how to cook or clean."

She glanced at him curiously. "I'm surprised you live alone when your parents own such a huge house." The Raos owned a mansion with several bedrooms.

He shrugged and took a sip of his coffee. "What can I say? I like my independence."

"Maybe if Suresh had felt that way I wouldn't be in this situation today," Megha said thoughtfully. She wondered if Suresh would ever be really independent of his mother, in or out of her house.

"Suresh is entirely too attached to Amma," said Kiran, confirming Megha's thoughts.

After another awkward silence Megha inclined her head towards the drawing room. "You did a fine job of decorating this place."

"I don't know how to do that either—my mother did that. She's very artistic, as you know."

"I know." And she was also part of the clique that planned her murder. His mother was tight with Amma, and Megha had seen them huddled together gossiping often enough.

As if reading her mind, Kiran quickly added, "I know what you're thinking. My mother was part of the conspiracy. I'm not trying to defend her, Megha, but I distinctly heard her trying to talk Amma out of it."

"And she didn't think to warn me? She was going to sit back and watch me die an agonizing death?" The bitter resentment was hard to keep out of her voice.

Kiran folded his arms over the table and leaned forward so Megha could see clearly into his deep-set brown eyes and note the thickness of the lashes. His dark brows were pulled close together, forming a small ridge in between. "Like I said, what she did was wrong. She probably thought there would be a divorce. If she knew it was anything this dreadful, I'm sure she would have tried to protect you." He must have noticed her lingering skepticism, because he said with more conviction, "Believe me, Megha, she's not a monster. She's a good mother to me and a loving wife to Papa. She wouldn't stand by and see you get killed—or anybody get killed."

"I suppose you're right." Megha recalled the occasions when she had visited the Raos with the rest of the family, and how Kamala had been quite cordial to her. She was not nasty like Devayani, their younger aunt, and certainly nothing like Amma. But Megha preferred to reserve her judgement about Kamala. Maybe Kamala Rao wasn't a bad sort, but Megha still considered her one of the conspirators. At present the entire Ramnath clan and the Raos remained suspect in her mind.

"You know as well as I that once Amma gets something into her thick head nobody can talk her out of it," Kiran reminded her.

"God, don't I know that!" Megha rolled her eyes.

"Besides, my mother is very old-fashioned. She'd never oppose something her husband's respected elder sister was planning, barring murder, of course."

Megha nodded, agreeing that stringent traditions did indeed prevent a woman from standing up to her older sister-in-law or betraying her confidence. Swallowing the last of the Ovaltine, she rose from her chair. "Would you mind if I wash my clothes in your washing machine, Kiran?" She had noticed what appeared to be a washer and dryer outside the bathroom, another luxury she'd never had.

"You can wash your clothes tomorrow, Megha. You need to get some sleep now."

"What!" Tomorrow would be too late. And sleep? In his flat? What was he talking about? Suddenly, panic set in again. She needed to get out of here as quickly as possible. Daylight was only a few hours away and she had to disappear before then. *Time was running out.*

"No, I have to wash them now. And can I . . . uh . . . borrow some money from you?" Oh dear, it was so awkward asking for money, even if it was a small loan. "I need to get on the earliest possible bus to Hubli. I'll return the money as soon as I get there."

Kiran's brows snapped back together once again. "You can't go out there alone!"

"I have no choice."

"Yes, you do. You'll stay here."

"I can't! I'm a married woman."

"I will not let you out of here until I know you're safe."

"You can't dictate to me, Kiran. Technically, you're my cousin-in-law. And since Suresh and you grew up together almost like brothers, you're more or less my brother-in-law." What was he thinking? It was a ridiculous idea, even more absurd than her appearing on his doorstep, begging for help. All she'd intended to do was borrow some money and request him to drive her to the bus stop. She'd definitely not envisioned any of this. Even the shower and the food and clothes he'd offered her were unexpected and utterly generous.

She looked at herself dressed in his clothes and frowned. What was happening here? Things were spinning out of control. She needed to focus on what to do next and not sit here drinking warm milk and admiring Kiran's flat, much less wear Kiran's clothes. And allow him to bully her in the bargain.

He came around the table to stand beside her, his face still drawn in a serious scowl. "*Technically*, you would have been dead by now, too. I'm not letting you out of my sight, Megha. If Amma can find you and punish you, she will. She wants her precious son to be viewed as a grieving widower, not a divorced man. She'll come to Hubli and drag you home so she can finish you off. Is that what you want?" His eyes searched her face for a second, looking for a reaction. Perhaps satisfied with the alarm flashing in her eyes, he said, "I didn't think so."

He was right. She was the one who'd come to him looking for help, and not the other way around, so she didn't have a right to get defensive with him. She was stuck in Kiran's home then, at least for a day. But after that?

Evidently interpreting her silence as submission, Kiran motioned her to follow and led her to his bedroom. When he noticed the uncertain expression on her face he laughed, surprising her once again by shifting from grim annoyance to wry amusement in an instant. "Don't worry, Megha, I plan to sleep on the sofa. You can use my room."

"I've imposed on you enough, Kiran," she protested. "I can't throw you out of your bedroom, too. I'll take the sofa."

He nudged her inside. "Don't argue."

Kiran peeled back the bedspread and instructed Megha to lie down. She obeyed reluctantly, looking small and helpless against the stark white sheets in his large bed. Her face looked flushed. He knew it was from the embarrassment of lying down before a man other than her husband and also from baring her legs. He noticed she had beautiful limbs, long and slim and shapely. Several angry red scratches were evident in places. There would be scabs forming soon. He hoped they wouldn't leave behind scars, marring the beauty of that smooth, creamy skin.

Then his eyes came to settle on her feet. Her right sole appeared raw and bloody. He lifted the foot in his hand to examine it. "Oh no, Megha, there's a cut here."

Megha's gaze dropped. "I know my feet look disgusting. I must have stepped on broken glass or something on my way here. I had no time to put on my *chappals*," she said, referring to the slip-on footwear commonly worn in India.

He turned on his heel. "Stay right there. I'll get some bandages."

She put up a hand to stop him. "Kiran, I think I might have left trails of blood all over your flat. My foot has been bleeding for some time now."

"Why didn't you tell me sooner?"

She looked contrite. "I may have ruined your beautiful carpet, too."

"I'll clean the floor and carpet later. Your foot needs attention first." He hastened out of the room.

Within a minute he was back with a white, rectangular plastic box tucked under his arm. In his hands he carried a glass of water and two white tablets. Putting them in Megha's hand, he handed her the water. When she lifted a questioning brow, he said, "Pain relievers—they'll help to remove the soreness from your muscles. You fell down and hurt yourself, didn't you? And all that running—you're going to be sore by morning."

Nodding, she swallowed the pills and set the glass on the nightstand. Meanwhile he flipped the plastic box open and pulled out a tube of antiseptic ointment, a bottle of alcohol, and a variety of bandages and gauze. He sat on the edge of the bed, lifted the offending foot and placed it in his lap. What a dainty little foot, he thought, noticing her toes curl. No fancy nail polish or pampering with pedicures and lotions here. Although the skin was rough from all the abuse her feet had suffered, the toes and arches were nicely shaped, and the nails neatly cut.

Megha kept her eyes averted. She was probably embarrassed about her foot resting on his thigh. Such close contact between the two of them was strange, he had to admit. And disturbing. Right now, his thigh was tingling, sending out a few sparks from her closeness.

He thought of something as he examined the seriousness of the wound. "Have you ever had a tetanus injection?" He hoped to God she'd had a dose of tetanus sometime within the last few years. If not, he'd have to drag her to his doctor friend's clinic right away. Tetanus infections could become fatal.

To his relief, she said, "I accidentally cut myself with a kitchen knife two years ago and our family doctor gave me an injection." She held up an index finger to show him her scar.

"At least tetanus can be ruled out then." Suppressing his male reactions, he quickly soaked cotton balls with alcohol and swabbed the wound. She winced a couple of times.

He glanced at her. "Sorry, I know it stings like hell."

"That's okay." She observed in silence as he worked on her wound. Her expression didn't reveal much.

Kiran fell into deep thought, wondering what was going through Megha's mind. She had run for miles in the dark, probably fallen several times, then climbed over a wall, and managed to find her way here. Good heavens. He'd probably never know the depths of the horrors she had lived through during the night.

He inwardly fumed at the atrocities she had suffered. As if running from certain death wasn't bad enough, she had to fight off a drunken brute on the streets in the middle of the night. She was a brave girl. It took guts to do what she had done. Well, at least she was here now, in one piece and relatively safe. From now on he would protect her. If he'd had any doubts earlier about what to do with her, they had vanished now.

As he attended to her, he knew exactly what he had to do. He'd keep her here, where he could keep a close eye on her.

He liberally applied the ointment on her sole and put an adhesive bandage over the cut. Then he wound a strip of gauze around the injured area and secured the bandage. Satisfied that everything was in order, he pressed her foot, giving it a gentle massage and making sure the dressing wasn't too tight. Then he swabbed her legs, arms and hands with alcohol before smoothing a light film of ointment over them, all the while admiring the satiny texture of her skin. "There, that should make it better," he said, spreading a little of the salve on her scratched chin and withdrawing his hand before he was tempted to caress her face or do something entirely inappropriate.

Megha refused to look him in the eye. He could tell she was discomfited by his closeness, perhaps even a little puzzled by what she considered extreme coddling on his part. In the kind of background she was used to men didn't do things like this for women. But he wanted to do it for her—take care of her, heal her and ease her pain. There was something about Megha that touched the very depths of his heart and soul.

But then, what was that other, guarded look in her eyes? "Megha, what's the matter? You're not scared of me, are you?" She shook her head. "Don't worry, I would never dream of taking advantage of you."

This time she met his eyes. "I'm not scared, Kiran—I'm touched by your compassion. Suresh would never have done

this for me. Even when I had a miscarriage, he didn't bother—"
Her eyes widened, as if realizing she had inadvertently said
something she hadn't meant to.

"You had a miscarriage?"

She nodded with obvious reluctance.

"When?"

"I . . . uh . . . a few days ago. In fact, it happened the day you
and I ran into each other by the riverbank—very late that same
night."

He digested the information for a minute. He clearly remembered that evening, every tiny detail. She had looked sad and
tired and disheartened, but he'd had no idea she was expecting.

She sent him a soulful plea. "Promise you won't say anything
to anyone? Only my parents know about it. Amma would kill
me if she found out." The irony of her own words hit her instantly. "What am I saying? Amma was about to kill me even
without knowing about the miscarriage."

Kiran grunted in sympathy. His loathing for Suresh went up
another notch. "I'm sorry about the miscarriage, Megha. That
baby probably wasn't meant to be," he consoled her.

"Maybe it's for the best," she agreed, the faraway look in her
eyes telling him she was recalling that night.

"Get some sleep now." He returned the first aid items to the
box. "We'll talk tomorrow."

"But tomorrow—"

"I'm going to take a day off from work and we'll plan a
course of action together." He waited for her to settle back on
the bed and pull the covers over herself.

As he started to walk away she called, "Kiran."

He turned around. "Yes?"

"Thank you for taking me in."

"No problem."

"I thought you'd turn me over to them, but you've been . . .
very kind."

"I would never turn you over to them, Megha."

She was quiet for a moment before she said, "I'm such a coward, aren't I, Kiran?"

"Why would you think that?"

"I panicked and ran away from an impossible situation instead of dealing with it."

"Anyone would have panicked in your place. It's human instinct to be frightened of death, Megha. Even soldiers trained in combat often run from certain death."

"A brave woman would have stayed and fought back. She would have known how to protect herself," she argued. "She would have at least gone to the police."

He shook his head at her. "Megha Ramnath, you are braver than anyone I know. Do you have any idea how many thousands of young women don't have the guts to run away from a situation like yours? You, on the other hand, recognized that there was no way to save yourself from two evil and determined individuals, so you escaped to save yourself. That's courage."

"But what's the use of trying to escape? I'm sure they'll find me sooner or later."

"No, they won't," he said with quiet assurance. "We'll make sure that they don't. We'll talk about it in the morning. Now try to rest."

"Okay." She sounded like a worn-out and frightened little girl.

Somehow Kiran didn't think she believed him.

Chapter 7

Despite her earlier desire to curl up and rest, sleep eluded Megha. She lay staring at the ceiling, the night light casting moving shadows on it as the overhead fan rotated at low speed. The degree and immediacy of the terror hounding her had lessened somewhat, but to be lying here in Kiran's bed was also frightening, although the bed was more comfortable than any she'd ever slept in.

What in God's name was she doing here? In retrospect, what she'd done tonight was insanity of a sort. The survival instinct supposedly made people do the strangest things. And this was beyond strange.

She shut her eyes and tried to unwind. Perhaps a little sleep would enable her to think more clearly in the morning. But her mind remained on full alert, listening for sounds, conjuring up dark images. The sound of an occasional passing vehicle outside the window seemed magnified and made her sit up in panic. The feeling of being hunted was still very much with her. It would probably remain with her for the rest of her life.

For a while she wondered what her poor cat was doing. Should she have brought Kuppu with her? But that, of course, was a silly thought. She had no idea where she was headed when she had started to run. The instinct to get away from danger was so potent, she'd never given any thought to the cat. Poor kitty, he was probably looking for her, wondering why she'd abandoned him. In the short while that she'd lived in that house, Kuppu had somehow become her personal pet.

As she prayed for sleep to come, a succession of images of what her life had been for the past year paraded through her mind. Was it because on some level she was trying to justify her reasons for being here? Why she had risked everything and literally ended up in the bed of a virtual stranger?

She clearly recalled meeting her husband for the first time—on the day of her bride viewing. He had come to her parents' home with his mother, father and sister to meet and assess Megha as a potential bride.

Avva had been cleaning the house most of the day and then made special snacks for the guests: spicy round potato *bondas* and sweet wheat *halwa*. In a pastel pink silk sari, Avva had looked so pretty. With not many special occasions in her life, Megha's mother very rarely got dressed up, so it was heartening to see her in silk. Appa, too, had worn a clean, crisp white shirt and black pants for the occasion—he hadn't dressed that way since his retirement. His gray hair was slicked back with a touch of coconut oil and he had almost looked like his old handsome self.

Naturally, Megha had taken great pains with her grooming that day. She had chosen her favorite sari from amongst her mother's silks—the lavender *Benares* with a narrow silver border and silver peacocks scattered all over—the one that made her dark eyes and glossy dark hair look richer, and her fair skin fairer. She had to make a dazzling first impression on the man who could easily end up being her husband. He was a highly-placed bank officer and probably came across lots of well-dressed and impressive women.

With great care she had made the pleats of her sari fall just right—not so high that her ankles would show and not so low that they swept the ground. Just that once she would have liked to have a little makeup, but Appa condemned cosmetics of any kind, calling them *veshaa-astra*, evil weapons of seduction worn by prostitutes. But in spite of it, the small pearl necklace and earrings that belonged to her mother's modest jewelry collection, combined with the fresh white rose tucked in her hair, had served to make Megha look her best.

Though not vain, Megha knew she was a very pretty young woman and wasn't above admitting it. She had been blessed with good genes since both her parents were good-looking. And fair skin was valued highly by Indians, especially Brahmins, so she was more than grateful to God for giving her a light complexion.

However, a little later, with a sinking heart she had let her eyes rest briefly on the rather small, uncomfortable-looking man named Suresh Ramnath. Utter disillusionment had settled in at once. Good heavens, this was the man her Appa and Avva had picked for her! What were they thinking? Her parents had to be insane to think of this individual as potential husband material. "Please, God, tell me that's not the man I'm supposed to marry!" she'd whispered to herself.

Suresh barely made eye contact with Megha. She wasn't even able to see what color his eyes were. He sat slumped in the chair, kept his hands folded in his lap and nodded or shook his head appropriately when someone addressed him. Gaunt and oily-skinned, he had scant hair, a hooked nose and deep-set eyes. His khaki pants and baby-blue shirt were just shy of shabby. He seemed to swallow a lot, because his Adam's apple seemed to bob up and down constantly. He was a delicate man. In fact, he could hardly be classified as a man. Each time his mother made a remark and said, "Don't you agree, Suresh?" he replied, "Yes, yes, very true."

A boy still tied to his mother's sari, Megha concluded. How on earth had he managed to become an important official at a major bank?

Her father had assured her that Suresh was a responsible man with a master's degree, a fabulous job and a bright future. And yet, during the entire visit, Suresh's large, bossy mother did all the talking.

And God, what a formidable woman Chandramma Ramnath was! Dressed in a bright green *Dharmavaram* silk sari and heavy gold-and-diamond jewelry, she had filled the small drawing room with her presence and the odor of her overpowering perfume the moment she charged in. She looked as if she were ready to do battle rather than meet her son's potential bride. Her dark eyes bulged from their sockets and her skin was dark and scarred with acne. Thick hair sprinkled with gray was pulled back in a round bun at the back of her head. Her teeth were whiter than white against her wide lips. When she looked around the worn-out drawing room with an air of unconcealed contempt those lips had curled in what looked like a practiced sneer.

She had studied Megha for a long minute, as if she was a ripe tomato to be purchased from the *bhaaji* market. Megha had shivered from the close, unblinking scrutiny. Even now the thought of that meeting made Megha wince. Had she sensed the malevolent vibes coming from Amma even as far back as her first contact with her?

Although bride viewing typically involved asking the potential bride and her family pertinent questions about her education, hobbies, talents and such, Chandramma Ramnath's list of questions for Megha was endless, bordering on harassment. "Can you cook?" was her first question.

"Yes. My mother has taught me well." That was one thing Megha could be proud of.

"Good. Do you know how to play classical music? Sitar, violin, vocal music, anything?"

"No, I-I'm afraid I'm not . . . musically inclined."

Amma frowned. "Well, why not? Music is important in a cultural sense, no? The human mind needs some culture. Our Shanti has had lessons in playing the sitar since she was ten years old. Anyway, are you any good at mathematics then?"

"Reasonably good," Megha had replied, afraid of saying anything more. She had always fared better at languages and social science. And what the hell did the ugly she-donkey want, a wife for her scrawny son or a rocket scientist for the space program?

"What use is a woman if she cannot teach her children mathematics?" Amma retorted. "It is the basis of all rational thinking." That particular remark was accompanied by a superior look aimed at Megha's mother, who had limited formal education.

The grilling continued in that vein the rest of the evening, with questions about everything from sewing and embroidery to bargain-shopping and child-rearing.

When Avva brought out the snacks and tea for the guests, the men and Shanti ate and drank heartily, but Amma toyed with the food, perhaps to show she wasn't happy with the quality of the plates and cups they were served in. Or maybe she was nervous, too.

Megha felt emotionally drained from the Ramnaths' visit and especially from that long and painful interrogation.

Suresh's father, Vinayak, whom Suresh strongly resembled, ventured to add a few comments when his wife commanded him to do so. "Very important for the girl to fit in with our family, no? We are a very close-knit family, you see," he said mildly. In faded gray pants and a cream colored bush coat, he seemed to be a man of few words and very little personality. He looked puny compared to his wife.

Shanti, Suresh's sister, the meek and bespectacled teenager, also seemed to favor her father in looks and personality. She wore a pale yellow crepe sari with an ill-matching blouse and a thick gold necklace that looked awkward around her bird-like neck. After joining her palms in the customary greeting of *Namaste* when she was introduced to Megha and her parents, Shanti immediately grabbed the newspaper lying folded on the teapoy and read it with undivided interest all the while they were there.

Later, when Megha analyzed her own reactions to the Ramnaths, she realized disappointment had topped the list, followed by intimidation. She protested to her parents, "How can you expect me to marry that man? He looks old and emaciated. And did you see his mother? Oh my God, she's fearsome enough to make Palgaum's notorious cockroaches run for their lives."

"Old? Suresh is only ten years older than you," Avva

snapped, rolling her pretty eyes. "*Putti*, your father and I are fourteen years apart." *Putti* meant little girl; it was an affectionate term her mother often used with her. In fact, it was commonly used in many *Kannada*-speaking households to address female children.

"But your generation is different, Avva! People my age want some intellectual connection with their spouses besides the obvious sexual union."

"Shh, why you are talking dirty like that?" Her mother looked at her like she had completely lost her mind. Physical bonding between the sexes was not to be discussed openly.

Her father scowled. "Stop fussing, Megha. If he is a bit thin now, he'll put on weight with age. All men do. If you look at his fat mother there is no doubt he will also become like her later on."

Besides, the astrologer consulted by her parents had with supreme confidence informed them that Suresh Ramnath was the perfect match for Megha.

When her mother had asked if he was certain, the astrologer's eyes had widened with offended disbelief. "You are questioning my expert prediction, Mangala-bai! You know I always find most eligible boy for your daughter: educated, employed and also rich. Have I not made very best matches for your other two daughters? They are now happy in their husbands' homes, no?"

When Megha grumbled about having to marry an ugly man, one shorter than herself, too, her once-handsome father sat her down and lectured her sternly. "Megha, let me tell you something: I'm a poor man and I cannot pay a big dowry. Because of your good looks the Ramnaths are asking for a reasonable dowry. Even that small amount I cannot afford, no? They have agreed to wait so I can pay it in installments. In my financial condition this is the best husband I can find for you."

"But why does he want to marry *me*, Appa? There are lots of marriageable girls out there with big dowries. Can't Suresh Ramnath have one of them?"

"Oh, Megha, you silly girl, don't you understand that he wants to marry *you*?" her father said, the combination of impatience and frustration clear in his expression. "The Ramnaths want a beautiful wife for their son so they can have good-looking grandchildren. They are all ugly people and the only hope of having a better-looking second generation is to acquire a pretty daughter-in-law. You fit the need perfectly."

When Megha pouted and whined in protest her father frowned menacingly. "Stop this nonsense right now, Megha! You will have a highly-educated husband with an excellent job and his parents are well-off and they own a nice house, which he will inherit someday. You will lack nothing, so just be grateful."

"I'm only twenty, Appa. I have only a bachelor's degree. I don't want to get married right now. I want to get a master's degree and become a journalist. I want to earn my living."

"Good girls from orthodox families don't work for a living," her father chided. "They get married so their husbands can provide them with a respectable home and a comfortable life."

"But journalism is a good profession for girls, Appa—very respectable. My professor says I have excellent writing skills. I could easily get a job with a magazine or newspaper." She had pleaded her case passionately. "Please, Appa, if not a job, at least let me finish my master's degree. We can borrow a little money from Leela and Hema. After that I can help you and Avva pay off the loan."

The shock was apparent on her father's face. "I will never borrow money from Leela or Hema! No parent should ever borrow money from his children. Megha, I cannot afford to send you for another degree. I'm getting too old to support you. I might die soon. So stop arguing and get married, for God's sake!"

Pleading with her mother had proved just as futile. Avva's sad eyes looked sadder than ever. "We are married to our fate, child. Suresh appears to be your destiny, no? There is no escaping from what fate has written across one's forehead. We cannot run from it and cannot hide from it."

Megha was unable to come up with any more arguments. Professional writing classes were entirely out of the question.

Being bright didn't mean much because the small town of Palgaum didn't offer anything like graduate scholarships to gifted students. Job opportunities for young, middle-class girls were limited, and in any case, her old-fashioned father would never allow her to work. No matter which way she looked at it, she was being sucked into the dark, bottomless pit of Hindu Brahmin conservatism, and there was no way out of it. Survival meant only one thing: Total compliance.

Squelching her cherished hopes, Megha reluctantly agreed to the marriage. She didn't want to make her parents' life more difficult than it already was. Perhaps if she'd been born unattractive, this wouldn't have happened. For the first time in her life she considered her good looks a curse.

After some serious contemplation she made up her mind that if she was married to her fate, she would give it her best. She would try to accept it and make a life for herself. Maybe Suresh wasn't such a bad man. In private perhaps he was kind and gentle and loving. Maybe even romantic. Her best friend, Harini, who got married only a few months earlier, had bagged herself a sweet and kind husband, and she was very happy. Megha, too, would be happy. She'd try her best, anyway. Mother Superior at the convent had always emphasized the timeless adage: God helps those who help themselves.

The wedding took place a few weeks later and was very small and unpretentious. Again, because that's all Megha's father could afford. Amma, the center of attention, dressed in a gaudy pink sari with gold designs accessorized by lots of diamond jewelry, looked like a giant ball of cotton candy sprinkled with glitter. She made a point of broadcasting that she had magnanimously agreed to a frugal wedding despite Suresh's being her only son simply because of her kind heart. "This wedding is not much better than the *zopadpatti* or shantytown weddings. But I am trying to be generous. One has to make a few sacrifices for the sake of the children, no?"

Megha noticed that Amma carefully omitted mentioning the dowry she demanded, something Megha's father couldn't afford. Nor did Amma mention to anyone the fact that she was desperate for a good-looking daughter-in-law. She wanted a swan to join her family of hideous ducks. From the curious stares Megha inferred that most everyone had guessed the truth but hadn't expressed it. Nobody dared to question the formidable Chandramma Ramnath.

Following the wedding, Megha was shocked to discover that the Ramnaths lived in a small and drab house. Moreover, Suresh's salary was nowhere close to what she'd been told. So, where was all that grandeur the astrologer had mentioned? Where were all the servants she had expected? What happened to all the sophistication: the appreciation of music, art and literature Amma had bragged about? Other than the daily paper, the usual TV shows, and Shanti's mound of college textbooks, there was nothing that reflected the intellectual atmosphere Megha had anticipated. Had her parents even bothered to research the facts before marrying her off to Suresh?

And to top it all, her life with the Ramnaths turned out to be only slightly better than hell. She had to get out of bed at five o'-clock each morning to fill the bathwater cauldron, fire up the hearth to heat the water, and then make an elaborate breakfast for the family. This was followed by cooking for lunch, then snacks for teatime, then dinner. These were only part of the work assignments doled out by Amma. The routine continued seven days a week with no break. What good was her college education if this was the kind of work she'd be doing for the rest of her life?

Tukaram, the man servant, came in daily to wash the floors, clothes and dishes. He was the only bright spot in the tedium of Megha's life. She enjoyed his presence and his colorful stories picked up from here and there. Middle-aged and balding, he was stocky and muscular from doing hard menial labor for various neighborhood families all his life. He had a weather-beaten face and an upbeat personality. To Megha he was like a breath of fresh air.

Having left his hometown of Malvan as a young, illiterate orphan, he had made Palgaum his home nearly all his life, washing and cleaning for middle-class people his only vocation. He lived in a small, rented, windowless room in the heart of town. But to hear him one would think he lived the privileged life of a prince. "God give me strong hands and legs and back so I work hard," he said. "Always God is giving, no?"

Tukaram addressed Megha as Megha-bai, something that surprised and delighted her because nobody had ever given her the respectful title of *bai* before. He treated her with deference and warmth and she reciprocated the sentiments. She often offered him a cup of hot tea, which he appreciated.

Amma had frowned on Megha's fraternizing with the hired help. "Getting too friendly with servants is not done in our house, Megha," she had warned. "He is a useless, low-caste fellow, a *shudhra*, so you treat him like a servant, you hear? Don't give him any tea or coffee. He can buy his own."

Megha had tried to argue mildly once. "But he works hard, Amma, so what's one small cup of tea . . . and some conversation? It doesn't cost anything, does it?"

"*Thoo*," Amma had spat out, "it is not the cost of the tea, you silly girl! Offering him refreshment and conversing with him is like accepting him on our own level, no? Remember, low-caste people are not our equals—they are not even fit for us to spit on."

After that little confrontation, Megha had tried to comply with Amma's orders, but couldn't help herself when Tukaram had such a genial personality that seemed to draw her in. So while Amma napped after eating a giant lunch, and while Megha chopped and ground and boiled and stirred, and Tukaram washed the dishes and cleaned the floor, the two of them talked. At least, Tukaram did most of the talking, and Megha listened attentively. She managed to slip him a cup of tea every now and then, when she was sure Amma was snoring in the master bedroom.

A regular gossipmonger, Tukaram had filled Megha's afternoons with interesting tidbits about the other families he worked for: who got married; who was pregnant; who was cheating on their spouse; whose children were a menace; who was dying; whose son had stolen money from his own father and then run off with the loot; whose daughter was bringing shame upon the family by having a boyfriend. Maybe that's why Tukaram had remained a bachelor—to avoid the grief of cheating spouses and wayward children.

Tukaram's colorful anecdotes managed to shock, enchant, amuse, and sadden Megha. They were like watching the continuing family sagas dramatized on TV. She always looked forward to the time of day when he'd report for duty with his easy grin that showed a chipped front tooth.

Now that she had run away from the Ramnaths, Megha was sure that by the next morning Tukaram would get busy spreading the news about her own disappearance to the various families he worked for. Tukaram's verbal reports were more reliable than the local newspaper.

But despite Tukaram's help with the washing, Megha had rarely gone to bed before ten o'clock every night, after which she had to pleasure her husband and fulfill his needs before she could get some sleep. She had felt like an unpaid, unappreciated maid in her own house.

And yet, her father had firmly believed that he was placing her in a sound and happy home. He had been positive that a stable and mature man would take care of her and rid her of what he called "Megha's giddy-headed fantasies."

Ironically, that mature man had turned out to be Suresh. His level of maturity was only a few degrees above that of Kuppu the cat. Although, on certain occasions, Suresh could be quite calculating and sly, as when playing card games, for example. He could easily beat all of them at cards. He was outstanding at haggling. He could defeat a fast-talking entrepreneur any day and come home with a bargain, his eyes ablaze with triumphant jubilation. He was more frugal than a starving squirrel staring at a dwindling stash of nuts. The subject of money put a smile on Suresh's scrawny face on the worst of days. Perhaps that was the reason he worked for a bank.

There was never any meaningful conversation between Suresh and Megha beyond family talk at the dinner table each night. He never discussed his job or his coworkers with her. He didn't seem to have any friends. He never touched her other than in the privacy of their bedroom at night. She might as well have married a monkey for all the emotional and intellectual connection she felt to him.

In other ways, too, Suresh was a rather weird man. Although his clothes looked dreary and dull, his *chappals* had to gleam. He had a fetish about footwear. He polished them to a dazzling shine each night, sitting cross-legged on the drawing room floor with the tip of his tongue held firmly between his yellowed teeth in deep concentration as his slight hands passed over the leather. If the squeak wasn't audible, the *chappals* weren't shiny enough.

With some perseverance Megha had somehow trained herself to care for Suresh and develop a mild fondness for him over the last several months. It was her duty to love and obey her husband. If not love, maybe a little affection was in order. Love, to her, had to be special, an all-encompassing tidal wave of sweaty palms, racing pulse and missed heartbeats—just like in the movies and romance novels she enjoyed so much. What she felt for Suresh was far from that breathless, heady feeling, so it had to be affection—on a very mild scale, too.

Her father-in-law, Appaji, was a reasonable man. He didn't have much to say in any matter around the house though, despite being the chief breadwinner. A slight man with a hunch and a perpetual cough, he kept to himself. He was rather secretive in some ways. He watched people closely and the guarded expression in his eyes rarely changed. Megha could never tell what was going on in his mind and always suspected that his chronic cough was a result of nervousness rather than any physical condition.

He was an officer at the State Bank of India's Palgaum branch. He spent his evenings and weekends at home reading the scriptures or the daily paper, dressed in a thin white *lungi*—a *sarong*-like piece of fabric wrapped around the waist that reached down to the ankles, paired with a sleeveless undershirt. His arms hung like scarecrow limbs and his long neck became more obvious with the V-shaped neckline of his shirt. The *lungi* was made of a translucent material and his blue striped underwear was clearly visible through it.

Megha was a bit embarrassed at first to see her father-in-law dressed like that. A man's underwear so obviously on display was a bit vulgar, but she learned to accept it. She was in no position to make comments about the lord and master of the house—albeit a gutless lord and master who shook with anxiety in that very same underwear at the sight of his wife.

Every morning around ten o'clock, Appaji came out of the bathroom wrapped in a brown towel. He combed lots of castor oil through his thinning salt-and-pepper hair. Then he systematically applied copious amounts of talcum powder to his hollow, hairless armpits.

The ritual of putting on his clothes, too, was exactly the same each day. He put on his trademark mouse-gray pants sitting on the edge of the bed while he raised each leg so high that everybody in the room was subjected to more than they wanted to see. The first time Megha got a glimpse she had rushed out of the room, shocked to the core. He always got dressed with the bedroom door wide open. Didn't the old man have any sense of decency? After a while she'd realized that to him it was the only way to dress—he didn't know any better—probably didn't even realize that his young daughter-in-law was in the room.

After that Megha made it a point to stay away from the master bedroom when Appaji put on his trousers. It wasn't easy, since that room was also where the bulk foods were stored in the corner cupboard (Amma wanted to keep an eye on them because she was convinced Tukaram would pilfer) and where everybody's washed clothes were hung to dry on clotheslines that ran overhead from one end of the long room to the other.

Appaji always wore a bush coat, the one with the permanent grease ring around the collar caused by the castor oil dripping over it. He put on his thick glasses and ate an unhurried lunch at precisely quarter past ten before he left for work. He then thrust his feet in his *chappals* and bid his wife goodbye. "Chandramma,

I'm leaving now. Should I pick up any provisions on the way home?"

Despite his lack of a backbone, Megha had become genuinely fond of Appaji. He was a kind man. Quiet and undemanding, he was the only person in the house who showed her any respect. He never complained about her cooking or the temperature of the water she drew for his bath every day. He would ask her to sit down and rest if he noticed she had been on her feet in the kitchen for long hours, but made sure to say it only when Amma wasn't within earshot.

On one occasion, Appaji had found his voice to contradict Amma when she was particularly vicious in her comments about Megha's *chapatis*, the flat, unleavened bread made of whole wheat flour that was a regular part of their daily diet. "Chandramma," he argued, "the *chapatis* don't at all feel like shoe leather. Don't condemn the poor girl so."

Just for that show of support Megha would be eternally grateful to Appaji—not that it helped much. Amma became furious and more vindictive towards Megha after that incident. But it was a question of principle—Appaji had tried his best to defend Megha and she appreciated that. She'd eventually come to love him like she did her own father.

Amma, on the other hand, was a different matter. An involuntary shiver went through Megha at the thought of her mother-in-law. An intelligent and pious woman otherwise, how could she be so evil when it came to her daughter-in-law? The puzzling thing was, in the beginning, Amma had actually seemed to be proud of Megha. Amma had behaved like a little girl with a new doll to be flaunted and paraded to garner everyone's envy. She took Megha everywhere with her, to her religious hymns-and-chanting sessions known as *satsangs*, her tea parties, the temple, the movies, the relatives' homes and all sorts of social occasions like weddings, thread ceremonies and birthdays.

Amma had even shared her precious bottle of Charlie perfume with Megha once or twice, much to Megha's delight, and to everyone's surprise. To be given a dab of Charlie from Amma was indeed an honor. The perfume was a generous gift from Amma's best friend, whose son sent her a few bottles of it from America every year. The Charlie was put away with Amma's other prized items in a locked steel trunk that sat under the master bed, chained to the window grill for added safety. Nobody really knew what was in that trunk besides her jewelry, some silver dishes and her priceless Charlie.

Amma always opened the trunk behind closed doors. Anyone who dared to enter her bedroom when she had her head in the treasure trove opened themselves to a major rebuke. "Trunk-time," as the family referred to it, was next only to *puja* or worship time, and neither were to be disturbed at any cost.

Each morning, after a long bath, Amma put on loads of Fair & Fabulous skin cream, then covered it with a thick layer of face powder. The fairness cream had done precious little to help her dark and rutted complexion, but she continued to use it generously. Then she prayed devoutly before the altar in the kitchen, with its rows of silver idols and pictures of Hindu gods and goddesses and saints. Megha had always admired Amma's devotion and her capacity to recite by memory so many Sanskrit verses from the scriptures. Too bad the piousness didn't extend to other areas of Amma's life.

About four months after Megha came to live with the Ramnaths her outings with Amma came to an abrupt stop. Amma turned against Megha with unexpected vengeance. To this day, Megha hadn't figured out what it was she had done wrong. Amma was loving and affectionate with her brothers and their respective families, fawned over them even. With her husband and children she could be a bit stern and unyielding. But with Megha her attitude was bitter contempt combined with angry reserve.

There was only one occasion Megha recalled when she had disobeyed Amma, and that was when she'd gone to the neighbor, Sharifa Hamid's, house to help out when Sharifa had suffered an acute appendicitis attack. Amma had never forgiven Megha for setting foot in a Muslim household and then returning to taint their pure Hindu home. The already fragile relationship between the two women had crumbled completely then and Megha's position had been downgraded from contemptible daughter-in-law to domestic servant.

Megha was still Amma's enemy number one. And Megha didn't even know why. Granted, her father hadn't paid the dowry money yet, and she had failed to produce a grandchild as expected, but both the problems weren't entirely her fault, were they? Surely nothing she had done was so severe a crime that it had to be punished by death?

After stewing for a while over all the injustices she'd suffered, rebellious thoughts slipped into Megha's mind. Why had she put up with the Ramnaths' despicable treatment of her all these months? Why had she let Amma look upon her as her personal doormat? Why had she allowed Suresh to use her body nearly every night and then ignore her the rest of the time?

Well, she wouldn't tolerate it anymore! She was no weakling. She was capable of not only fighting back but giving in equal measure. She had a perfectly good brain, didn't she? She'd teach those mean, ugly bastards a lesson. Not today, perhaps not tomorrow, nor even next year. One day in the future she'd deliver her own brand of justice and watch the surprise leap into their eyes. At the moment she had no idea how she'd do it, but given time, she'd know what to do.

Never having hated anyone with such passion, Megha didn't quite recognize the strong tide of feeling rising within her. But it was potent, bitter. It took her a few moments to realize what the emotion was: Revenge. Two, or rather, three could play the game of wreaking misery on somebody else.

Finally, overcome by exhaustion and with the pain pills easing the throbbing in her foot, she fell asleep, but not before making a resolution to get even with Suresh and Amma Ramnath.

Chapter 8

Megha woke up with a sore feeling, like the bone-deep aching that comes with the flu. Gritty-eyed, she squinted at the bedside clock then sat up in alarm. 9:37 AM! What was she still doing in bed? Why hadn't Amma woken her? She looked at the empty space beside her on the bed. Where was Suresh? And why were the street noises so subdued this morning as compared with the daily din of automobiles, bicycle bells, rickshaws, the clanging of the *doodhwalla's* milk cans and people's incessant chatter?

Her sleep-addled brain took a while to remember she was in a strange bed. Then, as the faint scent of Kiran's aftershave met her sensitive nostrils and she felt the soft, luxurious sheets beneath her legs, it all came back to her. And along with it came the sense of panic once again.

Telling herself to calm down, she stretched, then stood up, and winced when her body tightened in pain, especially when her bandaged foot hit the floor. The pain shot all the way up to her upper thigh. Carefully examining the sheets, she found two ugly blood stains, dried to a rusty shade of brown. She'd have to wash the sheets thoroughly before leaving the flat. A closer look at the floor showed the stains there were gone. When had Kiran come in and cleaned up that mess? Poor man, he was probably disgusted with having her as a guest in his home. Well, hopefully she'd be gone within the next hour or two.

Megha studied the room with curiosity. What she'd failed to

notice the previous night in her dazed state of mind, she noted now. The slate blue curtains on the window were closed, but there was a narrow gap where the two panels came together and the bright morning sun threw enough light into the room to illuminate it.

The bedroom furniture was made of rich, dark rosewood, with the headboard, the bedside table, the dresser and matching mirror all coordinated. Megha ran her fingers over the headboard's rim, admiring its smooth curves and glossy finish. Nice. Next to the window a computer sat on a rosewood desk with a crammed bookcase beside it. Most of the books were about engineering, computer systems and software design. There were a few novels—John Grisham, Tom Clancy, Stephen King, and James Patterson—typical male tastes in fiction.

Two extra wide *almirahs* or armoires, also made of rosewood, sat against one wall. It was a utilitarian and simple room—a man's bedroom, but again, decorated in excellent taste. Kamala Rao's hand was unmistakable.

Megha glanced at herself in the mirror and nearly sprang back in shock. The scratch on her chin was a red diagonal scab. Her hair was sticking out in various directions. The scratches on her arms and legs matched the one on her chin. The T-shirt and shorts looked crushed now. All of the previous night's events came flooding back into her mind, once again bringing with them grief, hopelessness, and fear.

She returned to the bed and sat on its edge for several minutes, trying to get a grip on the turmoil of emotions. Now that the sun was shining and it was a new day, her situation didn't look any more promising than it had the previous night. If anything it seemed worse. She was in a lot of pain and hiding in a stranger's house. She was still a woman with no home and no family. And not a single rupee to her name! A good night's sleep was supposed to refresh her mind, allow her to think of some way out of this mess, but her brain still felt dead.

What the hell was she going to do?

Rising from the bed for the second time, she went to the window and drew the curtains aside a little. There was a small park-like enclosure with a children's play area across the street. Child-size swings, a see-saw and two slides were separated from the adult-size benches by a large sand-pit. At the moment the park was empty except for two men trimming the hedge along the perimeter. The occasional car, scooter, bicycles and pedestrians moved back and forth on the street below. The traffic on this street was sparse compared with Cantonment Galli. It seemed blissfully quiet here. No wonder she'd slept so well.

Turning around, Megha headed back to the mirror. Her eyelids were swollen from last night's weeping. She had cried and sobbed until there were no more tears left. But the crying had been cathartic to some extent, although thinking about it now brought an embarrassed flush to her face. She'd made an utter fool of herself in front of Kiran.

She wondered what she could do to tame her wild locks. Finding two combs on the dressing table, she picked up the sturdier one to draw through her hair. The tangles were hard to smooth out because she'd gone to bed with damp hair, but she managed to bring some semblance of neatness to it by braiding it.

Looking around for her clothes, she realized she had left them in a heap on the floor by the washer. In her strange getup she was diffident about stepping out of the room. She was convinced she looked like the little beggar boy in the bazaar, except, unlike him, the clothes she had on were expensive. Both shirt and shorts had the Polo logo embroidered on them.

No longer able to hide in the bedroom, she tiptoed to the door and carefully opened it wide enough to poke her head out. The fragrance of fresh coffee greeted her and she breathed in deeply to inhale the mouth-watering aroma.

"Good morning."

Startled, she turned her head to follow Kiran's voice coming from the drawing room. He sat on the sofa, his long legs stretched out in front of him and his big, bare feet parked on the coffee table. He held a writing pad in one hand and an uncapped pen poised in the other. Dressed in fashionably faded jeans and a navy T-shirt, he looked freshly shaved and bathed. Kiran's pleasantly casual attire made Megha feel even more ill-at-ease about her own. She smiled at him but didn't step out of the room. "I guess you didn't get any sleep, huh?" she asked him, hoping he wouldn't notice the embarrassing warmth seeping into her cheeks.

"I managed to get some." He gazed at her face for a moment. "I noticed you slept soundly."

"Hmm. I didn't even realize you came in and cleaned the floor." She offered him a rueful smile. "Sorry about making you do all that."

"No problem," he replied cheerfully. "Hope the bed was comfortable."

"Need you ask? It's the most luxurious bed I've ever seen."

His grin was amiable, making her feel less awkward. "Are you planning to come out of there anytime soon?" he teased.

"I can't come out. I feel funny in these clothes. They're very nice, mind you, but I look silly in them."

"Is that right?" He continued to look amused.

"Okay, I'm embarrassed to come out," she finally admitted.

"I saw you in those last night, remember?" Kiran's eyes sparkled with mischief.

She wrinkled her nose at him. "I remember."

"Come on out—I made fresh coffee." The jesting grin flashed again, showcasing his fine set of teeth.

The promise of coffee made her stomach rumble in response. She was starving. Arms tightly crossed over her chest to hide what she considered her nakedness underneath the clinging softness of the cotton shirt, she stepped out. Last night, under the dimly sophisticated lighting, it hadn't seemed that bad, but now, in the bright sunlight streaming in through the dining room window, she felt exposed. "I think I'll go brush my teeth," she mumbled and made a dash for the bathroom.

Inside the bathroom she found a little surprise. On the marble countertop she saw her sari, blouse, petticoat and underwear sitting in a neat pile—washed, dried and folded. They smelled wonderfully clean. When had Kiran managed to do it? Between that and cleaning the rug and floors, had the poor man slept at all?

The inexpensive cotton of her once-white undergarments had long ago turned to a dull gray from constant washing. Oh dear, Kiran had touched her bra and knickers! It didn't feel right that a man other than her husband had handled her most intimate garments. If her mother ever found out about this, she would faint from the sheer shock of it.

Turning away from the clothes, she took care of the necessities, then carried her folded clothes back to the bedroom and changed as quickly as she could. She knew Kiran's eyes had followed her as she'd darted across the dining room. She was also sure he'd grinned at her silliness.

Feeling a little more relaxed in her own clothes, she managed to enjoy the simple breakfast of buttered toast and mango jam Kiran prepared for her. The gnawing hunger in her stomach began to ebb. The coffee was excellent. She felt like a spoiled kitten with all this attention he was heaping on her. God, this was so much better than home.

The thought of home gave her a sudden jolt. That miserable place in Cantonment Galli was no longer her home. In fact, she had no home anymore. She had run away from her husband and she was no longer welcome at her parents' house. She was homeless. A wave of self-pity brought on the urge to start weeping again, but she suppressed it. Feeling sorry for herself wasn't going to get her anywhere. Besides, Kiran was already swamped with her tears and her innumerable problems. She took a few deep breaths and forced herself to calm down.

Looking for a suitable topic to break the awkward silence between them, she glanced at Kiran. "I thought you'd be at work by now."

"Remember I told you last night I was going to take the day off?" He poured himself a fresh cup of coffee and sat across from her at the table.

Recalling it through last night's turmoil, she nodded. "Thanks for washing my clothes. How did you manage it so quickly?"

He shrugged. "I have a washer and dryer."

"You didn't have to do it, Kiran."

"Don't look so guilty. I didn't do much." He watched her thoughtfully while she ate. "Megha, I'm trying to make a list of all the things you're going to need right away. You'll have to help me here. I don't know anything about women's clothes or toiletries." He pushed the pad and pen towards her.

She chuckled as her eyes traveled down the sheet of paper and the extensive list he'd drawn up: lipstick, mascara, rouge, foundation, face powder, saris, blouses, footwear, undergarments, comb, brush, beauty products. That's where the list ended for now. There were question marks next to two of the items: undergarments and beauty products. She suppressed her urge to laugh, but a second later a giggle erupted and she placed a demure hand across her mouth. It wasn't right to laugh heartily or giggle before a man—it would be considered unsuitable behavior for a young woman, in essence flirting.

She looked up to meet his amused gaze. His lips were twitching. All at once they both burst out laughing. She didn't care about proper behavior at that moment—it felt wonderful to laugh with someone who had a sense of humor. She hadn't laughed wholeheartedly in months.

He was the first to recover. "Told you I don't know much about girly things. Why don't you make your own list?"

She confidently crossed out the first five items. "These are totally useless to me. I don't use any makeup. The rest looks okay."

Kiran's brows shot up. "No makeup at all? Then how do you manage to look so beautiful all the time?"

"Who says I look beautiful all the time? Right now my eyes are swollen from crying and sleeping too much, and the scab on my chin is turning to an ugly shade of brown. As for my arms and legs, I can't bear to look at them."

He parked his elbows on the table and rested his face between his cupped hands. Leaning forward, he studied her face. "The scab on your chin is minor and will be gone in a day or two. Your eyes are dark brown with a wide black rim around the irises," he declared. "That's why I'd assumed they were black." He let his gaze dwell on her face for a few moments. "I don't see any swelling. Your eyes are just as big and pretty and mysterious as they always are. Your cheeks are glowing, too. Sleeping late agrees with you."

Her cheeks were probably pink because of the blood rising into her face and neck. "You're very kind, Mr. Rao." She laughed, flustered by his close scrutiny, but genuinely pleased by his compliments. Then the pleasure was replaced by serious distress as she considered the list lying between them on the table. "Kiran, how am I going to pay you back for all this? I don't have any money."

"I don't want to be paid back."

"I can't accept things from you," she argued. "It's . . . not right."

"Why not? We're family, and families help each other."

She shook her head, unable to accept his explanation. "But still . . ."

"Besides, I can afford it." He pushed the list forward again. "Now, go ahead and add whatever you like. I'll see that you get them," he announced, with typical male confidence.

Megha looked at him reflectively. Kiran was a manager at a major corporation and probably accustomed to issuing orders. But she didn't mind his bossiness somehow. It was rather endearing, especially because she knew now that she could trust him and he was trying so hard to help her. She started to add to the list. Hairpins, sanitary pads . . .

He rose from the table, but pivoted on his heel as a sudden thought struck him. "Why only saris? Why don't we buy you some *salwar-kameez* outfits, Megha?" he said, referring to the two-piece outfits with a shirt and matching drawstring pants topped with a long, flowing, boa-like piece that fell across the shoulders. They came in a variety of styles and fashions and colors that went from simple and plain to stylish and elaborate, loose and modest to tight and outrageously revealing.

"I'm a grown woman, Kiran, and married. I can't wear girlish outfits. Besides, they're expensive. I can't let you spend that kind of money on me."

"Sure you can."

"Then you have to promise me something. You have to let me repay you for whatever you spend on me. Otherwise, I won't let you buy anything for me."

"Oh, stop it, Megha! I won't take any money from you." He glanced at her speculatively. "But if you insist on paying me back . . . maybe you can in other ways." A suspicious scowl from her brought an amused grin to his face. "Get your mind out of the gutter, Megha Ramnath! And stop looking at me like that. My intentions are entirely honorable."

Megha felt foolish when he put it like that. "I'm sorry—I'm still on edge." How could she have doubted his intentions in the first place? Last night, even when she was at her most vulnerable, he had been the perfect gentleman.

"All right, since I have no talent for cooking, perhaps you can cook for me," he said. "Tell me what you need in the kitchen and I'll get it. You're a fantastic cook, by the way."

Relieved that there was a way to pay him back, she jumped up. "That's easy enough. I'll look through your kitchen and make a list of what we'll need."

As she began to search through the cabinets, alarm flooded her mind like it had earlier. Why was she fooling herself into thinking this was home, and that Kiran was some sort of surrogate husband? Her situation hadn't changed one bit in the hours between last night and this morning. Kiran was still a stranger to her in many ways and she was still someone else's wife. Playing house with this man was not the answer to her problems. Besides, how long could she stay in hiding? A day? Two?

She abruptly shut the cabinet and turned to face him. "Kiran, I'm sorry, but this isn't going to work. I can't stay here indefinitely. This is your house, not mine."

Kiran sighed and shook his head. "Megha, when will you realize that it's dangerous for you to venture out on your own? The police are looking for you. You have no money, no job, and technically, no home. You could easily get kidnapped and forced into prostitution."

He seemed to note with satisfaction Megha's eyes expanding in fear and her quick intake of breath. "Now listen to me. You'll be safe here. Except for one or two close friends nobody comes to visit me. They come very rarely and never without an invitation."

"But what will your neighbors think?"

"My only neighbor on this floor is a pharmaceutical sales manager who travels on business most of the time. The other residents of this building are mostly single professionals like me who work very long hours. Nobody will know you're here. In a few weeks we can go to Mumbai and stay in my flat."

"Mumbai's the same situation as here, Kiran. I can't stay with you indefinitely."

"I'll find a hotel or some other place for myself in Mumbai, so there won't be any impropriety, all right?"

"What about your servant," she argued, "the one who comes to clean your flat on Sundays?"

"I'll tell him I'll be out of town for several weeks and I don't need him until I come back." Kiran groaned in exasperation. "Are you finished with the thousand and one arguments?"

"Well . . . I'm not happy about this. How about if I go to my sister's house in Hubli? I could go there today," she countered.

"No, that's the first place they'll look for you. Both your sisters will be questioned about your whereabouts. This is still the safest place for you, Megha. Nobody will ever dream of looking for you in my home."

She nodded reluctantly, digesting everything he'd said. He made a lot of sense. She had no other choice. Last night she'd instinctively come to him for help. It was no different now. She'd have to take his advice and depend on his good sense and generosity, at least until they could come up with another solution.

As she leaned against the counter and speculated, she realized with a pang that she was a ship without destination and anchor. Despite the repressive atmosphere of her husband's home she'd had her rightful place there as Mrs. Suresh Ramnath. Now she didn't have a place in life. She was no longer a wife, a daughter or a sister as long as she was on the run and remained in hiding in this flat. How had her life come to this? All her dreams of becoming a journalist someday, even of a simple happy life with a husband and home and children, were reduced to nothing now.

The vague notion about leaping off the balcony flashed through her brain once again. Nobody would miss her. But just as quickly the thought left her. She was a fighter. She'd managed to hold her own against the neighborhood bullies in her childhood, and in her own way she had managed to keep her sanity intact under Amma's hulking domination. She hadn't come all this way only to kill herself now. And, contrary to her dark thoughts, there were one or two people in the world who cared about her.

Although reluctant to get in touch with her parents, and with her anger at her father still raw, she didn't want her mother to worry. Avva would make herself sick with despair if she didn't know her youngest child was alive and well. She was probably beside herself already if she'd found out about Megha's disappearance. So Megha sat down and wrote her mother a brief letter, explaining that she was alive and safe, and why she was driven to do what she'd done. She begged her mother not to tell the Ramnaths about the letter.

No return address was indicated on the outside of the envelope and Kiran promised to have it delivered to her mother by special courier. Thanking Kiran once again for his support, Megha breathed an uneasy sigh as she sealed the envelope.

It was hard to think of herself as a fugitive, but there was no other word for her.

Chapter 9

Vinayak Ramnath observed his wife as she shifted yet again. Chandramma had been restless ever since she had come to bed. At the moment her clasped hands rested over her protruding belly. Her eyes were shut but he knew she was wide awake. She seemed to be meditating. He wondered if it was her conscience bothering her, but then, as far as he knew, she didn't have a conscience.

Lying beside her, Vinayak glanced once more at the bedside clock. It was late, well past bedtime. "Can't sleep, Chandramma?" he murmured.

She opened her eyes. "I'm thinking."

"About what?"

"About the shame that has fallen upon us. We can't even show our faces in public anymore, no?"

"Why do you say that?"

"How can you even ask? Our daughter-in-law ran away. God knows whom she eloped with. It could be the sweeper, the one-eyed man who sells vegetables on the corner, the postman . . . who knows?"

"I don't think Megha is capable of that. She loves Suresh."

Chandramma turned her head and aimed a withering look at Vinayak, making him flinch. "Women who love their husbands do not run away in the middle of the night!"

"She must have a good reason."

Another look of utter scorn was his reward for opening his

mouth, so he turned away and let her think in peace. Thinking was just another word for scheming anyway.

Vinayak knew fully well what was going on in his wife's evil mind. She was plotting her next move: get hold of a solicitor who would file an application for Suresh's divorce. Chandramma had put out the word that her innocent son had been treated shabbily by Megha—a fine, upstanding man with a promising career and a wonderful family behind him had been shamed by his unfaithful and immoral wife.

As far as Vinayak's own limited knowledge of the law went, the abandoned spouse had to wait for a year or two before anything could be resolved legally in the divorce courts, but then who could say what Chandramma could accomplish in her quest for a new daughter-in-law with a fat dowry? The woman was enterprising when it came to such things. And she had two rich and influential brothers who knew how to pull a few strings when necessary.

Chandramma had made a deliberate decision not to decorate the house with the traditional oil lamps for *Diwali* or hang the paper lantern on the front veranda this year. Showing the world that the family was devastated by Megha's disappearance, and therefore in no mood to enjoy the season, was a brilliant strategy on his wife's part. It was a worthwhile sacrifice for the long run. Soon Suresh would have a new wife and all would be well. Maybe sometime after that there would be a grandchild in the picture. The memory of Megha was already fading into the background. His wife couldn't have planned it better.

But it made Vinayak deeply unhappy to think about Megha. He had his suspicions about what had happened to her. In spite of his timidity, he was no fool. When questioned by the police, he had pretended ignorance about where she may have gone. In many ways he was glad she had run away—escaped a horrifying death. He had become fond of her. She was so much more of a daughter to him than his own child.

As a young man, Vinayak had often fantasized about having a pretty wife and beautiful, good-natured children. Those dreams hadn't come true. And then, suddenly and unexpectedly, it seemed God had blessed him with one such special child in the guise of Megha. Alas, the joy was fleeting, like a shooting star that was gone even before one could think of making a wish. Megha was probably too good to be true anyway. His luck had always been rotten.

It served him right, too. He had proved himself useless in protecting Megha from Chandramma. When a young girl came to her in-laws' house, she was handed into their care. What had he done to fulfill his responsibility towards his daughter-in-law? Nothing. He felt acute shame every time the image of Megha's trusting face rose in his mind.

Vinayak had nearly become sick when he found out what had almost occurred the other night. Even now the thought made him shiver. He had slept through Chandramma's planning phase like a fool until he had heard her shriek that Megha had fled from home. "Ree, wake up, wake up!"

Startled by her screaming, he had awakened at once. "What?"

"Megha is gone. That inconsiderate little bitch is gone."

"What do you mean *gone*? Look in the bathroom," he had retorted grumpily.

"She has abandoned Suresh." Chandramma's eyes had blazed with raging fire. *Revenge* had been written all over her face.

But, like a fool, at first Vinayak had believed Chandramma. He had shot out of bed and called Megha's parents, her sisters, even her best friend. Then he had gone looking for Megha, walked up and down the street, knocked on the immediate neighbors' doors, and done all he could to calm Chandramma down. Finally, in desperation, assuming Megha had been abducted, he had called the police. Dear God, what if his young and lovely daughter-in-law had been kidnapped and sold into prostitution? What if she was raped and maybe even killed?

He had actually put his faith in Chandramma's story. Not because he believed Megha had done anything terrible, but because it was unlike Megha to do something quite so thoughtless. But as he had gone around the house and yard to look for possible clues, he had found the telltale wooden bed reeking of kerosene in the shed and nearly vomited in fear and disgust. It had taken him a few seconds to deduce the implications and then several minutes to recover from his reeling senses. Chandramma had found him there, clutching his throat and staring at the floor. She had quickly dragged him out and brought him back to the house. Then she had disappeared for a few minutes, obviously to get rid of the evidence before the police arrived.

She and Suresh had lied about everything to the police and the neighbors. Chandramma was fully capable of such behavior, but Vinayak's disappointment in his son was acute and painful. The boy had no backbone, but that he had aided his mother in such a horrific plot was hard to accept. How could he have produced such a callous child? Nevertheless, Vinayak could not betray his wife and son by voicing his suspicions to the police. Besides, there was no solid evidence. Wood and kerosene were part of the supplies always stored in the shed and Chandramma was clever enough to come up with a credible explanation for them. So Vinayak had kept his mouth shut.

The thought of what could have turned into the cold-blooded, gruesome murder of an innocent young soul haunted Vinayak now, and would haunt him forever. The smell of kerosene would invade his senses henceforth. His role in this cover-up would surely hang over his head during his future lives, too. He would have to pay dearly to make up for his lack of courage.

Thank God, Megha had fled! In his mind he applauded her for her brave decision. He had been wondering how she had managed to flee in time. Had she overheard something, or sensed danger perhaps? How was it that she had known about it, while he himself had been oblivious to the whole affair when it was going on right under his nose? Whatever it was that had saved Megha's life, he was grateful, assuming she had run away and that she was alive and safe.

He had his suspicions as to where Megha might be hiding at present. He clearly remembered the look on Kiran's face the other day and on other occasions, too. That boy had feelings for Megha. Vinayak had suspected that for some time. Kiran had always eyed Megha with a light of adoration and desire in his eyes and had defended her when other family members criticized or condemned her. Kiran was also a strong and bright man with a firm sense of loyalty, so unlike Suresh. Kiran would be the first person, and perhaps the only person she might have turned to in her attempt to escape.

Megha would be safe with Kiran, if indeed she had gone to him for help. Kiran, with his connections, would help her get away from Palgaum, perhaps even find her a job somewhere far away, where Chandramma couldn't touch her. Vinayak decided that someday, if God would grant him an opportunity, maybe he could make it up to Megha.

As Chandramma obviously hatched her own evil plans, Vinayak began to conceive one of his own. But he couldn't put it in to action yet. Not just now, he told himself. He would have to wait for the right moment and then tread with care, or Chandramma, with her sharp mind, would discover his plans and ruin them.

But he couldn't wait too long. His secret might be out soon.

Chapter 10

"Megha! Wake up, Megha!"

With a shudder Megha came awake from the sinister darkness of the foggy backyard to the brightness of the room, blinking—the scream still inside her throat. Her heart was beating so frantically it seemed ready to jump out of her breast.

"Megha, were you having a bad dream?" A pajama-clad Kiran was bending over her, frowning. His hands were on her shoulders, pinning her down.

Dry-mouthed and bathed in a cold sweat, Megha nodded. "I . . . I think so."

"You were thrashing around and moaning. You must have been terrified."

Puzzled, she looked at him, but then glanced around and realized she was in bed. It all came back to her in a flash. She'd been reading in bed and must have fallen asleep. The magazine still lay beside her. The clock read 11:29 PM.

"I didn't mean to disturb you, Kiran."

He slowly let go of her shoulders. "That must have been some nightmare. Let me guess: Amma again?"

"It must have been. I don't really remember." All she could recall was the dark shadow and its cold grip on her, and the cat hissing and arching its back. Shivering, she touched her right shoulder. It still felt cool.

But the voice at the end . . . the one that called out to her when she'd screamed for help, she'd recognized it, even in the dream. That voice was Kiran's.

Kiran strode towards the kitchen and came back a moment later with a glass of water. "Here, drink this. You're perspiring, you must be warm."

No, I'm shivering. The icy water was refreshing nonetheless and she drank it down to the last drop before Kiran took the glass from her.

"Feeling better now?" Kiran still seemed concerned.

"Yes, thanks." She was glad he'd woken her from that nightmare. She didn't want to be in the grip of terror like that. She didn't want to wake up in a cold sweat. "I'm sorry I interrupted your sleep, Kiran. You can go back to your bed now."

Watching him walk away from the room and shut the door behind him, she realized she wanted him to stay a while longer. Going back to sleep was frightening. It meant more nightmares.

The evening after the nightmare had come to disturb her, Megha stood at the dining room window, her thoughts going to Kuppu. He had appeared in the previous night's dream, if only for an instant. She missed the cat dreadfully and wondered what the fat little devil was doing. Was someone feeding him, or were they letting him go back to being the miserable, scrawny creature he was before Megha had come on the scene and started to fatten him up? Did he miss her? She knew nobody bothered to stroke his head or talk to him like she did. Starved for affection, he'd loved curling up in her lap every chance he got.

They'd made quite a team since the day they'd met—Kuppu and Megha, both melancholy souls, looking for a little attention. Kuppu had become her companion, and he had responded to her in his own feline way: licked her hand in gratitude when she'd fed him, pawed at her indignantly when she'd ignored him, and wagged his luxurious tail when she'd poured out her heart to him. She prayed he was okay.

Parting the curtains a crack, she took a peek outside the window. Nothing seemed any different out there since the last time she'd looked, only minutes ago. The sun had set a while back, giving way to the velvety darkness that usually came with a waning moon. The nightly fog was rolling in. The houses on either side of the building had their elaborate *Diwali* lights glowing bright. The children in the neighborhood played with seasonal fireworks. Cars honked and bicycle bells jingled to warn careless pedestrians; people walked along the footpaths as they always did. She observed the scene carefully. No one looked suspicious.

But her paranoia lingered; the world closing in on her continued to feel like a steel mantle. And for good reason. From his parents Kiran had deftly managed to ferret out the information that the police were still on her trail. In fact, their efforts had been intensified since Kiran's father had requested his friend, the DSP, to make the hunt for Megha a priority. Apparently the net had been cast wide. Megha's sisters in Hubli and Bangalore, respectively, uncles in Chennai, and cousins as far as Delhi, Nagpur, and Mysore had been contacted.

From Kamala's description of the developments, it appeared that "poor dear Chandramma" was on the verge of an emotional breakdown. Kamala had evidently painted a tragic picture of a tormented Amma, sorely wanting her family to rally around her in her time of need. Kamala had even requested Kiran to pay Amma a visit and offer his sympathies. Kiran had made a token effort to stop by Amma's house one evening and have a brief but sympathetic chat.

The disturbing fact was that Amma hadn't stopped looking for her. Megha would never feel safe until a divorce could completely sever her ties to the Ramnaths. Until then she couldn't let her guard down. And in the meantime she was stuck here, in a sense trapped.

Turning away from the window, she cast a critical eye over the kitchen and dining room. Having cooked one more well-planned meal for Kiran, she was now done with the dishes and the cleaning up. She had always enjoyed cooking, which her mother had taught her sisters and her at an early age. By the time Megha had become a teenager, she'd been able to produce elaborate meals.

Kiran appeared delighted with her culinary efforts. He'd been consuming large quantities of food. Blessed with a hearty appetite, he seemed to enjoy eating. But then that tall, muscular body had to have ample nutrition, didn't it? He exercised most days by playing an early morning round of tennis with friends and colleagues at the Palgaum Club. So those masculine muscles were in fine shape. Megha liked to see the pleased expression on Kiran's face whenever he took his first bite of whatever she served for dinner. He'd gone to his parents' home only once during the week, mainly to avoid suspicion. His weekly routine of dining with his parents had to remain in place if Megha's presence in his home was to be kept secret.

The kitchen and dining room looked spotless, yet she picked up the cleaning rag and gave the counter tops another quick wipe. It was when the sun went down and darkness descended that she became restless and started to pace—it reminded her of that fateful night a week ago. Amma had clearly been planning the murder for some time. And all the while Megha had been totally oblivious to what was going on. How could she have been so blind, so ignorant? There had to have been signs. Even Kiran, an infrequent visitor to the house, had noticed something different about Amma's demeanor that evening.

Kiran and Megha had fallen into a routine of sorts during the week. Since he left very early in the morning and didn't return till late in the evening, Megha was alone most of the day. It was the evenings that presented a challenge. Since the flat was compact, it was awkward the first couple of days. She hadn't known how to behave around him. He was a stranger yet not an outsider, family yet not a blood relative, comrade yet not a friend in the true sense, a cousin-in-law and yet more like a brother-in-law because of his closeness to the Ramnaths. He'd gone out of his way to make her feel welcome and comfortable.

Initially, the two of them had bumped into each other even as they'd tried to avoid direct contact. But somehow, by the third or fourth evening, they'd found a level of comfort around their mutual presence. By an unspoken agreement they kept out of each other's way. He worked on his laptop computer or read technical books and reports that were obviously part of his work.

Meanwhile, in an attempt to remain as invisible as possible, Megha confined herself to the bedroom or the dining area and ironed clothes or read one of the countless women's magazines or books Kiran insisted on bringing home for her. The two of them had watched a couple of television programs together in companionable silence.

The previous evening they'd played a game of chess at Kiran's suggestion. Megha had enjoyed that immensely. Both she and Kiran were highly competitive and the game had become heated, keeping them up well past midnight. Kiran had won the game, boisterously smug in his victory. Megha had delighted in his mock theatrics while accepting her own defeat. Mostly she'd savored the camaraderie they'd established with just a game. She'd had a chance to become acquainted with a very likeable side of Kiran: his zest for life and his sense of humor. Since she'd grown up with older sisters and not brothers, she hadn't realized until now how fiercely competitive men could be, even outside of their careers.

Now she had some fresh clothes to wear, too. Pramila Pai, wife of Kiran's colleague Ashok Pai, had gone out and bought some saris, matching blouses, petticoats, nightgowns, underwear and toiletries for Megha. When Kiran had first told Megha about his plan to confide in Ashok and his wife, she had turned to him agape with shock. "You can't tell anyone I'm here!"

"They're my friends, they won't betray us," he'd assured her.

"We can't be sure."

"Listen, Megha, we have to trust someone. I know nothing about buying women's things and I can't think of anyone other than Pramila. She's a very nice and discreet lady and she'll get you whatever you need."

Realizing that she couldn't live with one set of underwear and one sari, Megha had reluctantly agreed to Kiran's plan. "All right, but only Ashok and his wife, and nobody else. Promise?"

Kiran had given her his solemn promise.

Standing by the dining table, she studied Kiran across the

room. At the moment he had his head buried in the laptop computer set up on the coffee table, his brows drawn in concentration. From his expression he seemed to be puzzling over something. She'd noticed he worked long hours at his office and still brought work home every evening. His briefcase was crammed and he received work-related calls at home, sometimes even in the middle of the night.

Being ignorant about computers and technical matters, Megha didn't understand any more than the gist of his conversations with his staff. He seemed intense during those phone calls, very focused on whatever issue was brought to his attention. Another surprising thing was that even when obviously riled or disappointed with the caller, he never raised his voice or became abusive. At the same, time he remained firm and distantly polite—quietly conveying his disapproval. On another occasion she had heard him thank his staff and compliment them on a job well done. She also knew he had treated his entire staff to a lavish lunch the previous day as a Diwali gift.

To Megha these were all marks of a good manager. No wonder they liked him so much at his company.

Kiran wasn't exactly handsome in the conventional sense. His nose was a bit too long and narrow, his eyebrows thick, and his jaw was square and stubborn-looking. And yet his face, with its capacity to break into an amused smile combined with the warmth and humor in his deep-set eyes, had depth and character. Right now he looked rather attractive in a white Hilfiger T-shirt and khaki shorts. The stark whiteness of the shirt contrasted with his tan skin and sharp features. A dense mop of hair that always seemed to curl, no matter how hard he tried to brush it down each morning after his shower, only made him look all the more appealing.

With a mental groan Megha reminded herself it was inappropriate for her to think of her brother-in-law in terms like "attractive" or "handsome." He was a good man, a generous man, a trustworthy man. In fact, she shouldn't even think of him as a man. Okay, so he was a relative by marriage, even a friend . . . certainly a Good Samaritan. And that's where it ended.

There was a certain strength about Kiran that was comforting. He exuded confidence. Even in her nightmare, she had instinctively turned toward the sound of his voice.

Amma and the rest of the family had always proudly claimed that Kiran was super-bright and that he'd performed exceptionally well in school. He had an engineering degree from the prestigious Indian Institute of Technology and an MBA from an American school. At twenty-seven, he was already an executive at a high-tech company. Everyone in the family knew he would eventually take over his father's business. He had mentioned heading his father's branch office in Mumbai. His future seemed bright.

Kiran was so different from Suresh—wonderfully, refreshingly so. Megha couldn't help making that comparison every time she looked at Kiran.

Perhaps sensing her eyes on him, Kiran looked up from the computer. "Feeling restless, Megha?"

"A little," Megha admitted, the heat rising in her face at being caught staring.

"Still worried about being discovered?"

She moved to the drawing room and sat down in the chair across from the sofa he occupied. "The thought does cross my mind often."

He pushed aside the computer and leaned forward, looking her in the eye. "I don't want you to worry, Megha. Haven't I promised to protect you?"

"I trust you completely, Kiran, but Amma is a vindictive woman. I've lived with her for the past year. When she wants something, nobody can stop her. She's like a rock hurtling down a steep mountain."

"I know that. That's why I want you to move to Mumbai. It's so big and crowded, she'll never find you there."

"Maybe," she replied with an uncertain smile. The subject of Mumbai sent an involuntary tremor through Megha. It was a big, bustling city, an unknown place. She'd heard about the heat, humidity, crime and poverty existing side by side with unimaginable wealth, tall buildings, beautiful shopping areas, and the beach in Mumbai from friends and TV and movies. She'd never been beyond fifty miles of Palgaum in her entire life. Although she disliked the idea of big cities, Mumbai sounded like heaven at the moment, compared to Palgaum, but it also scared her to no end—the classic dilemma of the known versus the unknown evil.

Assuming she went with Kiran to Mumbai, what would her place in his life be? What was she to him now? Every day she asked herself that. She hadn't found an acceptable answer yet.

Kiran rose and stretched, then invited her to take his place on the couch. "Why don't you get on the computer and amuse yourself on the Internet?"

"But you're still working on it."

He stifled a yawn. "I've done enough for one day. You're free to use it."

"I—I don't know much about using computers." It was embarrassing for Megha to admit she'd hardly ever used something that was so commonplace these days. Even small children knew how to use a computer.

He frowned. "Really? They didn't have computers in your college?"

"In the computer science department but not in the liberal arts section. I never had my own computer either, and no one in Suresh's home has one."

"I'll teach you." Maybe because Megha hesitated, he said. "It's very simple. Come here."

So Megha sat on the couch. She'd always wanted to learn more about computers and this was the perfect opportunity.

Kiran settled down beside her and gave her a brief lesson in how a computer worked. After a few minutes, with his encouragement, she timidly picked up the mouse and learned how to navigate the screen without letting the cursor get out of hand. As she started to learn more about web sites, and search engines and keywords meant to retrieve any kind of information or entertainment, her spirits lifted. Kiran showed her how to look up movie reviews, the latest news, addresses, consumer reports, merchandise for sale, tracking down people and telephone numbers, even recipes and shopping.

She smiled to herself. The entire world was available at the touch of a button. How incredibly wonderful! It was much simpler to learn than she'd thought, too. Within minutes she was typing in keywords all by herself, and enjoying herself immensely. A couple of times Kiran's patience seemed to slip a bit with her non-existent typing skills, but other than that, she was more than pleased with her first computer session. She turned to Kiran with an excited grin. "You're right. It is fun! No wonder some people get addicted to this."

"If you learn how to type, it'll be even more fun. What took you an hour now will take no more than five or ten minutes."

"Is it possible to learn typing on one's own?"

"I learnt on my own. I was a two-finger man until I entered the field of software and started to practice touch-typing."

"Is it hard?"

He shook his head. "I can show you. You need to practice though, or you won't gain speed."

"I'm willing to do it. What else have I got to do all day? I really want to learn, Kiran." She giggled. "I want to watch my fingers fly, write letters and articles, make magic."

Chuckling, Kiran logged off, shut down the laptop and eased it into its leather case. "Looks like you're addicted already."

A tiny spark of an idea ignited in Megha's mind. What if she could learn typing—not just the basics, but enough to become a good typist? It could be her first small step towards independence. Maybe she could even get a clerical job somewhere.

A computer! Why hadn't she thought of it days ago when she'd noticed the one sitting on Kiran's desk in the bedroom? "Maybe you can teach me some more tomorrow?" The next day was Sunday, and Kiran would likely be home all day. "Then I can practice typing on your desktop computer."

He thought about it for a moment. "Let's leave the computer lesson for another day. You've been cooped up in this flat too long. I'll take you out somewhere for the day."

She swallowed hard as terror replaced the earlier euphoria. "I can't go out!"

"We'll get you dressed in different clothes, change your hairstyle, and get some big sunglasses. Nobody will recognize you."

Her heart was beating loud and fast. No, she couldn't step out of this flat—not when she was just beginning to feel somewhat safe. "I don't want to go out, Kiran."

He shook his head. "It's not healthy for you to sit here day after day and worry yourself sick over Amma's next move. You'll lose your mind if you constantly think negative thoughts."

"Yes, but . . ." He'd never understand what paralyzing terror felt like. Nobody would understand unless they'd experienced it firsthand. "Wouldn't you rather use your precious Sunday to socialize with your friends or something?" she suggested.

"I socialize with them every morning when I play tennis," he reminded her gently. "We'll find a way to deal with that demented Amma."

"Dealing with Amma is not easy, Kiran. Poor Appaji has turned into a quiet, gutless little man in doing just that," Megha said. But she didn't want to dampen Kiran's spirit entirely when he was trying so hard to cheer her up. "Maybe we could go for a late evening drive or something, when it's dark outside."

"No. We'll go shopping. I hear shopping always cheers up women."

"I'm not like other women."

Kiran clenched his teeth for a moment. "As if I don't know that!" he murmured. But before she could question him, he quickly added, "Trust me. I'll call Pramila and see if she can lend you a *salwar-kameez* outfit."

Loath to turn down every one of his suggestions, Megha conceded. But she was convinced this was still wrong, maybe dangerous. Entirely wrong. Thoroughly dangerous.

Chapter 11

Megha slid into the passenger seat of Kiran's car. It felt strange. The outfit she had on didn't fit. Ashok's wife was obviously a lot shorter and plumper than she. Megha also wore a pair of sandals that belonged to the same woman and they were one size too small, making them pinch her toes. The still-necessary bandage on her foot didn't exactly help matters.

Sitting beside Kiran made her uneasy. This scene should have had Kiran's wife or fiancée sitting beside him, excited about going shopping with him. Instead he was escorting her, his runaway cousin-in-law. She felt like a common thief. She was going against everything she'd been taught since birth. They were both defying their traditional Hindu moral code. She could only hope the sum total of her sins didn't affect Kiran's future lives. He was merely playing the role of protector and didn't deserve to be punished by the bad *karma* surrounding her.

As Kiran eased the car out from the parking garage and out the gates, she turned to look outside the window, anxious eyes scanning the immediate area for Amma's spies. When she recognized no one and saw nobody looking their way, she settled back in her seat.

Flipping down the visor, Megha glanced at herself in the attached mirror. She had to admit her camouflage was quite effective. Dressed in the loose, lemon-yellow outfit with the flowing *chunni* covering the top of her head, her hair pulled back into an austere bun, and the huge, outrageously gaudy sunglasses perched over her nose, she was indeed unrecognizable. Even her own mother wouldn't be able to tell who she was.

Kiran turned to her. "Like what you see?"

"Not at all."

He gave her a wicked grin. "You could join the circus . . . as a clown."

She wrinkled her nose at him. "Hardly! I look very mature." She saw through his attempt at putting her troubled mind at ease.

He chuckled. "A very mature clown then."

Megha frowned as she noticed the route Kiran was taking. "Where exactly are we going? The bazaar is on the other side of town."

He kept his eyes on the heavily traveled road as he merged in. "To Dharwar. Nobody knows either one of us there. We can shop without any fear of somebody recognizing you."

"Hmm," she grunted and cleared the frown off her face. Again, she trusted his superior judgement. Actually, she had to admit it was nice to have a strong man she could trust. Suresh had turned to his mother in even the smallest matters. This was very refreshing—having someone so practical and resolute making decisions for her. She leaned back and closed her eyes for a minute, giving in to the luxury of being driven somewhere in air-conditioned comfort.

From behind her big mirrored sunglasses she could study Kiran surreptitiously. In the bright sunshine coming through the windshield, she could see every minute detail of his face. He had a tiny mole under the left jaw. Despite the morning's shave, his cheek was already showing a hint of a shadow. The long nose had a slight bump over the bridge. His lower lip was full and wide. His fingers were long and tapered, yet there seemed to be tremendous strength in them. The lean muscles in his arm and shoulder rose and fell each time he handled the gearshift.

Kiran Rao was definitely an attractive man. She felt a slight ripple of sensual awareness go right through her. Oh, God! Quickly she switched her gaze back to the window.

In less than an hour they reached the outskirts of Dharwar.

The landscape changed. The tract became hillier and the vegetation was different from that of Palgaum. The air was much less humid, too. As in any other suburban town, there were large, spacious homes that belonged to the more affluent. As they neared the town's center, the homes got smaller, the roads narrower, and the traffic increased and eventually slowed to a crawl.

Kiran maneuvered the car through the thick mass of pedestrians, stray animals and street hawkers inside the bazaar. He managed to find a parking spot and they walked towards the shops displaying clothing, purses, *chappals*, accessories, and anything else that a body needed.

After looking at literally dozens of outfits, they bought six. She wanted two and he wanted her to have many more, so they settled for six and a couple of saris and some sets of undergarments and sandals. They toured several stores, Kiran patiently urging her to look at more clothes and try them on. She turned to him in disbelief at one point. "Aren't you tired and bored yet?"

He shook his head. "I like shopping."

"Liar!" she accused him with a laugh.

At the end of nearly five solid hours of shopping, they noticed it was getting dark outside and that they were hungry. After stowing away the packages in the car's trunk and back seat they made one last stop at an accessories shop, the *vastu bhandar*, as such shops were referred to. Loosely translated, it meant "variety store." Ignoring Megha's protests, Kiran decided that she should buy lipstick and nail polish. "You're so young, Megha— barely voting age. Indulge and pamper yourself for a change," he scolded, nudging her towards the beauty counter.

She threw him an exasperated look and started to walk away. "How many ways should I tell you this? I don't use makeup and I don't paint my nails!"

"All right then, I'll do it myself."

"What?" Agape, she watched Kiran calmly march up to the salesgirl at the cosmetics counter and whisper something to her. The young woman nodded and studied Megha across the room for a moment. Then the two of them laughed and chatted while

Megha remained rooted to her spot by the exit door and fumed at Kiran's high-handedness. And to make matters worse, he appeared to be flirting shamelessly with the woman while she filled his order and beamed at him at the same time. The sheer nerve of it!

Several minutes later, Kiran returned to Megha's side with a triumphant grin and thrust a package into her hands. "A small *Diwali* gift from me."

She looked inside the paper bag. Two expensive lipsticks and matching nail polish bottles nestled inside. She closed the bag and stomped out of the store with a scowl. Without a word Kiran fell in step with her.

But Megha's irritation didn't last long. She realized Kiran was only being generous, whereas her behavior was both immature and churlish. At the very least she owed him an apology and a "thank you." But it was her other response, the unexpected resentment at seeing him flirt with another woman, that bothered her more. Kiran was a young, attractive bachelor and he had every right to carry on with any woman he chose. Megha was in no position to condemn this, let alone feel pangs of envy. And yet, the rush of jealousy had been unmistakable. She had to curb any such feelings in the future.

As they approached the parking area, she gave him a sidelong glance. "I'm sorry about the outburst, Kiran."

"It's okay—you're under a lot of stress."

"That's no reason for rudeness. I appreciate the gifts. Thank you."

He responded with a slow smile. "I knew you'd come around. What girl can resist cosmetics?"

She had to admit his indulgence was endearing. "True."

Once settled in the car she glanced over her shoulder at the packed back seat. "This must be the best *Diwali* I've ever had. If you buy me any more presents we won't have room to put them."

"Don't worry, we'll make room." He flipped down the passenger side visor mirror and said, "Try on one of those lipsticks."

"Now?"

"Yes, now."

"So damn bossy," she muttered under her breath, unwilling to admit that she liked his kind of bossiness. It was refreshingly male.

"What'd you say?" He shot her a smug smile, meaning he'd heard every word.

"Nothing," she said with a fake smile of her own. "I'll try the lipstick." She fished one out of the bag. It felt cool and satiny smooth in her fingers, an entirely unfamiliar sensation. Twisting the gold-tone tube to force out the shimmering coral tip of the lipstick felt odd. Her hands shook, more from being closely observed by Kiran than from lack of practice. She hesitated, but at Kiran's nod of encouragement she carefully put on the lipstick. It glided onto her full mouth like melted butter, soft, creamy, fragrant . . . and such a vibrant, warm color.

For a fleeting second she imagined her father's image looming up behind her, his eyes filled with cold condemnation. *Makeup is for prostitutes!* Frowning, she stared at the image in the mirror, at her own puckered mouth now painted a rosy shade of coral. Right at that moment, was she any better than a prostitute? A married woman shamelessly living with her husband's cousin and letting him buy her pretty things was only a hair's breath away from being a whore, wasn't it? It hurt to think of herself in those terms. She lowered her gaze from the mirror and closed her eyes to shut out the distasteful image. No, dear God, she was not a prostitute!

Then Kiran's voice startled her out of this introspection.

"Beautiful, just as I'd suspected," he pronounced.

Buoyed by his enthusiastic reaction, she resolved to set her inhibitions aside and enjoy the day. Turning her face this way and that, she studied her image in the mirror, gradually beginning to like what she saw. "Not bad." A smile touched her face. Kiran was right. Shopping for pretty things was a lot of fun.

Kiran's throat went dry as he saw the smile light up Megha's face. Good God, she was gorgeous! He'd always known that, but that little touch of lipstick added a different kind of allure, more sophisticated, more mature, more every damned sexy thing he wasn't supposed to notice. His testosterone was spinning in tight circles, making him crazy! It was hard not to grab her and plant a kiss on those glossed lips. But he couldn't do any of those things. She was still fragile. And she was just learning to trust him. The last thing he needed was to spoil what had turned out to be a very pleasant day, despite her protests.

During the course of the afternoon she had smiled, she had laughed, and she had seemingly enjoyed her shopping spree. Her eyes had glowed with pleasure at all the things in the stores. She had looked like a little girl on her very first shopping trip. Then he realized this was perhaps her first shopping spree of this magnitude.

Right now Megha was wearing one of the outfits they'd just purchased. She had put away Pramila Pai's ill-fitting clothes in a bag provided by the store. The coral-colored *salwar-kameez* fit her perfectly and suited her well. Her flushed cheeks reflected the pinkish tones of the silky fabric. Her new lipstick and sandals seemed to blend in with the picture. The salesgirl at the store had judged the shade well. He nodded in approval. *Damn it, Rao, just keep your bloody hormones under control,* he told himself and put the car in gear.

As a fitting finale to an enjoyable day, he took Megha to a quiet restaurant outside town for an elegant dinner. Kiran watched with amused contentment Megha eat the rich *makhani* chicken curry, *alu matar* or potatoes with peas, the hot, puffy bread called *naan,* and the rice *pulau* and salad. She had become very thin lately, and if she ate like this more often maybe she could gain a little weight. He wanted to give her many more pleasures like today's. Who knew what the next few days and weeks would bring? He fully intended to enjoy every hour of his time with her.

After they returned home that night, exhausted from the shopping and stuffed from the sumptuous dinner, Kiran talked Megha into modeling her new clothes for him. Excited about her lavish new wardrobe, she did as he wished, showing off her lovely ensembles, one after another. "Oh Kiran, these slinky fabrics feel wonderful against my skin," she marveled.

"I'm glad," he replied, envying her childlike joy in simple things. He hadn't experienced that feeling in so long, not since he was a little boy and every new toy was an adventure. It was a shame he took so much for granted.

Megha appeared to be caught in a shimmering dream. She glowed each time she wore a different costume and paraded before Kiran's admiring eyes. His appreciation seemed to encourage her, because she strutted before him, emulating the runway models she must have seen on television.

Caught up in her mood, Kiran applauded heartily. "Absolutely gorgeous!"

She sank down before him in a mock curtsy at the end. "You're making my head swim, Mr. Rao, sir."

"You should wear things like this all the time," Kiran told her.

"Can't—"

"Nonsense. Did you ever think of becoming a model or entering a beauty pageant?"

She chuckled. "Every teenager dreams of being a model or beauty queen or even a movie star, Kiran. But then, what girl from an orthodox Hindu family gets to wear skimpy outfits and flaunt herself in front of millions of people?"

"True, but lots of decent girls go into show business these days, and it's much more exciting than being hidden away in the kitchen of some house in Palgaum."

"This private showing was fun, Kiran," Megha admitted. "But—"

The phone rang, interrupting her. Perhaps jolted back to reality by the shrill ring, she fled to the bedroom and shut the door with a snap.

The spell was broken. Kiran picked up the phone.

Just before retiring for the night, Megha and Kiran made up a list of provisions that Kiran could pick up on his way home from work the next day. "Need any special things for *Diwali?*" he asked as he added items to the list.

She shook her head. "It doesn't mean much this year." For her there would be no lamps and fireworks and sweets and ceremonial herbal bath. Not that the previous year had been much fun either. In spite of being a new bride, *Diwali* had been very mundane. She'd slogged in the kitchen for days, making a variety of sweets and savory snacks, then cooked an elaborate meal on the day of *Diwali* and later watched everybody else eat till they were ready to explode. She had been too tired and fed up to be able to enjoy the festival.

Even though her parents weren't wealthy, her childhood *Diwali*s had been fun and eventful. Her sisters and she used to put on new outfits after the scented herbal bath. Avva used to decorate the cauldron that heated the bath water with a string of marigolds and tuck a flower in each girl's tightly braided hair. Then there would be lots of sweets to eat. After the sun went down the family would light the oil lamps and place them on the front *veranda*. Appa would climb on the stool to hang the *akash-deep* and invariably get irritated when everyone had an opinion about where and how the paper lantern should be suspended. "Four women driving me insane," he would grumble.

Days before the actual event, Avva used to slog over the kitchen hearth and make a variety of rich sweets: round wheat-flour and sugar *undé* dotted with raisins, sticky *halwa*, and deep-fried *karcheykai* filled with sweet coconut and sesame filling.

When Megha, the only one among the children with a sweet tooth, tried to take a sweetmeat or two, Avva would gently smack her hand and pretend to admonish her. "Those are for the goddess. Unless she blesses them first, you cannot have them! You'll have to wait until *Diwali*," she'd say, but the twinkle in her eye told Megha that she didn't really mean it. A little while later, watching Megha pout, Avva would let her have whatever she wanted. "I suppose it is okay for small children to eat before the goddess does," Avva would say. In fact, by the time *Diwali* day rolled around, Megha tended to lose interest in the sweets, having eaten her share beforehand, her fingers often sticky and her mouth covered with crumbs.

Then there were the fireworks that Appa would bring home in a cardboard box—a small quantity compared to the rich kids' treasures, but still loads of fun. Megha found great delight in lighting a string of firecrackers and then tossing it as far away as she could before it exploded into a long, continuous bang-bang-bang. With her fingers stuck inside her ears, she'd stand at a distance and watch them pop. It was silly to set them off herself and then run scared—but that was half the fun—anxiously waiting for the first thunderous crack, her heartbeat soaring.

It was even more entertaining to watch her sister, Leela, run for her life before the explosion. Leela was scared to death of loud noises. She hated fireworks of any kind.

Alas, all that frolicking had gradually dwindled down to just the religious ceremony at her parents' home in recent years. Her father had put an end to all the fun things. Besides, all those trimmings were expensive. And both her older sisters were married and gone.

Megha looked at the nasty burn scar on her wrist. If she thought the previous year had been bad, this year was much worse. "If I were still home there'd be no need for fireworks, Kiran," she said to him. "My burning corpse would have provided enough fireworks for the Ramnath family's entertainment."

"Don't!" Kiran's voice cracked like a whip across the table. "Don't ever say things like that about yourself!"

A surprised moan escaped from Megha's throat at Kiran's sharp rebuke.

He abruptly shoved away from the dining table and came to stand in front of her as she leaned against the kitchen counter, his grim, scowling face mere inches away from hers. His tone was uncharacteristically harsh. "Not even as a joke, Megha! Not even a bloody joke!"

Megha trembled and took a step backward, her back pressing into the hard edge of the granite counter. "I . . . I'm sorry. It was in poor taste." She chided herself privately for upsetting him so. He had promised to protect her and he considered her family, but the emotion behind this sudden flash of temper was evidence of just how much he cared. For Kiran to fly into a rage, she had to have hurt him deeply. "I don't know what made me say it, Kiran. I apologize."

Blowing out a long breath, he backed off. "Apology accepted."

Afterwards, when things settled a bit following Kiran's unexpected outburst, they decided it would be best for Kiran to attend the *Diwali* day *Lakshmi Puja* at his father's office. The *puja* was the ceremonial prayer and obeisance to Lakshmi, the goddess of wealth and prosperity and every Hindu businessman's primary goddess. It was an elaborate annual event and the family would be there, along with all of his father's employees. If he didn't show up it would look suspicious. Besides, Kiran was devoted to his parents, and as their only son it was his duty to be there. Sadly, Megha would have to stay home by herself.

Kiran glanced at her. "I don't like leaving you alone at home at festival time. I wish you could come, too," he said.

"You're very kind, Kiran, but I want you to go and enjoy yourself. Make your family happy. I'll be okay," she assured him and got up to get ready for bed.

That night, for the first time since she had started to run for her life, she slept in peace, without the curse of dreams or nightmares.

Chapter 12

Alone and restless on *Diwali* day, Megha settled down to watch television for a while, but every channel showed footage of the festivities taking place in various parts of the country. Smiling people doing happy things crowded the TV screen. The radio stations, too, played devotional music. The daily newspaper was full of *Diwali* photos and articles. There was no way to avoid the festive mood all around.

She wished she had the freedom to go out there, join the throngs of revelers on the sidewalk, light some sparklers and watch them erupt into a thousand stars, laugh a little and share some sweetmeats. But what she really wanted was to be with the family, with Kiran. And yet, all she could do was imagine the celebration taking place at Kiran's father's office. It was probably packed with family and friends, loads of lights and flowers and food. Amma was probably strutting around in silk and diamonds, playing the role of queen bee.

Earlier Kiran had looked dashing in his traditional *shervani*, the long, gold-embroidered, white silk jacket worn over matching trousers. When Megha had offered to press his outfit, he'd been hesitant. "I don't want to put you to work any more than I already have, Megha," he'd argued.

"Come on, it's nothing," she'd countered, grabbed the hanger from him and proceeded to carefully iron the clothes. Kiran's gratitude for such a simple gesture had been touching. For all the slaving she'd done for her husband and in-laws, she'd never heard a single word of thanks from any of them, except from Appaji once or twice.

Shutting off the television, Megha went to look outside the window once again. The strong odor of burning sulfur from the fireworks crept in. The street below was a haze of smoke. With Kiran gone, the flat felt empty. Although he went to work every weekday, today was different. It was *Diwali*. There was nothing for her to be celebratory about, except, as Kiran had cheerfully reminded her that morning, the fact that she was alive and healthy. And that by itself was plenty to give thanks to the goddess Lakshmi for. So Megha had taken a leisurely shower and bowed her head in silent prayer. Maybe next year would turn out better.

She ate a light lunch and watched a movie video Kiran had rented earlier in the week. One of the scenes in the movie showed a boat tossing about on a turbulent ocean. The howling wind and rain that nearly sank the boat and killed the dashing hero brought to Megha's mind the unexpected cyclone that had struck Palgaum several weeks ago. The storm had swept in with violent winds and torrential downpours, and taken out the power lines for nearly two days.

In the Ramnath household, the storm had turned into a particularly notable event. The memory made Megha forget her gloominess for a moment. It even brought on an amused laugh as she recalled the rather comical episode.

For two straight days drenching rain had fallen over Palgaum. Rivers of slush washed up into the streets and consequently into people's yards and homes. Along with it a long, fat snake ended up in the Ramnaths' backyard and somehow found its way into their kitchen.

Although Megha and Amma were both in the kitchen at the time, Amma noticed it first and let out a shriek. Her body quivered like a giant mound of jelly and her eyes turned enormous with fear. For a split second, just before the scream erupted, Amma was rendered speechless, her mouth working without making a sound—something Megha saw with her own eyes, or she wouldn't have believed it. Fearing for her own safety, Megha retreated to a corner far from the creature that seemed to be in no hurry. It slithered around casually, sniffing, investigating, and probably looking for a meal: a nice, juicy mouse.

Hearing Amma's cries of distress, Suresh and Shanti raced to the kitchen and stood gaping at the serpent. A moment later Appaji valiantly rushed in to defend his family, his *lungi* pulled above his bony knees and tucked in tightly about the waist. "Stop screaming so much, Chandramma. I will take care of that bloody snake," he assured his wife with quiet confidence.

Then he bounced around the kitchen with a folded umbrella, swinging it wildly, vowing to pound the "bloody snake" to a pulp. Megha had never seen Appaji exhibit such male heroism, so she watched in amazement as he tried to do battle with a five-foot long reptile.

Unfortunately, the snake gave Appaji the slip by creeping under the woodpile beneath the raised hearth. Appaji poked at the pile several times with the tip of the umbrella, but the snake eluded him.

Thwack! The umbrella came down with brute force, scattering the logs, but the wily snake was nowhere to be seen. A warning hiss now and then assured them that it was still alive and curled up somewhere underneath all that wood.

After a minute or two, several fruitless thwacks later, Appaji stared at the pile, too cowardly to move the remaining logs with his bare hands. He stood scratching his head in puzzled embarrassment. "Oh dear, looks like the snake is here to stay. Bloody stubborn, I say!" But he wasn't done yet. He swung the umbrella one last time and brought it down with a determined thwack. Alas, it had no effect, other than make everyone groan in disappointment.

Amma shot Appaji a blistering look. "Maybe you should let Suresh handle it, no?"

Appaji's shoulders slumped in defeat. Megha felt her heart constrict. The poor dear had one chance in his lifetime to prove his manhood. And he'd lost it.

Suresh stood beside Megha and Shanti and looked on the

scene with a helpless frown. When Megha nudged him to go help his father, Suresh shrugged and glared at her as if she'd lost her mind. The woodpile stirred ominously, sending Amma into another screaming fit and Shanti cowering into the corner alongside Megha.

Fortunately, Amma's screams brought the neighbor's son, Arvind Jagtap, to the rescue. The young man took down the logs of wood one by one until the snake was uncovered, and then squashed its hood with one quick swing of a cricket bat. Since the creature's tail continued to thrash about, he struck the tail, and that, too, went limp. The result was an oozing, mangled mess on the floor and the surrounding walls that sent the hypersensitive Shanti straight to the bathroom to throw up. Paying no heed to everyone else's relieved sighs and Amma's dramatic grunts, Arvind offered to dispose of the dead snake.

Appaji offered him a plastic bag and Arvind used one of the logs to slide the dead snake into it. Amma sent Megha a silent signal to clean up the waste left behind. Swallowing the acid rising in her throat, Megha quickly got down to mopping up the kitchen before she too felt the need to throw up. She'd never seen anything like that before. Although snakes were common in Palgaum, they stayed away from the more populated areas. She'd seen one or two from a distance in her father's mango orchard, but this was her first close encounter with a real live serpent. It left her shaking for several minutes.

For a day Arvind was the neighborhood hero. Other neighbors who had overheard the ruckus and come out to investigate the cause of the commotion, stood outside the back of the house in ankle-deep mud and watched the scene unfold in the Ramnaths' kitchen. They applauded and showered Arvind with praise for his unusual feat. The rather modest Arvind, perhaps embarrassed by all the attention, quickly got rid of the plastic bag's contents and went directly home without another word.

But the snake episode didn't end there. A day later, Amma stumbled upon the possibility of the snake belonging to the cobra family, in which case, she decided they were faced with a serious problem. "Oh God, I wonder if the serpent was a cobra, no?"

"It didn't look like a cobra, Chandramma," said Appaji with a casual gesture of dismissal.

"What do you know about snakes, Ree?" Amma threw him a look of mild contempt. "And what are we going to do if the serpent god, *Naga*, was killed by mistake, huh?"

"I'm telling you, it was not a cobra," asserted Appaji.

"But what if it was? That, too, killed in our house! It is a big, big sin to kill a cobra," Amma declared, promptly falling before the altar and laying her forehead on the floor in submission to her gods. "*Ayyo, devré swami, kshama maadu!*" she cried. Oh Lord God, please forgive us.

"But we had no choice, Amma. Don't you see that?" argued Suresh in a rare show of logical reasoning.

"Well, now that a cobra is slaughtered in our Brahmin home, a curse will fall on us," Amma gloomily predicted, then continued to beat her head against the floor. It was difficult to say why she was behaving in that fashion—regretting what she considered a sacrilege or just plain theatrics.

Appaji rolled his eyes. "Snakes don't put curses on people."

"Let me tell you something. Cobras are highly revengeful creatures." Amma finally raised herself into a sitting position. "They mate for life and grieve for their dead partner. They seek revenge on the killer. The dead cobra's mate will come and punish us."

"Don't let your imagination frighten everybody, Chandramma," cautioned Appaji.

"What are we to do now?" Amma was convinced it was entirely Arvind Jagtap's fault. "That boy is so stupid—instead of taking the snake out alive, he went and killed it. On top of that, he had the cheek to behave like he deserved high honor. He had the nerve to smile and look superior when those idiot neighbors praised him, no?" she fumed. "Our Suresh would have somehow managed to get rid of the snake alive. Then we would not have to worry about the curse."

Suresh get rid of a live *snake*? Megha nearly burst into laughter at Amma's confidence in her precious son. Suresh started to sweat at the sight of tiny mosquitoes and ants, for heaven's sake!

After some deep contemplation Amma came up with a plan—a *prayashchith puja*, in other words, a ritualistic atonement. "I am going to have a talk with that Arvind's parents," she sniffed. "It is their son's fault, so they will have to pay for the ceremony."

Amma read with avid interest articles about Americans suing each other for all sorts of reasons and winning huge monetary settlements through their legal system. This was Amma's chance at pursuing a similar sense of justice. The Jagtaps had done something wrong, according to her—therefore they had to pay.

"The *puja* will include the ceremony to cleanse the house. We will have to get a priest. Plus, the list of necessary things will cost a lot of money." Amma counted the items on her fat fingers. Then, genuflecting before the altar, she asked for divine forgiveness one more time. After slathering an extra-heavy layer of Fair & Fabulous cream and talc over her face—perhaps her idea of war-paint—she strode over to the neighbors' backyard.

The rest of the Ramnath family stood on the veranda, waiting anxiously for the battle to erupt. They were amply rewarded, because the Jagtaps stepped outside to confront a clearly hostile Amma instead of inviting her into their home. Megha guessed they didn't want either the raging Amma or any resulting blood from the encounter inside their home.

Arvind stood apart from his parents, clearly mortified by what was unfolding outside his house. He was probably regretting his actions from the previous day. Megha felt sorry for the unassuming young man. He really was a nice fellow, a college student, wholesome-looking, studious and polite. His price for coming to the aid of a neighbor was a cat-fight between his mother and the very neighbor he had helped.

Meanwhile Amma was rattling away a list of complaints about his behavior, calling him a "useless boy with no brains."

Arvind's parents summarily dismissed Amma's ranting as

pure babble, ungrateful and vicious. In fact, an indignant Mr. Jagtap attacked Amma in his own way. "How dare you are coming to our house and accusing our son of bad things!" The stout, balding man's face turned a blotchy red, looking like it was going to explode any moment. His lips trembled with rage.

"He defiled our home!" yelled Amma.

"De-fi-led! Hah, you think I do not understand big-big English words or what?" said Mrs. Jagtap, whipping the edge of her sari's *pallu* around and tucking it in at her waist, preparing for a major brawl. "Completely stupid you are. Arvind killed the snake and saved you all! Did we not see with our own eyes your husband and son standing like *buddhoos*, complete fools? Did we not hear the shouting that woke up every neighbor for hundred meters, huh?"

"Don't raise your voice to me, Mrs. Jagtap!" Amma warned.

Megha glanced around in embarrassment as several of the other neighbors, hearing raised voices, came out to their own back doors to observe the fight. And sure enough, like she'd expected, they started to take sides. But Amma had no supporters; they were all solidly in the Jagtaps' corner—literally. Half a dozen men and women slowly walked up to stand behind them and nodded vigorously in agreement with whatever the Jagtaps had to say. Besides, most of these folks had witnessed the snake-removal drama and happened to know the facts firsthand.

"I will raise my voice if I want," Mrs. Jagtap hissed back. "And why you are thinking it was cobra? It was not having the big hood or color."

Megha believed Mrs. Jagtap was correct in her assertion. The reptile in question was yellow with black diamond-shaped markings and was too fat and long to be a cobra. With her limited knowledge she figured it was probably a python or something similar.

With a stern finger held up, Mrs. Jagtap ordered Amma off her property. "Next time you want help, do not come here! You will not get it, I tell you."

When Amma opened her mouth to retaliate, Mr. Jagtap shut her up with a single motion. "Get out! Out, now!"

Humiliated and quaking with rage, Amma stomped back home to spit foul expletives at her wretched neighbors. "Those blackguards should be shot for such behavior. They are not fit to be Hindus. They had the nerve to insult *me*. The serpent god will put his curse upon those good-for-nothing bastards!"

Although appalled at such uncivilized behavior on Amma's part, Megha derived a certain degree of amusement from the event. It was satisfying to note that someone had the courage to put her mother-in-law in her place. The folks standing beside the Jagtaps obviously felt the same way—they were trying hard to suppress their grins. A surreptitious glance in Appaji's direction revealed a veiled look of mild hilarity in his eyes and his lips twitched.

Overall, the snake-in-the-kitchen episode had proved to be quite entertaining. Megha had managed to chuckle, even though she'd been thoroughly embarrassed that a neighbor had to rescue them when there were two grown men in their own home. Mrs. Jagtap, despite her limited English, had been accurate in her description when she'd called Appaji and Suresh "*buddhoos*, complete fools." Well, at least Appaji had tried his best and that counted for something.

Suresh, as expected, had behaved like a coward and a moron. *Buddhoo* for sure!

After the memories of that snake event faded away, Megha's bereft feeling returned once again along with the restlessness. She turned off the video movie. Something was missing. She knew what it was: Kiran—his passion for life, his exuberance, his sense of fun and adventure. He made her feel alive and vital. In his presence she managed to forget her woes.

Was she using Kiran as a handy crutch? If so, she'd have to learn to wean herself from him right away.

She glanced at the clock. It was late evening and beginning to get dark outside. The sound of exploding firecrackers had escalated in the last hour. She didn't expect Kiran home until very late. The *puja* included an elaborate dinner and he was likely to be in the midst of it.

The unexpected sound of keys inserted in the lock sent a chill up Megha's spine. She shot out of her chair and sprinted to the kitchen. Heart racing madly, she listened.

"Megha, don't panic—it's only me." Kiran's voice sounded like music to her ears. She let out a sigh of pure relief.

Emerging from the kitchen, she greeted him with forced casualness. "What are you doing home so early?"

"I felt like coming home."

A happy note clanged in Megha's heart. "What about the *puja* dinner?"

"Right here." Kiran held up an enormous plastic bag. "You didn't think I was going to gobble up a *Diwali* feast while you sat here all alone, did you?"

Her lips curved in a delighted smile. "But . . . your parents?"

"I lied," he said, a mischievous glint appearing in his eyes.

"You lied on a religious day?" Megha shook her head, feigning incredulity.

Kiran grinned. "Told them I had to work on a project deadline for tomorrow. Naturally Mummy packed enough food for at least ten people," he said, placing the bag on the table.

She sniffed the bag. "Smells delicious. Your parents' cook must have been working since dawn."

He raised a brow at her. "Hungry?" When she nodded, he rubbed his hands in anticipation. "Me, too. Let's eat."

"I'll set the table while you get changed." Megha watched with aching fondness as he disappeared into the bedroom. His generosity was amazing. He had missed the time-honored Diwali dinner at his parents' home so he could eat with her. All that casual talk hadn't fooled her for one minute. Project deadline indeed!

He had come home for one reason only: Megha. The tears welled up in her eyes.

Chapter 13

Vinayak Ramnath sat hunched in his office chair, poring over a ledger. A blue ceramic teacup sat near his elbow. His forehead glistened with perspiration. It was a hot day and the ceiling fan wasn't much help, so it was hard to concentrate on his work. He wiped his brow with a white cotton handkerchief.

When a squeal of brakes followed by loud honking and assorted invectives on the street assaulted his senses, he peered outside the window, peeling off his silver-rimmed reading glasses. "Those bloody rickshaw drivers," he snorted angrily. "Dangerous *goondas*!"

Realizing his reaction was a bit extreme for something that routinely occurred several times a day on the crowded street, he settled back in his chair. His knee-jerk reaction wasn't his fault. Megha's disappearance had left him feeling uneasy and jumpy. The slightest provocation seemed to set him off lately. He hadn't been sleeping well. He was sure it was only a matter of time before the police arrested him and his family for attempted murder. Besides, Chandramma was plotting something big again. She was like a taut wire about to snap any moment. He could almost taste the tension surrounding her.

A couple of his nearby colleagues, noticing his uncharacteristic reaction, stared speculatively at Vinayak for a few seconds, then silently went back to work. Embarrassed, he returned to his duties. He had a strong suspicion that most of them already knew about the scandal in his family. Gossip filtered very quickly through the bank's rumor mill. And their man servant, Tukaram, was an expert at spreading news through the community.

Vinayak's only concern was his reputation—he didn't want his fellow bankers to think he had abused his daughter-in-law and forced her to flee. He had worked too long and too hard to have his good name ruined because of what his stupid wife and son had done.

Vinayak had been promoted from junior officer to senior loan officer some twenty years ago. He had not received another promotion since then, but he was happy where he was. His little niche consisted of familiar faces, comfortable habits like old shoes, and the office café—only a few paces from his corner desk. A nice cup of thick, milky tea with loads of sugar was always available when he felt like it. For an extra twenty-five *paise* the pug-nosed errand boy in the cafeteria even delivered it to Vinayak's desk. The luxury was well worth the extra expense.

People who came to Vinayak about applying for loans slipped him a little bundle of hundred-rupee notes under the table and he made sure their loans got processed without a hitch. His had been a satisfactory career in most ways.

He was now biding his time until he could retire, only one year and four months away. He could hardly wait. But . . . then again . . . he wasn't so sure. Circumstances had changed at home in the last few weeks. Home had turned into a grim, miserable place. It had never been a happy, cheerful household, but now he had begun to detest it.

Retirement would mean he would have to be in Chandramma's company all the time. That woman would be the death of him. She would cut him in little pieces and feed him to the dogs if she allowed her to do it. "Ree, do this; Ree, do that," she would say to him. "Ree" was the official husbandly title of respect she used to address him, but the tone of her voice was one generally reserved for servants and untouchables.

At least while he still had a job he could spend five days a week at the office. Plus, here in this familiar two-story building, despite his demanding young boss with the fashionable haircut and American clothes, Vinayak enjoyed some degree of independence, a little self-respect, even a couple of friends. As long as he got his work done and the small business loans department had no complaints, nobody bothered him. He came in at precisely eleven o'clock and left at six o'clock each day.

Vinayak sighed and closed the ledger, then shut his computer down. He would have to find some other form of work if he were to survive after retirement. By the following year he would start to look around for something. He was good with figures and accounting. With his banking experience, lots of businesses could probably use someone like him.

In the meantime he had his secret savings account.

Several years ago he had started to stash away the under-the-table gifts into an account under a fictitious name. Being a bank officer all his life had paid off. He had quietly fed the account on a regular basis. He had, at strategic intervals, used the cash to buy and sell stocks. Now, with the stock market having done its part to pad his account handsomely, he had a nice little reserve. He paid token taxes on it but took care of the paperwork from his office. Nothing about the account reached his home.

Chandramma kept a strict eye on their regular savings and Vinayak's provident retirement fund. The fund was substantial and, combined with the inheritance his father had left him, enough to live on—so long as they lived frugally. His secret money was his own and meant for any unforeseen disaster. Who knew what the future would bring? The Lord's ways were hard to understand. One's previous life could come to haunt the present and money would always come in handy.

He had decided some time ago to put some of it aside for his daughter. Shanti was a less than plain-looking girl and was not likely to receive any marriage offers. If at all she did, the marriage was likely to be rather humble. He had to admit it was unfortunate—poor Shanti had a bad pool of genes to draw upon—no matter which parent she favored she was doomed. Her thick glasses and sallow complexion combined with her withdrawn personality would be hard to sell in the marriage market.

To make matters worse, Shanti had chosen to major in English literature and a future in teaching. What a bloody stupid choice! If she had at least gone into computers or medicine or engineering, she could have earned a good enough salary to survive on her own, but the teaching profession paid next to nothing. However, she was his child, and he owed her a decent living. She was a naïve girl, too, but affectionate in her own way. A bit too withdrawn perhaps, but then so was Suresh and so was he.

Under Chandramma's thumb, most anybody would be withdrawn.

After taking a quick look around the office to safeguard against prying eyes, Vinayak quietly checked his passbook to make sure his secret account was doing as well as it should. He then slid it into his desk drawer and locked it before pocketing the key.

He would never take his passbook home. If Chandramma found it, that would be the end of his independence.

Although he cared about Chandramma in his own way, he didn't love her. He had been a faithful husband to her in spite of the fact that intimacy between them had been rare. The last time he had touched her in that way, she had turned to him and exclaimed, "What is the matter with you? Suresh and Shanti are now old enough to get married and have children of their own, and you are touching me in such a shameless way. You are too old for this kind of teenaged behavior, no?"

Vinayak had promptly reclaimed his errant hand and turned over to his side of the bed, then pretended to fall asleep. He was furious and humiliated. How dare she call him old! She was only three years his junior. With her unsightly looks it was a wonder he had felt any lust for her at all.

Until recently, he had envied Suresh. Surely no good father would envy his own son? But Suresh had a gorgeous wife. At least in the marriage department Suresh had done very well, much, much better than Vinayak. Megha was not only beautiful, she was a cultured and respectable girl who had put up with

Chandramma's demands, and she seemed very affectionate towards Suresh. Kind and gentle to Vinayak, she even treated Shanti like a younger sister.

But now she was gone.

May God bless Megha, Vinayak thought with a tired sigh. She was like a breath of fresh air in their weary household. It had been a stroke of luck that the astrologer, in his customary terse fashion, had mentioned the girl to Chandramma. "Very good girl she is, Chandramma-bai, very beautiful and virtuous. She has just finished B.A. degree. But father is poor and cannot afford dowry. Maybe he will agree for your Suresh, no?" he said, stroking his thin gray mustache with his finger, his calculating eyes trained on Chandramma.

Upon examining the girl's photograph, Chandramma had pounced on the opportunity. At last, here was a chance to bring home a good-looking daughter-in-law and ensure some decent-looking grandchildren to carry on the family name. "Does her horoscope match Suresh's?" she had asked the old man. "Is she healthy? And I hope they have a pure Brahmin atmosphere in the house?"

"Of course, perfect match, no?" he had assured her. "For you, I only bring best."

Thrilled at his words, she had offered the astrologer a large bonus if he could arrange the match. "Tell them Suresh has an M.Com degree and is a senior manager at the bank with good prospects." She had asked the old man to quote Suresh's salary as twice the amount he really earned, making Vinayak squirm. "And tell them we are wealthy people with very high status," she had added. "And my brothers are Krishna Rao and Rama Rao. Everyone knows my brothers."

Vinayak had turned to her in shock. "How can we lie about Suresh's salary and our financial status, Chandramma? What will those people say when they find out the truth?"

"They are not lies," she had retorted. "Are my brothers not rich and respected in this state? Is our son not a manager in a big bank?" Vinayak had rolled his eyes and shut his mouth after that. Protesting would do no good anyway.

The sly old astrologer had broken into a smug grin. He had planned this all along. And if truth were told, despite his discomfort about Chandramma's deceit, Vinayak had silently rejoiced, too. It would be nice to have a pretty daughter for a change. He hoped she had a good, friendly personality and would adjust to their frugal lifestyle. And he prayed she wouldn't resent them for the lies. A fussy young lady with costly tastes and a strong will that clashed with Chandramma's would be a disaster.

But by God's grace Megha had turned out to be a gem, far beyond his expectations.

After the wedding, however, instead of showing the daughter-in-law kindness and respect, Chandramma had treated her shabbily. Vinayak had cringed every time Chandramma had picked on the poor girl. She had made it her mission to make Megha's life a living hell—insulting and humiliating her, making her feel small and inadequate. He despised himself for being such a coward and not coming to Megha's defense. His poor attempts at defending her once or twice had only served to heighten Chandramma's wrath. He had merely ended up making matters worse. Since then he had decided it was best not to interfere. But then Megha had paid the price once again.

It was bad enough that Chandramma had demanded a dowry from Megha's poor, debt-plagued father. Before the wedding, Vinayak had tried to dissuade his wife from demanding a dowry. "Chandramma, the girl is beautiful, bright and educated. We should consider ourselves lucky as it is. Think about it. Do we really have to have dowry, too?"

Shocked at his comments, Chandramma had given him a good tongue-lashing. "No dowry! Ree, are you totally mad or what? Our Suresh is a bank officer. Our family is well known in the state. We are too good for that girl with only a bachelor's degree and no career. Those Shastrys have no social standing; they should consider themselves blessed to have people like us associated with them. For giving their daughter a good home and husband, they should kiss our feet, no?" As always, Vinayak had retreated in defeat.

Chandramma had won another battle. She always did.

Recently, Chandramma had resorted to drastic measures to get the dowry money. She had no conscience. She had even stooped to murder. It made Vinayak sick to his stomach to think of the horror of it all. He was convinced that his wife had a mental illness of some sort. He had read about sociopaths and psychopaths—for all practical purposes they seemed like ordinary people, but their minds were twisted. Was Chandramma one of those mental cases? She had grown up in an affectionate and affluent home. There was no explanation other than insanity for the hostility and greed she exhibited.

All he could do now was pray that some day Chandramma would recognize her evil ways and atone for her sins. They had indeed been lucky to have such a wonderful daughter-in-law. Why couldn't his wife have seen that, for God's sake?

A sense of urgency to make up for his own sins had begun to creep up on him slowly, silently. It had started to become more evident since the previous year, when he had visited his doctor to be treated for bronchitis. His tired and weakened lungs were beginning to do something strange again. Having fought tuberculosis in his youth, he was resigned to the fact that it would probably show up again sometime during his life.

After looking at the X-rays his doctor had said it was serious—most likely lung cancer. "To be hundred percent sure we have to do a biopsy, Mr. Ramnath," he had said grimly.

Vinayak was not surprised that his lungs had deteriorated further. His persistent cough had become worse in recent months, convincing him that he was dying. But he had made it clear that he didn't want to be treated. "No biopsy. I have lived long enough, doctor. I am grateful to God for giving me this much after my tuberculosis."

"But that is ridiculous," the astonished doctor had scolded him. "You have to start appropriate treatment immediately."

Vinayak had shaken his head. "No! If it is cancer, I don't want to know. Just treat the pain when it starts, if it starts." The doctor had reluctantly yielded to his wishes, but not without issuing dire warnings about the horrors of cancer.

What would be the point in resorting to expensive treatment anyway, Vinayak had argued with himself. He had read about the side effects of chemotherapy and radiation, about how the treatment was often worse than the disease. He had no one to worry over his health, hold his hand, soothe his aches and sit beside him in the hospital. His wife and children were not warm, kind-hearted individuals. They were likely to be glad to see him die quickly. He did not want to wake up in a hospital bed and see Chandramma's face, blatantly telling him to hurry up and die so she could have his money.

No, it was not worth it, he had assured himself. He would rather die sooner than later.

Returning his attention to the present, Vinayak realized it was time to go home. Rising from his chair, he stretched. He was tired. Lately he tired easily. It probably had to do with that wretched cancer, or whatever it was that had invaded his lungs. Then he bid goodnight to the other staff and headed for the bus stop.

As he sat in the cramped bus on his way home, Vinayak began to experience that strange sense of unease combined with guilt again. Megha's disappearance was mostly his fault. He had failed in his duty towards her.

How long before the police figured it all out and ended up on his doorstep? And how long before the cancer killed him off? Meanwhile Vinayak prayed for a quick and silent heart attack.

Chapter 14

Chandramma Ramnath was a woman on a mission. She strode down the decaying alley with the purposeful air of one who knew exactly where she was headed. Although not entirely sure if she was going in the right direction, she managed to move with relative ease, navigating around the filthy little urchins playing a game of street cricket, the mangy dogs lying on the footpath, the old beggar woman holding out her gnarled hands for alms, and the stinking rubbish strewn around. The discarded banana peels were particularly dangerous and she took care not to step on any. She hitched up the folds of her sari so the hem would not touch the ground.

"Ugh! This neighborhood is filthier than I had imagined," she murmured under her breath, a pinched look about her face. The street was not paved and there was red dust everywhere, including on her sari. She would have to take it to the dry-cleaners the next day. Open sewers flanking the alley emitted a foul odor. Her stomach was beginning to protest.

The other pedestrians stared at her for a moment then moved out of her way. Chandramma knew she looked out of place in this neighborhood with her silk sari and expensive jewelry, and her focused behavior. The low-class women here had their cheap saris covering their heads and walked with their eyes downcast.

She came to a stop, pulled a piece of paper from her black leather handbag and studied it for a moment, a crease appearing on her brow. Then she slipped it back into her bag and glanced at the building that stood before her: a three-story tenement grayed with age and black lines of mold streaking the front from years of monsoon rain coursing down. Faded and darned clothes and saris hung on lines on the balconies outside each crumbling flat.

Why wasn't she told the building was a dirty little hole in the worst part of town? Chandramma let out an indignant sigh. She would have to have a serious talk with her friend who had recommended this place. But it was too late to turn back now. She might as well get her errand over with before she changed her mind.

After a brief second of hesitation she lifted the hem of her sari even higher and began to climb the steep wooden staircase with great care, one hand tightly clutching the flimsy handrail for support. "God only knows why that man lives in this bloody awful dump!" She grimaced at the ominous groaning of each stair as she set a stout foot over it.

Reaching the second floor, she stopped to catch her breath. She was wheezing from the long trek through the winding alleys and up two flights of stairs. Perspiration broke out on her skin. Ignoring the discomforts of the moment, she walked down the narrow passage, trying to read the numbers on the doors and the names of each flat's occupants.

She let out a sigh of relief when she found the flat with the crudely handwritten number 10. The name on the door: Pandit Haridas.

Finally! It had not been easy finding this elusive man. The rickshaw driver had driven her round and round the area a few times before she had ordered him to stop his vehicle and alighted, giving him a solid piece of her mind and only eighty percent of the fare he had demanded. The idiot drove a rickshaw for a living and didn't know the addresses around town. How asinine was that?

After that she had wandered some distance, looking for the address without any luck. So she asked a group of rather nasty-looking men loitering in the area for directions. They had clearly been drinking cheap liquor—she had smelled it around them. For one breathless moment she had felt a sharp stab of fear right in her ribs. The men looked dangerous! But with no one else about other than beggars, she had no choice but to ask the lesser of the two evils for help, the gangster-types. "Could you please tell me where Bhujle Chawl is?" she had asked politely. *Chawl* was a word for tenement.

The gang's leader, a stocky man with a greasy, movie-star puff of black hair, and dressed in tight brown pants and a cheap T-shirt, had moved forward, his arms folded across his chest. He had the audacity to raise an eyebrow and look her in the eye. "How much you giving, *bai*?"

"What do you mean?" He had the nerve to ask for money just to tell her where a miserable *chawl* was? Her breath had hitched when he started eyeing her jewelry with a speculative gleam in his eyes. Thief! But she had managed to hold his alcohol-reddened gaze for a long time, not flinching for a single moment. "That depends on whether you give me correct directions." She had pulled out a ten-rupee note and waved it in the air.

He had frowned at her. "Only ten? Not even enough for one *beedi* packet, *bai*."

On a whim she had waved the note before a mild-looking fellow standing behind the leader, wearing tattered clothes, his thin face looking hungry enough to snatch the money. Miraculously it had worked; she had wormed the information out of that idiot with an additional five rupees. She had taught the damned leader, that rabid mongrel in the tight pants, exactly who was master! Apparently the *chawl* was only a short distance from there. She had just wasted fifteen rupees for nothing!

As she started to walk away the men had jeered at her back. "*Arre, yeh aurat hai ke rakshasi?*" Hey, is that a woman or a she-demon? Her temper erupting, she had nearly turned around and gone after them to beat the shit out of the mocking bastards. But she could not afford to take on half a dozen drunken brutes in a street brawl. They would pulverize her and take her belongings. She was forced to suppress her rage, hold her head high and keep marching. The familiar tears of humiliation had started to sting her eyes, but she had squelched those, too. Damn, damn, damn!

Well, desperate problems required desperate measures. If she weren't so frantic she wouldn't be in this horrible neighborhood to begin with. Apart from those thugs it was probably filled with prostitutes, pimps, and God knew what other kind of vermin that respectable women like her should not even think about.

In the end, she had managed to find the nameless alley and the *chawl*. She didn't even want to contemplate how she was going to find her way out of this ghetto and return home. Mr. Haridas had come highly recommended by one of her friends and Chandramma had tracked him down. That was all that mattered right this minute.

She knocked firmly on the door. There was no answer. After a harder knock the door opened a crack and part of a face appeared behind it. A low, gruff male voice asked, "Yes?"

"I'm Mrs. Ramnath. I want to talk to Pandit Haridas."

"What you want Pandit for?" The man refused to open the door any more than three inches or so. All Chandramma could see was a snub nose that stood on a level with her chest. The semi-darkness of the room behind him made it impossible to see beyond the nose.

Rumblings of anger started building up inside her once again. She had not come all this way for some strange little man to cross-examine her. She gave him her most intimidating glower. "I need to consult the Pandit. Now, is he here or not?"

The man opened the door wider. "I am Pandit Haridas. Why you not telling me you want to consult, huh?" The man clenched his teeth as if in irritation.

"You didn't give me a chance," Chandramma retorted. What an odd little fellow he was. And so annoying!

The rest of the man's face was visible now and most of his body. Chandramma started to have grave doubts about her visit. Despite the gruff voice the man was no bigger than a dwarf. He wore a saffron colored *lungi* and a matching pullover shirt with no sleeves. His complexion was an unhealthy shade of white, almost albino skin. He had a large forehead and thick pink lips. Small gray eyes the color of wood smoke looked at her with mocking suspicion. He didn't exactly inspire confidence.

A slight chill settled around her. Had she made a mistake in coming here?

Nonetheless she raised a haughty brow at Pandit Haridas. "If you don't tell me you are the Pandit, how can I mention what business I have?" When she noticed his sly eyes travel to her handbag she clutched it close to her chest. She would be damned if she'd let some stunted albino rob her blind. If she had managed to thwart an entire gang of thugs earlier, she could easily handle this one. She'd pound the dwarf into *chutney* if he dared to come anywhere near her handbag. "Mrs. Rajan gave me your name," she informed him.

"Humph."

The little man was rude and humorless, Chandramma decided. She couldn't quite see how her wise friend had recommended such a man. But now that she was here she might as well see what he had to say. At the worst, she would be out of fifty rupees or thereabouts if she was lucky. "Mrs. Shambavi Rajan? You do know her, no?" She put on her most tart tone. It almost always managed to get her what she wanted.

"Okay, okay, if you know Mrs. Rajan, then come inside," the man said with some reluctance and motioned her to enter his flat.

Chandramma took one step inside and breathed in revulsion at the clutter and grime inside the room. It was dark and dank. She couldn't see a window or a ray of natural light anywhere. A small lamp with a low-watt bulb was all there was to illuminate the place. She had heard somewhere that albinos could not tolerate light. The place smelled of grease and sweat and . . . oh heavens . . . sour milk. Didn't the man ever clean his clothes or his dishes?

It appeared that the dwarf was unmarried and lived alone. No woman would live in a filthy hole like this. When he asked

Chandramma to sit down she looked around for suitable furniture. There were only two easy chairs. She chose the cleaner one and sank into it. She would have preferred to stand, but she was tired and the dwarf might feel insulted. And if he felt slighted, he might get rid of her before she could state her business.

"So, what you want to consult about, huh? My fee is three hundred rupees for half hour." The man sat in the other chair and joined his short hands in his lap, his fingers resembling baby bananas. His chubby feet didn't quite reach the floor.

Well, the dwarf was obviously greedy. Chandramma would rather die than pay someone that kind of money. The other day she had put out two hundred rupees and the stupid family astrologer had told her practically nothing of use. All he had provided was a character analysis on Suresh. She knew her son better than anyone else—she didn't need an astrologer to tell her that her son was weak and needed her to guide him. On top of that the astrologer had gone and told her husband about her private consultation. Consequently, Vinayak had asked her probing questions and treated her like a common criminal. That was the reason she had to find this other little man and stoop to coming into this shady neighborhood. She couldn't afford to have her husband find out about her activities. He had this annoying, self-righteous way about him that made her feel defensive.

She warily eyed the Pandit once again. The man had the nerve to quote such atrocious fees! With those rates he should have been living in cleaner and more decent quarters at the very least. She would have to do some quick bargaining. "One hundred rupees I will give you—no more. If you cannot give a reading, I will have to go," she informed him with an imperious lift of a brow.

Pandit Haridas studied the Ramnath woman for a long minute, his shrewd eyes taking in the quality silk sari in a shade of sea-blue, the leather *chappals* encasing her feet, the gold bangles on her thick wrists and the diamonds in her ears. "People are paying four and five hundred for my service, Mrs.

Ramnath. I am giving discount for you because you are friend of Mrs. Rajan. Three hundred rupees—I am giving best service for you." To soften the harshness of his tone he offered her a tiny smile—a token of compromise.

She sighed and settled back in the chair, making its wood frame groan. "All right, three hundred, but you will perform complete services, forty-five minutes," she countered. "What do you have to say?"

Knowing when to seal a good bargain, Haridas nodded. "Okay, for Mrs. Rajan's friend, I do complete service."

The woman dug out a sheet of paper from her handbag and offered it to him. "My son's horoscope. I want you to study it and tell me what I should do about him."

Pandit Haridas turned the lamp towards him and put on a pair of glasses, the frame held together with cellophane tape over the bridge. The illumination from the light bulb was barely enough to read by, but he always managed somehow. It was all his eyes could endure, and it was nice and cheap to maintain.

As he studied the horoscope he made odd grunting and groaning sounds, a trick that generally managed to make his customers uneasy. Some of those sounds didn't sound positive, but they served a purpose. They sent a message: this was a difficult horoscope and he would need to invest more time and effort into it.

Haridas noticed the woman glance at her wristwatch a few times. "Is the horoscope that bad?" she finally asked, a frown settling over her face.

Managing to cover up his smile, Haridas nodded. He had been reading the horoscope for several minutes. The clock was ticking. His little act never failed to work. The fat woman looked thoroughly worried about her precious son's future.

After a long while, Haridas looked up and peeled off his glasses. "Your son is already married, is he not?"

The Ramnath woman cleared her throat and glanced away. "Yes . . . yes he is."

"Then what are you wanting to know, Mrs. Ramnath? About his job? His health?"

"Yes . . . and . . . about his wife and . . ."

"And what, Mrs. Ramnath?" Haridas was enjoying himself immensely. Putting this disagreeable woman on the spot was more fun than he had anticipated.

"Oh . . . future children . . . of course."

"Of course." By asking about Suresh's career Haridas had obviously made it a bit easier for the woman to introduce the delicate subject that she had probably been obsessing about. Almost all his clients had delicate subjects to discuss. They didn't exactly come to this neighborhood for anything simple or ordinary.

"Career is okay. He might be getting a promotion in about one year, but only if I perform some holy rituals." He remembered to throw that in—the all-important holy rituals. "Marriage is also good, but I am getting some feeling that you are not satisfied, no?" He leaned forward, focusing on the woman with narrowed eyes. He felt a sense of smug satisfaction when he saw the embarrassed flush blooming over what he considered an ugly face. A mean and ugly face.

Haridas had been in this business for many years and served enough greedy women and men like this one to know exactly what Mrs. Ramnath was here for. He had met women who wanted him to perform satanic rituals to force their daughters-in-law and daughters to abort a perfectly healthy fetus solely because it was a female child. He had met men who wanted to have their business partners eliminated by less than honest means. He had seen young people who wanted him to help them steal examinations. He had come across couples in love that wanted him to assist them to elope. He had even crossed paths with men who thought it was all right to kill someone for their own selfish purposes. There was precious little Haridas and these four walls hadn't heard or seen.

This woman was as greedy and ruthless as they came—maybe more so. Well, for three hundred rupees he would tell her what she wanted to hear. He feared to ask her the details of her plans. Despite his questionable profession and his rather unconventional means of making a customer pay for his services, he had a conscience, and he refused to get drawn into things he felt would ruin his own chances of a better life in his next incarnation. His knowledge of astrology and the scriptures was deep enough for him to know there was a thin line between dishonest and sinful.

She shifted uncomfortably in her chair. "You see, Suresh's father-in-law lied to us."

"Aha, I see." This appeared to be a dowry matter, if his instincts were correct.

"He told us that he will pay the dowry within one year after the marriage. Now it is more than one year and there is no dowry."

"You are tired of waiting, then?"

"Yes. And my son's wife is not even expecting. I suspect that she is barren, no? What am I to do? You tell me."

A peek at the small wall clock located behind the fat woman told Haridas that he was about twenty minutes into his consultation. He had twenty-five minutes left. He went back to studying the horoscope, this time with a pencil in hand, letting his almost non-existent brows form a sharp V over his nose, pretending to look entirely immersed in the horoscope. He got the feeling the fat woman wanted her son to divorce his present wife. She wanted another daughter-in-law, a rich one.

Several awkward minutes later, after listening to the woman squirm and cough and throw other little hints of impatience at him, Haridas gazed at her once again. "I think there is a chance that Suresh will have opportunity for another marriage."

At once alert, the woman leaned forward. "He will?"

"You can get dowry also. But I will have to perform rituals and cast a special spell. It will cost two hundred rupees extra."

Eyes lighting up, the Ramnath woman sucked in her breath. "Really? There will be no bad effects on Suresh? On our family?"

Haridas shook his head gravely. "If there is no pregnancy then there can be divorce with very little bad effects. Everything will be okay." Then, to kill more time, he told the woman a bit more about Suresh's career and gave her some information on

how his horoscope affected the rest of the family. Naturally, all
the rituals and spells to make things go in the right direction
would cost extra money.

"So, you are saying getting rid of Suresh's present wife will
not be a problem?"

"Uh . . . no."

"She will disappear and it will not bring any *kashta* for us,
problems and regrets?"

Haridas nodded, a knowing smile playing over his face. He
was indeed good at astrology, wasn't he? He made plenty of
money by doing these readings. His rituals and predictions were
fairly accurate. He had a knack for casting spells. How else
could he get business repeatedly and good referrals? He charged
extremely high fees to tell people what they wanted to hear. He
coated the truth with a little sugar, and his clients fell all over
themselves, ecstatic at being able to do whatever it was they had
planned to do in the first place. All they needed was a push from
him and a spell here and there, and in return his pockets got
fuller.

The only reason Haridas lived in this squalid tenement was to
fool the income tax people. He didn't pay a single rupee in taxes
since his was a cash-only business. They would never dream of
seeking someone in the middle of one of the poorest neighborhoods of Palgaum. For all practical purposes he was a destitute
astrologer with virtually no clients to speak of. His customers
were all like this woman, people who did not want to be known
as his clients. He grinned inwardly as he thought of the amount
of money he had stuffed inside his mattress—also inside a few
pillows and in a few kitchen containers. It was enough to last
him a lifetime.

His astrological calculations from this particular horoscope
told him that the young man in question, Suresh Ramnath, was
feeble and not very bright. It also showed that he had made an
excellent marriage with his present wife, with or without dowry.
His current spouse would bring him good fortune in the future.
Her stars were beneficial to whomever she married. But if he divorced her, his chances would vanish. Suresh would likely stay

in his present job for the rest of his life. Even if he married a second time, and that, too, seemed remote, the probability of getting a better wife than this one was slim to zero. His physical health showed rapid deterioration after the age of forty.

The Ramnaths were obviously too stupid to recognize their luck in having a good daughter-in-law. Too bad, Haridas concluded. If this domineering woman was going to force her son to divorce such a promising wife and go looking for another one, who was he to dissuade her from her goal? He would collect his fee and let the she-buffalo hang herself.

While she reached for her handbag to pull out the money and carefully count it, Haridas noticed the woman looking smug. This was working out quite well for her. She was probably pleased that she could go home and follow through with her plans. "Three hundred for the reading and four hundred for the two spells—for Suresh's promotion and remarriage," she said and handed seven crisp bills to Haridas. "Everything had better be like you said, otherwise you will be hearing from me and also from Mrs. Rajan," she warned him.

"Never doubt my reading, Mrs. Ramnath," he said with an equally intimidating ring in his voice and pocketed the money. He had done this too many times to be scared away by a witch who was desperate and willing to sell her soul. He had a feeling she would be back within a few months. Most of them did. His mattress looked quite fat lately.

Chandramma wished the little man a quick *Namaste* with her palms joined and then departed in haste. She had to get out of there quickly. Haridas made her hair stand on end. There was something curiously disturbing about him. And it wasn't just his strange physical appearance. It was as if he could read her mind, every little thought that flashed through it. It was unsettling. The man had stared at her in an odd way, his nearly colorless gray eyes seemingly sizing her up. His little brown teeth reminded her of rodent teeth—she could imagine them gnawing on something, even human skin. She didn't appreciate losing her self-confidence the way she had with him. And the stench in his house was enough to make her stomach go into convulsions.

Very few things in life made Chandramma feel uncomfortable or intimidated. Haridas made her feel both. And she didn't like the feeling.

Even if she had found what she had come to seek, this was not a safe neighborhood for her to be roaming around. A few curious faces stared at her from the windows of the neighboring flats as she made her way down the long corridor and then the rickety staircase. Sensing those eyes following her, she clutched her bag more tightly to her chest.

It took her several minutes to find her way out of the maze of alleys and back to the safety of the more familiar streets. In the process she had to shoo away two beggars, one stray dog and even a hungry goat trying to tug on her sari in its quest for food. Fortunately, the gang of thugs was nowhere in sight. She had been afraid they would be lying in wait for her at the corner, expecting her to return the same way she had gone in. She quickly hailed a rickshaw the moment she saw one and headed home.

She settled back against the vinyl seat and took deep breaths of blessed relief. Despite the awkwardness with Haridas, a large burden had been lifted from her shoulders. He had informed her that her plans could go forward. She had it all worked out in her mind some time ago but needed to be sure she was doing the right thing.

But despite Haridas's reading, she would still talk to the family astrologer once again. She would force him to give her some definite answers, just to be reassured that she was going in the proper direction and that Haridas's predictions were accurate. She never took chances and didn't like getting herself in trouble. She was alone in this venture. Both her sisters-in-law, Devayani and Kamala, in spite of being her confidantes, had no idea how extensive and complicated her plans were. Devayani was like a puppy, eager to please, but Kamala, with her snobbish ways, was likely to look at Chandramma's plans with contempt. To reveal her ideas to the two women would be disastrous.

Chandramma was definitely alone in this.

She was furious at the Shastrys about the dowry. She considered herself a patient woman, but there was a limit to her patience. She was not a fool and didn't like to be treated like one. To her, an agreement was a firm obligation, and not to be taken lightly. She didn't care how Shastry managed to acquire the dowry. She wanted her money. Now! To aggravate her further, one year had passed by and that good-for-nothing Megha hadn't even managed to become pregnant.

Chandramma was willing to wait a bit longer for the dowry if there was at least a grandson in the near future, but without even that small reward, what good was a daughter-in-law?

Chandramma was loath to admit that Megha was beautiful. That was why she had bribed the astrologer to lie to Megha's parents about Suresh's horoscope and his earnings as well as their own financial status. Megha's beauty had seemed like an asset at first, but no longer. In fact, each time she looked at Megha's flawless complexion, her large eyes and perfect nose, Chandramma shuddered within. Everything about that girl made Chandramma feel less like a woman and more like a hulking, misshapen object.

Hearing remarks like, "Oh, what a lovely daughter-in-law you have," or "She looks like a movie star—where did you find her?" made Chandramma sick.

She hadn't wanted to be seen alongside Megha anymore—people just seemed to notice the contrast. Although they were too polite to say it, she could see it in their eyes while they mentally seemed to appraise the two women. She felt like she had gone back to her childhood and teenage days—those hurtful, horrible days when the boys had spurned her and the girls had looked at her with pity-filled eyes. Every girl that had approached her with an offer of friendship had done it out of pity. In turn, Chandramma had shooed them away. She had never wanted that kind of mercy friendship. She would manage on her own.

She had assumed that those days of scorn and pity were well behind her, but Megha's presence in the house had brought back these dark memories. The wound had been reopened and the pain and flow of blood were worse than before. And Megha was responsible for it.

Following the wedding last year, Chandramma had taken her new daughter-in-law to her regular religious meetings and socials to show her off as a prize acquisition. She would surely be the envy of her friends, Chandramma had calculated. They would congratulate her on her good luck and fine taste. They would likely be jealous of her and her son because of Megha's beauty. Instead, Chandramma had only received their pity for her own shortcomings. Outright hostility she could endure, but not pity.

A few whispered offensive comments made behind her back had reached her ears: *Poor Chandramma! She and her daughter-in-law look like Beauty and the Beast. How did a girl like that end up with that puny Ramnath boy? Oh dear, but the girl looks like a lotus growing in a swamp. Couldn't the girl's father find someone more suitable than the Ramnaths?*

Chandramma had immediately stopped asking Megha to accompany her to her social gatherings. Humiliation and the long-dormant feelings of rage had stirred up inside her. How could God be so cruel and unjust? Hadn't she been a chaste and devout Brahmin woman and prayed and performed her duties like she was supposed to? So why had God punished her with this face and body? When her parents had been good-looking people and her two brothers were handsome men, why was she condemned to such an unsightly appearance? Why were the Meghas of the world given the looks of *parees*? Angels.

There had been times during the past few months when she was tempted to slap Megha's smug face just to see an ugly blue bruise appear on its perfect surface, or feed her kilos of pure butter and watch her slender body turn fat and round. She wanted to see that girl waddle about like an overweight cow. Maybe pregnancy would have done that to her, but that hadn't even come into question. Her flat stomach and slender limbs were still the same.

Tukaram, their stupid servant, was so devoted to Megha he

seemed nearly ready to kiss the girl's feet. He had never shown even mild respect towards Chandramma in the twelve years he had worked for them, let alone such devotion.

To make matters worse, Chandramma's husband, Vinayak, was like a ball of soft wheat dough around Megha—in his eyes the girl could do no wrong. He was always polite and generous to Megha, and smiled at her a lot. A man who rarely smiled had suddenly begun to do it often. How nonsensical was that? He even thanked Megha for serving him a simple cup of coffee. It was sickening to watch her husband tripping over his own skinny feet to please the useless little excuse for a daughter-in-law. A grown man acting like a teenager around a young woman was contemptible.

Her favorite nephew, Kiran, had a habit of staring at Megha with adoration, too. That little slut had probably done something to him as well. Those big, innocent eyes were nothing short of dangerous. What was it about her that prompted such reverence—especially from men?

Well, no more! Chandramma was going to make sure that Megha would be banished from their lives. The worthless chit could take her fancy English words and stuff them in her throat. Just because she had attended some upper-class convent school and had a college degree she liked to pretend that her English skills were superior to everybody else's and that she could write well. Hah, little Shanti had attended the same school, and she could read and write just as well, maybe better!

Megha and her deceitful parents would be taught a lesson very soon. Chandramma would find a rich young lady for her son—someone with a respectable dowry—someone who would show her mother-in-law the respect due to her.

But first Chandramma had to find out where that good-for-nothing Megha was. How had she managed to slip out of their fingers? Had she overheard something and made her own escape plans while Chandramma was cooking up hers? Or, worse, had she seen and heard Suresh and Chandramma in the shed that night? Oh God, that spelled trouble.

Well, Megha might be clever, but not clever enough to hide

forever and certainly not clever enough to outwit her mother-in-law. Chandramma would hunt the girl down, sooner or later.

She had a few theories about Megha's disappearance, and an idea had been forming in her mind for the past day or two. To put it in motion she needed to find someone reliable but inexpensive to keep an eye on a certain house.

That was the big problem. Whom could she recruit for the job? The police would never cooperate, and hiring someone was likely to be expensive. Was there a way to find anything like private detectives in a small town like Palgaum? And if yes, how did one approach them? What exactly did they do as detectives? She had seen them in movies and on television, but she knew nothing about them in real life.

As the driver maneuvered the rickshaw through a busy intersection not far from the house Chandramma had been speculating about, her eyes accidentally fell on someone standing on the footpath.

A slow smile lit up her face. Haridas's so-called spells were already beginning to work or what? The ugly dwarf was good. Damn good! She grunted in satisfaction.

She had found the perfect spy!

Chapter 15

The dark automobile rolled to a stop at the end of the residential street, Devi Galli. A few shops and small restaurants flanked the commercial street which intersected with it, Hanuman Galli. The late evening light had faded a while back, but the street lamps, fitted with yellow vapor bulbs, provided dull illumination for the footpaths. The mosquitoes and moths were out, buzzing around the lamps.

It was just before dinnertime and people were returning home from work, most walking briskly, some on bicycles. Aromas of curry, frying oil, and fresh fruit mingled with the smell of automobile exhaust on the streets. Palgaum's nightly fog was already making its way from the river to settle over the town, its dampness apparent in the way the car's windows were slowly misting up.

In the passenger seat of the car Megha sat stiffly, her hands tightly clasped in her lap. Kiran turned off the ignition and glanced at her. "We're here."

She continued to stare at her hands. "I'm not sure I want to go."

"After coming all this way?" He sighed and drummed his fingers on the steering wheel for a moment. He should have known she'd panic at the last minute. In fact, he was having one or two second thoughts himself. "Shall we go back home then?"

"No . . . yes . . . no. Wait." She shook her head and frowned. "I don't know."

"Make up your mind, will you please? The longer we sit here the more suspicious it looks. We're in a no-parking zone."

"All right, I—I'll go." Megha glanced about her, carefully searching for familiar faces amongst the men and women walking and talking on the street corner. "I don't see anyone I know." She turned a dubious face to Kiran. "Do you think it's safe?"

He wasn't sure but he nodded. "If you keep to the shadowed side of the street you should be all right." Kiran had decided that this rather dark and unobtrusive corner, about a block from Megha's best friend, Harini's house, and the busy shopping area, would be the best place for him to drop Megha off and later pick her up. One or two of Harini's neighbors knew Megha by sight, and if they saw her arriving in a car at Harini's doorstep, they were sure to get curious.

"I'm not so sure now, Kiran." Megha gave him another skeptical look. "I'm beginning to think this was a foolish idea."

Kiran tried to keep his tone casual. "It's a bit risky, but you've been cooped up in the flat for days, Megha. You needed to get out and see your friend."

"But I might be putting her in danger," Megha murmured, her eyes looking troubled.

"Just make sure she understands how important it is to keep your visit a secret." Kiran sent Megha an encouraging nod. "Now go. Keep the *chunni* over your head until you're safely inside her house."

"Okay. You will pick me up later?"

"Of course, Megha!" Kiran nearly laughed at the absurdity of her question. How could he not be there to take her home? "You know I won't leave you stranded here."

Apparently satisfied with his assurance, Megha pulled the long, silky *chunni* over her head and part of her face, took one deep breath and gingerly stepped out of the car. After another quick reconnoitering glance she jogged across the street to the mostly unlit side of the intersection and melted into the shadows. The pedestrian traffic quickly swallowed her up.

Kiran watched her, trying to keep his eyes glued to the slim, disappearing figure. It was disquieting, watching her go off on her own, outside his protection. This was the first time she was venturing out since their shopping spree a couple of weeks ago. Back then he had been beside her all the time, keeping a vigilant eye on everyone around, making sure they stuck to areas where nobody was likely to know them.

But this was different. This was their town, where folks knew each other, if not by name, then at least by sight. His parents were well-known in Palgaum society. But the good thing was that Megha was relatively unknown. With any luck, nobody on the street would recognize her, even if they managed to see beyond the veil.

And it was a good thing his car had tinted windows—they had proved to be a blessing since Megha had entered his life. She'd arrived like an unexpected rainstorm on a hot summer day, drenching yet delightfully refreshing. His quiet and drab bachelor life was suddenly full and bursting with color. It even smelled wonderful, like old-fashioned cooking and Megha's sandalwood scent—an enticing combination. At first he wasn't sure how he felt about the intrusion, but he'd begun to like coming home to her each evening. In fact, it was so pleasant he never wanted it to end. He could easily picture her in his home, as his wife, as the mother of his children.

Shaking off the fantasy, he turned on the ignition and slowly drove away. He was still uneasy about Megha's visit to Harini, but he had only himself to blame. Watching Megha pace the floor each evening like a caged animal, fretting about keeping her whereabouts a secret from her pregnant friend as well as her parents was beginning to bother Kiran. It was difficult to see that look of guilt and anguish on her face. Finally, he was the one who'd encouraged Megha to pay Harini a secret visit.

It would be good for Megha to get out and socialize for a while, he'd figured. Even now, despite his misgivings, he was convinced it was the right thing to do. Besides, according to his mother's update on the Ramnaths, Amma had finally calmed down and resigned herself to Megha's disappearance. The police had apparently given up their search, too, at Amma's request.

That was good news, the main reason Kiran had assumed it was relatively safe for Megha to step outside. Maybe soon she would be able to move around more freely.

Kiran assured himself that he was only a phone call away. When Megha was ready to come home, she would call him. He'd pick her up at the same street corner and whisk her home.

Everything would be all right.

Neither Kiran nor Megha noticed the little beggar boy skulking on the corner. His bare torso showed every rib through his dark chocolate-colored skin. His threadbare shorts hung down to his calves. A permanent fixture at this particular intersection, he harassed every pedestrian, bicyclist and motorist for alms and refused to relent until he got what he pleaded for. If his amiable, two-missing-teeth grin didn't do the trick, he resorted to tears to melt the hearts of the passersby.

Today, he observed with watchful eyes the tall young lady hurry past him. Instead of chasing after her for money, he merely followed her at a safe distance, making sure to keep to the dark shadows. He noted that she knocked on a certain door. When the door opened, she walked inside and the door was shut quickly behind her. The curtains on the windows in that house were tightly drawn, so even if he stood on his toes he couldn't see inside.

He had been waiting for her—for the last three days.

He had a twenty-rupee note in his pocket. He had kept it close to himself, hidden from his father's drunken eyes. For him, it was about ten days' worth of alms. It felt good to wind his tiny, rough hand around the note. It was crisp and warm and it promised good things. Tonight he would treat himself to real food, not just someone's leftovers. The thought of dinner made his hollow, concave stomach growl in loud anticipation. The smell of fried onions and potatoes from the tea shop down the street was calling him.

Soon he would make another twenty rupees. The ugly old woman who had given it to him had promised more if he brought her good news. And this looked like good news. The young woman was someone he knew well. Although she wore different clothes and hid most of her face, he knew who she was. He saw people passing by all day and he was good at recognizing the way people walked and talked and moved. This was the pretty lady who gave him a coin whenever she saw him here. He didn't really know why she was trying to hide herself behind a veil, or why she was walking so fast, or why the fat old woman wanted him to keep an eye out for her.

But he didn't care, because the old woman had shown him a photo of the young lady and asked him to watch out for her and report everything he saw. He would get another twenty rupees soon, maybe more if he could think of a way to make it worth it for the fat old cow. A smile touched his gaunt face at the thought—his own money, and lots of it.

Megha let her eyes wander over the familiar drawing room in Harini's home. She had missed it so much—the hominess and the warmth of it. The black vinyl couch with the hand-embroidered cushion covers—made lovingly by Harini's mother. The picture of Harini's late mother-in-law framed and hung on the wall above the couch, the small TV set that sat on a scarred table. The two wooden chairs with the faded pink and gray floral pillows looked just like they always had, dented in the middle where someone's bottom had sunk in deep. Although a humble room, whatever little it contained was neat and spotless.

Even the scents were the same—the day's cooking mixed with the smoky odor of the jasmine incense that Harini burned all the time to chase away mosquitoes. The old teakwood coffee table still held a week's stack of *Times of India* and the latest copy of *Femina* magazine.

It felt like coming home.

The wave of nostalgia that came over Megha was so overpowering that she turned around and hugged Harini one more time. What she'd never noticed before was now so precious. She'd visited her friend at least once a week in the past—a hurried detour before she went to the *kirana*, grocery shop, while Amma took her long afternoon nap. Harini and Megha had always shared a hot cup of tea, a homemade snack and lots of news and gossip during those visits. With Harini's husband and father-in-law at work, and her young brother-in-law at college, the house was all theirs.

It had been that way for the past year—Megha visiting Harini, and never the other way around, because Amma had made Harini feel unwelcome in the Ramnath home.

"What have you got yourself into, Megha?" Harini's forehead gathered in a troubled line as she grasped Megha's hand, pulled her into the drawing room and examined her from head to foot. Then apparently satisfied that Megha was still in one piece, she let go of her hand. "I still can't believe you ran away and never told me!"

"But I—"

"Do you know how worried I was?"

"I'm sorry."

"You should be!" Harini's lips trembled. "I thought you had been kidnapped or killed or something."

"I couldn't tell you where I was. Even now, I shouldn't be here."

"I'm so relieved to see you, you stupid girl. I was ready to have a breakdown when I heard you had disappeared. I had all kinds of nightmares."

"I'm sorry. I just couldn't get in touch."

"Never do that to me again, no matter where you are!" Harini's eyes filled up and she used her knuckles to brush the tears away.

"Okay," Megha said regretfully. She should have known Harini would be affected badly by her unexplained disappearance. Harini was always like that with her—so concerned, so maternal. "I didn't mean to hurt you. I was just too confused and scared to do anything but hide and protect myself."

"All right then. Let's have some tea." Obviously recovering from her fit of wounded indignation, Harini ushered Megha into the kitchen and poured her a cup from the deep stainless steel pot reserved for tea.

To see the familiar green ceramic cup again tugged at Megha's heart. She nearly cried as she smelled the tea, piping hot, sweet and fragrant—just the way she liked it. Simple things could bring back such poignant memories.

Gratefully accepting the cup, Megha started to pace the kitchen floor, drinking the tea in small sips. Restless pacing had become a habit with her lately. Her face felt warm from the fear and excitement of being here and the steam rising from the scalding liquid in her cup. Going to the small window, she made sure it was tightly shut. Warned ahead of time, Harini had done a good job of closing off the house from potential Peeping Toms.

Harini silently watched her pace for several seconds. "Sit down, Megha. Tell me what's happening."

"When I ran from Suresh and Amma, all I had in mind was to run and save myself. Nothing else mattered."

"Of course not!"

"Now I'm not so sure." She took a thoughtful sip. "I feel . . . oh . . . sort of homeless."

"Why didn't you go to your parents? Or one of your sisters? They're family."

"How could I? The first place Amma would look for me would be there."

"I suppose you're right." Harini settled back in a chair, looking sufficiently convinced for now. "But couldn't you have worked it out with Suresh? Maybe see if he and you could move out of Amma's house and stay somewhere else?"

A bitter laugh erupted from Megha's throat. "Move out of Amma's house? Are you dreaming? But then, you don't have a mother-in-law."

"I have a father-in-law."

Waving away what she considered Harini's weak argument, Megha said, "Your father-in-law is a pleasant, quiet person, and he's hardly ever home. Besides, your husband is a nice man. I envy you." She stopped to put her cup on the table and placed a hand on Harini's shoulder.

Harini Nayak was so very lucky. Megha studied her friend's rounded figure, well into its fifth month of pregnancy. Harini's ordinary face looked almost pretty with the soft glow of approaching motherhood and the happiness that put a shine in her eyes. Her dark, stubborn curls seemed glossy—perhaps because of the hormonal changes associated with pregnancy. She looked plump and sweet and wholesome—like a ripe, juicy mango in May. Lucky, lucky girl.

Megha and Harini had been best friends since they were seven years old. They had been classmates, played together, shared their deepest secrets, argued fiercely, and even fought aggressively at times. But they had stuck together like twins all these years. Despite having two older sisters, Megha had turned to Harini for moral support whenever she'd needed it.

Harini had three brothers and no sisters, so she too had looked upon Megha as more of a sibling. Even now, they looked to each other for advice. Harini, older than Megha by a few months, was fiercely protective of Megha. And so damned loyal! In spite of all the nasty things Megha had done to her in their youth, including putting her up to silly pranks that got her punished, Harini had not wavered in her devotion to Megha—a true friend indeed. Fortunately, Megha had discovered Harini's true worth in time and improved her ways, started to give back some of the friendship she had received for years, or she would have lost Harini forever.

At the moment Harini looked like a mother hen whose chick had been snatched by a hungry cat.

Although plain in looks and average in brains, Harini was born with better fortune than herself, Megha concluded. It only went to show that good looks and intelligence didn't necessarily guarantee a happier life. Everything in life was entirely predetermined by fate: who you were; what you did; whom you married; and where your life would eventually take you. *Karma. Kismet.* Destiny. They all boiled down to fate.

And yet, Megha loved her friend and was happy for her, truly glad that Harini had found a blissful home and a kind husband. Her dear friend deserved the best. Harini looked content and Megha knew for a fact that she was eagerly looking forward to the birth of her first child.

Like Megha, Harini had married immediately upon completing her degree, just a few months prior to Megha's wedding. Harini's husband, Vijay, worked as an engineer for the local public works department, or PWD as it was known, and they lived in middle-class comfort. Her husband's younger brother was an engineering student, a shy young man who was easy to get along with. All Harini had to do was make sure the house was clean and everyone was fed well. In fact, that was the main reason Vijay had married a homemaker and not a career woman. With no women to take care of their all-male family, the men needed someone like Harini with her housekeeping skills.

Glancing at Megha, Harini smiled wryly. "Envy me? What for? I've always wanted your model-like beauty and elegance. You're clever, too. I can't imagine why you would envy someone like me."

"Because you have such a quiet and safe life."

Harini's worried frown instantly returned. "Talking of a safe life, Megha, what are you going to do? You can't hide forever."

Megha stopped pacing and came to sit in one of the old-fashioned kitchen chairs. Harini's kitchen was somewhat like Amma's kitchen, ancient and small, but it felt so much more cheerful. There was a radio softly playing Hindi songs. A burning incense stick on the altar exuded the pleasant and familiar smell of jasmine. Gleaming stainless steel pots and pans were lined up face down on a three-tiered wooden shelf that had turned gray with age. A small blue refrigerator hummed in a corner.

A package of Monaco biscuits lay open on the kitchen table, but Megha had yet to eat one. This kitchen had such a cozy and warm look about it as compared with the Ramnaths'. Even the tea tasted so much better here.

"I know," Megha agreed with a sigh. "I can't hide forever, but I can't go back to my husband, Harini. That's not an option. One of these days I'll contact my parents, but in the meantime I don't know what to do."

"What made you go to Kiran Rao for help, Megha? Why did

you go to your husband's cousin when you had family and friends?"

Megha took a deep breath. Hadn't she asked herself the same question over and over again? "Because he is the only person who seems to understand me, the only one who has been on my side when Amma and her family picked on me. And like he says, no one would dream of looking for me in his house, whereas all *my* family and friends will be suspect."

"I see." Harini took a second to think about it.

"Kiran is very kind and generous," said Megha, "but that makes my hiding in his house even worse."

"Why?"

"I feel so guilty about putting him in this awkward position."

"Oh, Megha, I hadn't realized how hard this is for you. That horrible woman could have burned you to death. Why would she want to kill her son's wife?" Harini's eyes turned moist with tears once again.

Watching Harini shed tears for her, Megha's own voice turned hoarse. "In . . . in Amma's eyes, I'm worthless. I didn't come with a dowry, nor did I get pregnant."

Harini stared in contemplation at her cup for a long moment. Perhaps instinctively, she put a hand over the gentle swelling of her own growing middle before she turned to Megha. "I know the dowry business bothered her, but what is this fuss about you not being pregnant?"

"I was brought into the lofty Ramnath household for a purpose—like a prize cow. I was supposed to produce one or two good-looking grandchildren, preferably boys, for Amma and Appaji to bounce on their knees. If, God forbid, my children looked like their side of the family, I'd probably be tossed out on my backside in a minute. If I produced a girl, again a similar fate. No dowry and no grandchild—therefore I was to be killed off."

Sucking in an incredulous breath, Harini exclaimed, "They're lunatics!"

"Much worse—they're psychopathic killers. Now do you see why I had to run away?"

"Why didn't you go straight to the police when you started running? Those murderers should be put in jail."

"What proof did I have? Who's going to believe the words of a distraught, twenty-one-year-old runaway against upstanding, upper-caste citizens like Amma and her rich, influential brothers? The police would laugh in my face and have me back in Amma's possession in a minute."

Harini's mouth formed a visible O. She looked as if she'd finally begun to comprehend the situation. "But how are you supposed to produce beautiful children with those ugly genes coming from their family? They look like three anemic rabbits mixed in with one raging hippopotamus."

Despite her anguish Megha chuckled at Harini's apt description of the Ramnaths. "And you thought I had a flair for colorful descriptions?"

But Harini didn't seem to think it was funny. She still looked indignant. "And why did your parents marry you off into such a horrible family in the first place?"

"My father said the Ramnaths were well-off but were willing to settle for a smaller dowry than the other families they had considered for me. My father is also getting old and sickly. Amma never missed an opportunity to remind me that she made a big sacrifice by accepting me into their family in spite of the measly dowry and my lack of a career."

"So your parents married you off to the first man who settled for a small dowry?"

"Precisely."

"I didn't know all the details until now, Megha." Harini threw her an accusing glance. "You . . . never really told me."

"It's not something to be proud of." Megha bit her lip in misery.

A pained groan came from Harini. "Oh, Megha, no wonder you looked so tense all the time during the past year. And your lord and master did nothing to protect you from that fat hippo?"

"Which lord and master do you mean—senior or junior?

There are two in that house, remember. Senior quakes in his *chappals* at the sight of his beloved Chandramma. Junior simply doesn't care. To him I'm just a free sex slave, cook, and servant rolled into one."

Harini squeezed Megha's hand. "I wish I could do something to help. Does Kiran have any suggestions?"

Megha rose to put their empty cups in the sink. "Kiran thinks it would be good for me to stay with him for a while and worry about the future after I get a divorce."

"But divorce could take years!" Harini looked scandalized. "You can't live with a young bachelor in secrecy for that long. You have to get a job or something, Megha."

"What kind of job? A bachelor's degree in liberal arts is good for nothing these days. I have no money or influence. I'm a fugitive, so I can't even stir out of the house. I'm here today under cover of darkness, my face hidden behind a *chunni*."

"Maybe you can teach English? You're good at English, especially poetry."

"I don't have a teaching degree or a certificate, Harini."

"What about working for a newspaper or magazine? You always wanted to be a journalist."

"And exactly how many English language newspapers and magazines are there in this town?" Megha's laugh was dry. "Exactly one: *The Palgaum Messenger*. And that is a small, one-man operation."

"Oh! But you write and speak beautifully. That should help."

"A lot of good that did me! Writing and speaking talents had no place in the Ramnath household. Only culinary and drudgery skills were welcome. They eat like gluttons. Amma looks forward to each meal like a starved animal."

"Starved hippopotamus." Harini grinned for the first time, easing the mood for both of them.

They moved to the drawing room and settled themselves on the couch for a while, immersed in their own private thoughts. Then Harini slid a hand in Megha's. "I'm glad you came to see me today."

"So am I."

"And I'm relieved that Kiran is taking such good care of you."

Megha stroked the pudgy hand that lay on hers. "You must promise not to mention this to anyone."

"I promise. But you have to stay in touch, okay? Don't make me worry about you again."

Megha's anxious glance wandered to the clock on the wall. "I better go now. Kiran will start to worry."

"Can't you stay a little longer and eat dinner with us? I'm making your favorite—"

"No! Vijay will be home in a little while and we don't want him to find me here."

"He'll understand if we explain. And we'll call Kiran and tell him you'll—"

"No!" Megha held up a hand. "You can't tell Vijay. It's too dangerous—not just for us, but for him, too."

"All right. But at least stay in touch," Harini added, as she watched Megha reach for the phone to call Kiran.

After a few minutes, picking up her purse, Megha slipped into the *chappals* she had left by the front door. She gave Harini a tight hug. "I feel so much better now."

"You don't look like you're better. Something else is troubling you, isn't it?"

Megha closed her eyes for a moment. "I've been having nightmares lately. I have this . . . this feeling that something is about to happen . . . that someone is watching me. I can feel it in my bones. Amma is waiting to pounce on me. Even walking here this evening, I had a feeling someone's eyes were following me."

"It's just nerves, Megha. I don't know much about psychology, but I'm sure anybody who's had an experience like yours would have nightmares. You were almost murdered, for goodness' sake."

"Nearly burned to cinders."

Harini winced. "Thank heavens you're okay now. I'm sure Kiran will keep you safe."

"Kiran tries very hard to keep me safe, even to the extent of putting himself in danger."

"Oh, my God," said Harini, a strange look coming over her round face.

Megha frowned at her. "What's wrong?" When Harini said nothing, she grabbed her arm. "Harini, are you okay?"

"I just realized something. Kiran is in love with you, isn't he?"

"What!" Megha gasped. "Don't be silly—he's my cousin-in-law. That's as good as brother-in-law in our family."

Harini shook her head. "I noticed him during your wedding. He kept staring at you all day, completely fascinated. I thought he was admiring your good looks like everyone else at the time, but now I know why he's doing so much for you. He's crazy about you, Megha."

Afraid that Harini's words might have some basis, Megha hurried to the door and unlocked it. "No, no, there's nothing between Kiran and me. He's a perfect gentleman."

"I didn't say he was not a gentleman," Harini replied quietly. "Listen, call me. And tell me if I can do anything for you. I have a little money of my own if you need it."

Megha shook her head. "You're very generous, but I can't take your money."

"In case you need it, you just have to ask. And be careful."

Leaning against the doorframe, Harini waved goodbye, the worry clearly showing on her face. Her eyes still looked red with tears.

Keeping her well-covered head down and her eyes on the ground, Megha hurried to the end of the street. Her palms were damp and her heartbeat pounded in her ears. The sense of dread was worse than the kind that used to come just before a final exam while in high school and college. It went beyond anything she had felt in the past. Was she doomed to live like this for the rest of her life, looking over her shoulder, worrying over where she went and what she did and who saw her?

She quickened her pace, telling herself she had only a few more steps to cover before she'd be safely ensconced in Kiran's car. For a moment she panicked. What if Kiran wasn't at the designated spot, waiting for her? She noticed the starved-looking beggar boy on his usual corner and quickly crossed the street to avoid him. Surprised that he hadn't come after her, she kept walking. The little devil hadn't recognized her in her camouflage. Or this late in the evening he was probably too tired to run.

Her heart was racing at a giddy pace now. This secret visit to Harini was more stressful than she'd imagined. What Harini had said about Kiran just now was disturbing, too. The more Megha thought about it, the more sense it made. Was Kiran really in love with her? Was that why he was so kind and attentive, so generous and wonderful?

And if he was in love with her, what was she going to do? Her feelings for him were . . . well . . . what *were* her feelings for him? She appreciated everything about him. He was a highly attractive man. He dressed elegantly, too. She'd have to be blind not to notice his sex appeal. She had seen women, young and middle-aged, look at him with frank admiration. The pangs of possessiveness and jealousy that came over her whenever that happened were hard to deny. So did that mean she was interested in him, too . . . as a man and not as a cousin? She wasn't sure. Everything was so confusing these days.

She realized she had reached the end of the street. When Kiran's parked car came into view, she broke into an excited run.

Chapter 16

A s Megha slid into the passenger seat, panting, Kiran shot her a smile. "Calm down. You're all right."

"Thank . . . God! That was . . . quite an adventure," she managed to murmur.

"Take a few deep breaths. You're wheezing."

"Okay . . . okay." She did as he said and felt her frantic heartbeat settle a bit.

"So how was it?" Kiran put the car in gear and pulled out.

"Good. Really good."

"Is your friend doing well?"

She took another long breath and pushed the veil away from her face. "Harini looks wonderful. She's getting nice and round."

Kiran chuckled. "She's supposed to get nice and round if she's going to have a baby soon."

Megha sniffed and looked around. "Why do I smell flowers?"

Kiran stretched his arm onto the back seat and retrieved a small plastic bag. "Because I bought you these."

Opening the bag, Megha pulled out a handful of *champak* flowers. "Why, thanks, Kiran." Holding the pale yellow flowers with their long, pointed and graceful petals in her cupped palm, Megha leaned back in the seat and closed her eyes to inhale their fragrance. "Umm, they smell fantastic . . . so soothing." No wonder spas and salons offered something called aromatherapy these days for calmness and serenity.

Why was he giving her flowers? But then he kept giving her things all the time, some big, some small, but gifts nonetheless. Maybe Harini was right. If he wasn't in love, he was at least suffering from a crush of sorts. But was she worth it—worth the attention of a man like Kiran? He was rich, educated, sophisticated, a man of the world. So how could he have a crush on her? But if it was true—and it was a big *if*, there was a major hitch: she was married. She might be a runaway, but she was very much married. She looked down at the beautiful flowers in her lap. It was such a sweet, sentimental gesture. Damn, it was nearly making her cry!

The scent of the flowers reminded her of that other occasion when Kiran had given her a single *champak* flower. It was the night his cousin Mala had turned thirteen. There had been an elaborate birthday party—more a gaudy spectacle than a party. The evening had started on a sour note with Amma ordering Megha to wear a different sari than the one she'd had on.

"That sari is not suitable. I don't like it." Amma's nose wrinkled in disapproval. "Change into something more proper, Megha. This is a very special occasion. Mala is turning thirteen."

Megha looked down at her pale green polyester sari with the pink rose print. It looked fine to her. "But, Amma, this is—"

"Just change!" Amma snapped. "What will people think if they see my daughter-in-law in a cheap sari? That we can't afford to even dress you properly?"

So that was it—Amma's ego. Megha gave Amma an acquiescent nod and rushed to the bedroom to reach into the steel *almirah* for a silk sari. The choice was easy. She had only three decent silk saris. They were from her wedding trousseau. She preferred to save them for very special occasions, not birthday parties. But she dare not stand up to Amma, who had decided that her youngest niece's birthday was a momentous occasion that called for silk.

Hurriedly pulling out the turquoise sari with the orange border and gold motif, she changed into the appropriate orange blouse.

She wished she could enhance the sari with more elaborate jewelry, but she didn't possess anything beyond the simple *mangalsutra*, gold earrings, and four bangles. A coral necklace to highlight the orange border on her sari would have been nice. She had seen a beautiful one in the window of a local jewelry store. It had three rows of tiny corals that dipped to a V with a circular pendant surrounded by pearls. The matching, dangling earrings were equally lovely. She had yearned for that coral set since she'd laid eyes on it almost two years ago.

While she finished wrapping the sari around herself as hastily as she could, there was a harsh rap on the door. "Come on, Megha, we are late!" Amma bellowed. "The taxi is here and the meter is running."

"Coming, Amma." Megha made a dash for the door. It wasn't her fault they were running late. She ran to the drawing room, thrust her feet into her *chappals* and stepped outside. Suresh was pacing by the front door. Amma, Appaji and Shanti were already seated in the taxi. Suresh put the heavy padlock on the door, then both he and Megha hopped into the taxi. Or rather, squeezed in.

The taxi was a compact old model that shuddered and stalled as it lumbered up the street at a crawl with its overload of passengers. The cloying scent of Amma's perfume was stifling in the close interior of the automobile. Megha bit back a mild wave of nausea.

The party was in full swing by the time they arrived at the Raos' home. Although smaller and plainer compared to the elder Raos' mansion, it was still quite elegant and was located in a high-priced neighborhood.

While Amma haggled over the fare with the taxi driver, Megha stood aside and admired the familiar house. It had a garden abounding in flowering bushes, a sturdy *champak* tree with full, graceful branches, and a wrought iron fence with a red and white painted gate. Hot-pink and white bougainvillea covered an arbor. The second floor had a balcony that boasted Devayani's prize rose bushes in giant terracotta pots. Fat roses in every possible color were in bloom at the moment, lending the house a lush, tropical look. To give Devayani due credit, despite her spiteful ways, the woman had created a lovely home.

Megha reflected with a wistful sigh that if she could own a house like this some day, she'd be more than content. She could almost picture it in her mind: lots of flowers; a dream kitchen; two children; a cat . . .

Devayani appeared at the door, bringing Megha's fantasy to an abrupt end. She was decked out in a red silk sari, a jasmine garland tucked around her elaborate hairdo. Lots of heavy gold jewelry complemented the ensemble. Her overbite seemed a bit more pronounced today, perhaps because she had decided to use a generous layer of blood-red lipstick that was in stark contrast to her large, white teeth. Her brows were crimped in irritation. "Why so late? I was beginning to worry," she said with the usual sinus twang and sniffle.

Amma inclined her head towards Megha with a long-suffering eye roll.

Devayani glanced at Megha, taking in her appearance and passing silent judgment at the same time. "Oh."

Megha offered an apologetic smile. She disliked apologizing for something that wasn't her fault, but it had become a habit lately. She tried not to let the resentment fester, but some days were harder to endure than others.

Devayani's husband and Amma's youngest brother, Rama Rao, smiled and nodded at them. He was a quiet, unassuming man with a mop of dense gray hair and a pleasant face. Everything about him was low-key. In spite of being a successful businessman he seemed to maintain a modest image. That was probably the reason Appaji and he got along so well. The two men usually huddled together and watched everyone else do the talking, especially their wives.

Megha looked around the room decorated with pink and white balloons. Mala was dressed in a powder blue and silver *salwar-kameez* outfit. She looked ill at ease and unhappy—not at all like a young girl celebrating a birthday. Short and chubby, with coffee-colored skin and wavy dark hair, she was a plain-looking adolescent, but an affectionate one. She was also a bright girl and excelled in school, especially at mathematics and science. She had dreams of pursuing a career in medicine. Megha liked her best among her husband's female cousins. Although Mala was a coddled child and complained at times, she was fun to be with when they talked about topics of mutual interest.

After everyone else had wished Mala a happy birthday, Megha gave her a brief hug. "Happy birthday, Mala. Why do you look so sad on your big day?"

Grabbing Megha's arm and dragging her to a quieter corner, Mala whispered through clenched teeth, "I hate this. I got my first period last month and this silly party is to celebrate that. Can you imagine that, Megha? They're going to humiliate me by telling the whole world that I got my period."

Poor child, reflected Megha. This was never an event to be proud of. Some Hindu families liked to make a big splash over a girl's transition to womanhood. Fortunately for herself, her own family had never paid attention to such routine matters. Nobody had noticed when Megha and her sisters had gradually turned into young women. Besides, her parents didn't have a large family or scores of friends or money to go out of their way to celebrate anything in style. Obviously the Raos preferred to make this event symbolic. She gave Mala a sympathetic pat on the shoulder. "I'm sorry. I can imagine how awful it must be."

"I don't think anyone can imagine this."

"Try to grin and bear it. It's only one evening."

Mala cast an annoyed look at the crowd in the drawing room and especially at her mother, who was blowing her nose periodically and carrying on an animated conversation with a relative at the same time. "I'd love to disappear somewhere and come back after the party is over."

"It will be over in a few hours, Mala."

"Megha, will you stay with me through the evening?"

Surprised at the unusual request, Megha's brow flew up. "You want *me* beside you? Why not ask your sister?"

"Kala is a fat frog."

"Shh! She's your older sister; you shouldn't say such things."

"Kala is mean and fat and jealous. She always makes unkind comments about you and Shanti."

"I don't think she means any of it."

Mala pressed on. "She's jealous of you because you're pretty and tall and slim. And she can't stand Shanti because they're classmates and Shanti gets better marks than she does in all the subjects."

Megha laughed. "Why would your sister be jealous of me? She's such a smart girl and very ambitious. She has a brilliant future ahead of her. I'm only a housewife with no job and no interesting hobbies."

"Just stay with me when my mother makes the stupid announcement and distributes the ceremonial sweets, okay?" Mala rolled her eyes in indignation. "Uh-oh, here comes another one of our aunts."

Megha and Mala observed Kamala Rao, Kiran's mother, making her way through the crowd towards them. Both girls stiffened in response. Kamala had an impressive-looking gift-wrapped package in her hands.

"What are you two young ladies whispering about?" Kamala inquired, one shapely brow elevated. Then she gave Mala a hug. "Happy birthday, my dear. You are a big girl today, aren't you? I have something special for you, *putti.*" She presented Mala with the gift and beamed with pride.

The woman looked elegant in her peach sari. Diamonds glittered in her ears and at her throat. Rows of gold bangles jangled at her fair wrists. Her nails were perfectly manicured and painted a peachy pink. One slim, long finger showcased an obscenely large diamond ring better than any velvet-lined jewelry box. She was the rich one in the family. She was also a very good-looking woman, graceful and classy. Once again Megha could tell from whom Kiran had inherited his tall and refined looks. Suddenly her own apparel seemed cheap and gaudy when compared with Kamala's fine getup.

Mala put on her best faux smile and thanked her aunt. "I'm sure I'll love it."

"Of course you will. I had it brought in from Mumbai just for you," said a pleased Kamala. She gave Megha a polite smile and a casual once-over. "You look very pretty this evening, Megha." Then she moved on to the others in the room.

Mala and Megha let out sighs of relief and stood in their corner to study the other guests pouring in, mostly family members. The extended family added up to at least fifty people: Devayani's cousin Padma and her family; Padma's brother-in-law, Jayant and his brood; Amma's uncle Sadanand and his children and grandchildren; second cousin Raghvendra and his entire clan of six married offspring and their respective families. It went on and on. Megha nearly got dizzy trying to remember all the names. The family rule was that if one relative was invited, the rest had to be invited, too, or it could lead to bruised egos, family feuds and bad blood. So the safe thing to do on special occasions was to invite everyone.

A couple of the Raos' neighbors and close friends showed up as well. By late evening the house was packed to capacity. Some of them placed their gifts on a growing pile in the corner of the drawing room. Others insisted on coming up to Mala and handing their gifts in person, making Mala more uneasy than she already was.

Drinks and appetizers began to appear and took up the next couple of hours. Megha stayed with Mala as she had promised. Running out of things to talk about with Mala, she looked at the wall clock. It was nearly dinnertime—a grand catered affair with many succulent dishes, no doubt. The caterers had made the delivery earlier and the aromas from the kitchen were drifting into the drawing room.

Megha noticed when Kala decided to put in a late appearance, just in time for dinner. She emerged from her bedroom and came downstairs dressed in a pumpkin colored *salwar-kameez*, her face a picture of bored contempt. She stood at the base of the staircase for a long moment and surveyed the scene before she moved to a quiet spot, as if she couldn't find a single individual worthy of her attention.

Kala looked like a round pumpkin in every way. She had a nervous habit of rolling her long hair into ringlets around one stubby finger. She was not a friendly individual, and certainly not a happy one. Megha had yet to see her smile or laugh. The few words she chose to bestow upon people were usually full of venom. She vaguely reminded Megha of someone else: Amma. Did she resemble Amma, too? Was Kala another Amma in the making? It was a frightening thought.

"Ah, here comes Tamarind Woman," hissed Mala, using the cliché about the tart tamarind fruit to describe people of a cheerless nature. Observing her sister's progress from the staircase to the drawing room, she added, "I would gladly give her ten rupees each time she gave up the sour face and smiled."

Megha pressed her arm. "Didn't I tell you not to say such things about your sister?"

"She doesn't have one nice thing to say about me."

Changing the subject, Megha said, "I'll go help your mother with the food."

Megha couldn't help feeling sorry for Mala. The girl needed companionship and looked to her for support. Mala loved fashion magazines and movie-star gossip, the latest in clothes and American music. She had nobody to talk to although she had a sister nearer her age than Megha. Mala didn't seem to have any close friends either. Megha was the only one in the family who showed any interest in any of her favorite subjects. The two of them got along well. Somehow, at all the crazy family parties and frequent get-togethers, they gravitated towards each other. Kiran would join them when their talk turned to sports and movies. The three of them made a good team. Too bad they weren't all siblings.

As Megha assisted Devayani in setting up the table, she saw movement at the front door from the corner of her eye, and looked up to see Kiran striding in. He was very late. In fact, he was probably the last guest to arrive. As always, he looked striking in well-pressed tan slacks and a tobacco-brown, open-neck shirt. He stood on the threshold and let his eyes sweep over the crowded room until they fell on Megha. A smile touched his face. She nodded and looked away.

Dinner was elaborate. Several varieties of vegetable curries, rice, breads, pickles, salads and desserts graced the table. A long line formed at the buffet. Devayani beamed at all the guests. "Everybody, eat well and come back for seconds and thirds, okay?" she urged, in keeping with old-fashioned Hindu hospitality.

The ice cream cake was brought out last, a huge rectangle with thirteen pink candles and one white one for good luck. Devayani dragged a scowling Mala toward the cake and the guests formed a circle around her. After the birthday song and the candle-blowing were over, Devayani clapped her hands to silence the chattering crowd. "Thank you, all, for coming today. It is a very special and significant day for the Rao family. It is very sad that my mother-in-law, Mala's grandmother, is still in the nursing home and cannot join us in the celebration. Our little Mala is not only thirteen today but she is now officially a young lady. Please enjoy the party and the cake will be served as soon as we cut it up."

Mala's hand trembled and her face turned an angry red. Abruptly bursting into tears, she pushed through the crowd and scrambled up the stairs.

The guests fell silent and gaped, watching Mala's back as she raced up the steps and disappeared over the landing. Nobody spoke for a full second. Devayani broke into a taut smile. "Mala's a bit nervous, no? Everybody, come on, have some cake before it melts."

The anxious looks and strained clearing of throats stopped. The folks went back to their original places and the party continued on.

Megha quietly slipped away upstairs. She knocked on Mala's door and found it unlocked. "Mala, are you okay?" she whispered. There was no response. She knew Mala wasn't asleep—the sound of sniffling said so. So she proceeded inside and shut the door, then sat on the edge of the bed where Mala lay on her stomach, her face buried in a pillow. "Mala, it's okay. Everyone has forgotten about it already. They're all eating and socializing like it never happened."

Mala's round body slowly turned over and she lay on her

back, facing Megha. Her tear-stained face looked puffy. "I don't want to go back there."

Megha's heart ached to see this young girl crying because the world knew her secret. Some customs were so humiliating and unnecessary. "I'm sure they'll understand if you don't return." Megha smiled conspiratorially. "You know what?"

"What?"

She pushed the damp hair off Mala's face. "One good thing about this is that they'll expect you to behave a bit strangely. Hormonal changes in a woman are an excellent excuse for any kind of odd behavior."

She was relieved when Mala, instead of pouting, snorted a laugh. "That's good then. Tell them I'm tired and I want to sleep."

Megha rose from the bed. "I'll tell your mother that. Do you want me to get you anything before I go downstairs? Do you have any cramps or anything?"

"Not anymore. I had them earlier and I took some pills."

"Maybe you can come visit us sometime this week. Remember, you had asked if I could help you with your essay on India's democratic election process?"

Mala nodded. "After school on Thursday? I still need help."

When Megha went back downstairs, a frowning Devayani cornered her. "Megha, did you talk to her?" When Megha nodded, she asked, "Is she okay?"

"She's all right."

"What did she say?" Devayani still looked anxious.

"She's a bit tired from the excitement and a little overwhelmed by all this." Megha gestured to indicate the drawing room. "She said to tell you she wants to sleep and doesn't want to come downstairs."

Devayani bit her lower lip for a second, her brows drawn in contemplation. Then she turned around and went back to the drawing room.

Megha watched her make her way toward Amma and Kamala. The three women huddled to whisper. As Megha looked on, she felt that familiar, eerie feeling creep up her neck. The women took turns taking covert peeks at her and went back to whispering. They were talking about her again. It hurt so much when they did that—alienated her and whispered about her, right there where she could see them. For some reason she had never fitted in with the family. After spending a year in their midst, she still felt it was her against them. Or was it them against her, the oddity that didn't belong?

Feeling a deep need for some fresh air, Megha made her way to the kitchen, slipped out the back door and into the garden. The atmosphere in the house was stifling. The lingering food odors and the heat and noise from so many bodies crammed into a limited space were beginning to bring on a headache. Her stomach seemed to be a bit on the rebellious side, too. She walked around the side of the house to the flower garden in the front.

The night air felt refreshing and fragrant with the scent of Devayani's roses, *champak* and jasmine. The nearby streetlight cast a cool glow on the tiny, white, night-blooming jasmine clusters. But Megha felt worn-out. She was always tired lately. By the middle of the afternoon she felt like every ounce of strength was drained. The evenings seem to drag and at night she collapsed into bed from exhaustion.

Strolling up to the wrought iron fence, she crossed her arms over the rail. It felt slightly damp from the ever-present fog. Inhaling the cool, scented air made her nausea recede a bit. There was a slight breeze and the *champak* tree's leaves rustled. She gazed at the moon, which looked pale tonight. There was a hazy ring around it, lending it a mysterious air. It was not a night for loneliness and sighing over silly wishes. It was a perfect night for lovers—to link arms, to laugh and moon-gaze together. But then, she was always a hopeless romantic. Appa was probably right—her brain was influenced by too many sentimental movies and novels.

Suresh would probably snort in contempt at her silly notions if she ever suggested anything remotely romantic like a walk in the moonlight. They'd never even had a honeymoon. They had gone to Tirupati for two days immediately after the wedding, but that was mainly to pray for Lord Balaji's blessings at the famous Tirupati Temple.

Naturally Amma, Appaji and Shanti had tagged along. It was the old-fashioned way—the family accompanying the newlyweds. The only privacy Suresh and she had been accorded during those two days was a private room in the hotel where they had stayed. Thank goodness, at least Amma hadn't invaded their nights. If she had, Megha would most likely still be a virgin.

"Hello, Megha." The voice came from behind her.

Jolted out of her reverie, Megha stifled a cry of alarm and pivoted around.

It was Kiran. "You needed to get away from that madhouse, huh?" he said.

She swallowed in relief. "Kiran, y-you scared me to death!"

"I'm sorry. I didn't mean to frighten you."

"Have you been standing there long?" He stood a few feet away, beside the burly trunk of the *champak* tree, hands in his pockets. The dense shadow cast by the branches made him nearly invisible. No wonder she hadn't noticed him earlier.

"Only about a minute. I was on my way out to my car and noticed you gazing at the moon. You looked so peaceful, I didn't want to disturb you right away."

"That's okay."

"I'm not in the habit of watching women on the sly, if that's what you're thinking."

"Of course not! I was a little startled, that's all."

"Are you all right?" His voice took on a concerned note. "You look a little . . . tired."

"I have a headache and needed some fresh air."

"Would you like me to get you a painkiller from the house? For the headache, I mean."

She shook her head. "No thanks. I'm feeling better already." He was so kind and thoughtful, it amazed her. Suresh had never made her such an offer.

Apparently satisfied with her answer, Kiran moved on to another subject. "Poor Mala looked mortified."

Megha shrugged. "Antiquated Hindu customs . . . you know. They can be crude at times."

"I wonder why people continue to follow such ridiculous traditions."

"In the olden days, it was more or less an announcement to the world that a certain young girl was healthy and normal, and ready to take on the responsibilities of marriage and motherhood, an invitation of sorts to the families of eligible young men to come bride-hunting. But in this day and age it's unnecessary."

"I agree. And how do *you* know so much about such things, Megha?"

"One of my subjects in college was sociology. I like to know what different societies around the world do and why. Many other cultures celebrate this coming-of-age milestone, especially tribal cultures."

Kiran smiled. "I see you have a curious mind." He inclined his head at the house. "Is Mala still upset?"

"She seems okay now. I checked on her before I stepped out."

Kiran came to stand beside Megha. "You're a kind girl, Megha. I'm sure you were the only one who offered her support." His eyes traveled boldly over her for a second. "By the way, you look very pretty this evening."

She was surprised by her own sharp intake of breath. "Th-thank you, Kiran . . . but—"

"But what?"

"You shouldn't say things like that. I'm your cousin's wife—your sister-in-law in essence."

He laughed. "My cousin's wife happens to be a beautiful woman and I'm merely stating a fact. Anything wrong with that?"

She fidgeted with her bangles. "Maybe in America such things are acceptable, but it's not right. It . . . it's not really wrong, I suppose, but it's just that other people won't think of it like that. If Amma heard you, I'd be dead."

He chuckled again. "Why?"

"She won't chastise you for making a forward statement.

She'll automatically think I'm encouraging you to say things like that."

Kiran dismissed her comment with an exasperated wave of a hand. "Forget Amma, will you? Who cares what she thinks?"

"I do, Kiran. I have to. She's my mother-in-law. If I make her unhappy, I have to pay the price." Her eyes darted about, brimming with nervous apprehension. "I better go back inside before they notice we're both missing. Those sharp female eyes and ears are likely to draw the wrong conclusion. They're already busy gossiping about me."

His eyes narrowed suspiciously. "You mean my aunts and my mother?"

"Exactly."

"Did you get a chance to hear what they were saying?"

"No. If they're talking about me they're not likely to do it when I'm within hearing distance, are they?"

"You're sure they were talking about you?"

"Very sure. They kept throwing quick glances at me every now and then while they whispered. You know what I mean, Kiran. You can tell when someone's talking about you."

"So, the old ladies are at it again."

She narrowed her eyes at him. "What do you mean *again*? You know something about it then?"

He shook his head. "Not really. If I did, I'd tell you."

She shot him a wary look before turning to go back inside the house. "I better go in before Amma comes outside looking for me. Goodnight, Kiran."

"Megha, wait a second." He stretched his arm and plucked a *champak* flower off one of the lower branches of the tree—a pale yellow blossom with long, tapered petals. "Here, smell this. It has the most amazing scent." When she didn't make a move he picked up her hand and placed the flower in it.

A faint gasp escaped her throat once again. "Oh . . . I can't accept flowers from you, Kiran!"

"Stop fretting, Megha. It's not a gift or anything. No need to panic."

She stared at her palm for a second, looking undecided. Then she turned on her heel and ran all the way back inside the house, conscious of Kiran's eyes following her.

Setting aside her memories of their unplanned but interesting conversation on that moonlit night, Megha stole a glance at Kiran as he drove her home from her emotional meeting with Harini. Did today's flowers remind him of that scene in his uncle's garden? Was that why he had bought them for her? She couldn't tell because his eyes remained on the crowded road ahead.

She sent him a grateful smile. "I appreciate the flowers. Where did you get them?"

"I bought them from the young man who sells them on the corner."

"The blind boy who sits outside the tailor shop, you mean? I often bought flowers for Amma's *puja* from him. His name is Shashank." What a coincidence, Megha thought. Or was it deliberate on Kiran's part? Shashank meant moon, and she knew Kiran was aware of the fact. Was he trying to send her some sort of message?

"Shashank, huh?" Kiran turned his head briefly to glance at Megha. "Interesting, isn't it?" And the expression in his eyes said he remembered their encounter in the moonlit garden all too well.

Chapter 17

Panic swept over Megha as she heard footsteps approaching the front door. She had been living in Kiran's flat in relative safety for a few weeks and she had just now begun to relax. Life had fallen into a semi-comfortable pattern. Kiran was away at work most of the day and came home quite late on most evenings. She cooked, cleaned and dusted the flat, and did the dishwashing and laundry. To keep his parents from suspecting anything, Kiran religiously continued with his weekly visits to their home and also to the nursing home to visit his grand-mother.

Megha had learned to recognize the footsteps of the people who lived upstairs, the postman who delivered the mail to each individual flat in the afternoons, the milkman who left the bot-tles outside the door every morning, and the servants who worked for various residents of the building. Kiran had in-formed his own servant that he didn't need his services until fur-ther notice. He wanted Megha to feel safe. Besides, Megha had insisted on doing all the housework in return for his kindness. He had not wanted her to do anything other than the cooking, but she'd been adamant, so he had conceded.

She paused in the midst of her chores to listen closely to the footfalls. Hoping it was one of the neighbors, she held her breath. When the sound came close enough for her to be con-vinced that it was not someone going to the neighboring flat, she shut off the gas burner and without thinking picked up the pan of milk heating on the stove. She nearly screamed in pain and dropped the hot pan back on the stove with a thud. The milk sloshed dangerously in the pan, spilling a small amount on the stove.

Meanwhile, the ominous sound of a bunch of keys being fished out of somewhere became clearly audible outside the door.

Could it be Kiran, she wondered? No, those were not his footsteps, and he always called her ahead of time to warn her that he was on his way, just so he wouldn't frighten her. It was also too early for him to come home. This was someone else. Who else had a key? She had no idea. She began to shake. Hastily using the edge of her sari to pick up the hot pan once again, she shoved it inside one of the kitchen cabinets, shut the door, and raced to the bedroom.

She needed a place to hide. Her desperate eyes swept over the bedroom. The armoires were too small for her to fit in. The bathroom! But, what if this person coming in the door needed to use the bathroom? Dear God in heaven, where could she hide?

The front door opened and someone walked in. The door's click and squeak were unmistakable.

Realizing the only place she could possibly remain hidden was under the bed, Megha hit the floor and crawled underneath it. There were two large empty suitcases stored there, leaving very little room for her. Frantic to keep herself hidden, she scrunched her body into a tight little ball and slid as far back from the doorway as possible. Her elbow bumped into the hard surface of a suitcase and she bit her tongue to keep herself from groaning.

The edges of the bedspread did not quite make it to the floor, allowing a view of what was underneath, if one wanted to look for something there. Megha's heart thumped in alarm. The sound of her own heartbeat echoing in her ears was so loud, she was afraid the person now entering the flat could hear it, too. Her knees were pressed close to her chest and her cheek butted against the edge of one suitcase as she lay in a fetal position, her sari pulled tightly around her so its bright blue color wouldn't show.

Closing her eyes for a split second, she prayed. *God, please . . . let it not be Amma . . .*

She heard the front door shut and then the footsteps headed toward the kitchen. It definitely wasn't Kiran. He always called out her name as soon as he came in the door. Besides, there was a gentler sound to this person's movements. The footsteps were confident, yet soft, very soft, not like Kiran's purposeful, masculine tread.

Her mouth turned dry. Amma! But the gentle, silky steps couldn't be Amma's.

A burglar then! What was she going to do if he found her there? He was bound to look under the bed. Wasn't that where a lot of people hid their valuables? He would surely kill her. Her heartbeat went up another notch. But then, the person had used keys to get in. A burglar wouldn't have keys to the house. It had to be someone who had free access to the flat. But who? The blood continued to pound away in her head.

Megha's eyes turned wide with alarm when the person's feet went towards the stove and stopped at the exact spot where she had been standing moments ago. What she saw was even more shocking: the hem of a pale gray sari and a pair of expensive and elegant mid-heeled sandals peeking out from under it.

A woman! Damn it! What was a woman doing in Kiran's flat? Did he have a girlfriend and had conveniently forgotten to mention the fact to Megha? In spite of the nearly paralyzing fear, Megha felt a vaguely familiar twinge go through her. Jealousy—the same bitter, corrosive kind she'd felt when the salesgirl at the store had flirted with Kiran. The woman standing at the stove certainly had a key, and the way she'd confidently marched in indicated that she knew her way about the flat very well.

So who the hell was she? Girlfriend, that's who she was! She had to be. Damn!

Megha nearly passed out when she heard the woman exclaim to herself. "Oh dear! This boy has spilled milk on the stove."

She knew that voice. Kamala! Kiran's mother was in the kitchen!

Megha's heart did a terrified flip. Kamala had obviously discovered the milk Megha had spilled in her frantic efforts to hide the partially heated pot. Was the milk still warm, and would the hot stove give her presence away? In a tight frenzy, her brain hunted for a way to explain her presence to Kamala if she were to discover her under the bed.

And she realized there was no explanation. There was no way in the world to justify a young, married, female relative's presence under Kiran's bed. Megha was supposed to be missing, no less. Amma had spread the word around that Megha had disappeared. Kamala was Amma's sister-in-law, friend and sympathizer. Put the two together and it spelled disaster.

What was Kiran's mother doing here, anyhow? Megha could have sworn that Kiran had told her only one or two other people had keys to his flat. Well, how was Megha to know that his mother was one of them? She prayed again that Kamala would not enter the bedroom. But knowing what a devoted mother Kamala was, Megha knew it was wishful thinking. The bedroom door was ajar and Kamala was bound to come in to check on her precious son's room.

Megha's dread increased when she noticed one of the armoires in the bedroom was partly open. Kiran must have left it like that after he had got dressed for work that morning. Although she was crouching on the floor, Megha could still see the edges of her new outfits hanging in the armoire, side-by-side with Kiran's suits and formal jackets. She recalled the time Kiran had insisted that she hang them there. Their combined clothes in close proximity to each other in the confined space were a bit too intimate for Megha's comfort. But Kiran had convinced her that her lovely new outfits would be crushed and ruined if she folded them into tight bundles and shoved them into the chest of drawers.

Now Kamala was here, going through her son's house, and she was sure to find the colorful, feminine outfits. Megha's world would come to an end. Kamala was an astute woman and would surely guess about Megha's presence in the flat. The police would come and drag her back to Amma's house, so Amma could finally derive her pleasure from watching Megha's skin singe and scorch and hiss, one tiny millimeter at a time.

At the grisly thought, Megha trembled. No, she couldn't allow that to happen. She wouldn't allow it! If it meant standing up to Kiran's mother, she would do it.

She watched Kamala's movements in silence. Her soft, well-preserved feet in their expensive sandals went back and forth in the kitchen as she cleaned the milky mess on the stove. Or at least, that's what Megha assumed, since she couldn't see anything higher than Kamala's ankles, and the kitchen tap was turned on and off a few times. Her breath painfully trapped inside her throat, in the next second she noticed Kamala's feet coming directly towards her. They came to stand by the bed, right before Megha's petrified eyes.

Kiran's mother stood there for what seemed like eons. What was she doing there, where Megha could literally see the color of her nail polish and count the number of gold threads in the fine border of the sari?

Megha held her breath taut until her chest hurt from the pressure. And still the older woman did not move. All at once, Kamala turned on her heel and walked out of the room. The gray hem and heels disappeared into the dining area.

Gradually Megha exhaled all that oxygen she had held inside herself for so long. It didn't appear that Kamala had noticed the partly open armoire. But the woman was still in the flat—she still posed a serious threat. Megha was trapped under the bed, praying that Kamala would go away quickly.

What would she do if Kamala decided to stay until Kiran got home?

Finally, just when she thought she was about ready to come out screaming from under the bed and beg Kamala to end the torture of waiting and call the police, she heard the footsteps fading away and the front door being opened and then a moment later being shut. Another familiar squeak and click sounded. Still powerless to believe she was all alone again

Megha let a few tense moments go by before she found the courage to crawl out from under the bed.

There was a thin layer of dust gathered on top of the suitcases and her sari was coated with it in places. She brushed it off. The dust flew about her, the particles dancing in the sunlight and making her sneeze. She was lucky that sneeze hadn't erupted earlier. She ran to the bedroom window, hid behind the curtain and peeked outside. Kamala was climbing into the back seat of the Raos' car. A second later the chauffeured vehicle drove away.

Megha's body went limp with relief. She slumped against the window frame and then slid down to the floor. She wondered if this was how it felt to be near death and come back to earth. She had lived through this one ordeal. How many more were there to come? How long could she continue to stay in Kiran's flat undetected?

Once again she sneezed. Being a superstitious sort, she took it to be a bad omen. She was sure to be discovered. It was only a matter of time. Pondering the thought, she let her head rest on her raised knees for a while.

Exactly what had Kamala been checking out in this room? Curious to find out, Megha returned to the bed and positioned herself exactly where Kamala had stood a few minutes before and looked around the room. The armoire door was at an angle, where anyone standing in this precise location would not be able to see the clothes hanging inside, at least not the female garments. Megha had managed to escape detection by a mere inch or so.

"Thank you, Lord," she whispered.

Turning toward the kitchen, she found that Kamala had indeed cleaned up the spill. Then she noticed a plastic bag sitting on the dining table and opened it. Inside the bag was a round stainless steel container. A note was attached to it. *Kiran, the cook made your favorite almond halwa today. Give us a ring when you get home. Love, Mummy.* So, this was Kamala's reason for intruding on Kiran's privacy unexpectedly. She had to bring her darling son his favorite sweet, the rich and sticky ground almond and sugar squares flavored with cardamom. And why had Kiran never mentioned to Megha what his favorite dessert was?

Oh well, ironically, while she'd been rationalizing that Kamala was the intruder, it had completely escaped her mind that she herself was the intruder here. Kamala belonged in her son's home, while she didn't. And why should Megha expect Kiran to share his likes and dislikes with her?

Now that Kamala had come and gone, what was she to do? She paced the drawing room floor while she debated calling Kiran. Any minute she expected the front door to open once again and for Kamala to walk in—accompanied by Amma. Megha's hands still shook and the tension in her nerves refused to subside.

Should she tell Kiran that his mother had come by? Or would it be best to leave the matter alone? In the end she decided it would be prudent to inform him. If Kamala was in the habit of making unanticipated stops like today, then she and Kiran had to plan a strategy on how to prepare for them in the future. Besides, the sweets sat in the bag with its little maternal note: *Love, Mummy.*

When Kiran heard Megha's hesitant voice over the phone, his own seemed to become tight with concern. She'd never called him at work before. "Megha, is everything okay? Are you all right?"

"I . . . I'm okay, Kiran. I . . . we had a visitor today." She wasn't sure how to introduce the subject and wasn't at all certain of his reaction, either.

"Who?" His tone clearly held alarm now.

Fearing that she had caused him unnecessary anguish, she at once decided to subdue her own voice. "Oh, nobody came to actually visit me. Your mother came by."

"Mummy?" After a moment of silence he said, "So she saw you there?"

"I don't think she saw me. I hid under your bed when I heard her come into the flat."

"Are you sure she didn't see you?"

"Quite sure."

"Damn! I completely forgot that my parents have a key to my flat."

"Oh dear." That explained how Kamala had turned up there.

"I just realized this is going to be a problem, Megha. I have a meeting to go to in a minute. Let's discuss this when I come home, okay?"

"Okay." She wondered if she should have waited until he came home to spring this kind of unpleasant surprise on him. He was a busy man with a department to run. "Kiran, I'm sorry I interrupted your work."

"Don't be sorry. You did the right thing. It was my fault for not remembering that my mother has a key." Since Megha didn't respond, he said, "Stop worrying about it. We'll think of some way to avoid this sort of thing from happening again. Now just enjoy your afternoon. Watch some TV. Read a magazine. Relax. I'll see you later."

Hanging up the phone, Megha sank onto the sofa. "Relax? Enjoy? Easier said than done," she murmured to herself.

All afternoon she paced the floor, with short breaks to sit down and rest her overworked legs. The television failed to hold her attention for more than a few seconds at a time. Every time she heard a vehicle on the street she sprinted to the window. When she realized it wasn't a family member alighting from a car or taxi she collapsed with relief. Two cups of hot, strong tea didn't help calm her nerves either. To keep herself from going completely crazy she washed clothes, even Kiran's office shirts that normally went to the cleaners.

She starched and ironed the shirts with vigorous, deliberate strokes in an effort to get some of the agitation out of her system. She couldn't go on like this, couldn't live like a fugitive, a common criminal. She had done nothing wrong. All she was guilty of was running away from certain death. Anyone facing the death sentence would have done the same. And then she had come to the one person who was willing to help, that's all.

In fact, Kiran had more than helped—much, much more. He had given her shelter, clothes, spending money, everything that he owned—everything that he was, with no expectations in return. She recalled the shopping spree, the appreciation on his face, his kind touch, his softly encouraging words, the gentle humor he added to most everything. Warmth and gratitude filled her. Kiran was her very own angel.

She put his favorite blue shirt on a hanger and took it to the bedroom. The rich fabric felt soft and huggable. When she hung the shirt in the armoire next to his other clothes, the distinctive scent of his aftershave met her nose. They smelled like him. She felt an urge to touch them, gather them up and bury her face in them. How silly and sentimental was that? She'd never felt this way before, not even about Suresh's clothes. She was behaving foolishly—like a woman in love.

She stopped abruptly in her tracks then. Oh God! It hit her like a loaded truck, the most upsetting and mind-numbing realization: She was falling in love with Kiran! In fact, she *was* in love with Kiran. Deeply. Desperately.

She tried to tell herself this was all wrong. She had no right to fall in love with a man she had no claim on. Perhaps what she felt was only a crush, with its roots in gratitude, like a dreadfully ill patient imagining herself in love with her doctor. Could it be infatuation then? After all, Kiran was a striking man with lots of charm. It had to be infatuation. No, it couldn't be. But on the other hand . . .

Picking up a photo album from the bookcase, she flipped to a page where there was a picture of Kiran taken in America—his graduation day, when he got his MBA from Columbia University. His hair was a little longer then, but the smile was the same. He looked proud and happy and . . . so damned desirable. She closed the album and put it back. She'd never felt like this about any man before.

Wasn't it only weeks ago that she had thought she loved Suresh, or at least felt wifely fondness for him? Then why did she feel this strange detachment from Suresh now? In fact, it went well beyond detachment. She loathed him. The swine! The filthy, good-for-nothing bastard! Even as the vicious words crossed her mind, she cringed. Where had they come from in the recent weeks? She wasn't raised to use words like that, even think words like that. Her father would have slapped her face if he'd ever caught her using such foul language.

After some serious deliberation Megha gave up analyzing her emotions. It was hopeless. She had no choice but to face the truth. She was not infatuated with Kiran—she was in love with Kiran. She had felt a certain energy flow between them since the day she'd stepped into this flat. At first she'd dismissed it as her mind playing tricks on her. But his closeness in the last few weeks had brought a curious breathlessness to her lungs, a tingling to her limbs.

She found herself fantasizing about how it would feel to be touched intimately by Kiran. Sleeping in his bed made those fantasies more vivid. They left her confused. He was merely her friend and protector. She couldn't think of him as anything else. She wouldn't. It wasn't right.

In retrospect, there was always an inexplicable bond between them—right from the beginning. How had she not recognized it earlier? At Mala's birthday party, he had walked in late and their eyes had met across a crowded room and something like a surge of electricity had passed through her. It sounded like a trite cliché, eyes meeting across a room and all that sentimental mush, but it had happened nonetheless—and she had failed to acknowledge it.

Then there were several other occasions when she had noticed, or rather, sensed his eyes on her, and felt a mild rush of excitement. She remembered explaining it away as awkwardness and embarrassment. It had been neither; it was sexual attraction and love in its blossoming phase. Never having experienced anything like it before, she had been blind to it.

But now she knew. And she was trapped, ensnared by her own mind, her own heart. Married to one man and trying to hide from him, on the one hand—in love with another man and attempting to run from him, on the other. This situation was even worse than her predicament some weeks ago. Her heart had not been involved then.

Fear engulfed her. And this time the sense of dread was even more powerful than what she'd felt on the night she was to be incinerated. She had the option of fleeing then. Now she was truly trapped. How could she run from her own feelings?

But she had to do something.

Her sister Hema came to mind again. She had to reach Hema and find out if she would be welcome at her home. Maybe Hema's husband could help her find a job. He owned a prosperous land-development business; perhaps he could find her a position there. Granted she had no skills of any sort, but she was a fast learner. She had already learned quite a bit about using a computer from Kiran. Her typing skills were improving daily. If office work was not available, she could become a nanny, or work in a nursery school. She loved children and could make a good teacher.

But Kiran had pointed out that the police and Amma would be sure to keep an eye on both her sisters' homes. Megha's presence would surely be a threat to them and their respective families. And there was also the matter of embarrassing her sisters' families with a scandal—police arriving at their door and apprehending a fugitive. Both Leela and Hema's husbands came from prominent families. They couldn't afford to have their names dragged through the mud.

The phone rang, startling her out of her thoughts. As was her habit, she let the answering machine pick up the call. She picked up the phone only if she heard Kiran's voice. The familiar click-click of the machine came on after the sixth ring, and she held her breath. When she heard the voice that spoke following the outgoing message, the breath seemed to go out of her lungs.

Amma!

All Megha could do was gape at the phone while the message got recorded. "Kiran, this is Amma speaking. Give me a ring at once. It is very urgent that I talk to you. I tried your office but your secretary said you were in a meeting."

Unable to support herself on her weakening legs, Megha sank onto the chair.

Chapter 18

After the voice faded away and the answering machine clicked off, Megha sat rooted to her spot. It was not her tortured imagination. It really had been her mother-in-law calling. The blinking light on the answering machine was proof of that. Besides, that fearsome voice was unmistakable. It continued to haunt Megha's waking and sleeping moments. She'd never forget that voice.

Amma's message had sounded ominous. Urgent! She had clearly said it was *urgent*. Sudden panic flooded Megha's senses once again. Kamala had detected Megha's presence in the flat after all. Something had given her away. Was it the hot stove and the milk? Or was it the open armoire that had traitorously revealed its contents? Had she inadvertently left her new footwear in the room? To make sure she hadn't, she peered under the sofa. There were all her sandals, safely tucked away.

She had been extra careful with all her belongings. But while she'd thought she had managed to elude Kamala's keen eye, she must have grossly miscalculated. The woman wasn't stupid. She had most likely called Amma right away about her discovery— if not an actual discovery, then at least her suspicions.

Megha knew she was finished. The police were likely to appear at the door any moment. She heard a vehicle come to a stop outside the building, so she raced to the window. It had to be the police! What was she going to do?

Looking outside, she found it was a taxi. A broad, slightly

balding man stepped out of it. The driver opened the trunk to pull out a large suitcase and an attaché. The big man paid the driver, then picking up his luggage, headed for the front of the building. A minute later she heard heavy footsteps on the stairs. At the front door she listened with her ear pressed to it. With any luck he would go to the third floor? The footsteps came to a stop right outside Kiran's door and she sucked her breath in. She heard keys rattling. Good God, exactly how many people had keys to Kiran's flat? Who was the chubby man? Just as she got ready to bolt to the bedroom again, she heard a door open nearby and then shut with a thud.

It dawned on her after a moment. He was the neighbor—the man who traveled frequently. After being away for several weeks he had come home. Until then she hadn't realized she'd been holding her breath. She blew it out and went back to the drawing room.

The neighbor's return added another wrinkle to her already complicated situation. He would suspect her presence in Kiran's home. The cooking odors, the sound of running water in the bathroom, and the sound of her voice—they were sure to give her presence away. Chubby man was likely to get nosy.

But what did it matter now, anyway? Amma had found out and Megha's end was near. She'd be dragged away to her death. Her luck had run out and even Kiran wouldn't be able to protect her this time.

The phone rang again and the terror ripped through her once more. She walked away from it as if it were on fire. But this time it was Kiran's voice that came on the recorder, and she dived to pick up the phone. "Kiran! Oh God, Kiran!" she sobbed into the telephone.

"Megha, what's the matter?"

"It . . . it's Amma. She knows I'm here. She called earlier. She's coming, Kiran! She's coming to take me—"

"Shhh, stop it, Megha!" When she continued to babble and sob, he ordered, "Stop it! Listen to me. She's not coming to take you. She tried to call me at the office and when she couldn't reach me she called the house. After that she rang here again and this time she got me. You know how impatient Amma is when she gets something into her head—she refuses to give up. She's looking for a lawyer and knows I have a couple of friends who are solicitors. So calm down."

"She . . . doesn't know about me then?"

"Not a thing. Now stop fretting and I'll be home in a few minutes."

"All right."

"And Megha?"

"Yes?"

"Don't bother with dinner tonight. I'll bring home some Chinese food."

"But I already cooked dinner."

"We'll use it up tomorrow. You like Chinese, don't you?"

A tremulous smile came to her lips. He was trying so hard to make her feel better. He was the sweetest, kindest man she knew. She didn't deserve his kindness. "I love Chinese food."

"Good. Now cheer up. I'll be home in a little while." His deep masculine voice was so gentle he could have been talking to a baby.

"Kiran, thank you. I don't know what I'd do without you."

He laughed. "I'll see you in a bit."

She hung up the phone. Indeed, what would she do without Kiran? Where would she be if it weren't for him? Dead, she thought.

So, Amma was looking for a solicitor to free her precious son from a doomed marriage, was she? Megha broke into a chuckle. Suresh would get himself a divorce in a year or two. By slow degrees, the chuckle turned into hysterical laughter. Suresh would be free and so would she.

The laughter turned into sobs when reality began to sink in. Free to do what? Live with Kiran? Hardly! He would be the laughing stock of the Rao family and the entire community. Her latching onto him would be disastrous for him. His parents would surely disown him. As a divorced woman Megha would have no status in society, but she couldn't drag Kiran down with herself.

The ring of the postman's bicycle bell interrupted her thoughts. A few minutes later she heard the postman's familiar footsteps on the stairs and then the sound of the mail being pushed through the brass slot in the front door of the flat and falling with a thump on the floor-mat in the entry foyer. When she was sure he'd ascended to the third floor, she went to fetch the post. There were several envelopes and a newsletter.

Tossing them on the kitchen counter, she went to wash her tear-stained face and comb her hair. A little after half an hour later Kiran walked in. Besides his packed briefcase he carried a plastic bag that exuded the enticing, distinctive aroma of Chinese food. "Megha," he called softly after he shut the door. By mutual agreement, they kept their voices down as much as possible to keep the neighbors from hearing them.

She took the bag from him and carried it to the dining table. She was afraid of meeting his eye. The discovery about her feelings for him made her nervous. With her eyes downcast she asked, "So, how was your day?" She pretended to get busy removing the food containers from the bag.

Placing his briefcase on the chair, Kiran approached her. He retrieved a container from her hand and set it down. "Megha, look at me. Are you all right?"

Her slightly reddened eyes met his anxious ones. "I'm not sure. I still believe Amma knows I'm here."

"She doesn't."

"I feel it in my bones. Where Amma's concerned I have radar."

"Even if she does suspect something, so what? If she wants to free Suresh so he can marry again, then she's welcome to. I've given her the phone numbers of my lawyer friends."

"That's good." She didn't know what else to say. She lowered her gaze so he wouldn't see the deep hurt in her eyes. To be used and discarded like rubbish by one's husband—correction, to be disposed of as a handful of ashes, was not something to feel good about.

He laid a hand on her arm. "So you think that's good?"

"Yes. Suresh can be free of me." She brushed Kiran's hand away and turned to attend to the dinner table. His touch disturbed her, sent a warm shiver through her body. It was tempting to lean into him, ask him to hold her in his strong, capable arms. Kiran held a certain animal magnetism for her that she'd never felt with Suresh. Right now, with him standing close, she wanted him so badly it was all she could do to keep her emotions under control.

The tension between them at the moment was palpable. A sidelong glance showed his hands clenched into fists by his sides. Did he feel the strange vibes, too? Or was he only being his usual concerned and helpful self? She could have sworn she'd seen a quick flash of something in his eyes a moment ago. Harini's conjecture came to mind once again.

Abruptly Kiran moved away to get washed and changed before dinner. She sighed in relief. Another minute of him standing inches away from her would have been her undoing.

She quickly set the table. In a few minutes he came out, dressed in black shorts and a bottle-green T-shirt. Late evening stubble had grown on his cheeks and chin. The dark shadow made him look manly and appealing. She felt the urge to reach out and touch his face, feel the roughness against her palm. Everything about him screamed Man—the exact opposite of Suresh.

And that made it more dangerous for her to be around Kiran.

Putting on a cheerful smile she said, "Okay, let's eat this delicious meal before it gets cold."

They ate mostly in silence, with a few polite words thrown in. But he kept glancing at her, as if to read her thoughts. "What else is troubling you?" he finally asked.

"Nothing."

"Come on, Megha," he urged, "tell me what's wrong."

"It's crazy really. That silly cat, Kuppu, begged me for food and affection all the time, but I miss the fat little rascal. I hope they feed him regularly. He was a thin, miserable thing before I started taking care of him."

"How about if we get a kitten to keep you company?"

"Oh, no, please! Pets are too much trouble anyway." Besides, she wasn't planning on staying here forever. A pet would somehow make this weird arrangement seem permanent. She couldn't risk that.

After dinner, Megha cleared the table, put the leftovers away in the refrigerator, and washed the dishes while Kiran picked up the day's post and took it to the drawing room. He settled down on the couch to read it like he did every evening. Several minutes later, when she emerged from the kitchen, she saw him frowning over an envelope. "Something wrong?" she asked him.

He merely continued to examine the envelope. "Strange," he said, his brows still pulled in a knot.

"What's strange?"

"This envelope. It's addressed to you."

Instant terror leapt into her throat. "It can't be!"

He held it up. "Here, take a look."

She gulped hard. Someone had located her whereabouts and written her a letter! "No . . . no . . . you open it," she said, trying to keep her hands from shaking. It had to be from Amma. Megha found it hard to move, but dragged herself towards Kiran.

He grasped her by the wrist and forced her to sit beside him. "It's yours, Megha." He thrust the envelope in her hand.

She continued to stare at it for a long time.

"Come on, Megha, you have to open it some time." His voice was stern, almost paternal.

His words shook her out of her trance. She tore open the envelope, sure that something evil was going to jump out at her. She had read bizarre stories about exotic poisons, tiny bombs and even killer spiders sent to destroy people through harmless-looking letters.

Her hands trembled so much she thought the envelope would fall out of her grip, but it didn't. She gingerly lifted the flap and looked in. All she saw was folded paper, so she pulled out the sheets and unfolded them. Something fell into her lap, making her flinch. She picked up the rectangular piece of paper, afraid to look at it but drawn to it anyway. Gazing at it for a moment, she looked up at Kiran. "It's a check," she whispered, "made out to me."

"Really?"

"Uh . . . for a hundred—" Her head was reeling. "Oh God . . . hundred thousand rupees!"

"One *lakh* rupees!" He looked stunned. "Read the letter."

"I wasn't expecting a letter or a check." She set the check in the space between them and glanced at the two-page letter, her eyes traveling at once to the end for the author's name. Her jaw fell. Appaji! It was quite lengthy, too. Had he somehow discovered her hideaway? And if so, why had he not made a phone call? Was he the one who told Kamala and Amma about her? There was only one way to find out.

It was written in a small, neat hand on two sheets of ruled notepaper.

> *My dear Megha,*
>
> *I know you will be surprised to hear from me and probably shocked that I have sent the letter to you at Kiran's address. If my guess is correct, you are probably somewhere within his reach. Please do not worry. I will not reveal this to anyone. I have suspected for some time that Kiran cares about you. I could only guess that when you ran away, you perhaps went to him for help. I do not condemn you for it. In fact, I sincerely hope you did exactly that. He is a good man and I am sure he will help you.*
>
> *In case you are wondering about this letter and the reason for the check, let me explain. I have been a useless father-in-law to you. I never had the courage to stand up to Chandramma and protect you from her. There is no excuse for my cowardly behavior. I should have done more for you. My wife and son have treated you badly. I want you to know I never wanted a dowry from your father. I always thought that you were much too good for our family.*

I had no idea about Chandramma's evil plans until after you disappeared. I suspected that she was planning something, but never anything so horrid. It was only later that I realized what had been going on. I was shocked, but as a husband and father, I had to do my duty. I am not asking you to forgive any of us. What we have done to you is unforgivable.

I have been keeping a savings account of my own for some years. No one in my family knows about it. The money was meant mostly for Shanti. But since you are like a daughter to me, I feel you deserve some of it. Please consider it a gift. Perhaps it will be a small dowry for you in the future if you remarry. And in some marginal way I will have atoned for my sins. Chandramma is trying to get a lawyer to file for Suresh's divorce. I believe it is for the best. I sincerely hope you have a second chance in life.

As for me, I may not have too much time left. My doctor suspects lung cancer. Again, I have kept this from Chandramma and the children. I have refused medical treatment because I have neither the will nor the strength to fight. God has blessed me with more than I had hoped for. You were a brief and positive influence in our home and brought me much joy. Please do not try to return the money. I want you to use it for whatever you wish. My blessings will always be with you.

Appaji.

Megha read and reread the letter, then handed it to Kiran. Quickly scanning it, Kiran frowned. "I had no idea my uncle could write this well."

They both puzzled over the letter a while longer. Megha put it down and settled back against the cushion without uttering a word. When the shock began to wear off she turned to Kiran. "Can you believe that? Quiet little Appaji has been keeping so many secrets all these years. A bank account and lung problems? But then I always thought he was secretive."

"He seems to care about you. Look what he's done for you, Megha."

"He was the only person in that house who showed me any kindness." She glanced at the letter and sighed. "I can't keep his check though—I'm going to return it."

"Don't do that, Megha. You'll hurt his feelings. Maybe you can invest the money in something useful."

She sent him a cynical glance. "What do I know about investing?"

"I can show you how to make your money grow."

"I've never had one rupee to call my own in my entire life. Now I have one *lakh*. I don't even know how it feels to handle that much money."

He chuckled. "You'll know very soon. In fact, you should open a bank account first."

"I can't go to a bank!"

Kiran patted her hand. "Don't panic, Megha. You don't have to go anywhere. I'll bring the forms home. I'll help you complete them and I'll deposit the check for you. Then we'll go over some investment options and you can decide what you want to do." He put the letter in her hand once again. "There's nothing to be afraid of."

She rose to her feet. "I'll need to think about this, Kiran. I don't know if I want to keep the money. I feel like a thief, taking what rightfully belongs to Shanti."

"The decision is entirely yours, Megha." He picked up the check from the sofa and handed it to her. "Keep this in a safe place in the meantime."

When she went to bed a little while later, she felt exhausted. She hadn't done much around the house other than wash and iron some clothes, and yet she felt limp. It had to be the disturbing day she'd had. As she slipped between the sheets, her emotions were a tangled knot. Anger, sadness, fear, gratitude, and uncertainty warred with each other in her wide-awake mind.

She wondered if Kiran, too, was lying awake in the drawing room. Poor soul, he had permanently given up his bedroom to her. The sofa had to be very uncomfortable for a tall man like him, but he never complained. Whenever she brought up the subject of swapping beds, he insisted that he had never been more comfortable in his life. Liar! He was being such a generous host.

Megha still couldn't bring herself to believe that Appaji had sent her money. She was cross with him even now for not having told her about his suspicions regarding Amma. But then, could she really blame him? No one stood a chance against the charging bull named Amma. It was ironic that the check should come from the very family that had hounded Megha and her parents for money. Her own father-in-law was now giving her a dowry so she could marry someone else in the future.

She could some day be a dowry bride—a somewhat used and jaded dowry bride—if some foolish man out there was willing to have her. Hysterical laughter bubbled up inside her at the absurdity of it, but she suppressed it for fear of disturbing Kiran.

That night she had the dream again. She must have screamed or made some sort of noise, because she woke up to find Kiran standing beside her, his face filled with concern, whispering soothing things to her. After a while she convinced him to go back to his own bed, assuring him that she was going to be all right.

But she was not all right. She thought she had learned to handle the frightening dreams that continued to haunt her. After all these weeks the image of her would-be burning was still raw. Even during her waking hours the sheer horror of it tormented her, making her break out in a sweat. She couldn't talk to Kiran about it. It was too awkward to discuss, much too personal. Although he knew some of what had happened the night she'd escaped, she had still not told him much about the nightmares that plagued her, or the kind of treatment she had suffered at Amma's hands, or even her life with the Ramnaths for that matter. It was both painful and embarrassing to talk to him about that aspect of her married life.

On a few occasions she had caught Kiran looking at her with genuine anxiety in his discerning eyes. She knew he was aware of what was going on in her mind to some degree. But she also knew he was too much of a gentleman to pry into her private hell.

Tonight she realized her demons were still very much alive and well. Amma and Suresh still possessed the power to drag her back, soak her in kerosene and light a match to her. She felt the deep urge once again to pick herself up and run.

Questions popped into her mind. Was Palgaum safe for her anymore? As long as she remained in Kiran's house, was Kiran safe? Falling in love with him had complicated the situation to no end. Along with her own safety, could she put Kiran's safety on the line? What could she do to assure his security without seeming ungrateful?

She had to make a decision soon. Very soon.

Chapter 19

Kiran's brain churned with troubled thoughts as he tried to settle himself on the sofa once again. He wasn't entirely sure if it was wise to leave Megha alone yet. She was still shaking from the nightmare when he'd left the bedroom a while ago.

That must have been some hellish nightmare. Hearing the muffled scream emerging from the bedroom, Kiran had rushed in and found her thrashing around like a small animal caught in a trap. Probably mistaking him for the demon in her dream, she had fought him with all her might. It had taken considerable strength to subdue her. In the end, it was he who was scared out of his skin. Megha had some deep emotional scars that would probably stay with her for life.

What had the Ramnaths done to her that she suffered so much? Or was it something that went back to her childhood? She was very close-mouthed about her past other than telling him a little about that night she had escaped from Suresh and Amma.

Despite his conviction that he was Megha's savior, doubts and misgivings scratched at his mind. Reality had begun to rear its pragmatic head. Appaji's letter and the check had jolted Kiran into thinking hard. Suresh, who had started to fade more and more into the background in the last several days, was suddenly looming large once again.

Of course, Amma's hulking presence constantly hovered over them. This afternoon's phone call had made it all the more real.

His own breath had stopped for a second when she had called him at his office. Far from feeling satisfied with her explanation, Kiran was uneasy. He knew his aunt well enough to sense that she was up to something again—her answer had sounded too rehearsed. Had she guessed about Megha's presence in his house and called to verify it? Had she somehow discovered Appaji's secret letter to Megha?

Was it wise for him to shelter Megha like this? Was he doing her more harm than good? She obviously needed psychiatric counseling for her recurring nightmares and her growing paranoia. Then there was her reputation to consider. No matter what his personal feelings for her, Megha was right about one thing: it was unacceptable for a bachelor to have a young female living with him under these circumstances. But then, what other choice did he have? All the options had been examined and re-examined a number of times and they kept coming up empty.

But now, because of Appaji's eccentric sense of duty and generosity, Megha had some money. Kiran couldn't decide whether it was a blessing or a curse. He could no longer use Megha's lack of resources as an excuse to keep her in his home, but on the other hand, for the first time in her life she had some financial independence. Megha could now afford to leave town and live somewhere on her own. But she had neither the maturity nor the experience to make a career for herself, and her money wouldn't last long.

In the meantime, Megha was still his responsibility. He had promised her she could stay as long as she needed to. And he wanted her to stay, under his roof, under his protection. But it was also dangerous ground. His attraction to her continued to grow and trouble him. As it was, he had to nearly beat himself to stay away from her.

His eyes wandered to the closed bedroom door. Night after night, the temptation to join her in that big bed was hard to resist. He took a deep breath and closed his eyes, trying to let reason replace desire. She needed him, not as a man but as a guardian. All his protective instincts were on full alert—he wanted to take care of her. His male instincts, however, were another matter—they were going completely crazy. Were his erotic feelings tantamount to moral turpitude? Was his need to touch and love her grossly inappropriate?

Well, of course it was, he told himself in silent exasperation. He couldn't take advantage of her helplessness. Never!

Then he heard the click. Shifting, he saw the bedroom door open by slow degrees. His pulse shot up. In the semi-darkness, he watched in silence Megha's nightgown-clad figure tiptoe around the dining table and disappear into the kitchen. He heard the refrigerator door open and its faint light illuminated the dining area for a second. Then the door closed with a muffled whoosh.

She probably needed some cold water.

With his breath reined in tight, he waited for her to come out of the kitchen and creep back to the bedroom. No sense letting on that he was awake and watching her. Several minutes later there was no sign of her. Finally, convinced that something was wrong, he threw the cover aside and rose.

To make sure he didn't startle her, he called out to her softly. "Megha, are you all right?" His question met with silence. "Megha?"

This time he heard a slight rustle, so he proceeded to the kitchen, calling her name again. He found her standing beside the sink, leaning against the counter with a glass of water in her hand, staring into space. Her stillness told him she was lost in some private world.

Moving to stand directly in front of her, he pried the nearly empty glass from her hand and put it on the counter, then took both her hands in his. "Did you have another bad dream?" He kept his voice quiet and gentle.

Megha shook her head.

"What is it then? You can't sleep?"

Shaking her head once again, she seemed to emerge from her trance. Her eyes came to focus on him. In the dim glow of the streetlight filtering through the window, Kiran couldn't quite see the expression in them, but he sensed that Appaji's letter had something to do with her present condition. All he could feel was her need for comfort and assurance. So he dropped her hands and placed his on her shoulders. "Tell me what's bothering you. Maybe I can help."

Her hands came up and she flattened them against his chest, as if to push him away, but after a moment's hesitation she sighed and laid her forehead on them, tucking her head under his chin in a childlike move. "I'm so confused, Kiran."

"About what?"

"Until last night I had no choice but to stay here, but now I have some money. What do I do with it? If I go off on my own, what will I do? I've never held a job. I've been alone in my whole life."

Oddly his thoughts were along the same lines as Megha's, Kiran reflected. Now she no longer needed him in the most desperate way. And yet, if she moved out of his life, what would become of her? He was just as anxious about her options as she was, perhaps more, but he couldn't very well tell her that.

She looked like a lost child. What she seemed to need was someone to tell her everything would turn out all right. So he said, "Listen, you don't have to make any decisions right away. Take some time; do some serious thinking. You and I can look at some options and then you can decide what's best. Meanwhile, consider this your home."

"You've been more than generous, Kiran. But I can't stay here forever."

"There's plenty of time to think about this. You shouldn't rush into anything you'll regret later." On an impulse he added, "And don't forget Amma is still out there."

Amma's name seemed to send a shiver through Megha. She appeared to surrender to her need for closeness, so Kiran put his arms around her. Never having held her before, his body reacted with a pleasant tremor of its own. Damn! She felt small and soft, so defenseless.

An odd mixture of tenderness, protectiveness and primal desire filled Kiran. This was what he'd been contemplating, dreaming about, fantasizing over for the longest time. Now that Megha stood within the circle of his arms, he realized that reality was far more enchanting than his wildest fantasies. And far more frightening—like the nervous apprehension of gazing at something beyond one's reach, and wondering if it's real or just a fleeting illusion. And whether it will crumble when touched.

Oh, she was real all right! Her fragrance was unmistakable, her warm breath on his chest disturbingly real. He tried to remind himself that she was off limits to him. Megha was hurt and vulnerable; she needed his sympathy and support, not his less than honorable attentions.

She stirred, and he wondered if she was going to push him away this time. If so, perhaps it was for the best. Instead, she lowered her hands from his chest and wrapped her arms around his waist, hesitantly at first, then more firmly, pressing closer against him.

That final gesture on her part was his undoing. Was she trying to snuggle closer for warmth and comfort or was she feeling the sensual, pulsing current between them as he was? He closed his eyes and hoped she couldn't hear his heart pounding, his breath sounding labored. Despite his resolve not to go any further, he felt compelled to place a soft kiss on the top of her head. Her hair was silky and smelled sweet. So bloody irresistible!

Abruptly she disentangled herself and pulled away from him. But her hand lingered on his arm. A puzzled look came over her face and her hand trembled. Had he gone too far with her? Had he repulsed her with that foolish kiss? "I shouldn't have done that. I'm sorry, Megha," he mumbled.

But she continued to look bewildered. Her hand remained on his arm. Was she trying to assess his expression? Was she wondering why his arm wobbled just as much as her hand?

A light seemed to flicker in her eyes. In that instant Kiran realized that Megha had felt something during that embrace— perhaps not with the same intensity as he had, but he could sense her rigidity, her pulse picking up momentum.

The electricity between them intensified then sparked.

* * *

Kiran held Megha with his eyes, a silent message in them she couldn't ignore. Was that desire burning in his gaze? Love? Anticipation? So, Harini had been right in her assessment of Kiran's interest in her. Her own instincts were right on target, too.

Something inside Megha snapped. She knew she was treading on dangerous ground, and yet . . . recklessness seemed to override prudence.

Kiran must have experienced the same desperation to touch her because he pulled her back into his arms and lowered his mouth to hers. "I'm sorry," he whispered, "but I have to do this."

The tension that had built up and hummed for so long between them finally broke loose. Guilt and trepidation were forgotten as their feelings for each other buzzed and swirled around them in circles.

As they kissed, Kiran's hands caressed her, tenderly at first, then with rough urgency. One large hand curled around her nape, the other traveled to her back, her hips, her shoulders, her breasts, touching, stroking, exploring. "Forgive me, Megha—I can't help myself."

Lost in the moment, Megha vaguely wondered why Kiran was so apologetic. She was participating in it just as much as he. "It's okay," she said and looped her arms around his neck. She puzzled over why she had never experienced this kind of physical and emotional high with Suresh. But then Suresh had never kissed her like this, held her like this, or touched her like this. This was different. And although her brain warned that it was wrong and immoral, her heart said otherwise. Casting all other thoughts aside, she responded to Kiran with a curious hunger.

In the next minute, Kiran broke the kiss, making Megha wonder if she'd repulsed him in some way. Had she behaved like a wanton slut? But she was caught by surprise when he put one arm behind her back, the other beneath her knees and hoisted her in his arms.

He was taking her to the bedroom. She knew it; she saw it in his face.

Kiran was a large, strong man and it felt wonderful to be cradled in such powerful arms. Despite their obvious strength they held her with the utmost care. Kiran's eyes looking into hers as he strode toward the bedroom had an intense, provocative gleam in them. Suresh was so puny he could hardly lift a log of wood, let alone his wife. And yet Kiran held her like she weighed next to nothing.

He carried her to the bedroom, all the while mesmerizing her with his gaze. She couldn't have broken the eye contact if she tried. A distant bell of alarm clanged somewhere in her brain. But at the moment only her need to stay close to Kiran prevailed. Her other life was merely a blurred and unpleasant dream. This was now and it was infinitely more desirable. More seductive. More captivating. She wanted this, wanted Kiran as she'd never wanted anything in her life.

In her eyes, Kiran put all those movie heroes to shame. Those Mills and Boon men paled in comparison to him. Kiran was her personal hero. And at the moment he was all hers—all six feet of hard muscle and hot, captivating maleness. A ripple of excitement shot through her veins.

In the bedroom, he put her gently on her feet and caught her once more in his arms. "Megha, are you feeling what I'm feeling?" he asked.

Words failed her. All she could do was stare at him. Sensual energy flowed over her, setting every nerve on full alert, yet she remained speechless. *Yes, I'm feeling what you're feeling and more. Much, much more!*

"I want to make love with you, Megha—" He halted, probably because her eyes turned wide. Then he continued, "But only if you want it as much as I do." His voice sounded hoarse as he unbraided her dense mass of hair, lifted a handful and watched it sift through his fingers. "You have lovely hair . . . so soft . . . like silk."

A smile touched Megha's lips. She'd never paid much attention to her hair, and yet, the way Kiran was fingering it, admiring it, it was one of the most erotic gestures in the world.

For a moment, she was almost consumed by the powerful longing to surrender completely to him. The need was startling in its intensity. She'd never felt such an overwhelming hunger to make love before. This kind of yearning was new to her. She tried to think hard for a second, even to fight the wave of desire, but realized it was a losing battle. Her feelings for Kiran would win in the end. She loved this man deeply and she wanted him.

Watching the conflicting emotions doing battle in her eyes, he cupped her face in one firm hand. "I know what's going on in your head. I'm just as confused as you."

"You, too?" But he was always so decisive, so sure of himself.

Kiran smiled at her. "Yes. But let me love you, Megha. Let me give you what you need."

Oh dear God, she wanted that, too. Was her need for love so nakedly visible in her eyes that he could read it with such clarity? Whatever, it was too compelling to deny him or herself. Her body was already trembling with anticipation. She nodded yes.

He must have sensed her lingering reluctance. "Are you sure?" Again she nodded. "I don't want to hurt you," he murmured.

"I know."

"And I certainly don't want you to regret it for the rest of your life."

"I won't."

"You can still say no. Just say the word and I'll go back to the couch."

"I-I'm sure."

He studied her for a moment, perhaps wondering whether he'd heard correctly. Then he crushed her to him once again. "I love you, Megha. I've loved you since the day I met you."

She shook her head at him in disbelief, despite Harini's observations about him. "Love at first sight? But . . . it can't be. That was my wedding day."

His fingertip traced the line of her jaw. "I know, and I've loved you since then. You were the most beautiful woman I'd ever seen, the most charming bride. You still are."

His words puzzled her. Expressing love so overtly was not the Indian way. Men and women rarely professed love to each other—it was expressed in actions, in expressions, perhaps even in writing if the occasion presented itself, but never verbally. And yet, here was Kiran, baring his heart and soul to her. Maybe that was the American way he'd learned while he lived in New York. But he loved her! It was thrilling to hear him say it. And that was all that mattered.

"I wouldn't want to make love to you if I didn't care for you deeply, Megha," he said. "I'm not the sort of man to treat sex as a pastime."

"I know."

"And I want to marry you when you're free. I want to give you everything."

Marriage! And he sounded perfectly serious about his intentions. He was remarkable, everything any woman could ever ask for in a man—so honorable, so strong, so caring and capable. And yet, she'd ended up with his rotten cousin. Where was the justice in that? But Kiran was miraculously here with her now and he loved her. She'd worry later about the propriety of being intimate like this with him. For some odd reason, familiar lines from Omar Khayyam's *Rubaiyat* drifted through her mind:

Ah, my beloved, fill the cup that clears
Today of past regrets and future fears;
Tomorrow? Why, tomorrow I may be
Myself with yesterday's seven thousand years.

"May I take your nightgown off, Megha?" Kiran's voice was a hoarse whisper.

"But . . . but I . . ." How could she casually bare herself to him? What was she supposed to say?

"Let me look at you, all of you," said Kiran.

Instinctively she agreed, unable to resist the whispered words, her sense of modesty overcome. He slowly unbuttoned her nightgown and slid it off her shoulders. It fell to the floor, leaving her naked, covered with goose bumps.

She heard his sharp intake of breath, saw his eyes turn darker. "You're more beautiful than I'd imagined," he said. Letting his gaze rove over her in the blue-green glow of the night light, he took in every inch of her body, making her skin burn with embarrassment. But there was wonder and reverence in Kiran's expression as he gazed on her. He made her *feel* beautiful, exciting and desirable.

Within seconds Kiran undressed himself and it was Megha's turn to gawk. It wasn't as if she'd never seen a naked man before, but she couldn't help staring in fascination, couldn't believe how magnificent his body was. Unconsciously, she couldn't help comparing him to Suresh. Kiran was a marvelous example of a young, healthy *male* in every sense of the word.

Then he scooped her up once again and laid her on the bed. "My God, Megha, you don't know how long I've waited for this," he breathed, proving to her over the next several minutes exactly how eagerly he'd waited and how desperately he wanted her. When Kiran finally joined his body with hers, he made her shatter into a thousand glorious pieces, then fell apart himself.

When she managed to open her eyes through the blissful haze, Megha realized that without being conscious of it, she, too, had waited a long time for exactly this. It was what her body and mind had craved, to be filled, to be satiated, to be taken completely, to be loved as if there was no one else in the world but the two of them. The pressure of Kiran's weight on her felt sweet. She was home.

An incredible mix of laughter and sobbing rose high in her chest. Tears spilled from her eyes. He brushed them away with his fingers. "Did I hurt you?"

"No."

"Are those tears of joy then?"

"Yes."

"I never want to see you shed tears of unhappiness, sweetheart. I want to fill your life with nothing but joy."

He'd called her sweetheart! It had the most magical ring to it. She closed her eyes and smiled, silently assuring him that what she felt was pure joy. She had never thought physical love could be like this—beyond the mere joining of two bodies—a sublime experience that touched the soul—a glimpse of heaven.

She knew then that no man other than Kiran would ever be able to give her this. If only she could tell him that, convey what she felt for him. But she couldn't say it aloud. It wasn't right for her to confess to him her innermost feelings as he had done with her. He was a free man, while she, although she'd offered herself to him, was not a free woman.

As their sated bodies gradually separated, Kiran rolled over, but pulled her close to him and settled her head on his shoulder. They both lay quietly for a while basking in the afterglow of love, letting their bodies and minds settle. Then, having discovered the wonder of passion, they turned to each other instinctively once more. They made love again and again, taking it slower each time, giving themselves an opportunity to savor every moment. Eventually they fell asleep.

Sometime in the middle of the night she woke up, groggy and slightly disoriented. Feeling Kiran's hard, warm body beside hers, she came wide awake. She had never slept in the nude before, let alone in the arms of a naked man. Living with her in-laws had made nakedness impossible, even in the privacy of the bedroom.

Reality slowly began to seep in, and the first stirrings of the moral significance of what they'd done began to claw at Megha's brain. She had just slept with her husband's cousin.

Dear God! What had she done?

Chapter 20

Megha lay wide-awake beside a sleeping Kiran for several minutes, his arm still binding her to him—a very male and possessive gesture. Her mind was now racing. She knew exactly what she had to do. On the one hand she was elated to learn that Kiran loved her. The physical experience of making love with him still tingled along her nerves. It was deeply touching. He had made her cry with the sheer joy of it. Why couldn't she have been married to him in the first place?

One couldn't change one's destiny, however. She wouldn't let her curse become Kiran's curse. He deserved better than the spoils left behind by his cousin. He deserved a good, unsullied woman for a bride and not used goods like her. He needed an educated and refined girl from his own upper-class background. As a matter of fact, Megha had gathered from Amma's boasting that families of many marriageable girls had approached Kiran's parents regarding an arranged match—families able to provide large dowries. But Kiran had shown no interest in any of those girls.

Megha could never aspire to measure up to the lofty Raos' standards of culture and sophistication. They would want a girl with the proper connections for their precious son. Besides, this kind of scandal, Kiran marrying a once-married-and-separated woman, would ruin him and his family. The sacrifice he was willing to make for her was too high a price to pay. She couldn't let him destroy his near-perfect life for her.

With great reluctance she removed Kiran's arm from her. It felt muscular and heavy. He stirred and rolled onto his back but fell once again into deep sleep. Relieved, Megha gingerly sat up in bed to judge if the bed would squeak. It didn't. The ceiling fan was on and it spun around with a humming noise, muffling other sounds.

Kiran continued to sleep soundly. His bare chest rose and fell in a slow, steady rhythm. With minimal movement she slid out of bed and glanced at the heap of clothes on the floor. They'd been in such a rush to rid themselves of them that they hadn't cared where they fell. It was embarrassing to look at them now; they reminded her vividly of the wild and passionate love she and Kiran had shared only a short while ago. It was a love that had no place in either of their lives—an illicit love that was as tainted as it was magnificent, like the flowers of the foxglove plant, beautiful yet deadly.

She changed into a sari, folded Kiran's pajamas and laid them on the bed. Then she knotted her loose hair into a tight coil.

For a long minute she stood by the bed to study Kiran's face in the semi-darkness—so strong, so unselfish and so very dear. He slept like a young boy, his mouth soft without its wide-awake stubborn firmness. The arm that had rested on her belly was now flung above his head. His chest was broad but lean, with a dusting of hair. Was it only an hour ago that she had touched it and laid her head on it? What a contrast to Suresh's puny, hairless, concave chest. The desire to run her hands over him and feel the texture of his skin and muscle and hair just one more time bubbled up inside her. Quelling her errant thoughts, she tiptoed away.

Opening the door with infinite care, she stepped outside the bedroom. With the door open, she stood still for a second, watching for movement from Kiran. He didn't stir. With the blood pounding in her brain, she gently shut the door.

She took several deep breaths to keep the threatening tears at bay. Enough tears had been shed. She wanted to carry this image of a peacefully sleeping Kiran in her mind forever. He'd be furious when he woke up and found she was gone. But this was her only chance to do something for him. Some day he would thank her for it.

As she let herself out the front door the hinge creaked as usual. She froze for an instant then pulled the door shut and went down the staircase. The street was deserted this time of night. Strangely she was not afraid anymore. The familiar hunted feeling of the past few weeks was curiously absent.

She didn't run but walked briskly in the direction she felt inclined to go. Shivering a little in the cool night air, she drew her sari tightly around herself. As if pulled by a magnet her legs carried her directly toward her private refuge. When in trouble, the invisible compass in her mind magically steered her to the river. On the way there she stood for a minute at the end of the street where her parents lived, wondering if they slept in peace despite knowing their daughter was missing for several weeks. Again the deep sense of detestation kicked in. They had willingly sent her to hell, with no thought for her safety or her welfare. Poverty and bad health were no excuse for tossing one's child into a snake pit.

As expected, it was hauntingly quiet by her favorite spot near the river. The beggar, who was a permanent fixture there, was probably fast asleep in the sanctuary of the temple. Dense fog always surrounded the area, so she could see next to nothing. The damp, solitary darkness of the riverbank would have frightened her ordinarily, but tonight she felt at peace. The sound of flowing water was clearly audible in the calm of night. A dog started to howl in the distance. Did it sense her presence?

She walked toward the sound of the gurgling waters, sank to her knees and said a quick prayer, asking God to bless the people she loved and forgive her for taking the coward's way out. She had tried to be brave, tried to do what was right, but in the end nothing had worked. It all came around to death. Her death. By living she continued to be both a burden and a threat to everyone around her. It was best for her to leave. *Yama*, the god of death, would succeed in his quest after all.

Suicide went against her Hindu beliefs, but she was convinced that in her case it was the only right thing to do. Didn't the holy book, the *Bhagvad Gita*, preach that doing one's duty towards family and society without giving thought to one's own needs was the ultimate test of a true Hindu? In that case, she was doing what she felt was her duty—looking out for others, especially Kiran.

Drawing upon an inner strength she never knew she possessed, she took a step into the river. Her face contorted when the cold rushing water lapped at her feet and sent an icy shiver up her body. Her sari whipped around her legs as the breeze lifted its folds. With a cleansing breath she took another step forward.

"Megha!" A distant voice reached her through the fog. She ignored it. It was only her conscience telling her something she didn't want to hear. She continued ahead.

"Don't do it, Megha! Stop!" The voice was faint above the bubbling ripple of the water and her own heartbeat. She blocked it out again. A hazy band of light seemed to come through the fog from behind her and flashed for an instant. The water churned around her ankles and leapt at her calves. She closed her eyes and took a shaky breath. Suicide was so damn hard.

Abruptly the wind went out of her sails. She screamed when she felt herself being grabbed from behind and hauled backwards. With all her might she tried to fight the force that pulled her, but it was stronger than she. Her arms were pinned to her sides and her feet dragged through the silt. She was towed with ease although she squirmed and kicked. She felt herself being lifted and deposited roughly on a hard surface, making her wince. Then she heard the same voice she'd heard seconds earlier, calling out her name, but this time it sounded angry.

"Megha . . . Megha . . . can . . . you . . . hear me?"

"Wh . . . who . . . Kiran?"

"Are . . . you out . . . of your . . . bloody . . . mind?" the voice gasped, desperately trying to catch a breath.

It was indeed Kiran's voice. And it sounded furious. In the dark she could barely make out his silhouette against the river. "Kiran? H-how did you find me?"

He threw himself down beside her. She could feel the warmth of his arm, his hip and thigh next to her own. He was here in the flesh. He wasn't something her disoriented mind had conjured up in a fevered state. His breath came in hard gulps. No wonder—he had literally carried her all that distance from the river to the rock and that too while she had fought him hard.

"It . . . didn't take . . . a freaking genius . . . to figure . . . it out," he wheezed.

"How did you get here so quickly?" Her own voice wasn't steady either.

"I have a car, remember?" He was still enraged, but now, since his breath had begun to stabilize, his voice was laced with bitter sarcasm.

She flinched at the acidity of his tone. Cynicism and hostility were so unlike him. His deep voice almost always conveyed patience. Earlier that night, she had heard that same voice turn warm and gruff with desire and tenderness. Except on that one occasion when he'd blown up at hearing about Amma's attempts to burn her, Megha had never seen him intensely angry— testy yes, but never livid. Now he was enraged at her. He had every right to be upset, of course.

"Damn it, Megha! What are you doing to yourself? What are you doing to me? You tried to kill yourself, for God's sake! What Amma and Suresh couldn't accomplish, you wanted to carry out on your own? Is that it?"

"I'm sorry."

Kiran picked up her cold, damp hand and held it in his own. "Why, Megha? Was making love with me so hateful?"

"No." Oh God, he sounded so hurt.

"If it was so disgusting, then why didn't you say so before I went all the way? I would have left you alone. I asked your permission before I took you."

"That's not it at all, Kiran."

"If it isn't that then what the hell made you want to end your life?"

Megha pressed his hand against her face. "Making love with

you was the most beautiful experience of my life, Kiran. I'm grateful to you for giving it to me."

"And this is the way you show it? You know I couldn't bear to lose you—especially not after what we just had."

"But you don't seem to understand something, Kiran. I would bring you misery—utter shame. Marrying me would be disastrous for you."

"Where did you get that stupid idea?"

"Listen to me. Your parents would disown you, Kiran. You're their only child. They have all their hopes and dreams pinned on you. The entire Rao family looks at you as their son and heir. You would always be known as the man who slept with his cousin's discarded wife, a dowryless, runaway wife, a whore who shamelessly seduced you, and the woman who almost became a mother but miscarried."

"Shut up! Just shut up, will you? Why don't you let me decide what I want? I'm a grown man and I don't give a damn what other people think."

She clucked impatiently. "But what they think matters in a society like ours! What your parents think matters even more."

"My parents are not as rotten as you've made them out to be either."

"But your mother conspired with Amma for months. She wanted me dead as much as Amma did."

"You're wrong. I told you my mother thought Amma was planning a divorce. I realize that right now my parents are part of your in-laws and so, in your mind, enemies. But trust me, Megha. They'll come around when they get to know you, when they realize my happiness depends on having you in my life."

The cool air blowing from the river made Megha's sodden sari cling to her legs, sending a shiver through her. She stared into the foggy darkness, listening to his passionate argument. Slowly she began to understand the magnitude and depth of his feelings for her. If he was willing to make such sacrifices for her, he loved her more than he loved himself, more than he loved anyone else. She had done him a grave injustice by trying to commit suicide. Although she'd convinced herself that she was doing it for him, she had also been cowardly in her reasons for wanting to disappear—she was too scared to face an uncertain future.

Kiran had saved her life. Again. That was twice in a span of a few weeks.

But now what? After all, nothing had really changed. She turned to him with a tired sigh. "I'm still married to your cousin. That fact still remains, you know."

"That will change soon, trust me. Amma said she was going to file for divorce immediately. She called me looking for lawyers, remember?"

"I bet Suresh is going along nicely with her demented plans."

"Of course. Suresh is a spineless ass," Kiran ground out through clenched teeth.

"Assuming things will fall into place like you say, what do we do now?"

"Nothing at the moment." His arms came around her in a tight clasp. "I was frightened out of my mind. At first I thought you had merely started to run. But then I remembered that look of intense regret that came over your face after we . . . uh . . . were finished. I knew exactly where you'd go. I drove like a demon, praying you'd stay alive until I got here."

"I'm sorry," she repeated. What else could she say?

"Thank God I made it in the nick of time. Finding you alive and breathing makes me want to give you a thorough spanking and lock you up, you silly idiot."

"Maybe you should." She felt like an idiot. "I don't know what I was thinking, Kiran. All these feelings . . . and then what happened between us . . . I was scared and confused."

"Don't you think I'm scared, Megha? Being in love with my cousin's wife, a woman who's like a sister-in-law, is the scariest thing I've ever known. I'm scared of what will happen to you, to us in the future. I worry about the wisdom of keeping you concealed in my home and I fear for your safety all the time. But you have to understand something—suicide is not the answer to any of those problems. Death is nothing but pain for everyone around."

"I'm beginning to realize that now."

"Besides, shouldn't you continue fighting Amma even harder?" he said. "Show her how brave you are. Don't hand Suresh and her an easy victory. Give them hell—defeat them at their own dirty game."

"You're right . . . you're right . . . and I'm sorry." It made perfect sense now. Why hadn't she thought of all that? What had happened to her resolution to seek revenge against Amma and Suresh? And how could Kiran be so young and yet so wise?

"You'll never try anything this insane again?" he asked.

She buried her face in his chest. "I won't." His heart was still racing. She could feel the rapid rise and fall of his ribs against her face. Shame and guilt knifed through her. How could she have even dreamt of hurting this wonderful man? A fine way to repay him indeed, after all he'd done for her!

"You promise?"

She nodded yes into his chest.

"Good. Now let's get out of here and go home."

Home! The word sent a mild and unexpected pang of longing through her. It sounded so good, and yet so wrong, corrupt somehow. She was going home to her cousin-in-law's house, not her own. Even so, she knew she had to go with him. Maybe someday soon it would begin to feel right. As long as he said he would make it right, she would trust him. He was the most trust-inspiring individual she knew.

They walked hand in hand to his car. Engulfed in fog, they had to carefully feel their way over the rough terrain in near-total darkness. He had on shoes but her *chappals* had been carried away by the river. Although he had brought a flashlight with him, it had fallen out of his grip while rescuing her. It took them several minutes to locate the car because he couldn't quite remember where he'd parked it. She followed him in silence, letting herself be led like a small, rebellious child chastised by a loving parent and then hauled home—forgiven, but expected to be on her best behavior in the future.

She turned to Kiran as he started the car. "You were fast

asleep when I walked out of the house. When did you find out I was gone?"

He raked unsteady fingers through his already disheveled hair. In the dull radiance of the car's dashboard lights, she noticed he was in pajamas. They were wet and muddy below the knees. His expression was grim. He looked exhausted.

"I woke up and noticed you were gone," he said. "It meant only one thing: you had started to run once again. I had this ominous feeling that what happened between us caused you to go away, perhaps even harm yourself." He turned to her, his eyes dark and bleak. "I thought I'd be too late. I prayed all the way here, Megha."

"I'm not as brave as you think I am."

He fixed her with a thoughtful look for a moment. "Let's just call it a minor lapse in judgement—caused by severe stress."

"I didn't mean to hurt you. I promise I won't try it again."

"Okay." He threw the car in gear and started to drive down the rutted path that led to the main road. They drove home in silence. She noticed he wore a brooding scowl on his face. Tonight's strange events would hang between them for a long, long time.

Once they reached home, things got awkward. Only hours earlier they had slept in each other's arms. But now what? They both glanced at the bedroom door then looked away.

Kiran made the decision for both of them. "Go to bed, Megha. I'll sleep on the sofa as usual." Perhaps noticing the look of hesitation on her face, he added, "Don't worry—I won't be disturbing you."

Chapter 21

The sound of children playing in the park across the street drew Megha to the window. Standing at a safe distance behind the curtains, she observed the scene outside. Half a dozen little boys played cricket with tot-sized bats while a couple of nannies, *ayahs,* kept a watchful eye on them. In this affluent neighborhood, *ayahs* minding children was the norm. Every morning and afternoon Megha noticed the *ayahs* walking the kids back and forth to school or to the playground.

Megha looked wistfully at the children. Would she ever be blessed with any of her own? Not likely, now that she was going to be a divorced woman with no real chance of remarriage.

That single night of passion with Kiran several days ago came to mind. Oblivious to everything but their desperate need to touch and explore and discover each other's bodies and make love, neither she nor Kiran had thought about protection. Passion had overruled common sense. She had lost sleep over the possibility of pregnancy, obsessed about it, until this morning, when her period had arrived as a blessing. She'd never been this relieved to see it. A quick prayer of thanks had come to her lips.

God, what a catastrophe it would have been if she'd become pregnant with Kiran's child. On the one hand, it would have been the most joyful thing to happen and, on the other, it would have made an already difficult situation entirely impossible. A fine way to start off the New Year, which was coming up in a couple of days!

Ironically, her sense of relief was in direct contrast to what she'd felt while she was married to Suresh. Then she had longed to conceive. And when it had finally happened after nearly a year of waiting, it hadn't lasted very long. Now that she thought about it, the puny and unhealthy-looking Suresh probably had some problems in the fertility department. Had Amma ever given thought to the possibility that her son could be a poor sperm producer? Even if she had, the stubborn woman would never admit it.

Megha remembered the one time she was pregnant, and hadn't even known it until that miserable night, not that long ago. It was the same day as her first wedding anniversary. God, what a dreadful day that was—she remembered it well. Things had gone so wrong. The half-inch long scar on the inside of her right wrist was a cruel reminder of that day. Most people recalled their first anniversary with fondness. Hers had been eventful all right. But sentimental? Sweet? Hardly!

Megha leaned against the window frame and closed her eyes as she reconstructed that day in her mind, image by image. It was all so painfully clear, and likely to stay that way for a long time.

By the time the Ramnath family had finished breakfast and Megha was well into preparing lunch, she knew with a sinking heart that her first wedding anniversary was going to be a disappointment. Nobody had remembered it was a momentous occasion for her and Suresh. Not even Suresh.

She had awakened with a mildly optimistic feeling that morning. It was exactly one year to the day since her wedding. Nothing noteworthy had occurred during the year, but it was a significant milestone nevertheless. A first anniversary was meant to be celebrated. But not in this house apparently.

As she had lain in bed at dawn, she had remembered how Harini's husband had surprised Harini by giving her a gold chain with a lotus pendant and then whisked her off to Goa for a couple of days of fun and romance by the sea. Harini had returned with stars in her eyes and even more love for Vijay than ever before.

Although Megha had no such romantic illusions where Suresh was concerned, she had hoped he would remember the occasion and perhaps mention a simple but private dinner at a restaurant or at least a movie. She was not looking for expensive trinkets; something unpretentious and cheap would have been sufficient to make her happy. Even a long, romantic walk by the river would have been better than nothing. But Suresh had entirely forgotten their anniversary. How could he! Her easy-to-stir temper began to simmer at his negligence.

Nobody else from the family had remembered the anniversary, either.

An indignant pout settled over her mouth as she went about her morning duties. Tukaram must have noticed her sullenness, because he, too, worked in silence. She chopped the potatoes with a rare vengeance and carelessly tossed them in the pan, causing the hot oil in it to splatter and land on the inside of her wrist. She winced in pain. This time the angry tears managed to spill out unchecked. Oh hell! Nothing was going right!

She quickly held her wrist under cold running water for a few minutes. An angry red blister, the size of a large grape, was already beginning to form. The fiery pain shot right through her forearm. It would likely turn into an ugly scar and last for years, maybe forever. She wiped the stubborn tears away with her knuckles.

On the other hand, the burning sensation in her wrist prompted her to do something, anything, to combat the gloom hanging over this dismal day. She wanted a break from the dull routine she had sunk into. Seven days a week she did the same things, over and over again. She needed to get away from this depressing place and its occupants. If she didn't, she'd explode. The walls of the tiny house felt like prison, with Amma the chief warden and Suresh the prison guard. She decided she'd give herself a day off—an anniversary gift to herself. She'd consider it her private celebration.

That afternoon, as Amma readied herself for her customary siesta, Megha approached her. "Amma?"

"Hmm?"

"I-I'm planning to go visit Appa and Avva today."

She winced inwardly when Amma's eyebrow shot up. "What did you say?" The voice was threateningly soft.

Megha knew Amma had heard it right the first time. "Since it's my first wedding anniversary, I'd like to be with people who care about what it means to me." Megha was shocked at her own effrontery when the words escaped her mouth, but she had just about had it with Amma and her witless son. Even if she had been somewhat undecided until that point, she was now convinced that she'd spend the rest of the day . . . and, oh yes, the night as well, with her parents. She was going to exercise her rights. At the moment she didn't care if she was dismissed as a rebel. She didn't even give a damn if Amma decided to raise a hand to her. Rebellion—hot, kick-in-the-stomach rebellion— welled up inside Megha at Amma's stern expression. She was even prepared to get into a fist fight with the witch if she had to.

Amma shifted on the bed. "Going to your parents' house, huh? What about my afternoon tea . . . and the family's dinner tonight?"

Casually slinging her overnight canvas bag over her shoulder, Megha managed to hold Amma's gaze. It was an outward calm, to be sure, because her legs trembled and her heart thudded madly. There would be a heavy price to pay for her impertinence, perhaps for the rest of her life. But she wasn't about to give up now, not when she had come so far. "Your tea is in the thermos on the kitchen table and I made plenty of food for lunch, so there should be enough leftovers for dinner."

"What about Suresh? He is your husband, no?"

"My husband doesn't even realize it's his first anniversary, Amma, so I'm planning to spend it with my parents. I'll be back tomorrow," she said and turned around.

Thrusting her feet into her *chappals*, she stepped out the front door, her back rigid, her head held high. The last thing she heard as she walked away was Amma's piqued voice talking to herself. "Who does the silly chit think she is—the maharani of Palgaum or what? What is this anniversary nonsense, anyway? We never had anything like that when we were young."

Although Megha's parents lived some two kilometers away and the afternoon sun was hot enough to scorch her skin, she decided to walk instead of taking the bus. All the pent-up anger was roiling inside her and she needed to work it out of her system. She also needed to think. The noisy, crowded bus with sweaty bodies crammed in like pickled limes wouldn't allow her to think clearly.

The perspiration running in droplets between her breasts and down her back was annoying. The burning in her wrist hadn't ebbed one bit, but she ignored it and kept walking at a brisk pace. By the time her parents' modest home came into view she felt faint and nauseated. She told herself it was only the sweltering heat that made her feel sick. She'd be okay once she had a chance to sit down and have a glass of cold water. A nice afternoon nap in her old room sounded blissful. That's what she badly needed—sleep.

When Megha knocked on their door, her mother opened it. Caught by surprise, she stared wide-eyed for a moment, then smiled. "Megha! What brings you here today, *putti?*"

Megha shrugged. "Just felt like it."

Her mother pulled her in. "You look so flushed. Did you walk all the way in this heat, dear?"

Nodding, Megha discarded her *chappals* by the door and tossed her bag on the floor. "I was in a mood for walking."

"Oh," said her mother, looking at Megha's face with apparent concern. "Your face looks so . . . uh . . . let me get you some cold water."

Megha sank into the lumpy cushion of one of the chairs in the drawing room and watched her mother go to the kitchen and return with a stainless steel tumbler filled with water. How pretty her mother still managed to look, Megha marveled, as she accepted the tumbler. Despite having crossed fifty, she was slim. Her large eyes still twinkled brightly when she smiled, her thick hair had no more than one or two strands of gray, and her figure could hold its own against a group of thirty-year-old women any day. Even in a rough, faded print sari, her elegance was quite evident. Her skin still had a youthful glow.

Unfortunately, Avva had ended up in a lackluster marriage. She had a difficult life, Megha knew. Giving birth to three daughters in a male-obsessed society had not been easy. Her in-laws, Megha's paternal grandparents, had apparently been harsh about Avva's inability to produce a male child.

But at least Appa and Avva, despite their disillusionment, had been caring and loving parents. Her grandparents, on the other hand, had been distant and cold. They had never shown the girls any affection. It was almost as if female children had no emotional needs. They were always treated as unwelcome additions to the family. Consequently, Megha and her sisters had never been close to the old folks. After their deaths some years ago, there was no real mourning to speak of. Only Appa had grieved for them.

Money had always been tight, too, but somehow Avva had managed to raise her daughters with grace and dignity. She had sacrificed a great deal to make sure her children had a good education at a convent school. Mangala Shastry wanted her girls to speak and write fluent English and gain general knowledge, become more sophisticated—something she'd never had.

Swallowing large gulps of the deliciously cold water, Megha glanced at her father reclining in his favorite easy chair. Now he, unlike Avva, looked gray and old from rheumatoid arthritis and chronic heart disease. He used to be a handsome man until a few years ago. He had been a tall, distinguished-looking individual with an aristocratic nose and an air of proud masculinity. In fact, the rest of the family as well as friends had, in the past, made frequent comments about what a handsome couple Megha's parents made. The two had been brought together as very well-matched individuals in an arranged marriage.

Their three daughters were considered lucky to have inherited their tall and slim good looks from such remarkable-looking parents. Megha's older sisters had made excellent marriages because of their beauty. Megha probably would have done the same if circumstances had been different.

Noticing Megha's blister, her mother drew a hissing breath. "Oh Lord! What happened to you?"

"Cooking accident this morning," said Megha with a tired sigh.

"I have some cream for that. Let me get it." She returned in a minute and applied some yellowish stuff over the blister, all the while lecturing Megha on the importance of being careful while working with hot oil. Then taking the empty tumbler from Megha's other hand, she set it aside. "It is your first anniversary today, Megha. Shouldn't you be with Suresh?"

"Suresh went to work as usual, Avva. He didn't even remember it was our anniversary."

Her mother's anxious eyes met her father's bespectacled ones across the room for a brief moment before they returned to Megha. "Maybe he'll remember later."

Shaking her head, Megha buried her face in her hands. She couldn't trust her voice. She knew the tears would start flowing soon. Seeing her parents had reopened the still-throbbing wound of disappointment that had formed that morning. The long trek in the sun had not helped in the least. If anything, the exhaustion made her feel shaky and a headache was setting in. Her legs and lower back ached. The glass of cold water she'd just finished, instead of easing her stomach, was making her queasier. The burn on her wrist felt worse with Avva's cream smeared over it.

Her mother came to sit on the armrest of the chair and ran her hand along Megha's back. "I'm sorry, *putti*. I know you are disappointed."

"Sorry is not going to make Suresh a better man, is it?"

"But Suresh is not a bad boy. He may bring you something nice when he comes home from work. He may be planning a surprise, no?"

"He won't! He doesn't care about anyone but himself. And his mother is even more selfish than he. I hate her, that fat, waddling bitch."

Her mother's shocked gasp was unmistakable. "Megha! You should not talk about your mother-in-law like that!"

"She deserves that and more. She treats me worse than a servant."

"*Ayyo*, you poor child!" Somehow Avva's clumsy efforts at comforting her made the situation worse instead of better. Megha burst into bitter sobs.

Her mother continued stroking her back. "Shhh . . . shhh . . . everything will be all right, *putti*. You wait and see."

Megha looked up to note her father's reaction to her tears. He eyed the scene briefly and then looked away. Uncertainty seemed to flicker in his eyes. He slowly rose from his chair and went to stand by the window, with his back to her. His thinning gray hair badly needed a cut. At the back it lay in limp wisps over the frayed collar of his once-white shirt. His appearance seemed to fit in with the shabbiness of his house by the river, with its peeling paint, its dusty, framed photographs, and its meager furnishings. There was never enough money to live comfortably.

Realizing it was hopeless to expect her old-fashioned parents to understand, Megha blew her nose in her handkerchief and jumped out of the chair to face her parents. "You two don't understand! For your generation an anniversary is like any other day. I'm twenty-one years old. Things are different nowadays. Young people celebrate anniversaries and birthdays with parties and cakes and candles, and they have real honeymoons after their weddings."

"But, Megha—"

"Nobody bothered to acknowledge my birthday two months ago. Now nobody cares about my first wedding anniversary. The family made a big deal about Mala's thirteenth birthday and her puberty, but I might as well be the untouchable slave in the house. They don't care, Avva—they just don't give a damn. Those selfish bastards!"

Mangala sighed in helpless frustration and repeated, "I'm sorry."

Megha wearily picked up her bag and headed for the room that she and her sisters had shared when they were growing up. "I'm going to rest for a while and then go out for a walk by the river." She turned around to face her parents for a moment. "Is it okay if I stay here tonight?"

Her mother nodded. "Of course. You look tired, dear. Have you eaten any lunch?"

Megha said yes even though it wasn't true. She hadn't eaten anything, but the very thought of food was making her sick. All she wanted to do was curl up and sleep. She glanced once again at her father for his response to her request to spend the night.

Her father stood rooted to the spot like a statue. He was even more conservative than his wife. Megha knew precisely what he was thinking: he was wondering why she was here when her place was with her husband, especially on the day of her anniversary. At that moment, she felt nothing but apathy for her father. He didn't seem at all concerned about her. He was only a notch above the Ramnaths where emotions were concerned. He hadn't said one word to her since her arrival a few minutes ago. He had displayed mild pleasure at seeing her at first, even smiled a bit, but had turned cold and silent when she had explained why she was there. In his mind this was not a social call—she was running away from her husband—and for ridiculous and childish reasons, too.

Did her father have no feelings for her at all? Was she so much of a liability to him, that much of a dark cloud hanging over his head?

She turned on her heel and strode into the bedroom, entirely disgusted with her father. Then she shut the door and sat on the extra-large bed she had shared with her two sisters. The mattress smelled musty from lack of use. From the chest of drawers she pulled out clean sheets and pillowcases. Stubborn grease stains still marked the pillowcases—stains made from years of coconut-oil-glossed heads resting on them. Avva had always massaged coconut oil into the girls' scalps and woven their long hair into tight plaits secured with ribbons on the end.

Then Megha heard her parents talking about her. She wondered what they were saying. The need to know why they behaved the way they did, rather than idle curiosity, made Megha crack open the door and observe her parents in secret.

Mangala glanced at her husband, a crease in her forehead. "What did we do, Ree? Did we make a mistake by marrying her off in a hurry to the first man who was willing to accept a small dowry?"

Yes, it was a mistake, Avva, Megha silently pleaded. *Don't you two realize I'm miserable there?*

Lakshman finally turned from the window. "I'm not sure, Mangala. We did the best we could. We had just finished paying off the last part of the loan we took out for Hema's dowry. We should consider ourselves lucky that Suresh accepted our Megha for only fifty thousand rupees. Most others were asking for *lakhs.*"

Lucky! Was her father blind, or entirely insane?

Sinking into the chair Megha had just vacated, Mangala cupped her face in her hands and stared at the floor. "Still, maybe we should have let her study some more and look for a job."

"No! Definitely not a job!"

Why not, for heaven's sake? I'd have been happier working for a living.

"She wanted a master's degree and a job, but we forced her to get married. If not a degree then perhaps we should have looked for a boy elsewhere. She is a beautiful and bright child. We might have found someone good for her with no dowry."

Lakshman glowered at his wife. "Are you dreaming, Mangala? Who would marry a girl without a dowry in our caste? Even if she got another degree, she would have to get married *sometime.* How could a young woman stay single?"

"Girls work and remain single much longer these days," Mangala gently argued.

"Not our girls. It is unthinkable in our family. We would still have to pay the dowry—if not last year, then two years from now. No matter how educated and forward-thinking our caste is, when it comes to money and dowry matters it will never change."

"Still, we could have waited for another year at least, no?"

Lakshman Shastry closed his eyes wearily. "I'm already sixty-five years old. I have been retired for five years now. We had to make sure she was settled before I die."

"Ree, please don't talk about death," Mangala pleaded.

"Face it, Mangala. I could die tomorrow, and then what would you do? You would be a burden on Leela and Hema yourself. How would you support Megha and marry her off, too?"

A shadow crossed over Mangala's face. "But the Ramnaths have not turned out to be what we thought. Every time I see Megha she looks more unhappy. Leela and Hema are happy girls. They have good husbands and children, and big homes with servants and cooks. But our Megha has ended up in a small home where she works like a domestic servant day and night. Did you see that burn on her wrist just now? She never smiles anymore. She used to be such a cheerful child."

Cheerful? What is that?

Mangala shook her head. "Ree, I am convinced the astrologer lied to us. Why else would our Megha end up in such a house?"

"I know he lied to us, Mangala," said Lakshman. "I believe he may have been bribed by that Ramnath woman to find an attractive and intelligent girl for their ugly and dull son. He must have told us that Suresh is a good match for Megha just to make more money."

"It is too late to do anything now, no? I think poor Megha is going to suffer all her life because of somebody's greed."

Suffer all her life! Megha shuddered. Good Lord! It was entirely possible that the fat old witch had paid the astrologer to lie about Suresh's horoscope. Why hadn't Megha thought of that? Devious as Amma was, she'd do anything to have her way. And what about that bloody astrologer? Could he be that unscrupulous? Would he willingly ruin a girl's life for money?

Lakshman stared at the street scene outside the window once again. His hunched stance seemed glum. "Why has God been so unkind to our family, Mangala? I have tried my best. I am only a simple man with very large debts and failing health. I could die of heart failure any time. As a responsible father, what else could I do but marry our youngest daughter off as quickly as I could?"

I know you're poor, Appa, but you could have at least asked me what I wanted, couldn't you? I would have gladly worked and given you my entire salary to pay off your debts.

With a resigned shrug Megha's father started to lumber towards the master bedroom. His arthritis made his gait slow and cumbersome. "Girls these days read all those silly magazines and see too many Hindi films. Then they think their life is dull because their husbands don't sing to them like movie heroes and don't buy costly presents. Once Megha gets over this childish phase, she will be okay."

No, Appa. I'll never be okay. I'll wither and die in that miserable house in Cantonment Galli.

His wife fixed him with a skeptical frown. "I'm not so sure, Ree. Her mother-in-law is a mean and cruel woman. Everyone is afraid of her."

Not just afraid but terrified.

Lakshman made a familiar gesture of dismissal with his withered hand. "I think that Ramnath woman is abusive to Megha because I have not been able to pay her dowry. Next year, if the mango harvest is a little better, maybe I can pay the first installment. After that, everything will be okay. Just wait and see. It is all about the money, I tell you."

"*If* the mango harvest is better? When is it ever better?"

Shaking his head as if in obvious defeat, he pressed his gnarled fingers to his eyes. "I wish I had money to give now. Those people . . . so very greedy . . ." He disappeared inside the bedroom for his afternoon nap. His wife watched him for a moment then followed him.

Megha shut her door quietly and settled down on the bed. The room was dark and cool and silent, like a deep cavern. She closed her eyes and slipped into glorious sleep within seconds, sleeping for nearly three hours.

A cup of steaming hot tea and some biscuits that her mother gave her after her long nap left Megha feeling somewhat refreshed. She hadn't slept so long in the middle of the day in years. She began to accept the fact that her anniversary was going to be like any other day—gray and cheerless. As they sipped their tea, her mother kept up a steady chatter about Megha's sisters and their respective children, the neighbors, and the fast-approaching *Diwali* festival. But her father's brows were drawn in deep thought. Or was it disapproval? He barely glanced at Megha, making her feel further unwelcome.

She went back to her room to get changed and comb her hair. As she applied the symbolic red dot on her forehead she paused for a second. Wasn't that ironic? Here she was, religiously putting on the traditional marriage symbol of a *bindi* while her husband was out there somewhere, entirely oblivious to the fact that he had a wife.

Once or twice she had wondered if Suresh had a girlfriend or a keep somewhere, but then she'd dismissed the idea immediately. He was too cheap and too stupid to carry on an affair. And what woman would want an unattractive and stingy squirrel like Suresh, unless she was blind, or uglier than him, or just plain desperate. And he was an appalling lover, too. No sane woman would want that cold, inconsiderate pile of skin and bones in her bed.

Megha briefly stuck her head in the kitchen to tell her parents she was going for a walk and headed out the door.

"Be careful, and come home before it gets dark," her mother reminded her.

Megha took a deep, cleansing breath outside the door. The afternoon heat had ebbed and a slight breeze from the river was blowing her way. It was pleasant, the perfect time of day for a stroll. She waved at their neighbor across the street. Mrs. Shanmugam, wearing a maroon sari, her dark hair oiled and combed back in a bun, was sitting on her stoop as always and waved back. Noticing the curious look on the woman's face and how she adjusted her glasses, Megha kept walking at a brisk pace. If she stopped to say hello, she'd be subjected to the older woman's stories.

She was in no mood to answer inquisitive questions and feed the local gossip mill. She certainly didn't want to hear about how Mrs. Shanmugam's daughter's rich husband had bought a new car or that he had given his wife a new gold necklace.

Megha wasn't an envious sort, but today was a bad day to hear about someone's blissful marriage and what their money could buy.

In a little while the river came into view, immediately lifting her spirits. It made an awesome sight as it cut a wicked path through the town, like a cool, flowing ribbon of water, making a gurgling sound while it slithered over rocks and driftwood. Megha loved the river. Since she was born and raised in her parents' house nearby, the riverbank had served as a childhood playground. It was also a very short distance from her father's modest mango grove.

She studied the orchard now as she walked past it. The mango season was long over. The grove looked pathetic sitting next to the lush rubber plantations belonging to the maharaja of Palgaum. The royal plantations were abundantly healthy, neat and professionally maintained, while her father's mango trees, without proper fertilizing and pruning, looked droopy and produced very little fruit. Despite the maharaja's offer to buy the land, her father stubbornly hung on to it for sentimental reasons—his family had owned it for generations. Besides, it was his insurance policy—in the event of his death, his wife could sell the plot of land to the royal family and have a little money to live on. With each passing year the land became that much more valuable, but it didn't do the Shastry family any good in the meantime.

Megha's father had worked as a horticulturist in the district horticulture department. The family's mango orchard had provided a small additional income over the years. Like all government employees, he had been forced to retire at the age of sixty and now all her parents were left with was a small pension and an unreliable crop of mangoes that depended solely on the erratic weather. Whatever fruit the vagrants didn't steal, and the birds and insects didn't destroy, were sold for a pittance in the open market. It was hardly enough to get by on.

Things hadn't been so bad when Megha's older sisters were growing up. Her father's government salary had provided the family with a decent enough living. But educating the girls and getting the first two married had been expensive. The dowries alone had cast her parents into heavy debt. Megha had always abhorred the idea of dowry—now she hated it even more. It was a curse—it had brought her nothing but grief. If she ever gave birth to a daughter someday, she'd never pay dowry; she'd find her a kind man who cared more about integrity and family values than money, a man who would love and cherish his wife.

She walked steadily for a while until she came to the giant banyan tree with its extra wide branches that looked like tentacles. She was tired from the brisk exercise. Her feet and back still hurt, despite the long nap.

Finding her favorite boulder under the tree unoccupied, she sank onto it to catch her breath. It felt good to rest. From centuries of use as a seat the surface of the rock was smooth as butter. At the moment it was warm from having absorbed the afternoon heat.

As a young girl she had often come to this spot to contemplate or regain her composure after a quarrel with friends or sisters. Except for Harini, she had lost touch with most of her friends in the past year. Lucky girls, they were still single and carefree souls. Some of them had jobs while others were pursuing advanced degrees. She missed them. She missed her sisters, too, although they had married and moved out years ago. Hema and Leela couldn't make frequent trips to Palgaum because of their children's school schedules.

Noting the time on her wristwatch she figured Suresh would be home by now. Had he wondered why she wasn't home or didn't he even notice that she wasn't there to greet him with the customary cup of tea and snack?

Amma was probably sulking about having to serve tea to the family. Well, Amma would have to manage. It would do her good to move that mammoth body once in a while. Today was *satsang* day, singing spiritual songs and hymns and chanting with a religious group, so she would probably head out with her sisters-in-law and her lady friends to chant for an hour or two and then the women would let their tongues wag. Amma was likely to come home in a foul mood because there would be no fresh meal waiting for her. She would have to warm up the left-overs from lunch for the family's dinner and then clear the table and clean up the kitchen—in other words, do what Megha did every evening.

The old battleaxe would no doubt work herself into a ferocious mood.

As Megha's breath became even and the perspiration on her face evaporated, she lifted her gaze to the horizon. The sun was getting ready to set. It was a blazing orange ball, gently hovering over the river's edge, appearing hesitant about retiring for the day. The waves on the river shimmered—long slivers of undulating russet and gold.

This part of town was much quieter than the one she lived in, but there were still a few people moving about. Several women, having finished washing their clothes in the river, passed her by with their wash-baskets. She marveled at how they balanced the baskets over their heads with old saris rolled into tight round coils to cup them, so their two hands could be free to lug other articles. They were probably heading home to fire up their hearths to cook supper. Megha watched their sunburned children moan and protest about having to return home.

The old beggar sat on the ground under a nearby tree some distance away and hungrily consumed a meal off a tin plate—someone had likely given him their leftovers from lunch. It was probably the only food he'd had all day. Although he looked wild with his long, unwashed hair and tattered clothes, he didn't frighten Megha. He had been living under the protective shade of that tree for years. She'd seen him there since she was a child. He looked older and scrawnier now. In the monsoon season and at nights he moved to the shelter of the nearby temple. She continued to sit there because she knew the beggar was harmless.

"Megha." A deep male voice jolted her from her reverie, making her turn her head.

It was Kiran, Suresh's cousin.

"Hello!" She was surprised to see him. "What are you doing here, Kiran?" She quickly surveyed his tall, athletic figure dressed in a tan open-neck shirt and crisp brown trousers. He walked towards her with a confident stride.

"I was going for a much-needed walk after sitting in a cramped airplane seat. I just returned from a business trip to Mumbai," Kiran explained. "Mind if I sit down?" His brows were raised in question.

"Not at all." She slid over to the far end of the boulder to make room for him. Always the gentleman, she noted. He even asked for permission before he sat down. "So how was Mumbai?"

"Hot and crowded and stifling. And the return flight was delayed."

"By then it was too late to go to the office, I gather?"

He nodded. "I decided to take a walk along the river instead, stretch my legs a bit and enjoy the sunset."

She smiled. "Me, too. I came to visit my parents and needed to get out for some fresh air."

"This is a beautiful spot, isn't it—the most scenic view of the river and the temple? I'm sure your poetic mind appreciates it more than the rest of us."

"As a matter of fact it reminds me of something written by Sara Teasdale."

"Teasdale, the American poet?"

Megha looked at him in pleased surprise. "You know about her?" Indian men and even women typically were not interested in poetry and poets, let alone one who wasn't all that well-known outside the literary and academic communities. Most people knew names like Wordsworth and Byron and Tennyson, but Teasdale?

Kiran shrugged. "My English teacher in high school might have mentioned her once or twice . . . I think." He quirked a brow at her. 'You actually remember the poems you studied in school?"

"Not all of them. Teasdale just happens to be one of my favorite poets."

"Can you recall enough to recite something?"

"You don't mean *now*!"

"Why not?"

Megha threw him a wry look. Was he pulling her leg? No one other than her poetry teacher at school had ever asked her to deliver a poem. "Come on, Kiran, you don't really want to hear someone reciting poetry."

"I happen to like it." He grinned at her. "Contrary to popular belief, real men do like poetry."

"Oh, all right," she said with a chuckle and tried to recall something that was appropriate for the moment. "Stop me if you're bored," she warned him, "but this one is called *Dusk in June*. I think it suits the present setting:

Evening, and all the birds
In a chorus of shimmering sound
Are easing their hearts of joy
For miles around.
The air is blue and sweet,
The first few stars are white.
Oh let me like the birds
Sing before night."

Kiran looked delighted. "That was beautiful, Megha. And to think you remember it so well! I'll be damned if I can think of a single line."

"But I bet you remember all your mathematical equations and formulae from high school. I can't recall anything beyond long division." She rolled her eyes. "I'd have preferred to have a mathematical brain like yours instead of the one I have."

Kiran feigned a puzzled look. "Hmm, I've always wondered why beautiful scenery tends to inspire poetry and not geometry. Pythagoras could be so much more exciting than Keats, don't you think?"

Megha snickered. "Oh yes. Amma always reminds me, 'Mathematics is the basis of all rational thinking.'" Megha managed to do a convincing imitation of Amma, including the imperious raised eyebrow and fists planted on the hips.

Amused by her antics, Kiran laughed out loud. "Well, despite

Amma's philosophy I still think the sunset here is worthy of poetry."

"I agree. Even as a child I often came here to think. I still come here to contemplate," she told him.

"You must have been contemplating a serious matter or composing a poem of your own before I showed up," he teased, "judging from your frown."

"I tend to frown when I think." Was it becoming a habit lately? Too much frowning caused early wrinkles, according to Harini.

"This used to be one of my favorite places, too, especially during my summer holidays. How come I never saw you here before?" he asked.

"My friends and I played around this general area." She motioned with one hand. It would have been hard for a well-to-do boy like Kiran to mix with the likes of her. He had probably mingled with his own kind: children who were educated in exclusive boarding schools and played sophisticated sports like cricket and tennis and golf—not street hopscotch and card games played with dog-eared cards, as she had. Besides, he was a few years older than she was.

"I generally met my friends over there." He pointed toward the royal plantation.

She laughed gently. "If that's where you played your games, you probably socialized with the royal princes."

"I went to school with Suraj Kane, brother of the present maharaja of Palgaum."

"I thought so. Even if you saw me in those days, how would you know who I was, Kiran? I looked just like dozens of other little girls."

"Believe me, if I'd seen you when I was in my teens, when I had nothing but girls on my mind, I'd have turned around and taken a second look—a pretty girl like you. The rest of the girls would be nothing like you." A wicked sparkle in his eye told her he was merely indulging in a little harmless flirting with her.

"You're very kind, Kiran." Despite knowing it was friendly ribbing, her cheeks felt warm at the unexpected compliment.

His gaze suddenly came to settle on the red blotch on her wrist and his expression turned serious. "What happened to your wrist?" He studied the blister for a second then sent her a wary look.

Embarrassed, she laid the wrist face down in her lap. Was it her imagination or did he seem suspicious? Surely he didn't think Suresh was physically abusing her? Suresh was an indifferent and thoughtless husband, but he had never raised his hand to her. "Hot oil splatter—I got careless while cooking."

"Have you put any kind of medicine on it?" Kiran's tone was filled with concern.

She nodded. "My mother put some cream on it."

He slid closer to her, picked up her wrist and examined it. "The blister looks fresh. It must hurt like hell. You'd better take good care of it, Megha. Burns can easily get infected if you neglect them. Didn't Suresh notice it?"

Megha gazed out on the water for several long seconds before she spoke. "It's a minor burn—it'll disappear in no time."

"Megha, I asked you if Suresh had seen it." His voice was one of quiet authority—something she'd never heard before. Was that the managerial tone he used in his office?

"Not yet. It happened after he left for work. But then Suresh notices very little. He didn't even notice that today was our first wedding anniversary."

Kiran's eyes widened with outrage. "That thoughtless bastard!" He immediately offered her an apologetic shrug. "Sorry . . . pardon my language."

"Don't be sorry. Those were my sentiments, too. I was so upset at Suresh's behavior that I decided to get out of there and go to my parents' house. I'm planning to spend the night there, just to get even with him."

"I'm sorry to hear that, Megha. I expected better than that from Suresh."

She shrugged it off and glanced again at the setting sun, now only a thin, salmon sliver. Dusk was beginning to settle around them, the mosquitoes becoming more abundant. The twittering birds in the tree overhead had quieted down, indicating they were settled for the night.

Nearby, the temple lights came on. There were no lights by the river and the fog had a way of rising unexpectedly after sunset. Getting lost in it was like walking with a blindfold on. So she quickly rose from the rock. "I better head on home. It's getting dark."

Kiran sprang to his feet. "I'll walk you home."

"I can find my way," she assured him with a smile. "I'm a grown woman and I'm familiar with the neighborhood."

"With the fog rolling in it's not safe for you to walk alone, Megha. I'm going to see you home."

"That may not be a good idea. I appreciate your concern, but . . . my parents won't like seeing me with you." She fixed him with a regretful look and plunged into an explanation. "Nothing personal, but you know how it is—old-fashioned customs and all."

He brushed the dust off the seat of his slacks. "Don't worry—I won't go all the way to your door, only to the end of your street. I just want to make sure you're safe."

How considerate, Megha reflected. No one, not even her own father had walked with her in recent years to any place to ensure her safety. "Thank you."

They began to walk back slowly, watching the lights come on in homes and businesses in the distance, listening to the sounds of rushing water, observing the fireflies make weird illuminated patterns in the rubber plantations.

Despite the awkwardness of strolling on a balmy evening with her cousin-in-law, Megha realized with a pang that it was pleasant. Kiran was fun to be with. He had even managed to get her mind off the anniversary fiasco.

But she shouldn't be enjoying his company, she admonished herself. How could she? It was wrong for her to appreciate any man other than her husband. It was unnatural.

It was going against everything she'd been taught.

The loud honking of a truck passing by jolted Megha out of her reverie.

Chapter 22

Kiran's mind refused to dwell on work. His hands remained on his computer keyboard, but they barely moved. His secretary had looked at him strangely a few times—sort of a perplexed look combined with curiosity. When one of his analysts had popped in earlier to ask a question, he had more or less brushed him off. It wasn't Kiran's nature to ever neglect his work or his staff, but it had happened. He'd have to apologize to the man later.

Megha often monopolized his thoughts, but lately it had become worse. Perhaps because he knew now what it felt like to hold her, love her, feel her body come alive under his hands. Or was it because he'd nearly lost her? He continued to worry about her emotional state. Would she attempt suicide again? Thank God he'd reached her in time and drummed some sense into that beautiful but stubborn head the last time, when she'd tried to drown herself in the river. The experience had shaken him. The river. It held some powerful memories.

The walk along the river with Megha not too long ago came to mind. He remembered it vividly.

Kiran stole another glance at Megha as she strolled by his side in silence. Being a tall woman, her stride nearly matched his. She had a graceful walk.

It had been an unexpected joy to find Megha by the riverbank. Alone. His mind had gone into a tailspin the minute he'd recognized the lone figure sitting under the banyan tree. She had cut a forlorn image, her profile against the setting sun looking grim. At first he'd assumed his mind was playing tricks on him. His sensual dreams and thoughts about Megha had been playing havoc with his brain. When he'd realized it was indeed Megha in the flesh, he had stopped just short of running towards her.

He had missed her while he was in Mumbai. When he'd passed by the clothing stores with their willowy mannequins in the windows wearing chic outfits, he'd thought of Megha dressed in them. She'd have looked superb. When he'd eaten a particularly enjoyable dinner at a popular restaurant, he'd wondered if she would have enjoyed it, too. When he'd picked furniture for his new flat in Mumbai, he'd wished Megha had been there to help him choose it.

Now, she had mentioned the forgotten anniversary. That explained her sad look. How could Suresh have forgotten his own wedding day, especially when he had Megha for a wife? Most men would be thrilled to celebrate having a woman like Megha in their lives. Kiran's jaw hardened in anger at what he considered Suresh's gross negligence of his wife. Suresh needed to have his skinny little ass flogged for his carelessness, or at the very least have his ignorant head examined.

They left the riverbank and reached the paved road and footpath, then continued to walk at a less leisurely pace. It was a little more difficult to walk together now, with other pedestrians weaving their way in and out. A young man sped past them on his bicycle, whistling a familiar tune. Kiran threw her a sidelong glance. "Remember that song? What was it . . . about five years ago that it became so popular?"

She nodded. "It used to be one of my favorites. But then, at sixteen, every other movie song seemed to be the favorite." She chuckled. "Until a new one came along."

Sixteen? Of course! Only a child, he thought unhappily. She was so young—and already married a year. A bright and spirited girl like her should have been enjoying her youth, acquiring advanced education, perhaps even pursuing a career. Once again he wondered why her parents had married her off to his pitiful cousin. Was it only the question of dowry or was there something else underneath the surface?

As they drew closer to town and its clusters of homes, a flower vendor approached them with dainty jasmine *gajras*—small garlands that women wore in their hair as adornments. "*Saheb*, *gajra* for your missus? Very fresh," the vendor called out. The heady, seductive scent of jasmine was potent as it floated across the way from the florist's basket.

Kiran noticed Megha stiffen and shift away from him.

The florist had assumed they were married, since they were walking together along the riverfront. Romantic walks in this town were reserved for the married. Besides, the *mangalsutra* around her neck clearly announced to the world that she was married. The florist's blunder didn't bother Kiran in the least, but Megha looked mortified.

Who else could have seen them together and jumped to the same conclusion? A quick glance around showed there were lots of people walking about. Neither he nor Megha had been paying much attention to the scene around them.

Despite his mild concerns for Megha's reputation, on an impulse Kiran pulled out his wallet to buy a *gajra*. "Take your pick, Megha," he said, motioning her to come forward.

She frowned at him and shook her head. "No, please."

"Then you'll have to settle for my choice." He picked one with snowy white jasmine and tiny red roses contrasted with the fragrant, grayish-green herb called *marva*. It seemed like the prettiest one in the bunch.

But when he held it out to Megha, she refused to accept it. "I can't take that from you, Kiran. But thanks, anyway." She must have seen the puzzled look in his eyes, for she added, "Why don't you take it to your mother?"

He smiled. "Consider it a small and insignificant anniversary gift, Megha. Had I known it was such a special day, I would have brought a proper gift for you and Suresh."

Upon Kiran's insisting, Megha reluctantly accepted the flowers, but tears gathered in her eyes, surprising him, making him wonder if buying her flowers was a mistake. She looked down at the ground and bit her lower lip, perhaps to control the tears. "My parents will wonder where I got it."

"Tell them you bought it for yourself," he said, hoping to make light of the situation.

She gazed at the garland in her hand as if it was priceless gold. "Thank you. It's thoughtful of you. You're very kind, Kiran."

"It's nothing." Kiran realized this was the second time she had referred to him as kind. The sentiment tugged at him. Was she starved for appreciation, and never received any? His aversion to Suresh was increasing by the minute. In fact, it was turning into full-blown loathing and Kiran didn't like the feeling. It wasn't like him to feel animosity toward anyone, and so it irritated him even more.

Megha tucked the *gajra* in her braid. Perhaps from seeing the look of frank admiration in Kiran's eyes, the color seemed to rise in her face. "It's not right for me to accept gifts from a man other than Suresh or my father, Kiran," she said, raising a nervous hand to her hair to make sure the flowers were secured properly. The tears were now rolling down her cheeks.

His eyebrows arched. "Why the tears, Megha? Have I made you feel that guilty?" Now he was really feeling like a heel.

"No, it's just that . . . no one's ever bought me flowers before." She sniffed and dried her eyes with a handkerchief. "Don't pay any attention to me. For some reason I'm more emotional than usual today."

"There's nothing wrong in being emotional. Everyone needs a little emotion in their lives. If Suresh missed spending this day with you, it's his loss."

As they approached a busy intersection, she threw a cautious glance over her shoulder. "My father usually takes a walk at this hour. If he catches me talking to you, he'll have a fit." After another quick precautionary look around, she said, "Thanks again, Kiran. I can see my way home from here."

"Megha."

"Yes?"

"Make sure you take care of that burn on your wrist."

"I will. Thanks."

"And . . . try to cheer up."

She nodded and turned to cross the street.

"Happy anniversary, Megha," he whispered, knowing for sure that she couldn't hear it. She was already striding in the direction of her father's house.

He waited and watched until she disappeared around the bend. What a sheer waste of beauty and brains, he rued for the hundredth time since he'd met her. Strange that he should be the one to spend her anniversary evening with her rather than her husband. It had taken every ounce of his self-control to keep himself from touching her. She had looked so utterly vulnerable this evening. He couldn't believe a simple string of flowers had reduced her to tears. Well, it certainly had been a memorable evening.

An odd sense of loneliness and disquiet settled over Kiran as he walked home.

Chapter 23

Brushing aside her memories of the walk by the river with Kiran, Megha forced her mind to return to the present and moved away from the window and the sight of the children in the park. She spent long moments observing the kids each day. As much as she liked watching them play and hearing their voices, it was painful, too. Her miscarriage still haunted her.

That ill-fated night, after Kiran had bought her the flowers and escorted her home, she'd felt drained. The exhaustion was beyond ordinary fatigue. After eating a small meal at her mother's coaxing, she had gone straight to bed, hoping the tiredness would diminish after a night's rest. Maybe she was coming down with the flu or something.

Megha remembered that night all too well. Just thinking about it made her stomach cramp up—even now.

She was deep in sleep when the first stab of pain speared through her middle. She came wide awake in an instant. What in God's name was *that*? She rolled onto her side and the pain eased a bit. She took a deep breath and exhaled slowly. Just as she tried to go back to sleep another vicious stab penetrated her abdomen.

Easing herself into a sitting position, she took a few deep breaths. That didn't help either. One sharp spasm of pain after another started to rack her body. She tried to rise to her feet, but ended up collapsing to the floor, feeling dizzy and weak. She frowned in panic. Something was terribly wrong with her. Was it something she had eaten earlier that night? But then, her parents had eaten the same things. They were sleeping peacefully in the next room. Her father's snoring was unmistakable.

Should she awaken her mother? When the next wave of agony washed over her, she had no doubt she was in serious trouble. She had no choice but to disturb her parents, so she knocked on the wall that separated her room from theirs. There was no response. She could hear Appa's snoring continue uninterrupted.

Waiting for the next surge of pain to pass, she knocked again—harder this time. In the next room she heard her mother's startled reaction. "Ree, did you hear that?"

Then her father's sluggish voice responded, "Hmm? Someone . . . knocking on the door or what?"

Realizing her parents were disoriented from their abrupt awakening, she desperately pounded on the wall once again. A second later her mother rushed into the room and switched on the light. She gasped in shock when she saw Megha sitting on the floor, clutching her abdomen. "*Ayyo*, Megha!" She sank to the floor beside her. "What is it, *putti?*"

"I . . . I'm in pain, Avva," she managed to whisper. Her face crumpled in agony.

Her mother managed to help her up and move her back to the bed. But she looked at the sheets and stopped short. "Oh my God! You are bleeding!"

Megha cried in pain again, but waited to let the cramp ease before she glanced at the blood. Good Lord! Where had all that blood come from? She drew in a ragged breath. "It—it looks horrible!" Dismayed, she frowned at her mother. "What's happening to me, Avva?"

Her mother looked too stunned to say anything. She was silent for a full minute before she spoke again. "Did you miss your monthly cycles recently?"

Despite the pain, Megha tried hard to think. She recalled wondering why she had been so late this month. She calculated the dates in her mind. It had been several weeks since her last cycle. After a few moments she nodded. "I think I'm about six weeks late."

Mangala examined the sheets once again, still looking dazed. "Oh, God! I think you are having a miscarriage."

"Miscarriage!" Megha stared agape at her mother. "But . . . but how can I have a miscarriage when I'm not pregnant?"

"It looks like that, no? I can't think of anything else for this kind of bleeding."

Megha puzzled over her mother's remark. Was a very late cycle a sure sign of pregnancy? She wasn't sure. She'd felt extremely tired lately, and that was because of all that hard work . . . or so she had assumed. She hadn't experienced any cravings or bloating or any of those other symptoms Harini had described to her. She had been getting lessons from Harini about what to expect when one got pregnant. But then, her mother was knowledgeable about these matters—much more so than young Harini. Avva was probably right. She gripped her belly as she felt the next cramp seize her.

Visibly shaken and distraught, her mother rose to hurry out of the room. "I better get your Appa."

Megha's father looked pale when he came into the room. His hair was sticking out in various directions and his nightshirt looked a hundred years old as he approached the bed to study Megha's plight. "I'll get dressed and walk over to Dr. Sanghvi's house," he murmured. "I hope he can come straight away." He gave Megha a long, anxious look before leaving.

While they waited for the doctor to arrive with her father, Megha rested her head in her mother's lap. "Oh *putti*, this is all my fault," Avva said ruefully. "I should have noticed you looked different when you arrived this afternoon. You were more upset than usual, your face was flushed. I should have guessed that you might be expecting a baby. I should not have allowed you to walk so much. I think you strained yourself, no?"

"It's not your fault, Avva. I'm the one who should have known. How could I be so stupid?" It wasn't fair, this gut-wrenching agony. Damn it, it just wasn't fair! She had tried to be a good person all her life. She had been taught by her parents and the nuns at school that being upstanding and decent always brought one good things. Except for a few minor lies, she had led an honest life. She said her prayers each day. To make sure she covered all bases, she said her Hindu prayers as well as the Lord's Prayer and a Hail Mary. And what had she got in return? Grief! And more grief!

Her mother pushed a damp lock of Megha's hair off her face. "Don't blame yourself. You are so young. How would you know how to recognize the signs of pregnancy? When I was pregnant with your eldest sister, I was only a teenager, and didn't realize until I was almost three months along that something was different."

Megha glanced in disgust at the bloodstains on the sheet. She had waited so long to get pregnant. Her mother was probably right. She had walked a long distance—first the walk from her in-laws' home to her parents' in the merciless afternoon heat, and then the evening walk along the river. In the process she had inadvertently hurt her unborn child. Dear God, why had she not recognized the signs of pregnancy? Another cramp sliced through her just then, and she squirmed.

Would Suresh even care if he found out? Or would he be furious with her?

As if reading her daughter's thoughts, her mother stirred. "Maybe I should go over to the neighbor's house and use their phone to call Suresh."

"No!"

"He should be here with you."

Megha grabbed her mother's wrist. "Please," she cried, "I don't want Suresh here."

"But Suresh is your husband, dear. He should be told."

"No, it's best that he doesn't know. He'll run to tell his Amma and she'll blame me for this. She hates me. Now she'll hate me more. She'll say I've robbed her of a precious grandchild."

"But how can she blame you for something like this? It can happen to anyone."

Megha shot her mother a wry look. God, for a mature

woman her mother was so incredibly naïve, almost pathetic. "Avva, believe me, I manage to get the blame for everything that goes wrong in that house. Amma sees to it. Suresh lets her see to it."

Mangala leaned back against the headboard and let out a deep sigh. "What kind of *naraka* are the Ramnaths giving you, Megha? Oh baby, you look so sad these days."

Megha knew *naraka* meant hell "*Naraka* is what it really is, Avva," Megha said and closed her eyes.

Dr. Sanghvi and Megha's father arrived a while later. The doctor had treated their family for years. He was a small, bald, tired-looking man who should have retired years ago, but continued to work. He looked as if he would die healing people— he was that dedicated to his profession. He confirmed her mother's suspicions after questioning Megha about various things.

"It's my fault, isn't it? What did I do wrong?" Megha asked him anxiously.

He shook his head. "It can happen at times for no reason. That is why we call it a spontaneous abortion."

"Then it was not my fault?" she said, badly needing confirmation.

"No," he assured her. "Sometimes, if the fetus is malformed or abnormal, nature aborts it for a good reason. Occasionally a lack of the hormone progesterone can also lead to a miscarriage."

Megha sank back against the pillow, feeling the first wave of relief sink in. It wasn't her fault. Thank God!

Dr. Sanghvi then carefully examined her, the bunched-up sheets, and the undergarment Megha had been asked to discard. "Early stages of pregnancy. It looks like the fetus has been completely expelled."

"Are you sure, Doctor?" Megha's mother looked at him with an uncertain expression.

"Quite sure," the frail doctor replied. "I'll give her something for the cramps. The bleeding should stop within a day or two." He rummaged through the contents of his well-worn brown leather bag, pulled out a sample of some tablets in a foil pack and handed them to Mangala. "Give her one right now. The pain should ease and she will sleep. She might be sleeping a lot, so don't worry if she does. Let her stay in bed until the bleeding completely stops, okay? She needs to rest."

Megha quietly swallowed the tablet with the cold water her father fetched in a tumbler. At this point she was willing to do anything to get this over with. Then her mother helped her up and to the bathroom to get washed. After making the slow trip back from the bathroom, she changed into a faded kaftan that belonged to her teenage years and sank onto clean sheets that her father had spread over the bed. The simple effort left her feeble and shaky.

Her eyes settled on the soiled sheets heaped in the corner of the room. All that she had hoped for during the past year was reduced to a tiny ball of bloody mucus, swaddled in old, faded sheets. How could a fetus, a living, breathing, baby-in-the-making be eliminated so easily? She had never given serious thought to conceiving and giving birth. It had always seemed like an easy and logical thing: one got married, had sex and then there would be a baby. Who would have thought of serious setbacks like a miscarriage? The sheets seemed to mock her even as they lay huddled on the floor. She couldn't even carry a baby to full term.

In that moment—Megha truly believed that nothing she did would ever come out perfect. Amma was right: her fate was flawed and her life would end in failure. Mistakes made in her past incarnations were catching up with her.

She turned to her mother and found her shedding silent tears. At seeing Avva so grief-stricken, her own sobs erupted. She put her arms around her mother, both to give comfort as well as to receive.

The two women held each other and cried. They wept for the baby that would never be, for Megha's cursed fate that had placed her amidst the Ramnaths, for the complete waste of a young and beautiful woman's life, and for the physical and emotional pain this episode had brought. They shed tears until there were none left, then Megha slid back down on the bed and lay down, exhausted.

She sensed her mother sliding in next to her and pulling a sheet over both of them. She felt Avva's arm come around to hold her. Avva hadn't done that in years. Did she, too, need the warmth and comfort as much as Megha did? "Avva?" she said.

"Try to get some rest," whispered her mother. "I will stay here with you."

"Do you think God is punishing me for something I did when I was little?"

Her mother was quiet for a long time. "You were a good girl when you were little, Megha. You are still a good girl. I think we all bring our punishment with us . . . you know . . . to make up for sins from our previous lives. It follows us through every life, again and again, making sure that we pay for everything, the good and the bad, until we have finished paying. Then we are free to become pure, and go to God . . . forever."

"Hmm." Megha pondered that bit of deep philosophy for a minute. It was rather complicated to comprehend. "Do you think there is a lot more bad fate for me, or do you think this is it?"

"Only God knows that." Avva patted her hip. "Shh, go to sleep now. Perhaps things will get better after today, no?"

"Do you think if I pray to Lord Ganesh he will remove all my hurdles, my bad *karma*?"

"He may or he may not, but prayer is never wasted. Even if God does nothing, it always makes you feel better. Prayer is good for the *atma*. Soul."

Megha cuddled close to her mother and said a quick prayer. Her father must have taken care of the doctor's fees, she figured, as she tried to block everything else out of her mind except the need to get rid of the physical pain. She would repay her father later. She didn't want to be more of a burden to him than she already was.

Then she closed her eyes. There would be plenty of time later to grieve the loss of her potential son or daughter. At the moment she just wanted to sleep and forget it ever happened. She was lucky this had occurred at her parents' home. She needed her mother, now more than ever. If it had happened at her in-laws' house she would have choked from the sheer lack of sympathy and their disdain. She preferred not to speculate about what Amma would have said and done.

As the medicine started to take effect and the cramps began to ebb, she started to feel lightheaded, like she was floating in a white mist. Images began to dance across her delirious mind. Pleasant images . . . from her childhood . . . things she'd done when her father was a handsome man with a capacity for laughter . . . games she had played with her friends and sisters. Avva was even more beautiful then and so much happier.

It felt good to let Avva hold her like this. Her mother was saying something in her soft, gentle voice, just like she had when Megha had been ill when she was a little girl. Yes, it was nice to be with Avva—she always smelled of talcum powder and spices. She smelled exactly the same now.

Megha's last image before she fell asleep was of herself reaching out to touch the cool water of the river, but what she felt in her hand was not the ripple of water—instead, it was a delicate string of fragrant jasmine and *marva* and miniature roses. A deep male voice said to her, "Consider it a small and insignificant anniversary gift." She couldn't remember who had said that. She tried to jog her memory. For some reason it was important that she remember it. But her mind refused to cooperate and she gradually sank into oblivion.

The doctor's prescription must have been potent, because the next two days passed in a haze. She spent them in a semi-awake state, hallucinating off and on. Her mother gave her more of that medicine each time she complained of discomfort and helped her to the bathroom. She vaguely remembered Suresh's visit on the evening following her ordeal. Appa must have informed him.

She recalled Suresh sitting on the edge of the bed for a while and staring at her thoughtfully. Then he said something that sounded like, "So, when do you think you will be well enough to come home, Megha?"

She wasn't clear about her exact words, but she believed she had said, "I'm not sure. Perhaps in a day or two?"

Suresh had looked at her with very little sentiment in his insipid eyes. He could very well have been gazing at a rag doll. There was no physical contact, no apology for forgetting their anniversary, no mention of being worried about her, and no sympathy for her plight, either. All he cared about was her return home so she could go back to her daily grind of churning out elaborate breakfasts, lunches, teas and dinners for the family. In other words, he wanted the Ramnath family's unpaid servant to get back to her job as quickly as possible.

She longed for Suresh to hold her, tell her that he loved her, and assure her that she would get pregnant again soon. She would have settled for a mere touch. But she would never get that from him. She had to console herself by thinking she was lucky he had even bothered to visit her. He was probably convinced he had more than performed his husbandly duty by coming to see her and sitting beside her for a few minutes.

Maybe he didn't even know she had a miscarriage. Perhaps her parents had made up some other malady to protect her from Amma's wrath. She hoped they had concocted some credible story. Coming so soon after her defiant attitude towards Amma the other day, a miscarriage was not likely to make her popular with the Ramnaths. All at once she felt hopelessly tired and started to turn away from her husband.

Suresh rose to leave. "I have to go now, Megha."

Even now, as Megha worked in the kitchen, listening to the children's high-pitched voices across the street, her anger simmered. She had suffered a trauma the night she'd had that miscarriage, and all her husband could say was, "I have to go now." Damn him! And then, to top it all, he had tried to kill her. She'd get even with him someday. By God, she'd teach that stunted, heartless bastard and his beastly mother a lesson! Their karma would catch up with them, too.

Chapter 24

Chandramma lay sprawled on the bed, her head cradled in her locked hands on the pillow. Vinayak cast a brief glance at her. His wife appeared to be deep in thought.

The iron bed with its tall headboard and the four posts that held up the white mosquito net looked a bit cramped for her size. She occupied about two-thirds of it while he had to make do with the remaining one-third. Good thing he was a small man.

Vinayak stood before the mirror hanging over the dressing table, massaging castor oil into his scalp, trying to coax every little nerve and follicle to respond to his nurturing touch. The massaging action, *malish*, was warm and soothing and made him sleep better at nights. He had learned the trick from a professional *malishwalla* or masseur. Even if it didn't do much for his memory cells or his falling hair as the *malishwalla* had promised, it helped him sleep through Chandramma's earsplitting snoring. The woman could blow a hole in the roof with her honking and hissing.

He was vaguely aware that Chandramma's coconut-sized breasts were clearly visible through the thin fabric of her white blouse, and the bright orange sari had hiked up to expose her thick calves. But his eyes remained on his own image in the mirror while his bony fingers moved up and down his scalp rhythmically.

He continued to ignore his wife even when he heard her

sharp, dramatic intake of breath. Vinayak had given up looking at his wife with anything but mild disgust for some time now. That episode a while ago when she had spurned him came to mind. Not only had he married an ugly shrew, he was stuck now with an enormous ugly shrew, whose sex drive was all but non-existent. Always a plump woman, she had started to gain more weight immediately upon giving birth to Shanti and hadn't stopped gaining since. Her passion for food had replaced her passion for her husband.

Well, he wasn't exactly a handsome man, and then there had been that terrible and near-fatal illness during his childhood that had more or less sealed his fate. The best he could hope for in a wife in those days was someone like Chandramma. In fact, even Chandramma was a blessing then, considering the predicament he had been in. She even came with a substantial dowry, which had made it possible for him to buy this house all that many years ago. Additionally, she gave him two children, one of them being a son to carry on the Ramnath name. The son had turned out to be a major disappointment, but Suresh was his child, nonetheless.

Vinayak felt he really had no right to complain about his lot. His mind went back to his teenage years. He shuddered like he always did when he recalled that miserable period in his life. It had all started with that scratchy cough. At first his parents thought he had a simple cold. His mother coddled him with vile concoctions made of ginger, lemon grass and every kind of medicinal herb and spice she could think of.

When his problem continued she put poultices on his back until his very sweat reeked of onions and spices. The doctors prescribed shark liver oil, nutritional compounds, and *ayurvedic* elixirs. Nothing helped. His cough became persistent; he often coughed up blood and his already thin shoulders and chest began to hollow out and sag. He took to his bed for months after that, too weak and exhausted to go to school. After a while, even getting to his feet became a trial.

When his breathing became shallow, everyone decided he was at death's door. His mother became frantic. "Oh Lord, why are you doing this to us? Have we done so many bad things that we have to be punished so much?" she often cried as she pleaded with her mute gods and goddesses. They sat on her altar and offered no answers to her pitiful questions.

Vinayak's parents had already lost a son in infancy and a daughter to typhoid when she was barely five years old. They could not afford to lose this son as well, their only living child. They even named him after Vinayak, another name for Ganesh, the elephant-headed god, the remover of obstacles, so the child's path would be clear and allow him a full and healthy life.

When Vinayak reached the age of seventeen and very nearly died, a bright young physician, Alphonso D'Souza, diagnosed Vinayak's illness as the dreaded disease, the ominous T word: Tuberculosis.

Vinayak was promptly dispatched to a sanitarium for intensive treatment. He spent three precious years of his life in that prison-like brick building in a remote rural area forty miles from Palgaum. Life was miserable at that dreadful place, if it could even be called life in the first place. It was more like living death.

The stern, humorless nurses poked and prodded him all the time; the food tasted like crushed blotting paper; and he was never allowed any visitors, not even his parents. "We cannot allow the dangerous germs to spread to others," they told him when he demanded to see his family. The only pleasure he was permitted was to sit in the sunshine on the small area of grass in the afternoons and read his mother's letters.

Her notes to him carried more or less the same optimistic sentiments every week. *My dearest son: You are getting better each day. I miss you so much. I pray for you daily. The Lord will hear my prayers and you will come home. You will look handsome again, my little boy. Keep your faith in God and do what the doctors tell you to do.*

He read and reread such words and he cried each day—for his lost youth, for his mother's voice, even his father's iron fist. He had taken all those things for granted while growing up. If God would make him well he would never again take his life for granted, he resolved. He would never question his father's authority or his mother's smothering love.

By some miracle he began to improve. Something was working. Perhaps it was the medical treatment, or it could have been his own will to recover and leave the place he had come to detest. He gained a little weight and could keep the food down. He stopped coughing and gagging. Slightly more than three years later he was discharged from the sanitarium. They said he was cured.

He could go home and start a new life. His mother and father performed a *puja* to Lord Balaji to mark the special day and to offer thanks to the Lord. All the relatives and neighbors came to rejoice and offer their blessings.

Vinayak was convinced that most of them came to see for themselves whether he was truly cured and what he looked like after spending three years in that much-feared place called a sanitarium. To them, it was most likely a case of someone who had died and gone to hell, and come back to tell his story.

After the excitement died down he finished high school and then went on to college to get a degree in accounting. A bit older than his classmates and introverted by nature, he felt like an outcast, but he had promised himself that he was going to make the most of what destiny had given him as a rare gift. Every hour of every day was something to be cherished and he intended to do exactly that.

He managed to find a clerical job with the State Bank of India immediately upon graduation. However, when all his contemporaries got married and settled down with a wife and children, he remained single. But not out of choice. He longed to have a family of his own. Alas, once a tuberculosis patient, always a tuberculosis patient. He found that out soon enough.

Nobody wanted to have anything to do with a former "TB patient," as one was referred to even after one was cured. The stigma never left him. Prospective brides and their respective families shunned Vinayak. His emaciated looks didn't help matters either.

His sweet and devoted mother would often try to soothe his

wounded feelings. "Why you look so sad, *putta*? There is a nice girl somewhere just for you, no? You wait and see."

So he waited. But the girl never materialized. God hadn't made one "just for him."

His father was a more practical man. "Vinayak, do something with your life, son. Work hard and become a bank manager, maybe even the general manager. It does not look like marriage is in your stars. At times God just overlooks some people. What to do? It is your fate—that is all I can say."

His father's words had made sense. But philosophical thoughts did little to alleviate the deep need for love and sex and companionship. With no one to confide in, he became lonely and depressed.

Then one day, a surprise envelope arrived from Bangalore. A man called Mr. Rao had written to his father and sent him his daughter's horoscope to be matched with Vinayak's. Vinayak was stunned when his father told him about Chandramma and her parents and their interest in him as a prospective son-in-law. "Are you sure they have the right name and address?" he had asked his father, sure that his luck couldn't have changed quite like that—overnight. "It could be some silly mistake."

"It is definitely for you, son," assured his father. "There is no mistake."

A rare smile broke out over Vinayak's face. Here was a girl with a college education, the daughter of a successful businessman from Bangalore, interested in marrying him. Her parents were even offering a generous dowry. There had been no photograph of the girl or any indication of what she looked like. But Vinayak and his parents were so relieved and thrilled that someone at last wanted to marry him, they at once agreed to the match. They didn't even bother to have the horoscope read by the astrologer.

On the day of the official engagement, the Rao family from Bangalore arrived in a big white Ambassador car. They wore expensive clothes and had a chauffeur. Even the way Mr. and Mrs. Rao greeted them and conversed was more polished and sophisticated than anything Vinayak and his parents had ever heard or seen. However, what emerged from the car behind them was a rude surprise for the Ramnaths. The girl was chubby, with bulging eyes, dark, rutted skin, and a sullen expression. But then the Raos appeared equally taken aback at seeing Vinayak. The boy was skeletal, had scanty hair and yellow teeth, and was quiet as a ghost. And he was smaller than the girl.

Both parties probably came to the conclusion that this was the best they could do under the circumstances. The wedding took place a few weeks later. Chandra, or Chandramma as she was affectionately called, turned out to be a woman with a mean streak and an iron will. Vinayak, already a timid man, withdrew into his shell even further.

It broke Vinayak's heart to see Chandramma mistreat his aging parents, but his timidity prevented him from intervening most of the time. Whether it was Chandramma's abuse or something else, Vinayak couldn't say for sure, but both his parents died within a few years of the wedding, within a year of each other, too. In some ways Vinayak considered it a blessing. His parents didn't have to put up with their evil daughter-in-law for too long.

But like many arranged marriages of convenience, this one had managed to work. With Chandramma's constant nagging that he better himself, Vinayak went from bank clerk to loan officer; the dowry money was sufficient to buy a modest house; and two children were born to them. They were born twelve years apart, but that was okay—to Vinayak they were still two small miracles in his pathetic life. Even if he wasn't blessed with a good wife, God had seen fit to give him the priceless gift of fatherhood.

Every time he felt rueful about the choice he had made in a marriage partner, he reminded himself that technically he'd had no choice. Chandramma was the only woman brought to his attention. If he hadn't married her he probably would have lived a bachelor's life. At least now he had a family to call his own. He had a lot more than many other men had—especially men who had TB—men who languished in a wretched sanitarium till the day they died.

And yet, despite the philosophizing, a few misgivings had started to enter Vinayak's mind, especially lately. He was beginning to feel very restless.

He glanced at his wife through the mirror. Her lips were curved in a satisfied smirk. She had been looking smug like that all evening. Something had gone well for her. She had also been a bit excited most of the day, like a little girl who had accidentally discovered her *Diwali* present before its time, but didn't want her parents to know that she had.

Vinayak knew his wife well. Too well. The suppressed excitement meant only one thing: she was planning something important. And again, knowing her, she was up to something questionable. Good deeds were not something Chandramma casually indulged in, at least not unless there was something in it for her. Since her attempt to do away with Megha, Vinayak's contempt for his wife had doubled.

Although he preferred to keep his counsel to himself, curiosity got the better of him. His wife looked a bit too complacent for his liking. Most often that look translated into problems for him. He was not in a mood for more problems. His boss had become quite unreasonable lately and demanded a ridiculous amount of attention to details. "Customer service, Vinayak, remember customer service above all else," Eric Gonsalves reminded him frequently in his hoity-toity American-accented English.

His boss had the cheek to call him Vinayak, too—not even the courtesy of addressing him as Mr. Ramnath. After all, he was Gonsalves's elder and deserved at least that much respect. Hah, that American influence again, addressing everyone by their first name! What kind of nonsense was that? Vinayak preferred the conservative British way of conducting business.

He admitted to himself that he was bored with his job, tired of his boss and becoming dissatisfied with his life in general. The last thing he needed was for his bossy wife to start something that would cause him more problems. "Chandramma, you look very pleased. Your errand must have been successful.

What was that important errand you had this afternoon?" he asked cautiously.

The smirk vanished from her face. "Nothing for you to worry about."

Vinayak frowned in disapproval but his voice remained passive. "I know you are making trips to the astrologer lately and it is not to match our Shanti's horoscope with that of a suitable boy. What are you planning now, Chandramma?"

"I am not planning anything, Ree. I already told you that."

He finished his oil massage ritual and carefully wiped his hands on a small towel. "Then why are you going so many times to the astrologer?"

Chandramma turned to face him, defensive as ever. "How did you know I went to see the astrologer?"

"He came to the bank this afternoon to deposit the cash you paid him to do a special reading. He told me about your recent visits. He seemed to assume that I knew."

"So the old bastard couldn't wait to run to you about my consultations!" Chandramma's brows descended over her nose in annoyed contempt.

Climbing onto his side of the bed and sitting cross-legged to do his usual bedtime yoga exercises, Vinayak replied, "He didn't run to me. He was at the bank today to make a deposit and I noticed him on my way to the café, so I stopped to talk. I asked him about his business and he said it was doing quite well, especially this week. Thanks to your three special readings, he made two hundred rupees per sitting." Noticing the hooded look in his wife's eyes, Vinayak continued, "So, what were the special readings about? For six hundred rupees they had to be important, no?"

Chandramma stuck her double chin out. "Have you forgotten that we have a daughter of marriageable age? A good mother is supposed to go to the astrologer to get horoscopes matched for her grown children. He is the best astrologer in town and he has a computer now, you know. He charges more lately to recover the cost of that computer."

"Never mind the cost. I didn't know we had any boys' families inquiring about our Shanti. Besides, Shanti has made it quite clear that she is not interested in marriage right now. She is only nineteen."

Chandramma was a pathological liar, but Vinayak knew she was not one to let herself get caught lying. "Marriages take a long time to arrange, Ree. Just because I didn't tell you it does not mean there are no prospective boys for Shanti. Before we know it she will be twenty years old, a college graduate, and ready to marry." She sent him a defiant glance and waited for his reaction.

Too tired to argue further, Vinayak dismissed the matter with a shake of his head. He closed his eyes, did his deep-breathing exercises and meditated for five full minutes. Then he turned off the light and pulled the covers over himself. He could never win with Chandramma. She had the mind of a stubborn donkey. Just before he drifted off to sleep he wondered whether it would be wise to keep a closer eye on Chandramma in the next several days.

He had the uneasy feeling that his wife's latest activities might have something to do with their daughter-in-law. Was Chandramma still trying to hunt Megha down and kill her? Did Chandramma's New Year's resolution include another murder plot?

Vinayak's hand trembled in fear. What kind of hell was his wife dragging him into? The thought was frightening.

Chapter 25

Despite all her attempts at getting the depression out of her system, Megha failed. Kiran came home from work and seemed to guess at once that she was in a bad mood.

Tossing his briefcase and suit jacket on the chair, he studied her face across the room. "What's the matter, Megha?"

"Nothing," she replied and went back to her task of setting the table. A man would never understand a woman's emotions.

His frown deepened. "You're not . . . uh . . . you're . . . how should I say this?"

She sent him an uneasy glance. "What are you trying to say?" It wasn't like him to dance around any issue.

Kiran looked uncomfortable. "You . . . um . . . don't have any morning sickness or anything, do you?"

So that's what had him so worried. It wasn't just she who was troubled about her becoming pregnant from that single night they had slept together. He had obviously been under the same kind of strain. "No, Kiran, I'm not . . . I'm not having a baby, if that's what you're asking. Everything's okay," she informed him. She couldn't help the telltale surge of heat in her neck and face. This was an awkward topic.

His frown eased a little but his eyes were still watchful. "Are you sure?"

"I'm positive."

"Well, that's a relief!" he murmured. "I was so damn worried that I might have got you . . . landed us both in trouble."

"You can't blame yourself for what might have happened, Kiran." She was too embarrassed to meet his gaze, so she continued to go back and forth between the kitchen and dining areas, bringing the food to the table. "I was an equal and willing participant."

"But you're so young and innocent. I should have known better than to talk you into doing something so entirely foolish."

"What!" She couldn't let him shoulder all the responsibility for this. She wouldn't. They were two young people in love, with normal, healthy reflexes. It was only a small miracle that had kept them apart for so long in the first place. She'd be damned if she'd let him live with a guilty conscience all alone.

She left the plates on the table and came to stand before him, so she could look him in the eye. "Look, let's get this straight: I'm a grown and married woman, not an innocent child, Kiran. And you didn't talk me into anything; I did it on my own. We both acted impulsively that night, but it's never going to happen again. We won't let it happen, so stop worrying. Besides, I'm not pregnant, so let's not talk about it anymore, okay?"

"Fine. But I want you to know something first," he said.

There was such a sad and regretful note in his voice that it tugged at her. "What?"

"Although it's a relief that it didn't happen, in other ways I'm disappointed."

She knew the exact feeling. "Why, Kiran?"

"If the circumstances were right . . . I mean if you were my wife, discovering that you were carrying our child would be the most wonderful news in my life. Nothing would make me happier." He must have seen the look of intense longing in her eyes, the one that matched his own, because he laid a hand on her arm. "We'll make it happen someday . . . when the time is right."

Hearing him voice her own sentiments so candidly brought a lump to Megha's throat. *Oh, Kiran! I would give anything in the world to have your baby.* But she couldn't say it aloud. Instead she said. "The circumstances are far from right, so it's best not to dwell on it."

"All right," he agreed. "If it's not that, then why are you so tense? You're not—"

"No! I'm not planning to run away or attempt suicide again, if that's what you're insinuating," she interrupted, at once reading his thoughts.

"I'm glad to hear that. But something's still bothering you. I can tell."

"Don't pay any attention to me; I was just indulging in a bit of reminiscing and self-pity. It's a woman thing—we tend to get emotional for no particular reason sometimes."

"Let me get changed and we'll talk." Kiran plucked his jacket off the chair and disappeared into the bedroom. Several minutes later he came out, wearing jeans and a T-shirt. Pulling out a chair, he sat at the table and sniffed the food she'd just finished ladling on his plate. "Umm, this smells wonderful. *Aviyal* is one of my favorites." Then he spooned some of the mixed-vegetable curry cooked in a white, ground-coconut gravy into his mouth. "Excellent."

"Glad you like it." Relieved that Kiran had temporarily forgotten her glumness, she started to eat her own dinner. She knew he planned to go out later to visit his grandmother. Ajji, as everyone referred to the elder Mrs. Rao, was in a nursing home, where she was recovering from a heart attack followed by a crippling hip fracture. He diligently visited his grandmother every Wednesday. Each member of the family picked a different day of the week to visit Ajji, so the old lady would have someone for company every day.

"I have an idea," Kiran announced after a few seconds of quiet introspection.

"If it's more shopping, forget it, Kiran," she said. "I have all the clothes, toiletries, makeup and footwear I'll ever need."

He shook his head. "Not shopping, but a visit to someone special."

She looked at him sharply. "Visit?" Her furtive visits to Harini's house were enough to keep her in a constant state of nervousness. Still suspicious that someone, most likely Amma, was watching her every move, she couldn't stand another clandestine outing. Her nerves couldn't possibly handle it.

"Don't look so scared, Megha. I'm sure Ajji would love to see you."

"Ajji! You must be joking! Your grandmother is family. She'll tell the rest of them that I'm still in town and that I'm staying with you."

"No, she won't—not if I tell her not to."

"But she's Amma's mother and your grandmother! Why would she protect *me*?"

"She's a very bright and astute lady. You'll be surprised at how good she is at keeping secrets. She's known many of my childhood secrets. She hasn't divulged a single one yet."

"You don't have any real secrets. I'm probably your first and only dirty secret."

"Don't put me on a pedestal, Megha." He looked amused. "I wasn't exactly a saint in my adolescent days, and I'm not one now either. You should know that better than anyone else."

Megha flushed furiously, recalling their naked bodies tangled amidst the sheets the other night. "But this is not the same. I'm her grandson's runaway wife being sheltered by her other grandson. How is she going to react to that?"

"Listen, I know how serious this is." Kiran put his spoon down and leaned forward. "But believe me, Ajji is one person you can trust. She's the only one who is likely to believe that Amma is capable of murder. And, she's also the only individual in the family, besides me, who'll be willing to protect you."

Toying with her food for several minutes, Megha deliberated over the idea. The thought of going out of the house in itself was enough to give her heart palpitations. On top of that, visiting the Rao family matriarch? How could she manage that? The old lady was an elder, most likely a woman of honor with conservative ideas and a stringent code of ethics. She probably believed Brahmin women had a role to play and it certainly wouldn't include abandoning one's husband and in-laws.

But on the other hand, Megha argued with herself, maybe it

was time she met Ajji, got to know her a little. If Kiran said she could be trusted, then it was probably safe to do it. Also, it would feel good to get out for a change, breathe in some fresh air. She looked at Kiran hesitantly. "I . . . I guess I could go."

"Good. We can wish Ajji a Happy New Year together—cheer her up a little," he said with an encouraging nod.

Megha vaguely remembered meeting Ajji a year ago, on her wedding day to be exact. That was the one and only time she'd met the old lady. Almost immediately after the wedding, Ajji had gone off with other elderly relatives on a pilgrimage of the famous temples of central and south India. Then, at the end of the trip, she had stayed with her widowed sister in Chennai for several months. A few days after her return, Ajji had suffered a severe heart attack followed by a fall in the bathroom that ended in a fractured hip. The doctor had advised her to remain in a nursing home for several weeks while she recuperated because the family was not capable of giving her the constant care she needed.

Although Amma visited Ajji every Monday and Thursday, sometimes accompanied by Appaji or Suresh or Shanti, she had never invited Megha to go with her. Whether it was because Amma wanted to make her feel like an outsider or some other reason, Megha had never been able to comprehend. Although Megha had wanted to visit Ajji and get to know her, she hadn't had the courage to ask. What if Amma denied her request in that brusque way of hers, saying she wasn't welcome? In recent months, everything that Megha did or said had set Amma off.

Ajji, the tiny woman with soft gray hair pulled back into a bun at the nape of her neck and dressed in a simple widow's white silk sari, had sat in the front row at Suresh and Megha's wedding, an honored place reserved for the eldest member of the Rao family. The old lady had very sharp features and despite the wrinkles, had an expressive face that was still attractive. Somehow Ajji had reminded Megha of a delicate and exotic white-plumed bird. When Megha, the new bride, had bowed low to touch the lady's feet in the reverent Hindu tradition, Ajji had beamed. "What a beautiful girl you are! You will make our Suresh a very happy man, no? May God bless you with a long marriage and many healthy children."

When Kiran pulled into the parking lot of the single story building that housed the nursing home, Megha glanced around to make sure no one else from the family was there. Kiran, noticing the look on her face, said, "I'll go inside and make sure nobody else is visiting her. I'll also explain to Ajji about what's happened between you and Suresh recently."

"She must know that already. Amma will have filled her in on all the details—her own twisted version of them."

Kiran shook his head. "Doesn't seem that way. I've been seeing Ajji every week, and she hasn't brought it up. Maybe Amma didn't want to upset her."

Megha rolled her eyes. "Oh, come on, this is too big a thing for Amma not to have mentioned it to her own mother."

"As of last week, Ajji had no idea. She makes kind inquiries about you all the time, asks why you've never come to see her." He seemed to think the matter over for a second. "I'll just tell her the truth now."

"Do you think that's wise?"

"Better to tell her the whole story before she sees you, don't you think? Otherwise, she's sure to mention your visit to the others since she'll have no idea you're hiding from them. I have to first make sure she understands that she can't tell another soul about you."

"I'm afraid she'll hate me, Kiran. How can a woman her age accept something like this?"

"She's very modern in her thinking, Megha. She's really quite amazing—sharp as a dagger, you'll see." He stepped out of the car. "Stay here; I'll be right back."

Several tense minutes later, he returned and opened her door. "I told her everything."

Megha closed her eyes for a moment. "She's thoroughly upset and doesn't want me anywhere within a thousand meters of her, correct?" She should have known this wasn't going to work. Kiran was too damned optimistic.

"Wrong," he said. "She's enraged at Amma, but she's very sympathetic to your situation and says she wants to tell you something."

"What is it?"

Kiran shrugged. "I don't know, but she's being very mysterious—says she has been meaning to tell me something for a long time, but didn't know how. Now that we're both here, she says it's best if she shares it with both of us. 'Highly important,' according to her. Come on."

Megha hesitated for an instant then pulled the veil partly over her face and followed Kiran around the building to what appeared to be an inconspicuous side entrance, perhaps an employees' door. He had obviously decided it wasn't wise to enter through the main door. All visitors used that entryway and they could run into someone they knew.

Now that she was here, Megha wondered what she should say to Ajji. Despite Kiran's assurances that his grandmother was a modern woman, Megha wasn't sure of her welcome. What would the old lady think of her grandson living in sin with his cousin-in-law? Or hadn't Kiran mentioned that part yet?

She began to have serious doubts. Maybe she could still go back to the car and wait for Kiran to visit his grandmother alone.

As if reading her thoughts, Kiran shook his head at her. "Don't worry. She'll be happy to see you. She told me that herself." He escorted her down a short corridor with rooms opening out on either side.

A few wheelchairs were lined up on one side of the aisle. The overhead fluorescent lights were bright, making Megha even more apprehensive about being seen. The smell of antiseptic combined with traces of chlorine cleanser and urine was unmistakable. Memories of visiting her father when he'd had bypass surgery came to mind. The hospital he'd been in was crowded and not particularly clean, but that was all they could afford. Seeing Appa in pain and all those tubes attached to him had made Megha weep. She could picture him now, looking gaunt and lying on the narrow bed, his eyes glazed. She had thought he was going to die, but he had survived and returned home, a pale image of his former self, both physically and emotionally. Life at home had never been the same since.

No matter how upscale, all health-care facilities smelled the same. For a nursing home in a small town in India, this one was surprisingly clean and modern. But then it was a small and exclusive facility for the wealthy, so they probably provided better care.

Voices emerged from a few of the rooms. Megha instinctively pulled the *chunni* lower to cover most of her face. Visiting hours were on and she could easily end up running into a familiar face.

A stooped old man, walking with the help of a metal walker, shuffled along, entirely oblivious to their presence. A heavy-set nurse dressed in a starched white sari marched by, frowning oddly at Megha, making her feel like an object in a shop window. The veil over her face was bound to be an odd sight. An anxious thought struck her just then. What if Amma questioned the nurses about anyone new coming to visit Ajji? She tried to put it out of her mind. The nurse hadn't been able to see her face.

Moaning sounds coming from somewhere made Megha shudder. This was depressing. Poor Ajji! She had been confined to this convalescent home for weeks now. No wonder Kiran said she looked forward to his visits. He was also her favorite grandchild, from what Megha had gathered.

At the end of the corridor, Kiran steered her into a large square room. It looked spacious as compared with the other rooms they had glimpsed in passing. Megha guessed that rich folks probably got the bigger and more comfortable rooms. This one had a cream tiled floor and two curtained windows that overlooked several trees and part of a street. A cool breeze stirred the cream and gray checkered curtains and brought in some fresh air, helping to dispel the antiseptic odor. Kiran quickly shut the door behind them and moved to the windows to close the curtains. Megha sent him a grateful look. He had become so adept at shielding her.

A picture of Lord Balaji sat on a bedside table. Holy incense sticks burned in a silver holder, emitting a woodsy smoke— probably a good thing to drive away mosquitoes and sweeten the air while it was being offered to God. Next to it was a dog-eared copy of the verses of Purandardas, the sixteenth century poet-saint. From the looks of the book and the reading glasses placed on top, Ajji read it often.

Megha's eyes were drawn to the huge bed sitting in the center of the room. Ajji reclined on it, leaning back against a stack of pillows. In a white cotton gown she looked even more frail and bird-like than Megha remembered. The silver hair looked a bit disheveled and her arms were loose skin and bone, but the keen eyes that peered at her were the same ones from the previous year. The old woman struggled to sit up.

"Don't try that on your own, Ajji," chided Kiran before rushing forward to lift her into a more upright position. "Megha was a little afraid of how you would react to her."

For a moment, a hush fell over the room. Megha let the pastel green *chunni* slide off her head and fall around her shoulders. The two women gazed at each other for what felt like eons to Megha. The stillness was thick and taut. Her heartbeat thumped. What now? Was the old lady going to faint or something? Was there time enough to turn back and run before grandma ended up having another seizure?

But an unexpected smile came over the old woman's face. "Megha."

Megha put her palms together and greeted Ajji with a *Namaste*.

"Come here, *putti*."

Hesitating, Megha took a small step forward.

"Do not be afraid. Come, come, sit here." Ajji indicated a spot beside her on the bed. "Let me look at you."

Instinctively Megha cast a glance at Kiran, then seeing his encouraging nod, she proceeded to sit on the bed beside Ajji, but not before she touched her feet. It seemed to please Ajji, since she smiled. "Very nice . . . your mother has taught you to follow our old customs, Megha."

Kiran pulled up a chair close to the edge of the bed and made himself comfortable, stretching his long legs in front of him. Megha found his closeness comforting.

Grabbing Megha's wrist with her rough and bony fingers, Ajji brought her face closer. The intensity in Ajji's eyes made Megha tremble a little. "Still very beautiful, but you have become very thin," she remarked. "You would have made Suresh very happy and made the Rao family also happy. But Chandramma spoiled it. What a pity, no? She always does that. She destroys her own life and destroys other people's lives." The old woman shook her head sadly. "When she will improve, God alone knows."

At a loss for words, Megha merely looked toward Kiran for direction. He said nothing, clearly letting Ajji set the tone and pace.

"Megha, Chandramma treated you very badly, no?" said Ajji. Probably because she noticed the hesitant look in Megha's eyes and received no response, Ajji let go of her wrist and went *tsk-tsk* with her tongue. "She was not always so bad, my dear. She has bad blood in her; that is what makes her like that."

"Bad blood?" What did that mean? Megha turned to Ajji with a raised brow. Amma always boasted about her family tree, her pure, clean Brahmin roots.

Ajji's eyes unexpectedly filled with tears and she used her fingers to brush them away. "Oh, Meghamma, what I can say? It is a very long and sad story."

Megha nodded, remembering that Ajji wanted to tell them something "highly important."

"I will tell you and Kiran something if you both promise not to tell anyone."

"We won't, Ajji," prompted Kiran, "but are you sure you feel up to it?"

"I am old and tired, Kiran. If I don't tell someone now, then nobody will know after I die. At least this will make you understand why Chandramma behaves in this manner. You may not forgive her, but at least you will have more understanding, no?"

"Whatever you tell me will stay with me." Megha patted the

old woman's hand to emphasize her oath. But she wondered what could be so highly secret in Amma's past that even her own brothers didn't know.

Megha felt immensely relieved that Ajji had been cordial to her so far, and pleased at being addressed as Meghamma, an affectionate variation of Megha. No one had called her that in years. It brought back poignant memories of her early childhood. Her father, in his younger and happier days, used to call her his little Meghamma. He used to let her accompany him to his mango orchard and help him supervise the mango picking. School was always closed for the summer holidays at the time of the mango harvest, which was wonderful. He would call out to her on those hot and steamy May afternoons, "Come on, Meghamma. Help me make sure the mango pickers are doing a good job. If you are a good girl, you can keep two of the best mangoes for yourself."

He would help her lace up her special black shoes with the thick soles so the thorny weeds growing under the mango trees wouldn't prick her tiny feet. He would hold her hand all the way to the orchard. He would hoist her up on his wide shoulders if she complained of being tired. Sometimes he would tickle her ankles just to hear her giggle hysterically and squirm, then beg for more. "Tickle some more, Appa, tickle some more." Then he'd tickle her once again and laugh along with her.

She loved to hear the high-pitched screech of pure joy erupting from her own throat, followed by her father's gruff, amused chuckle. Perched high atop his shoulders, she could reach the luscious mangoes in the trees with little difficulty. In fact, from way up there, she could see the whole world, and she would feel like a pampered little princess without a care in the world. Appa was all hers—he would love and protect her forever. At least it had seemed that way then.

After sitting under the cool shade of the mango trees and eating the lunch packed by her mother, Megha would attack one of her prize mangoes with greedy zest. The mangoes always tasted like heaven right off the tree—warm from the sun, golden in color, heavy and sweet and fragrant. Her father would watch her indulgently and then with infinite patience wash the sticky mango juice off her face and hands with a rag dipped in cold water. Most often the juice dribbled over her clothes and shoes, much to Avva's disapproval. But Appa always appeased her mother with gentle words. "Never mind, Mangala. Let the girl enjoy the mangoes while she is still a child. Just wash the clothes and wipe the shoes."

As the girls grew up, his pain from arthritis escalated, the debts from medical bills and dowries started to mount, and her father gradually turned somber. Somewhere along the way he entirely lost his health and with it his sense of humor. A kind man filled with gentle warmth turned cold and bitter as the years turned leaner and harsher. Since the heart attack and the bypass surgery he had become even more austere. As a matter of fact, lately, he seemed downright callous. Where had the marvelous father of her childhood years gone, the man with the kind brown eyes and the wide, smiling mouth?

Setting aside the moments of nostalgia, Megha forced herself to return to the present and turned to Ajji, her eyes softening as they met Ajji's pleading ones.

Ajji took a quivering breath. "I have not told this to a single person in my life—not my husband, not even my children."

Kiran shot a mocking smile at his grandmother. "What is it? Amma stole something expensive and you didn't tell the police and now you're feeling guilty?"

"I wish it was something simple like that, Kiran," said Ajji wistfully. "But what I have for you is a secret. A very shameful secret."

Chapter 26

Megha watched Kiran's eyes go wide with shock. She herself shifted uncomfortably. She knew what was going on in his mind, because she had the same thoughts. What kind of shameful secret would a sweet, old-fashioned grandmother have? Once again she touched the old woman's hand. "Ajji, why do you want to tell *me* this? I'm practically a stranger to you."

"Because you are the one who has suffered the most under Chandramma. On the day of your wedding, when I saw how pretty and charming you were, I knew Chandramma would dislike you. Kiran tells me you almost died at her hands. Chandramma hates you for a reason, *putti*. You are everything she would have liked to be and could not." Tears pooled in Ajji's eyes. "If I tell you my story, maybe you will understand why Chandramma is like that—full of bitterness and hatred."

Kiran offered his handkerchief to his distraught grandmother.

"I was a very young girl when this happened, only seventeen," said Ajji. "I was beautiful, just like you. Our home and business were in Bangalore, but my husband was going to different places to buy goods for his general store. He was always traveling to Bombay, Poona, Delhi, Calcutta—all kinds of places."

"Were you often left alone in a big house then?" Megha asked.

"No, we had one servant who lived with us. There were two

others who came every morning and left in the evenings. My mother-in-law was also there, but she was very sick and bedridden."

"She had cancer," Kiran added.

Ajji nodded. "I was a new bride, but because my mother-in-law was disabled I had the responsibility of running the household."

Not knowing what to say when the old woman stopped to blow her nose, Megha looked at her attentively, encouraging her to continue. She noticed Kiran doing the same.

"Lingayya was the *bhangi,* the untouchable sweeper who used to clean the toilets. When I first came to the house, he was very respectful towards me. He was always joining his hands and remembering to say *Namaste* to me, always bowing his head and never making eye contact. After one or two months, he started to raise his eyes and look at me. He started to make me very uneasy. He began to look at me with greedy eyes. He frightened me, Meghamma. I began to hide in my room whenever I knew he was outside, cleaning the toilets. I did not want to have anything to do with him. But he would stand near the window to our room and stare inside. Whichever room I was hiding in, he would stand outside the window of that room. He would smile at me and lick his lips."

"Why didn't you tell Thatha?" Kiran asked, referring to his grandfather, and voicing Megha's thoughts. It would seem logical for a young woman to go to her husband with something that disturbed her so much.

"I was too scared to tell that to my husband and my mother-in-law. Then they would surely blame me for encouraging him to look at me like that, no?"

Megha knew exactly what Ajji meant by being blamed for something unfairly. She'd had that problem while in college. When she complained to her father that some of the boys made passes at her, he thrashed her for it. "It is not really the boys' fault, Megha. When you flaunt your beauty that is exactly what happens. The boys will leave you alone if you behave like a good Brahmin girl." It always came down to the girl; it was always her mistake. In a male-dominated society it was never the man's fault.

Refocusing her mind on Ajji and her narrative, Megha wondered what Ajji's story had to do with Amma. Where was all this leading? She was curious to find out.

"Then my mother-in-law died. It was a blessing for her, poor thing." Ajji stopped for a few moments, as if to gather her thoughts. "Some weeks after that, my husband went on a trip to Bombay for several days. And the next day, our servant, Gauri, received a telegram. Her brother had died in a bus accident. She had to leave for her village immediately to attend his funeral. Everything started to go wrong at the same time."

"Fate," murmured Megha. There were no coincidences in life, as her mother always said. Everything happened for a reason.

"Exactly," agreed Ajji. "Suddenly, I was alone in that big house. I could not sleep that night. All the sounds in the house kept me awake. It was a dark, new moon night, *amavasya*—a night for bad things to happen."

Amavasya. One of those evil, moonless nights, sighed Megha.

"Then the doorbell started to ring," Ajji said. "I was terrified to open the door and hoped the person would try a few times and then go away. But the ringing did not stop. The person began banging on the door, too. So I decided to be brave; I opened the door."

Megha's heart missed a beat. "It was Lingayya?"

"Yes. I almost fainted from fear when I saw him. His eyes looked red and his teeth very white in his ugly, dark mouth. I tried to close the door, but he pushed his way in. He was drunk and stinking like the low-class *bhangi* he was. He . . . oh God—"

Noticing the look of terror flashing in Ajji's eyes, Megha instinctively knew what was coming next. She took Ajji's frail hand in hers and squeezed it. There was no sense in making the old woman relive an obviously traumatic experience. Noticing the concerned frown on Kiran's face, she said, "Ajji, just forget about it. Let's talk about something else."

"No, I want to tell you both. I *have* to tell you, no? Please, listen to me," begged Ajji. "I told Lingayya to go away and tried to push him out of the door, but he was a big, fat man, too heavy for me. He came inside the house and closed the door behind him. He pushed me down to the floor and dragged me to the drawing room by my arms. I screamed and kicked, but nobody heard me. We had a big walled compound and the nearest house was far away. And it was late, so nobody in the neighbor's house was awake. I begged Lingayya not to touch me. Oh Lord, how much I begged him nobody will ever know!"

Ajji's eyes took on a faraway look. "I told him I would give him money, even my diamond necklace and earrings, if he left me alone. But he only laughed at me and grabbed me again. He tore my blouse." Ajji put a frail hand to her mouth, her agitated eyeballs starting to bounce back and forth across the room as if she were surveying the scene repeatedly in horrifying slow motion. All at once, deep, violent sobs erupted from her.

Megha took the trembling old woman in her arms and rocked her like a child. "I'm so sorry."

Kiran rose from his chair and paced the room for a bit before returning to the chair. He was scowling, clearly touched and upset just as Megha was by Ajji's tale of horror and tragedy.

After a few minutes of shedding hot, cathartic tears, Ajji recovered a little. Despite Megha and Kiran's efforts to stop her from torturing herself with her disturbing memories, she insisted on relating the rest of her experience. "No, you must listen. Lingayya was a horrible man. He had no morals, no character. After all, he was a *bhangi*."

"Not all *bhangi*s are bad people. In fact, our *bhangi* was a very nice man," Megha protested in response to Ajji's prejudiced statement.

"Meghamma, you are too young to know this. Untouchable men are more horrible than most other men, my dear. Do not ever forget that! They have no culture and no education; they are as violent and unpredictable as wild animals. They do not have strong morals like upper-caste men. That Lingayya had his eye on me for a very long time and he found a chance to get what he wanted. I was alone and I was helpless, no? So he took what he wanted."

"Oh dear God!" Megha felt her stomach take a dive. In spite of guessing exactly how Lingayya's unexpected visit had ended, Megha was still in shock. How could anyone, even a detestable brute, do that to a helpless woman—subject an innocent young girl to such unspeakable violence? What horrors had poor Ajji suffered as she relived that single episode over and over again all these years? It was too hard to imagine. Rape was not meant to happen in a respectable, upper middle-class household. All Megha could do was stare at Ajji in disbelief.

Kiran, on the other hand, looked furious, silently raging at a man he'd never known, a man who'd defiled his dear grandmother. His hands were tightly clasped together, the knuckles looking pale.

Ajji's swollen eyes came back to rest on Megha. "Afterwards, Lingayya quietly left the house. After stealing what he wanted, he just walked away, Meghamma! He had lost nothing and I had lost everything, no?"

"Yes, yes you had," whispered Megha, trying not to start weeping herself.

"I stayed on the floor for a long time, cold and miserable. There was blood from the attack; my blouse was torn to pieces; my sari was heaped next to me. I cried and cried, but what did it do? Nothing! Crying was not going to wash away the shame or the pain. I was ruined for life. How could I face my husband when another man had taken my body? As a Brahmin woman I was not fit to even touch my husband's feet after what happened.

"I could smell Lingayya's ghastly stench on me. His toilet-cleaning fingers left black bruises all over me. My body was fit for the toilet. But after praying hard for a while, very slowly I realized that it was not my fault. I had to keep telling myself again and again—it was not my fault . . . it was not my fault. Before the sun came up the next morning, I took a bath, burned my clothes in the fire that heated the bath water, and pretended as if nothing had happened."

"What about the next day? Didn't the other servants suspect anything?"

"Shivrama, the gardener, was too old and almost blind to notice anything. Indira, the cook, looked at me with curious eyes. I told her I fell in the dark on my way to the bathroom the previous night. She kept staring at me suspiciously. I tried to stay in my room and told her I was in pain from the fall. I don't think she believed me. I was thankful to God that my husband was not there to see my bruises. He was not going to come back for many more days. I prayed for the ugly marks to go away by the time he came home."

"But what about Lingayya? Did that bastard come back the next day?" Kiran asked.

"Oh yes, he returned to work, looking very pleased with himself. But after that night I made sure at least one of the servants stayed with me all the time while Gauri was away."

"Didn't you have Lingayya dismissed?" Megha said.

Ajji looked at Megha as if she'd lost her mind. "How could I, *putti*? It was not that easy. I had to have a reason for dismissing him. How could I tell my husband that Lingayya had raped me? How could I tell anyone? After my husband returned home, I had to pretend like nothing extraordinary had happened. Every time my husband touched me it killed me a little bit. I almost told him a few times to get away from me, that I was a dirty woman, not fit to be his wife. Slowly, very slowly I became quiet, tried to forget it ever happened. But I could not forget it— I just could not. Even now I have horrible dreams. I still see Lingayya's face."

Knowing all about bad dreams and the terror they could generate, Megha sighed. "Of course you do."

"After the attack, Lingayya continued to look at me with the evil look, but luckily I was never alone in the house anytime after that. I thought I would be okay . . . until—" Ajji sent Megha a quick glance then looked at Kiran. "You two know what happened then, don't you? You can almost feel it, can you not?"

Megha nodded, experiencing an ominous feeling about what was about to come next. In fact, she knew exactly what had happened—woman's intuition perhaps. But Kiran looked puzzled. She could tell he wasn't quite sure what to expect.

Ajji turned to Kiran, probably because he seemed to have no clue. "I conceived, Kiran. My husband's seed had not made me pregnant all those months, but Lingayya's had."

"But how could you know for sure that it was Lingayya's? Thatha came home soon after that, didn't he? You said he . . . you and he . . ." Kiran's voice sounded hollow.

"I knew, my dear. From the timing of my pregnancy I knew the baby was Lingayya's. Only I knew. I had to pretend that the child belonged to your Thatha, no? He was happy about my being in the family way. He fussed over me and made sure that the servants took good care of me while he was away. In fact, he hired another woman servant to look after my needs. He pampered me every night after he came home from work. His kindness broke my heart, a little bit at a time. In those days there was no abortion, no? Even if there was, where could I get one? How could I explain to the doctor why a respectable, married woman like myself wanted an abortion? I pretended to be happy, but I cried secretly every day of my pregnancy."

Megha's heart ached for Ajji. God, what a nightmare! A long, nine-month ordeal that must have seemed endless.

"Then I gave birth to Chandramma," said Ajji. "There was no doubt about whose child she was. The baby looked just like Lingayya. My nightmare was to continue. In fact, it had become even more frightening. I said to God, 'Why me? Why did this happen and why could the child not look like me, at least? Are you going to punish me all my life for something I had nothing to do with?' Of course there was no answer from God."

Karma once again—merciless, unpredictable and unjust.

"I knew people talked about my child," Ajji continued. "Relatives looked at Chandramma with pity. I even heard the servants gossiping about how my child was so ugly when my husband was a handsome man and I was a pretty woman. They believed it was a *shaapa*, a curse on the family. I knew it was a curse, too—the curse that had come in the shape of Lingayya."

"But . . . but you loved the child, anyway?" Megha was curious to know.

"Of course! Chandramma was still my child, no? I even named her *Chandra* after the moon, hoping her looks and personality would turn beautiful and calm like the moon. My husband loved the child, too. He never questioned her unusual looks or her strange temperament. He thought she probably looked like some unknown ancestor."

"Didn't Lingayya get suspicious when he saw your baby?"

Ajji seemed to shiver as she tried to recall the facts. "He knew. Oh dear God, he knew! I could tell from the way he always looked at Chandramma. I was afraid he would kidnap her or something. I have never wished bad things on people, but that time I did. I prayed that something evil should happen to him so he would leave us alone. Then he got into some drunken fight one night and got his leg broken. After that he never came back. The other servants told me that his leg was so badly smashed that they had to amputate it. He could not do *bhangi* work anymore. We never saw Lingayya again. I felt guilty afterwards because my prayers had made him a cripple. In a few years I got over my guilt, but I never got over what he did to me."

How could you forget, Megha thought, *when Amma was there as a cruel and constant reminder?*

"A missing leg was too good for the bastard, Ajji. He should have been shot to death!" fumed Kiran in true male fashion.

A distant look came into Ajji's eyes and she glanced pensively at the Lord's picture. "Sometimes I think it is our fault that Chandramma is so strange. Because she was an unhappy child with no friends, we felt sorry for her. The neighborhood children called her names and never asked her to join in their games. She was always alone, always angry. When she tortured insects and small animals we scolded her, but never punished her. Maybe we should have taken her to a psychiatrist or something, but in those days we didn't even have any psychiatrists, and it never occurred to us then, anyway. Also, she was our only daughter. We spoiled her. We let her have her way. To our sons, Krishna and Rama, she was the big sister. She was very good to them because they let her boss over them. She still bosses over them."

She bosses over everyone!

Ajji turned her gaze to Megha. "I worry about you, Meghamma. As soon as I saw you I started to worry about you."

"Why?"

"Chandramma is jealous of you because you are beautiful and intelligent, because people admire you. I have seen her look at you with those eyes. She even resented me for the same reason when she was young. Thank God she changed after she got married and left our home."

"Jealous of you? But you're her mother!" Megha wondered how anyone could be jealous of one's mother.

"She is capable of hating her own mother, so you be careful, my dear. When Chandramma wants something, she will get it, by whatever means. And she takes revenge on people that she feels have wronged her."

"But I haven't wronged her in any way," murmured Megha, a sense of cold alarm creeping up on her at Ajji's words.

"No, Meghamma, you have not. But Chandramma will think you have because you ran away and ruined her plans, no? And in her mind it is a reason for revenge. I want you to be very careful, Megha."

"I'll try."

"But please don't hate her. It is not her fault that she is like that. Blame me if you like. I always worry about her. Someday, she is going to destroy herself." Ajji breathed a sad sigh and blew her nose. "I hope I don't live to see that day."

Tears welled up in Megha's eyes. She looked at Ajji with new-found respect and admiration. The woman had lived through a long, endless nightmare, practically all her life. She continued to suffer from the trauma inflicted upon her years ago. And yet, she had managed to preserve her dignity and honor. She had found it in herself to love the child borne from that inauspicious union. She had done the right thing by that child. Here she was now, sharing her innermost secret with her grandson's wife, so she, Megha, could find it in her heart to forgive Amma for the many wrongs she heaped on her.

By confiding in Megha, Ajji had broken her sacred oath of never revealing her shameful secret to another living soul. Megha knew that in her own way Ajji was trying to protect both women. She quickly dried her eyes. "Now I understand why Amma is so different from her brothers, so different from you."

The old woman's smile was tremulous. "I am glad you understand, Meghamma. But that is not all of it. As Chandramma grew older, she was looked at like an outcast by the servants in the house, by the neighbors, and by the girls at school. The more they rejected her, the more malicious she became. Then, when all her classmates got married and settled down, she had no suitors. She must have felt hurt and unwanted. I prayed to God to find her a good husband."

"But she did get married," prompted Kiran.

"Yes. One day, when someone suggested Vinayak Ramnath for her, we wondered why. They explained to us that Vinayak had tuberculosis during his youth and his parents had no luck in finding him a bride. When we approached his parents about matching horoscopes for a possible marriage, they agreed at once. For us it was a miracle." She let out a long, relieved breath and glanced again at the holy picture on her table. "Because of the Lord everything has been okay for my Chandramma after that. She may not be rich like her brothers, but she has a kind husband and children now. If she can stop being so greedy and evil I believe she will be okay. My sons also have good wives and good children." She threw a fond look at Kiran. "When my husband passed away some years ago he died a contented man."

Agape at what she'd just heard from Ajji, Megha whispered, "Appaji had tuberculosis?"

"They did not tell you that? Chandramma and Vinayak kept

that a secret from your parents or what?" Ajji seemed genuinely surprised.

All Megha could do was nod. Tuberculosis! And yet, nobody had seen fit to tell her parents about it. Not that it mattered much, especially since Appaji was cured now. She loved Appaji dearly and didn't think any less of him. The fact remained that if she and Suresh had any children, they could have been susceptible to the disease. Her knowledge of TB was extremely limited, but she knew in some cases the propensity for it could be genetic and that it was highly contagious. Suresh was a thin and weak man just like his father, and so was Shanti. Could they be carriers of the disease, or even future sufferers?

Megha wondered if it was horribly selfish on her part to feel relieved that she was no longer pregnant. Pregnancy was a non-issue now anyway, since she would never again sleep with Suresh, and never go back to the Ramnaths.

All at once she felt emotionally exhausted. It was too much to digest: Amma's strange parentage; Appaji's childhood illness; Ajji's sudden desire to confide in her and Kiran about a long-held secret. Everything had come at her in one single evening. Her sympathy for Ajji was so acute that it formed a tight ball in her chest. And to think that she herself had a hard life—poor Ajji had endured much worse in some ways.

She thought about Amma's obsession with caste and class. The incident with their neighbor's appendicitis attack came to mind. Amma had called Megha a sinner because she had entered a Muslim home and come back to pollute the pure Brahmin environment in their own.

It was ironic that the devout Amma's father was not a pure-bred Brahmin but an untouchable whose job was to clean people's toilets. Well, being a *bhangi* was not the man's fault, but he was a heartless rapist who had left an innocent young woman shattered for life, and for that Megha could find no kind sentiments for him in her heart.

Sometime later, when Megha and Kiran felt Ajji had calmed down sufficiently, they decided to leave. Visiting hours were over and the nurse had knocked on the door then checked Ajji's blood pressure and pronounced it normal. Then she had given Ajji her nightly medicines. The old lady was comfortably settled amongst the pillows, a serene look on her face as they wished her goodnight. Megha touched her feet in a respectful salute. Ajji's tears had dried and the agitation from earlier was gone. She smiled at them and held their hands briefly. "Be careful, both of you. Go home and have a very good New Year, okay? God bless you."

"Hope your health improves in the coming year, Ajji." When Megha said, "Would you like me to visit you again sometime?" Ajji merely dismissed her with a casual wave.

Megha wondered if the visit had been too traumatic for the elderly woman. Somehow she felt it was odd that Ajji was so calm, unnaturally tranquil for a woman who'd had an emotional evening.

The old lady's sudden decision to confess and then her rapid transition from agitation to resigned calm left Megha puzzled. Was she on some kind of medicine that affected her mind? Exactly what kind of pills had the nurse given her? She threw Ajji one last, troubled look before pulling her *chunni* over her head and walking away with Kiran. Ajji looked like she was ready to doze off.

Chapter 27

Disturbed by fitful sleep and strange dreams, Megha tossed about on the bed. Her eyes traveled to the bedside clock frequently. She could not get Ajji and her story out of her mind. And there was the other thing: the gentle old lady had warned her more than once about Amma. *I want you to be very careful.*

There was some rationale for telling Kiran and Megha her sad tale. There had to be. Why else would she unburden herself for the first time in her life after so many decades of silence, and to someone so young and practically a stranger? The horror and tragedy of Ajji's rape continued to trouble Megha.

She had never come across anyone who'd been raped. She hadn't even heard of anyone who'd been through it, until now. In the kind of cloistered environment she'd been raised, no one talked about such things. If a rare case of rape ever occurred, it was likely to be hushed up quickly. The man responsible for it would never be punished because of the secrecy surrounding the incident. The violation of a woman's honor was a matter of shame and degradation, therefore pretending it never happened seemed to be the only way to deal with it. The sad part was that the victim was left to cope with the trauma all alone. Ajji was a classic example of how lonely the life of a rape victim was—a life of humiliation, guilt and helplessness.

Thoughts about Ajji left Megha with a tight feeling in the pit of her stomach. That ominous sensation had set in when she had bid Ajji goodbye and then it had stayed with her.

The shrill ringing of the telephone made Megha jump. The time was precisely 2:07 AM. That feeling of foreboding immediately sprang to the fore, stronger, more urgent. Through the closed door she heard Kiran's voice answer the extension in the drawing room, first sounding drowsily muffled then alert. She strained her ears to listen to the conversation. Kiran's concern was unmistakable as he spoke for a few seconds and ended the call. Then there was silence.

Something was clearly wrong.

Unable to contain herself any longer, Megha climbed out of bed, opened the bedroom door and hurried to the drawing room. She found one of the floor lamps turned on and Kiran sitting on the sofa, his arms hanging loosely on his pajama-clad knees, staring at the floor. "Kiran, what's wrong?"

Kiran appeared dazed. He glanced up when he saw her. "I can't believe this."

"What is it?"

"Ajji's gone, Megha."

"What do you mean?"

"She had another heart attack and they couldn't resuscitate her. She passed away half an hour ago." The dismay on Kiran's face told Megha the news had hit him like a slap in the face. It also indicated how deeply he cared for his grandmother.

"I'm sorry, Kiran." She went to sit beside him.

"But she looked so well when we left her, better than other days when I've visited her." He scrubbed his face with one hand. "I don't understand."

"Neither do I." Though Megha had experienced an uneasy feeling for the past few hours, the news still came as a shock. Ajji had seemed to be in reasonably good spirits for a woman in her condition. Had that emotional confession been too much for her fragile constitution? Had she intuitively known the end was near? Was that the reason she had bared her soul to Megha and Kiran? She had a resigned look on her face when she had wished them goodnight. Hopefully that meant her soul was at peace.

"Do you think telling us her secrets was too exhausting for

her?" Kiran asked Megha, echoing her thoughts. "I should have stopped her, Megha. I shouldn't have let her go on and on, reliving that nightmare from more than half a century ago."

Kiran looked so miserable that Megha gently touched his hand, hoping to offer some comfort. "If anyone is to blame, it's me, Kiran. It was my visit that started all that confession business, remember? Besides, I think she needed to tell her story to someone, get it off her chest. She seemed to be at peace with herself afterward. If you recall, she was no longer agitated when we left her."

"I thought that was because of the medicines the nurse gave her."

"At first I assumed that, too, but the more I thought about it the more it seemed like a sense of relief from having rid herself of a burden she had been carrying around for most of her life. Look at it from her point of view. She had a full life; she was tired of living in pain; and she was ready to give up. She probably wanted to confess to someone she trusted before she passed on." When he still looked glum, she squeezed his hand. "We all have to die sometime, Kiran."

He seemed to ponder that for a long time before he said, "I guess you're right. It was her time to go." With a deep sigh Kiran rose from the sofa and headed for the bedroom. "I better get ready for the funeral. They're transporting her body to my parents' house right now."

"Kiran," Megha called out.

He turned around. "Yes?"

"I'm so sorry. I know you loved her very much."

He gave her a long, thoughtful look. "I'm glad you were with me when I visited Ajji for the last time. I always wanted her to get to know you better." He shook his head. "I just wish you and she had a chance to meet a few more times. She was an educated woman and liked reading, and for her age she spoke good English and had a nice sense of humor. You two would have found a lot to talk about."

Megha smiled, remembering Ajji's words. "I was impressed

by her. Do you think she guessed . . . you know . . . about the two of us?"

He shrugged. "I'm quite sure she knew how I felt about you all along. She is . . . was a very perceptive and intelligent woman."

Megha watched him disappear into the bedroom then removed his sheets from the sofa, folded them and set them aside along with the pillows. She pressed her fingers to her eyes, feeling the first ripple of grief. But her heartache was more an extension of Kiran's emotions. She hadn't known Ajji long enough or well enough to feel deep sorrow. Tears pricked her eyelids, but she kept them under control so Kiran wouldn't see them. He'd have more than his share of weeping women at his parents' house.

Naturally, Kiran had to go to the funeral alone. A few minutes later, dressed in sober gray slacks and a white shirt suitable for a funeral, Kiran left with a promise to call Megha later.

But his call never came. And she understood why. The viewing was likely to last many hours since the Rao family had scores of friends, customers, acquaintances and contacts. As soon as the news spread through town, people were likely to show up in large numbers to pay their respects. Kiran would have to play his part in accepting condolences on behalf of the family and taking care of the visitors. Distant family members would arrive from out of town and they would need some attention as well.

One good thing was that Hindu customs didn't allow the body to be preserved for several days, drawing out the funeral process endlessly. The cremation was conducted as quickly as possible after an individual's demise, bringing with it closure. No matter what, Kiran was likely to be occupied for the next several hours.

Nonetheless Megha sat by the phone and waited for his call. A feeling of helplessness had engulfed her since the sad news had come in. A much-loved member of the family had died, and she could do nothing. As a daughter of the house she would have liked to be involved in helping with the funeral, grieving with the family, but she could do none of those things. She was no longer one of them.

It only served to magnify the sense of wrongness of her presence in Kiran's house, the sense of alienation. The only consolation was that she and Kiran had helped somewhat in diminishing Ajji's guilt and easing the painful burden she'd carried all of her adult life. Ajji had lived a long life, albeit a life tainted in a lot of ways. As Kiran and she had agreed earlier, it was Ajji's time to go—a quick and relatively painless death. The only regret was that she had died alone in a cold nursing home instead of in her own house, surrounded by family.

When the sun came up and the phone still remained silent, Megha quietly rose and took a shower. She hoped Kiran, amidst all the chaos, had remembered to call his office and explain his absence. While she made herself a cup of coffee, she wondered if he'd had a chance to have a cup of anything yet. Then she started cooking. With so much going on, Kiran was likely to neglect his stomach and would probably come home exhausted and hungry. She could at least feed him a decent meal and make sure he got some rest.

Late that evening, just after sunset, Kiran returned, looking predictably spent. "It's finally over, Megha," he said and headed straight for the shower. Bathing immediately after a funeral was a must.

When he came out of the bathroom sometime later, shaved and scrubbed clean, dressed in shorts and T-shirt, he still looked dog-tired. His eyes were red-rimmed. Collapsing into a drawing room chair, he put his feet on the coffee table and threw his head back against the headrest.

Concern for him made Megha go to him and kneel beside his chair. "I'm sorry I couldn't go with you, Kiran. I know this is hard for you."

"At least she didn't suffer, according to the doctor," said Kiran. "Her heart just stopped. In fact, she looked like she was merely sleeping."

"I told you she was at peace. By the way, how is Amma holding up?" Curiosity got the better of Megha, despite telling herself she couldn't care less what Amma did anymore.

Kiran rolled his eyes. "Making it look like she's the only one affected by this, of course. She's quite an actress, my aunt. If I didn't know her true nature, I'd be inclined to believe her tears and emotions were real."

"Maybe they were real, Kiran. Ajji was her mother, after all."

"True. She's very affectionate when it comes to family."

"I know." Megha made a face.

Kiran touched her cheek. "Wish she'd recognized the fact that you are family, too."

"How is everyone else handling it?"

"They're all resigned to the fact that Ajji was old and ill and had to pass on. Papa is naturally very upset."

"Of course, because Ajji lived with him and your mother all these years, they were close."

"That and the fact that, as her eldest son, Papa had to perform the last rites with the priest."

Megha knew what that involved. Funeral ceremonies were rather complicated. Hindus believed that one had to have a son to perform the last rites, or one's soul would never find *moksha*—salvation. In fact, that was one of the prime reasons Hindus obsessed over producing boys. It was a good thing Ajji had two sons.

"You look worn out, Kiran. Would you like something to eat?" Megha rose to her feet. "I did some cooking so I'd have a meal ready whenever you came home." When he shook his head, she said, "A cup of tea or coffee then?"

After a long moment of what appeared to be contemplation, Kiran grasped both her hands and tugged, pulling her onto his lap. Megha went rigid, ready to slide off and scoot away. He hadn't touched her in this manner since that night. But he put his arms around her now and drew her close, positioning her firmly against his chest. "I know you don't want me to do this, Megha, but please, just stay with me."

She shifted. "How about something to eat first?"

He shook his head. "All I need is you right now."

Although the closeness sent a brief sensual flutter through her, Megha stayed within his embrace, with his face buried in her neck. His breath was warm against her skin, and it was a pleasant sensation. He smelled of soap and aftershave.

They sat in total silence, and yet she knew they were connected in the closest possible way. Despite the tight physical bond, there was nothing carnal about this. It was all about offering consolation to Kiran, and about comforting each other, she told herself. He needed her in a way no one had ever needed her. *All I need is you right now.* Only she could give him what he wanted, and it was precious little. And by God, she'd give it to him.

After several minutes, she felt his hold on her slacken, and his body begin to relax. His breathing had gradually gone from shallow to deep and even. He had fallen asleep. An almost maternal rush of emotion swept over her. She gently removed his arms from her. He stirred when she slid off his lap, but she placed a warm, soothing hand over his forehead until he fell back into a deep sleep. He needed to sleep off the exhaustion and grief.

Tiptoeing to the bedroom, she picked up a light blanket and returned to cover him. On a sudden impulse she bent down to place a soft kiss on the top of his head. His abundant hair was still damp from the shower. Then she turned off the lamp and returned to the bedroom to practice typing on the computer.

Chapter 28

Several days after Ajji's passing, Megha, dressed in her usual camouflage, carefully stepped out of Harini's house. From sheer force of habit she made a quick survey of the immediate area before starting down the footpath. A few remnants of New Year's celebrations were still on the ground: muddied pieces of streamers, bits of colored latex from popped balloons, a gaudy, neon-pink *Happy New Year* sign in a store window. It reminded her of Ajji wishing Kiran and herself happiness in the coming year. Had Ajji known then that death was near, that she wouldn't be around to usher in the new year?

Megha must have been walking for no more than two minutes when all of a sudden a large hand clamped over her mouth, effectively cutting off her startled scream. A strong arm banded her from behind, immobilizing her right arm. She found herself held against a chest that felt like a thick, solid brick wall.

Instinctively her free arm shot out, blindly trying to fight off the attacker, but all it managed to punch was air. Then that arm, too, was grabbed and pinned to her side. She tried to kick, but she was trapped between a car's fender and someone's big, tough thighs. Her body was a dead weight while her heart exploded into a frightened pounding. She was tightly restrained by a large man, a man she couldn't see.

"You make noise and you will die, okay?" whispered a gruff male voice in her ear. Numb with terror, Megha abruptly quit squirming and went still.

In the next instant she was roughly shoved into the back seat of the dark car, a big hand pushing her down, slamming her face into the seat. Then the man got in beside her and shut the door. The engine was already running. She was whisked away. With her nose squashed into the vinyl upholstery and her body hunched over at a painful angle, she couldn't even see who her captor was. He was crowded against her rear end, practically lying on top of her back in an effort to keep her silent and still.

The car was moving erratically. Megha could feel the thrust of the engine and the weaving motion required to maneuver the car at high speeds around vehicular and pedestrian traffic. The driver kept blowing the horn continuously. The brakes squealed a few times, people yelled, and she heard the driver curse under his breath. And all the while her subjugator remained firmly on her back, making it hurt like hell. Her slim body was getting crushed under his weight.

The hand across her mouth shifted, but before she could work up a scream the voice whispered again, "No making sound and no moving, or you die."

When she made a slight move to lift her head, the voice barked, "Stay!" So she stayed, motionless, her eyes shut tight. Something foul was stuffed into her mouth, then a smelly rag was placed over it and bound tightly. Next her hands were tied behind her back with rough rope. Only when satisfied that she was safely bound and gagged did the man yank her up by her braid and throw her head against the backrest.

Despite the pain associated with the brutal handling, she realized she was at least sitting upright now and his immense weight was off her back. But it was too damned shadowy in the car to see the man beside her. All she could make out from the corner of her eye was a balding head and a huge, wrestler-type body. She was too scared to turn her head and get a good look at him. He could be carrying a knife and cut up her face or stab her eyes.

Stunned, Megha stared into space. Her heart hammered a thunderous beat in her chest and her breath was all but cut off by the filthy piece of cloth covering her mouth. Despite the heat, she had broken into a cold sweat. *God, what happened?*

One minute she was scurrying down the footpath and in the next instant she was grabbed and hauled into an automobile.

Her throat burned from the gag that penetrated deep into her esophagus. Her ribs ached from being crushed with such brute force. Every time she tried to inhale, all she managed to get was foul fumes from the gag that smelled like sour sweat.

After her brain adjusted to the shock and the paralysis eased, Megha dared to turn her head and cast a cautious glance outside the fast-moving car's window. They had left the familiar streets of Palgaum and moved on to less-traveled ones. She had no idea how long she'd been sitting in the car. She was completely disoriented. Something was making her brain dull.

The car bounced over something, her stomach lurched, and a wave of nausea struck it hard. Megha closed her eyes for a moment to let the churning in her belly recede, then gingerly looked around her in the muted light of the car's dashboard. Very slowly she began to comprehend her plight.

She had just been abducted. And the terror she'd felt only weeks ago came back with twice the intensity.

Telling herself to close her eyes once again and breathe, she prayed, then took a few shallow breaths. It was the only way she could think rationally. *Breathe in . . . then out . . . breathe in . . . out . . .* It was hard to draw breath with her mouth completely covered but she tried.

Surely someone on that busy street had seen her being ambushed? At least one individual would have the sense to note down the vehicle's license number and call the police? Every other middle-class person these days carried a mobile phone. Somebody had to have witnessed the crime? She desperately hoped they had.

Summoning enough courage, she ventured to steal a wary glance at her abductor. A huge, bald man sat beside her. He reeked of perspiration. From the looks of the car's interior and the meter obvious on the dashboard, they were in a taxi. Her only view of the driver was the back of his head, a rather small head with longish, curly black hair. The rearview mirror was at an angle, so she couldn't see his face.

Who were these men and what did they want with her? She had heard of big-city thugs that abducted young and pretty women and sold them into prostitution. But here in the rural town of Palgaum? And if they were professional kidnappers and pimps, where were they taking her? She had heard sickening stories of young girls sold as slaves to Middle Eastern sheikhs, who then whisked the girls off to their harems and did hideous things to them.

She stole another peek at the fat man. Was he in the flesh trade? What did men in the flesh trade look like anyway? Was she headed for some secret airport where she'd be put on a plane destined for some remote city somewhere on the globe?

Oh God! This couldn't be happening to her!

Panic welled up like hot lava inside her and she wanted to struggle and scream for help. But no sound could emerge from her gagged and bruised throat. Her hands were bound solid and the most she could do was stare helplessly at the man. He returned her stare, silently telling her it was futile to struggle. She was at his mercy. When she looked meaningfully at her feet resting on the floorboard, he shook his head, essentially warning her, "*Don't even dream about trying to kick me, you idiot. You'll die if you try.*" Her sense of panic shot up by several degrees. This was no joyride. These men were serious.

The bald man went back to carefully observing the passing street scene, his watchful eyes moving back and forth. He seemed taut as a rubber band about to snap. Maybe all that sweat on him was from nervousness. His dark shirt looked damp and clung to him like a wet rag. It was the only positive sign: he was scared and tense about something.

Turning his head every few seconds to look behind them through the windshield, the man blew out short breaths. Was he checking for police or was he waiting for more of his accomplices? From his anxious frown she could only conclude it was the police he was concerned about. She wished there were police around. Maybe she could do something to get their attention. But what? She was bound and gagged. The stink going up her nose and mouth was only getting more potent and sickening. Soon it would nauseate her so much that she was likely to choke on her own vomit and die.

Hopelessly she slumped in her seat once again, the tears beginning to cloud her eyes. How in heaven's name was she going to get out of this?

The driver inclined his head slightly to address the bald man. "*Kidhar, saheb*?" Where, sir?

The bald man's voice was low and urgent. "She said to take her directly to the burning ground."

She? Who was the man referring to? Who had ordered him to take her against her will? And burning ground? That's where they cremated dead people!

In a flash the truth came to Megha. Amma!

With a sinking heart she realized Amma had won after all. Amma had hired these men to abduct her and burn her to death. What Amma couldn't do on her own she would now accomplish through hired killers. Could the woman have gone to such bizarre lengths to get what she wanted? And how in God's name had Amma known where and when to find her? How had the old witch managed to orchestrate a perfect abduction?

The taxi was moving faster now, and the chance of rescue grew more remote with every kilometer they covered. There was practically no traffic here. It was pitch dark outside except for the pools of light created by the taxi's headlights, but the smell of hay and cattle instead of the familiar street odors told Megha they were on the highway, far from town. She had never been to the burning grounds. Hindu women never went to the cremation site; only men were allowed there. She had no idea how far it was.

Stark alarm made her sit up. She was alone with two killers and she was headed straight for her funeral pyre. Was this what a sheep headed for the slaughterhouse felt like?

A few moments later resignation began to set in. She was as good as dead. Why in heaven's name had she made the stupid mistake of setting foot outside Kiran's flat? Today was Thursday and Thursdays were supposed to be special. Megha got to visit Harini one evening a week when Harini's father-in-law attended a religious meeting and her husband worked the second shift. Her brother-in-law never came home before eight o'clock on any evening.

The two young women had met on the sly the last two Thursdays and today was the third. After obsessing for days over the safety of meeting clandestinely with her friend under the cover of darkness, Megha had finally come to the conclusion that she couldn't live like a recluse forever. Kiran was delightful company in the evenings, but his nearness was more of a threat than a comfort. Besides, Megha needed a friend to talk to, a female friend, someone who would sympathize and advise and provide solace. And Kiran had encouraged the visits, too.

In retrospect, it had been a grave mistake to venture out of the house, especially when her sixth sense had been prickling. She had sensed that she was being watched every time she'd stepped out of the flat. It was stupid to assume Amma might have given up on her and that the danger was behind her. She should have recognized that Amma was nothing short of tenacious, despite the fact that she was supposedly still in mourning for Ajji. Like a rabid dog, Amma went after what she wanted with a ferocity that bordered on pathological. God, why hadn't she listened to Ajji's advice? Hadn't Ajji cautioned her emphatically about Amma's viciousness, her capacity for revenge? Why had Megha not anticipated this sort of thing?

But it was too late to rue the fact now. The stench of perspiration jerked her back to the present reality. With a pang she remembered Kiran would be waiting for her on the street corner. In the trauma of being abducted, she had forgotten that he was expecting to pick her up at the designated place. Immediately the fear mounted once again. Kiran! Oh Lord, where was he? Was he patiently waiting for her in his usual spot or had he started to look for her? What would he do once he realized she wasn't coming back from Harini's house?

Her only hope now was that Kiran would recognize foul play

and do something. Deep in her heart she knew Kiran would do everything in his power to locate her. But could he find her in time to rescue her? Would he even dream of looking for her in the funeral yard of all places? Not likely.

Gradually the taxi slowed down and made a sharp right turn onto an unpaved surface. The vehicle bounced around on the uneven surface for a while. The fat man barked out instructions to the driver as to which direction to take. Then the taxi came to a slow stop, but the engine stayed on.

A fresh surge of fear spiked through Megha's brain. They had reached their destination!

The driver turned to ask the fat man if he should wait, to which the man nodded yes. "Wait here and make sure she stays! And you keep the headlights on," he ordered. Then he opened the door on his side and got out, leaving Megha alone with the driver. With her breath coming in short, frantic puffs, she turned her head around to the back, and saw the man open the trunk, pull out a metal can and walk around to the front of the taxi. He stopped next to something that looked like a stack of wood.

A muffled moan escaped her, making the driver turn around and glance at her. He had a thin face, a hooked nose and a mustache, and eyes she could barely see. She struggled and whimpered some more. He continued to stare at her, but said nothing. He had installed a small picture of the goddess Lakshmi on his dashboard. He was obviously a Hindu and believed in God. How could a devout man take part in killing an innocent woman?

She said a silent prayer to that picture of Lakshmi. What was it her mother had said—that in the long run prayer was always good? If nothing else, she could at least ask for forgiveness before she died, ask the goddess to give Kiran the very best in life.

Meanwhile, in the golden pools of light cast by the taxi's headlights, she watched the bald man stack the wood to construct a platform of sorts. Her funeral pyre!

The hopelessness of her situation struck Megha. She was going to die a gruesome death. Here on this dark and lonely cremation ground she was going to die, all alone and totally helpless to save herself. Despite having escaped from a similar fate earlier, the gods had destined for her to die just such a death. Tears of frustration formed in her eyes again and began to roll down. Sobs formed in her chest, but all that came out were pitiful muffled sounds because of the gag.

Although her legs were unbound, how far could she run in the dark with her hands tied behind her back? She didn't know her way around here, in any case. And the taxi would overtake her in a second.

She wasn't sure whether it was the sobbing or something else that drew a response from the driver. Maybe it was her heartfelt prayer to Lakshmi. His expression changed—even in the semi-darkness she could see that. She thought she saw something like guilt flash through his eyes in the dull light coming from the dashboard. Or was it pity? She couldn't say, but there was something in his look that told her he was getting uncomfortable with the situation. His mouth opened once and then closed immediately.

She continued to hold his stare, hoping that she could convey to him her desperate plea for help. She'd take his pity or whatever it was that could move this man to help her. The wooden platform for the pyre was steadily building up.

Dear God, she was going to die! Five minutes from now? Ten?

She tried to send the driver a frantic, pleading look. *Do something. Please! Drive away. Take me far from here. Please . . .* Perhaps it worked, or maybe it was the man's conscience that wouldn't let him stay still. He sent a guarded look at the bald man, who was now positioning the last of the logs on the platform. The uppermost layer toppled and Megha saw the fat man curse and bend down to retrieve the logs. Although she couldn't hear him, she knew he'd muttered something foul under his breath. All of a sudden the driver whipped out a mobile phone from his pocket and dialed a number, his bony fingers shaking.

Megha's eyes bounced between him and the fat man. Who was the driver calling? Was it the police or Amma? Was he calling for help or to report that things were progressing as planned? Then she heard him say, "Hello, police station?"

Haltingly the taxi driver told the police his location and what was happening in Hindi, all the while casting anxious looks at the other man, who continued to work steadily. Because the old, clunky engine was still running and making a racket, the fat man had probably not been able to hear the driver's whispered conversation with the police.

Once or twice the fat man turned and looked directly at the vehicle, giving Megha another panic attack. The driver looked terrified, too. He had barely shoved the phone back into his pocket when the fat man returned. Megha noticed the look of dread on the driver's face, the perspiration on his dark nose and forehead. He had made that phone call just in the nick of time. Or had he?

The wooden platform was ready. The fat man opened the door on Megha's side and grabbed her arm. He reeked of gasoline. It could only mean one thing. He had poured the liquid over the platform and had come to drag her out. She went limp in an effort to resist him. Dead weights were supposedly harder to move. He tugged on her arm, but she fought him, desperately kicking him in the chest and thighs. He groaned in pain when her foot connected with his groin, but recovered in the next instant and turned more vicious. In retaliation for her aggressiveness, he grabbed her hair and yanked it till the pain burned in her head. Meanwhile the wrenching on her arm was putting pressure on the rope binding her wrists, cutting in deeper.

Even as she fought, Megha's eyes flew to the driver. One last plea! The man obviously had a conscience, or he wouldn't have called the police. Would he help her any further or was he afraid for his own life? Would he just sit there and expect the police to rescue her? But the police were in town and this was miles away outside the town limits. Would they ever make it here? Even if they did, she would be burned to cinders by then.

All at once the taxi lurched forward, the rear door still open. With the vehicle's abrupt motion, the fat man's head knocked against the side of the cab with a dull thud. He cursed, losing his hold on Megha's hair, but refused to let go of her arm. She tried to pull away from him so she could slide over to the other side of the seat, but he had a firm grip on her arm. The taxi gained speed, going over what seemed like bumps and holes in the dirt and grass of the cemetery.

The vehicle continued to drag the fat man alongside it, his thick fingers fastened on her arm. Megha pressed her back into the backrest and pushed her feet against the front seat to gain leverage in her efforts to fight the pull on her arm. She had to somehow lose the fat man, even if she died trying. Gathering every ounce of her strength, she managed to draw up one leg and kicked him in the ribs.

The recoil motion combined with the taxi fishtailing at that moment sent her sliding over the vinyl seat straight to the other end. The right side of her head and face slammed into the window. She saw stars for a moment. Her head seemed to explode and her arm felt like it had come out of its socket. It was torture. Through her own excruciating pain she clearly heard the fat man's cry of agony. She must have hit him in a sensitive spot, but she hadn't managed to shake him off—yet. He now had a hold on her foot. Persistent bastard!

She watched in horror as the taxi speeded up some more, bouncing forward unsteadily in the dark. The fat man must have stumbled on something, or lost his footing, because abruptly he let go of her ankle, and then fell away from the vehicle. She heard a thump as he struck the rear fender before falling off.

The open door hung loose, its hinges squeaking and grinding. Was the fat man dead? She didn't really give a damn. He was no longer in sight, no longer chained to her ankle, and that was all that mattered. And she didn't care what direction the taxi continued to go in, as long as it was away from the cremation ground. She was still alive and wanted to stay that way. The same partial sense of reprieve she'd felt when running for her life the first time some weeks ago came to mind.

And the pain . . . oh God, the pain was roaring through every inch of her body. She knew for sure that her arm was either broken or dislocated. She started to feel faint but fought to keep her eyes open. She couldn't afford to lose consciousness now. What if she woke up and found she was still under the fat man's control? What if she woke up to feel flames licking at her?

The ride seemed to last forever, with the driver hunched over the steering wheel, presumably trying to peer in the dark, looking for the main road. Megha prayed some more.

As if in answer to her prayers, headlights appeared in the distance, dozens of them with golden halos around each. Such bright light! She'd never seen anything like it. Had that knock on her head killed her by any chance? Had she died and gone to *swarg*? Heaven?

She hadn't even had a chance to thank Kiran properly for all he'd done for her. If she'd known she was going to die, she would have told him how she felt about him. He had a right to know that his feelings were reciprocated. She would have made love with him again, experience the sublime beauty of it . . . one more time. She would have admitted to him that she, too, would have liked to have a child. His child.

And she was too damn young to die! She couldn't be dead. Perhaps her brain was badly injured and she was merely hallucinating?

Everything after that appeared to go so fast it became a blur. She was vaguely aware of the taxi moving onto steadier ground, slowing down and finally coming to a stop. All at once they were surrounded by vehicles. Uniformed men came at them from everywhere. She heard a jumble of voices, speaking in Hindi, in English, in Marathi, cars honking. Her vision was blurred. Was she going blind, too? She desperately tried to keep her eyes open.

Someone came to the open door, slid into the seat beside her and exclaimed, "She is here! She is alive!"

In an instant the other door opened and two men were untying her hands and removing the gag. Blood pounded in her head. And it hurt . . . horribly. She screamed in pain when one of the men touched her shoulder.

"Does your shoulder hurt?" he asked her gently. She nodded. *Yes, damn it! I'm dying from pain.* She heard him say to the other man. "She may have a fractured arm or shoulder, no?"

"Looks like some respiratory damage with her breathing cut off," said the other man.

Despite hearing their murmured conversation, she remained silent, mutely staring at the back of the driver's seat, shivering. Oh God, it was so cold.

"Breathe!" one of the men said. "Try to breathe deeply." She tried to do as he asked, but she couldn't. There was no strength left and the shivering had become more intense. She was freezing. Then, more briskly, the same voice commanded "Breathe!" while he thumped her gently on the back.

"I—I . . . can't . . ." she whispered. She just couldn't. She wanted to close her eyes and die.

"Please try, come on!" the man urged. "You need oxygen in your lungs."

It was hard to concentrate, but she focused every bit of energy on breathing and managed to swallow some air. Her chest felt like it was on fire—the pain was that intense. The smell of sweat remained in her throat. She still couldn't see very well—everything and everyone around her appeared hazy, as if they existed in a dream. And she couldn't stop shaking. A pair of strong arms hoisted her out of the taxi, once again making her cry in pain. She was in agony.

"Let us get her out of here." Someone yelled, "Get a blanket or something—she is in shock."

Then she saw Kiran, or rather someone who appeared to be Kiran, standing among a number of men looking like a row of tin soldiers all exactly alike. They were so out of focus she wasn't sure if this was not just another hallucination. Was it really Kiran?

"Megha!" Kiran stepped forward, his arms held open to receive her. It was he! It was his voice calling her name. He had been looking for her after all. She knew he'd come for her. Her guardian angel! She promptly passed out.

Chapter 29

When Megha opened her eyes, she found herself in the familiar bed in Kiran's bedroom. Gingerly she reached out to touch the pillows, the sheets, her face and arms, to make sure this was not a dream. She was alive. Alive and reasonably well. Her muscles felt sore, especially her right shoulder and arm, and there were ugly cuts and bruises on her wrists. That was only four days ago, or was it five?

She looked at the bedside clock and grimaced. It was mid-afternoon and she was still in bed!

No, this wasn't a dream. And what happened to her some days ago was not merely a nightmare either. It was as real as the sounds of vehicles and people outside that open window, as real as the nagging ache on the side of her head. She put a hand up to her temple. Sure enough, there was a lump, still painful when touched. But she wasn't seeing hazy images anymore. The digital clock's readout was clear and sharp. Everything else in the room showed a single, crisp image.

She had lived through another harrowing experience. That added up to three: two serious ones engineered by Amma and one minor episode involving a drunkard in a dark alley—and all within the span of a few short weeks. Would there be another? Yes. Knowing Amma and her demented doggedness, she would keep on trying. And if it happened again, Megha's chances of coming out of it alive were next to zero. Amma wasn't that big a fool. She'd failed twice and learned from her failures. Plus, even *Yama*, the god of death mentioned by the astrologer, couldn't be that generous after so many attempts.

Outside the room she heard the click-click of Kiran's computer keys—a monotonous, comforting sound. He was nearby. He had come for her, to bring her home. When she'd been pulled out of the taxi and seen him, or rather the blurry image of him, it was as if she'd glimpsed heaven. All she wanted to do was hold on to him and forget everything else. She'd done exactly that and then fainted like a weak fool.

She had woken up in a small private hospital that belonged to one of Kiran's friends, where she'd been treated for concussion and shock in addition to a dislocated shoulder. She recalled screaming in pain when her shoulder was manipulated back into the socket. She clearly remembered Kiran staying by her side, talking to her. He had assured her that her presence at the hospital was a secret. His doctor friend would be very discreet. The next evening, when her vision had cleared up, the shivering had stopped, and her headache and shoulder pain had eased a little, he had carried her to his car and brought her back to the flat under cover of darkness.

She'd been sleeping a lot since then, although Kiran had tried to keep her awake with strong tea and coffee, and pills of some kind. "You need to keep your eyes open . . . you had a concussion . . . come on, open your eyes . . . try to sit up . . . look at me, Megha. You must stay awake . . . do it for me, sweetheart. Do it for me." She could hear his words, especially the endearments, and remembered obeying them as much as she could, but it had been a tough battle.

To her embarrassment, he had helped her to the bathroom several times. The poor man had gone to ridiculous lengths for her.

As she slipped in and out of consciousness, her memories of the last few days were vague and wispy, like clouds. One thing she was sure of—she had talked to Kiran about her past. Although she had kept a lot of it to herself while she had lived in his flat, somehow during her recuperation she had felt the need to confess. Maybe it was the combined effects of the concussion and medicines, or perhaps she believed she was going to die and, just as Ajji had felt the need to confess before dying, Megha had experienced the same desperate need to tell someone. And who better than Kiran, her friend and confidant?

She remembered telling him about her life with the Ramnaths, the nasty barbs from Amma, getting reprimanded for the most ridiculous mistakes, the way Suresh ignored her most of the time and then how, at nights, in the darkness of their bedroom, he would grab her body as if she were a whore. There was no love, no tenderness, not even a kind look or word—just a minor bruise or two around her hips where his thin fingers had gripped her. He would take what he wanted, roll over and start to snore.

She recalled Kiran's soothing touch, his voice telling her everything was all right now—she never had to go back to Amma's house, never had to put up with Suresh's callousness. Kiran promised he would take care of her; he would never treat her like Suresh did; he loved her.

Now recalling the extent of her confession, she put her hands over her eyes. Oh God! She had gone on and on. Her story had been told in bits and pieces, whenever Kiran had fed her caffeine and asked her to talk, to stay awake, and keep her eyes open.

How had all that nonsense about her intimate life with Suresh come into the conversation? How stupid was that, telling Kiran what had occurred in her marriage bed? And exactly what had Kiran thought about her babbling? He must have been embarrassed to death, hearing the shameful details of her life. He had probably wondered what in heaven's name had compelled him to take her to *his* bed. Ugh! This was beyond embarrassing. She'd never be able to face him again!

Nothing seemed to make sense about what had happened after coming home from the kidnapping. Then, to add to everything, there were the nightmares, more intense than before, more real, more terrifying. Her screams still echoed in her brain. Each of her experiences had been worse than the one before.

Now they were all turning into one giant nightmare—dark and deadly.

The bedroom door opened slightly, making her jump. Kiran's

face appeared in the door. "Sorry, didn't mean to scare you, but I thought I heard you stirring," he said softly. Probably seeing she was wide awake, he stepped in. "How are you feeling?"

"Very sore, but otherwise okay." Megha offered him a smile to prove it. Even smiling seemed to hurt. Carefully she pulled herself up into a sitting position. The room seemed to spin for a second before it righted itself. Oh God! She took a quivering breath. She wasn't altogether okay yet. "Sorry for all the trouble I've been causing you."

"Don't worry about it."

"When you took me in I bet you never dreamt of all the problems you were taking on, did you?"

Approaching the bed, he sat on its edge. "Your problems are my problems, Megha. We're a team now, remember?"

"Being a team shouldn't include having to play nursemaid to me." The blood rushed to her face. "Or playing psychiatrist, either."

He smiled. "I don't mind."

"I'm sorry I embarrassed you and myself by telling you the nasty private details of my life, Kiran. It wasn't right. I don't know what came over me."

"I needed to know that. I'd been wondering what went on in that dark Ramnath house and how you were treated while you were married to Suresh." He patted her hand. "I'm glad you told me. Now I have a better understanding of who you are."

"You're not disgusted then?"

"No. In fact, I'm proud of how you managed to stand tall despite the humiliation you were subjected to." He gingerly touched her shoulder. "Painful?"

"Somewhat."

Tracing a gently probing finger along the bruise on her temple, he frowned. "Still very swollen and discolored. Does it hurt a lot?"

When she nodded, he said, "I promised to ring Santosh and give him a progress report. He said he'd prescribe something else for the pain if it didn't subside." He lifted her chin to face him. "Can you see me clearly?"

"Yes."

"You see only one long nose and one set of beady eyes?" he teased.

She nodded. "And only two fierce eyebrows," she said, working up a grin. She could also see the way his gray T-shirt hugged his muscles and how the light from the window put a gleam in his hair. He looked wonderful—extraordinarily dear.

His smile widened. "That means you're feeling much better. You don't know how relieved I am. I'm not a praying man, Megha, but you had me saying my prayers. I'd forgotten every Sanskrit verse I had learned in my childhood, but one came to mind. I prayed to Lord Ganesh to remove every obstruction from your path. I recalled *Vakratunda Mahakaya Suryakoti Samaprabha . . .*"

"Very impressive! At this rate, you'll turn into a *pukka,* genuine Brahmin, besides being a search-and-rescue expert," she told him, trying to keep her voice cheerful. Inside, she was anything but cheerful, but didn't want to trouble Kiran any more than she already had. He worried about her enough.

"I didn't rescue you, Megha, the police did. And there won't be any more danger from Amma. She's learned her lesson."

"But she's relentless. She'll try again. For some absurd reason she hates me. She won't rest till she's cremated me. You heard what Ajji said."

Kiran took Megha's hand and examined the bruises on the wrist. "Amma spent a couple of days in a filthy Palgaum jail. My father and uncle threatened to leave her there forever if she did anything more to hurt you or anyone else."

"Oh, she must have loved that, getting chastised by both her brothers. Her *younger* brothers."

"She should be grateful. If it weren't for Papa's connections, she'd be brought up on charges of attempted murder. The police commissioner has personally warned her about any more criminal activities. Plus, in spite of Papa's efforts to keep this quiet, her story made headlines in the local papers, embarrassing her in front of her friends and neighbors. Her picture was in the papers, too. She's afraid to show her face in public now. She won't come anywhere near you, near us."

"I'm not so sure, Kiran."

He continued to examine her wrists. "I had a serious talk with her, too."

Wide-eyed she looked to him. "You?" She'd never thought he'd go to such lengths.

"I threatened to have her and Suresh put in prison for life if they as much as looked at you again. I even let them think I have the police watching them around the clock."

"How did Amma react to that?"

"Her eyes bulged even more. I've never seen my aunt that petrified in my entire life. Between my father and me, I think we've got the monster caged." With an amused chuckle, he added, "And Suresh—he looked like he was ready to wet his pants."

Megha started to laugh, although it sent intense pain shooting up her temple and into her brain. "I would have liked to see that." She patted his hand. "Thank you, Kiran!"

"My pleasure. I rather enjoyed that."

"What exactly happened that night? How did Amma find me? I've been sleeping so much I don't really know anything other than what directly involved me."

"You know that little beggar boy on the street near Harini's house? Amma paid him to keep his eyes open in case you showed up."

"How do you know that?"

"Amma confessed to the police when asked how she knew where and when to find you."

"I see." Megha recalled something. "No wonder that boy wasn't harassing me or anyone else on the street for money lately. Amma was taking good care of him. But I didn't think he recognized me."

"He must have, especially after he saw you there the second time, entering and exiting Harini's house. He reported it to Amma and she hired some wrestler-cum-ex-convict to kidnap you."

"And then kill me."

"I told my father that he should force Amma to see a psychiatrist. Even if psychiatrists were rare in her youth, we have plenty of them now."

"You know something? I think this latest episode was more a matter of revenge than anything else. The fact that I thwarted her carefully laid-out plans by running away at the last moment was what enraged her. Just like Ajji said, I had made a fool out of Amma, so she had to teach me a lesson and kill me off."

"Good Lord, I think you're right! The woman is clearly sick. It must have something to do with the genes she inherited from that bloody bastard who molested my grandmother. I can't think of any other explanation for why Amma is a psychopath when my father and uncle are gentlemen."

"But why do I get stuck with the psychopaths of the world?" Megha groaned. "Am I some kind of magnet for such people?"

"What do you mean?" Kiran was frowning at her. "Who else?"

"The drunkard in the street the other night."

"Oh, that one. You never really told me much about him."

"I wasn't in any shape to talk about him that night, Kiran. I was sitting on the footpath, crying and feeling sorry for myself when I noticed him observing me. He had this predatory look on his face. I ran as fast as I could and then jumped over somebody's compound wall and hid there. He came looking for me. I heard him . . . and then . . ."

She remembered it well—the ice-cold terror of being pursued by a man in the dead of night.

Kiran, clearly disturbed by her experience, tightened his hold on her hand. "Did he hurt you?" When silence followed, his jaw tightened, a reflex indicative of rising internal distress, as Megha had begun to discover. Nevertheless, his voice was gentle when he said, "Tell me, Megha. I won't hold it against you. Remember what Ajji said? If an innocent woman is attacked, it's not her fault."

The memories of that night still seemed fresh to Megha, perhaps because her recent trauma had stirred up those images. Or was it because she'd been sleeping and dreaming so much and so vividly in recent days? "He probably would have attacked me, but I managed to escape."

"He didn't touch you then?" She shook her head. Kiran let out a deep breath. "Good. Let's hope you'll never have to go through anything like that, ever. Three terrifying experiences within a few weeks! You must have set some kind of record."

"This third time I thought I was definitely going to die. God, it was dreadful . . ." She began to cry softly.

Kiran slipped his arms around her. "Shhh. It's over, Megha. You fought back. You did something to make the taxi driver feel guilty and call the police. He was promised a thousand rupees. I guess he didn't think the money was worth having murder on his conscience." Kiran tucked her head under his chin and held her close. "You and I will be leaving Palgaum soon. We can put all these nightmares behind us."

Megha buried her face in his chest. "Maybe. If the night-mares don't follow me forever, that is."

"If they do then we'll find a good psychiatrist to treat you in Mumbai. We'll make sure they leave you alone."

"I wouldn't be alive if you hadn't come for me, Kiran. I don't know how you found me, but you did."

"When you didn't show up at the usual place on time, I called Harini. When she told me you had left several minutes earlier, I knew something was wrong. Then I noticed a taxi fishtailing down the street, honking away, scattering frightened pedestri-ans. I called my friend, the district superintendent of police, right away. And then I started to follow the direction the taxi had taken, but I lost it in the heavy traffic somewhere. Some twenty minutes or so later, my friend rang me to say the cab driver had called in for help."

"Took him forever to make that call," she grumbled. "I had to literally sob and beg him to help."

"I'll tell you something, Megha—it was the longest and scari-est twenty minutes of my life, waiting and not knowing what might have happened to you. After I heard from my friend, I drove like a maniac towards the cremation ground, but the police got there before I did. In any case, the taxi driver had enough sense to try and rescue you before Amma's hired killer could get you."

She pulled back to blow her nose. "Was the cab driver arrested?"

"Yes, but they let him go when he told them the whole story and I talked my friend into going easy on him. The fellow has a wife and children, and although he was slow to react, he did rescue you, didn't he?"

"Whatever happened to the evil fat man?"

"They picked him up in the cemetery, injured and bleeding. He's in the hospital with a broken leg and several other injuries. He confessed to being hired by Amma for a fee of three thousand rupees. After he recovers, he goes back to prison."

"The greedy old bat, Amma, never gives up, does she?"

"I think she's tired now."

"So how are your plans with the move to Mumbai coming along?" Megha felt guilty about forcing Kiran to move to Mumbai sooner than necessary. If it weren't for her, he would have been happy doing things at his own pace. She had turned his world upside down.

"They're going very well," Kiran replied.

"Is that what you want, Kiran? Or are you doing it for me? I want to know the truth." She searched his eyes and saw nothing but warmth and honesty.

"It's exactly what I want, Megha. In any case, the plan was for me to join Papa's business and try to expand it, and now is a good time to do it." Perhaps because he saw anxiety in her eyes, he added, "Don't worry, no one knows you're with me. I told them you left town right after you were rescued by the police."

"And they believed you?"

"They had no reason not to. They thought you wanted to get out of Palgaum and away from Amma as quickly as possible. Even before that, they thought you were hiding out somewhere on your own and that I was the only one in the family you had contacted."

Looking at her incredulous expression, Kiran laughed. "I

swear they never once guessed you were staying here. They're still scratching their heads, wondering where you were for the last few weeks. They keep asking me, but I tell them I promised you I'd never reveal your address. Only Appaji probably knew about it, and even he was guessing, I believe. He doesn't seem sure."

Letting go of Megha, Kiran headed for the door. "I'll heat up some food. You must be hungry. You've eaten practically nothing in the last few days."

"Been sleeping too much to eat or bathe," she said, sniffing at the sleeve of her nightgown then wrinkling up her nose. "I badly need a bath."

"Then go take a hot shower and I'll get lunch on the table." He hesitated. "You, uh . . . need any help with the shower?"

She flushed at his offer. "No, no, I can manage."

"After you eat we'll start packing some of your things. You have a flight to catch early next week, remember?"

"Yes," she said, watching him leave the room and close the door behind him. Soon she'd no longer be living in this flat, or sleeping in this room. She slowly got out of bed, holding on to the headboard and giving herself a minute to get over the brief wave of dizziness. She walked over to the dresser, or more like, shuffled. Every muscle in her body ached. She gasped at the image she saw in the mirror. One side of her face was entirely swollen and purple. The area around one bloodshot eye was a darker shade of purple. No wonder Kiran had looked worried.

Letting her fingers run over Kiran's hairbrush, his bottle of aftershave, and his shirt hanging over the bedpost, she absorbed them, the colors, the textures and the scent of them. Despite all the bad memories of outside the flat, the inside, especially this room, held the most precious ones.

In a few days she'd be leaving for Mumbai. A week after that, Kiran would empty out the flat and move out, too. Their lives would alter once again. Within a short span of time their individual lives had clashed, intertwined and changed completely.

She picked up a clean set of clothes and made her way to the bathroom.

Chapter 30

Megha's heartbeat did the little flip-flip—that familiar beat that spelled excitement. The late morning sun looked particularly brilliant outside her small window, its long golden fingers reaching into the trees and the thorny shrubs that skirted the property. Music played on someone's radio. It was a beautiful Sunday.

She checked herself out in the mirror. Satisfied that she looked her best, she smiled at her image. Yes, she had on lipstick; yes, she was wearing fashionable high-heeled sandals; yes, her nails were painted; and oh yes, she had sprayed herself with perfume. She closed her eyes and sniffed her wrist in delight. It smelled delightful—naughty, even a bit wicked perhaps.

She was wearing her lavender crepe sari with the vertical, white swirling design that draped attractively, enhanced her tall and slender physique. She had on a matching sleeveless blouse. Until a year ago she had shunned sleeveless blouses. She had always been taught that baring one's arms all the way to the shoulder was wanton. But now she wore sleeveless blouses proudly since they showed off her long, smooth arms—all the scars were gone, except for the burn on her wrist. She knew she looked beautiful because . . . well, because she felt beautiful.

Kiran had convinced her that she was young and pretty and vibrant, and deserved to dress up and take pride in herself. And so she did. Every moment of her transformation was delicious. He made her feel sexy and desirable.

She looked at her slim, gold-tone watch—another luxury she'd never had in the past. A plain watch with a thick, black vinyl strap was all she'd ever had.

It was nearly time for Kiran to arrive. He was always punctual, unless the traffic was unusually heavy. She had not seen him in nearly five weeks—a distressing length of time. She couldn't wait to see him. That was another sensation that had been alien to her until recently. It felt marvelous to experience the heady feeling of anticipation without the accompanying guilt.

She slipped on a simple silver chain around her neck and put on her silver hoop earrings. Everything that had been taboo to her was not so anymore. The prison wall erected around her had been demolished, one suffocating brick at a time.

But she had still not dispelled her nightmares completely. They came back to disturb her sleep now and then. Thankfully, their intensity seemed to be diminishing. She even experienced a pleasant dream or two once in a while.

The thought of Amma didn't frighten her as much either. In fact, Amma in some ways had gone from being a menace to a pitiable soul. All her life Amma had been shunned, ridiculed and alienated because of her looks. Her hostile demeanor had added to her lack of appeal. The resulting bitterness had channeled itself into the most destructive acts—self-destructive for the most part, if only Amma would take the time to stop and think. That's probably what Ajji had meant when she'd said she worried about Amma destroying herself one day.

Getting arrested and thrown in jail had hopefully put some sense into that demented head of hers. Loss of face in her social circle must have been a more bitter lesson in humility, than getting arrested.

For now, just the fact that she was away from Palgaum made Megha feel as if she had shed a particularly confining mantle. She had come a long way, learned a few valuable lessons, grown in so many ways since her escape from the Ramnaths. There were occasions when the deep resentment and need for revenge still rose to the surface, but those times were becoming less frequent. Besides, making her life an outstanding success was a fine way of avenging herself.

She was no longer the cowering, sniveling young girl the Ramnaths had taken to their home as a private slave. There would be no better revenge than standing before Amma and Suresh as a thriving career woman, and perhaps as the well-loved and indulged wife of a good-looking and wealthy man— especially the man who was their nephew and cousin. Wouldn't that be a fabulous feeling? A beautiful baby in her arms—a prod- uct of Kiran's and her love would be the ultimate triumph, if she could pull it off.

She had to remind herself that if it weren't for that horrific night, she wouldn't be here today. She would have been in the Ramnaths' kitchen even now, giving up the best years of her life, slaving away, perhaps playing mother to one or two skinny, un- healthy babies that looked just like Suresh. So in retrospect, she had plenty to be grateful for. Besides, it was easier to forgive when one was happy.

Kiran had made all that possible. He had helped her to heal by teaching her the meaning of deep and selfless caring. He was the one good, shining thing that had come out of all that misery.

Sitting at her plain desk in the small room, Megha reread the printout of the e-mail message Kiran had sent her. The women's hostel in which she now lived did not allow telephones in the in- dividual rooms and it wasn't easy to use the single public phone in the lobby. But such was life on a busy college campus. She had refused to allow Kiran to buy her a mobile phone, but she had purchased a used computer at a good price and set up an e- mail address for herself. Besides, receiving a letter was more fun. She could read it whenever she wanted to.

The most recent one was brief but sweet. *My dearest Megha: I'm sorry I can't make it this Sunday. I have to meet some out- of-town clients. I'll miss seeing you, but I know you have to study for your final exams. Only a few weeks left before you get your degree! Imagine that, the master's degree you always wanted. Looking forward to seeing you next Sunday. I have a small surprise for you. All my love, Kiran.*

Another surprise? She chuckled. Each time he drove down from Mumbai to see her, he insisted on bringing her gifts. No amount of scolding stopped him from buying more. It was a nice feeling to be remembered and missed and spoiled by someone special. Maybe someday soon she could start giving him something in return.

After re-reading the letter one more time, she folded it with care and put it in the large envelope in which she kept all his letters. She missed him so much: his sense of humor, his sage advice, his warmth. She missed his teasing, too.

Until Megha had fallen in love with Kiran, she had never imagined herself to be a passionate woman. Now she felt differently. She yearned for him. But she still couldn't bring herself to touch him intimately. Not yet. She couldn't trust herself with him. Once she touched him in that way, she'd want more. Much, much more.

She was a graduate student now at a college in the big city of Puné. Her name was Megha Shastry—her maiden name. She never ever wanted to be associated with the name Ramnath again. Being young, she looked like one of the regular students. And yet, she was far from being one of them. She kept to herself and didn't have any close friends. She was polite in her demeanor, but kept her distance from the other girls. They were all carefree and single and had parents who supported them. They looked forward to careers and marriages. A runaway wife like herself, with a shameful secret past, would never fit in with them. She was afraid they would ask her awkward personal questions, so it was best to remain aloof.

Aside from all that, she had to study harder than the others because she had been away from the college scene for some two years before joining the program. It was simpler to stay in her room and study or read or listen to her radio.

How had she ended up here? First of all, there had been the timely psychiatric counseling. Once they had arrived in Mumbai, Kiran had insisted that she see a doctor about her nightmares and her lack of appetite. After the kidnapping she had lost a lot of weight and become depressed.

She had gone to see Dr. Rege reluctantly, but in the end the gentle doctor's nudging and prodding had been of immense help. A middle-aged woman with kind eyes and a wealth of common sense, she had made Megha realize that what had occurred was a part of her life she could separate and set aside—a past that need not affect her future. She had also helped Megha recognize that blaming her parents for everything that had gone wrong was not healthy for her—holding a grudge was detrimental to personal growth. Very slowly she had begun to eat better, gain a little weight, take an interest in her surroundings, read more books and do some writing.

After the therapy had ended, Megha had done much soul-searching and come to the decision that she had to put some distance between herself and Kiran. Being within touching distance of the man she had come to love and desire, but couldn't have, had become pure torment. She would never be able to plan any kind of a future by living under his roof.

While staying in Kiran's Mumbai flat for several weeks, she had done some research on colleges and come to the conclusion that she wanted to go back to studying. She had longed to get that journalism degree for a long time. Maybe there was hope yet.

Getting a master's in journalism and then working for a magazine or newspaper was her goal. Mainly she wanted to become independent and never be at someone's mercy ever again. Not even Kiran's. She would never put herself in a vulnerable position. All her life, men had made decisions for her—first her father, then Suresh (at Amma's direction), and most recently, Kiran. She'd be the one in charge of her life henceforth. She would use Appaji's gift to pay for her education and living expenses. It would be a worthwhile investment in her future.

After reaching a decision, the thrill of adventure had bubbled up inside her. She could do some of the things she had dreamt about all her life. For that she was immensely grateful to Appaji and his rare generosity. Yes, it was rare—he was a frugal man as far as her knowledge went.

When she had mentioned her plans to Kiran he had given her a dubious look. "College, Megha? Are you sure?"

"Yes, I'm absolutely certain. I want a master's degree, Kiran. I want to be able to take care of myself. I can't depend on you forever."

"But you won't depend on me. You can work for me," he had protested. "I'll pay you a salary. You'll earn your money."

"I don't know anything about working in an office. I need to get a degree and then maybe I can still work for you after that," she had countered, hoping that concession would sound more convincing.

"How and where are you going to attend college?" he'd asked, still reluctant to accept her idea.

She realized that his concern sprang from the fact that she was naïve and inexperienced and that the threat of Amma, although diminished, was still there. Kiran was being his usual protective self, but Megha couldn't lean on him any longer, at least not in this fashion. "Appaji said I could do whatever I wanted with the money he gave me. I've calculated everything, Kiran. It will be more than enough to support me in Puné."

"Why Puné? Mumbai has some of the best colleges in the country. You can pick any one you want."

"I need to be on my own for a while, Kiran." She didn't know how to explain to him that she couldn't stay with him without the right to love him or touch him. "If I live on a small budget, I may even have a little bit left at the end. I'll stay at the women's hostel and get my degree," she had said, with an air of certainty.

"But what about us?" Kiran had asked.

"I've decided on Puné so we can still see each other as often as we wish," she'd replied. "It's within driving distance, isn't it?"

"And when did you figure out all this?" The combination of hurt and irritation in his eyes was obvious.

"I've been doing some serious thinking for quite some time, Kiran. I don't want to live with you while I'm still married to Suresh. I feel like . . . like . . . a cheap . . . a kept woman," she had confessed. The Mumbai flat had two spacious bedrooms with their own bathrooms, and they had never been intimate with each other after that one episode, but being under the same roof still felt like living together.

"Megha, I'm sorry you feel that way. My intentions were entirely honorable, I swear."

His distressed expression had deepened and stabbed at her even more fiercely than it had earlier. "Oh, Kiran, it's not your fault. You've been wonderful to me. It's just my conscience that can't accept this strange arrangement. You understand, don't you?" she'd pleaded with him.

When he'd realized that she'd already made up her mind, he had yielded to her. In fact, he had helped her download the college application forms, complete and then submit them. Then he had celebrated with her when the college had accepted her. As usual, he had offered her every kind of support he could give.

She had also picked Puné because it was a large enough city without being overwhelmingly big. And she had no family or friends there, so she could remain anonymous. She had informed her mother, again by a simple courier letter, that she was safe and healthy and that some day she would be in touch. Although Harini had a computer in her home, Megha had kept contact with her by letter, too—and no return address. Naturally everyone in Palgaum continued to ask Kiran about Megha's whereabouts. He had informed them that he'd lost touch with her. She had simply vanished from their lives.

During his last trip to Palgaum several weeks ago, Kiran had discreetly managed to find out that Harini's baby boy, Shyam, was going to be celebrating his second birthday soon. Megha wondered if he had his mother's almond-shaped eyes and his father's angular jaw. Had he inherited Harini's fierce sense of loyalty?

Megha had been at college for nearly two years and had performed exceptionally well. And now, final exams were around the corner and she was nervous. The proverbial light at the end of the tunnel was getting brighter while her nerves were getting shakier. After graduation Kiran wanted her to return to Mumbai and to him, where she could start working for his company.

But that wasn't going to happen. She had yet to inform him that though she appreciated his offer, she had other plans. She would surprise him today with her news.

How would he react to it, she wondered?

Chapter 31

Looking outside the window, Megha noticed the familiar car coming around the sharp bend in the road. Before it could come to a stop outside the building, Megha locked the door to her room, flew down the stairs and out the front door. She stood at the top of the concrete steps and watched as Kiran parked the car and stepped out from behind the wheel. He was wearing jeans, a dark blue T-shirt with some kind of logo on it, and sneakers. His short hair was a little windblown. His designer sunglasses gave him a bold, racy look. She noticed how the group of girls standing outside the hostel gawked at him.

It brought on a feeling of intense satisfaction to know that other women admired the man who was here to see *her*.

She went down the half dozen steps and approached the car with a smile. "Hi, Kiran. Did you have a nice drive?" she asked him, feeling shy all of sudden. It always hit her like this. She rushed out to meet him and then wondered if she was being too forward in making her pleasure at seeing him so obvious.

He peeled off his sunglasses and hooked them on his shirt pocket. "The traffic was manageable." He let his eyes roam over her for a long, lazy minute before flashing an approving grin.

She blushed. "It's the sari you gave me for my birthday."

"And I knew it would suit you well." He pushed his hands in his jeans pockets, as if to keep them from straying to touch her. The two of them never touched each other in public. Even in private it rarely went beyond a light touch on the hand or the arm.

The girls standing on the steps were staring at them curiously. They had been busy chatting until they'd noticed Kiran stepping out of his car and Megha sailing out to meet him. Then the twittering had come to an abrupt halt and everything had gone quiet. It happened every time Kiran came by to visit.

"I believe the girls are admiring you, Kiran," she said and inclined her head towards the group of women.

He laughed—the easy laugh of a man accustomed to attention from females. "It's just curiosity about who I am. I bet they think I'm your boyfriend," he said, with a wink. Opening the car door, he ushered her in. "Come on, get in before they can speculate any more about us."

She settled herself in the passenger seat. "We'll let them speculate then, won't we?"

Kiran got behind the wheel and grinned at her. "That's the spirit."

They went into town for a leisurely lunch at a restaurant popular with students. It was crowded, but they managed to find a table after a short wait. They ordered the restaurant's famous veggie-cheese sandwiches—fat slices of toasted bread slathered with butter and topped with sliced cheese, tomato, cucumber, and hot-and-sweet chili chutney.

As they ate their thick, rich sandwiches, he produced an ancient pen from his pocket. "Your surprise."

Her eyebrows flew up. "My surprise . . . a pen?" She had become used to insanely extravagant presents. She was more than a little surprised to see a weary-looking pen.

"Not just any pen. It's my lucky pen. I've had it all through my high school and college days. I even had it with me in graduate school in New York. As long as I used it for my exams, I got outstanding marks."

She stared at the pen for a few moments. Then her mouth curved. "Are you saying I should use it during my exams?"

He made a big production of rolling his eyes in long-suffering exasperation. "Why else would I give it to you? You have final exams coming up, remember?"

"How could I forget? It's just that this lucky thing is so unexpected. You believe in *abshakhun* and all that? I didn't think you were the superstitious type." She twirled the pen and looked at him with a mildly challenging look. "Are you . . . really?"

"I'm the most superstitious man you'd ever want to meet. I make wishes upon shooting stars; and as a good Brahmin boy I refuse to cut my nails and hair after the sun goes down. And, this last one is significant—I never look at a woman if she doesn't at least measure up to an eight point five on my scale of one to ten." He stared at her with a deadpan face, his arms folded and resting on the table as he leaned forward to meet her mock challenge.

"I see." She suppressed the desire to giggle.

"And in case you're wondering, Miss Shastry, your score on the scale is a perfect ten," he added with a disarming smile.

The giggle erupted. "Thank you, Mr. Rao. I'm flattered. What about the girl at the cosmetics counter in Dharwar? How did she measure up?"

"Who?" He looked genuinely perplexed.

"How soon we forget! The girl you flirted with for a good ten minutes—the one who sold you the lipsticks and nail polish."

"Oh . . . oh, that one. She was barely a four on the scale. I don't even remember her."

"Typical male. That poor woman was ready to fall at your feet, too," Megha said with a shake of her head. She slipped the pen into her purse. "Thanks, Kiran. I'll return it after my exams are over." Then she sent him a sly smile. "I have a surprise for you, too."

"I love surprises." He put an eager hand on the table.

"It's not a gift. I can't afford gifts yet. It's another kind of surprise."

"What is it?" When she continued to smile, he said. "Come on, the suspense is killing me."

She pulled out a letter from her purse and handed it to him. "Tell me what you think."

He read the letter and let out an excited whoop. "You'll be writing for *The Daily Herald!* This is better than any gift. A whole series of articles, no less!"

"I couldn't believe it either. I still have to pinch myself to make sure I'm not dreaming. The series is titled *Greed and Misdeed—Abuse and Death Stalking India's Dowry Brides.*"

"Catchy title."

"I called it *Greed and Misdeed,* but the editor wanted the more dramatic add-on."

"It certainly grabs the reader's attention. If they put it in bold headlines, they could sell a whole lot of newspapers." Kiran narrowed his eyes at her, a troubled look replacing the euphoric one. "You sure you want to get into that sensitive subject? You're just beginning to put that behind you."

"It's something I want to do—have to do, Kiran. Literally thousands of helpless females suffer horrific deaths and un-imaginable abuse because of dowry. The media calls them Dowry Brides and Dowry Victims. People talk about them and recoil in horror, but nobody does a thing to try and stop them. The legal system is equally hopeless in bringing the hideous practice to a halt."

Kiran folded the letter and set it on the table. "You're sure it won't be too disturbing for you?"

"I'm positive. In fact, it might be good for me, therapeutic in some ways."

"I wish you all the luck then. I'm sure you'll do very well. I always knew you could do it. You're so damned bright." He laid a hand on hers across the table. "I'm proud of you, Megha."

His hand felt warm and reassuring. "Your approval means a lot to me." She was proud of herself, too, come to think of it. *The Daily Herald* was a small but reputable newspaper with a loyal readership, and the editor had offered her a contract after seeing several samples of her writing. Of course, he'd made it clear that editing on their part to suit the layout and audience was inevitable, and they'd pay her the minimum rate based on her complete lack of experience. But it was a start, an exciting first step towards the career in journalism she'd dreamed about for years.

"When does the first article come out?" Kiran asked, sipping his iced coffee.

"In three weeks. It wasn't supposed to come out for at least two months, but the latest news headlines gave me an unexpected advantage."

"What news headlines?"

"Kiran, don't tell me you haven't heard the biggest and most sensational story of the decade!"

"Am I missing something here?" Kiran pushed aside his glass, looking mystified.

"The bride who had the groom and his family arrested and jailed for demanding a dowry, and then sued them for the pain and emotional trauma caused to her own parents, made international headlines. The media's giddy about it. The young bride is going to be on American and European television soon. There might be a movie in the works."

"Oh, that story—I know about that. I must say she and you are two very brave women—crusaders in a way."

"She deserves the praise, not me. She had enough courage to call the police while I merely ran and hid like a frightened mouse." Megha made a face. "I'm still in hiding."

"But I'm prejudiced about you," said Kiran, making Megha feel incredibly pleased. "I hope your articles will be given a good spot in the paper."

"I doubt that, since this is my debut attempt. I'll get page ten or twelve if I'm lucky. By the way, I've decided to write under the name M. Shastry. I've chosen to remain semi-anonymous for obvious reasons."

"Wise decision. You're taking on a daring project here."

"It's time the world was told about the horrors of bride and wife abuse." She looked out the window and sighed. "I'll be happy if my insignificant articles could just initiate a debate on the topic. If I can just touch a few dozen minds, I'll feel like I've done something."

"I'm sure you'll make it happen—stir up public opinion," Kiran said. He spoke as if he had infinite faith in her.

After lunch Kiran talked Megha into going to a movie. Then they took a long walk in one of the public gardens and discussed Megha's upcoming articles some more before going to a quiet dinner. When it got dark outside and the street lights came on, Megha looked at her watch. "Kiran, it's time I got back to the hostel."

"Already?" He settled the bill and got up from the table. "You're right. I have a long drive back to Mumbai, too." They climbed in his car and headed back to the campus.

As always, Megha turned quiet and introspective when their special Sunday came to an end. Although she was the one who had put this forced distance between them, she felt bereft when he left for Mumbai after a day of being together. She fought the urge to beg him to take her with him.

He glanced at her after turning onto the street where her hostel was located. "Something bothering you?"

"It was such a relaxing day. I hate it when you have to leave," she admitted.

"I know the feeling."

"You, too?"

"Yes. I miss you, Megha. I love you." After a moment he added, "I didn't want to tell you this yet, but maybe I should. A friend's father is a high court judge and has promised to pull some strings to speed up your divorce from Suresh."

She turned to him, her eyes wide. "He has?"

"He thinks it will happen in six to eight weeks if things go smoothly."

If things go smoothly. Things rarely went smoothly for her, but something in Kiran's tone made her want to believe him. He never lied to her.

A delicious feeling of warmth and optimism began to spread through her. At last, she could be free of her shackles. She could be a young, single woman again. She could dream, laugh and do whatever she wanted, including flirting with Kiran. On an impulse she did something she'd never done before. Leaning over, she kissed him on the cheek. It was a light and brief kiss, just a brush of lips on his skin. "Thank you. I don't know what else to say."

Obviously pleased and surprised at her unexpected gesture, he in turn grasped her hand and placed a kiss in her palm. He couldn't do any more than that while driving in traffic. "No need to thank me. Just say you'll marry me as soon as you're free." Probably wondering if he'd said the wrong thing, he cast a quick, hesitant glance at her.

She smiled at him. "Let's get the divorce out of the way first, shall we?"

They drove in silence until the hostel came into view.

She touched his arm. "Kiran."

"Hmm?"

"I . . . I love you, too."

Kiran's foot seemed to trip over the brake and the car skidded to a stop before her building, scattering the gravel underneath. He turned to her slowly. "You mean that?"

"You know I do."

"You've never admitted it before."

"That's because I didn't have a right to." She looked away. "I still don't."

"You have every right to express your feelings, Megha, and I needed to hear that." He cupped her face in one hand and turned it around, forcing her to look at him. "You know I've loved you for a long, long time. I always will."

"I've loved you, too," she said quietly, "a long time." It felt strange to say it at last. Women weren't supposed to express their feelings so openly, and neither were men for that matter. But then her life had been anything but the norm. And the world had changed. Kiran was a modern man with a western-ized outlook on life. He even believed in something called Valentine's Day and he'd bought her red roses to celebrate the event. Besides, if Kiran could be so candid in expressing his feel-ings, why couldn't she? It was well worth it, too, just to see the look of joy spring into his eyes.

"Glad to finally hear that after all these years of waiting,

Miss M. Shastry," he teased. "So come here—show me you mean it." He put his hands around her face and brought his mouth down over hers. He kissed her thoroughly, making her slip her arms around his neck and cling to him.

She never wanted the kiss to end. They hadn't kissed in well over two years. There was so much hunger there, such intense need. She felt like a starving woman who hadn't eaten in months and was suddenly offered a morsel. And from the way Kiran's mouth moved over hers, she knew he was just as starved as she. She pressed as close to him as she could get over the gearshift separating them.

"Umm, I do believe you mean it," he said finally and let her go with great reluctance. The look in his eyes was one of raw desire. "God, it's hard staying away from you. You know how frustrating that is?"

Her heartbeat sounding like war drums, she nodded. "Yes, I do."

"All the more reason why we should get married as soon as possible."

She didn't want to address that topic at the moment. "There's plenty of time for that."

"Uh-uh. Life is short, Megha. And I want to give you everything you deserve and want: a comfortable home, a garden, children, books, a cat . . . whatever. I want us to be together for the rest of our lives."

"Sounds like a wonderful dream, but it's too soon to think of that."

"You know something?" His eyes narrowed on her thoughtfully. "Sometimes you scare me, sweetheart."

Megha laughed. "Why?" The endearment made her all wobbly and weak.

"Since you moved to Puné you've become increasingly independent." He caressed her cheek with his knuckles. "Not that it's a bad thing. I'm proud of you but I'm also scared of the evolving Megha, the one that's emerging from underneath that terrified one who came to my door that night more than two years ago."

"I've learned a lot of valuable lessons in living since that night," she said. "And if it weren't for your love and kindness and support I wouldn't be here today."

"That's not true. You'd have found a way to get here." He gave a wistful sigh. "Sometimes I feel like a doting parent watching a fledgling try its wings and succeed. And I start to wonder if you're going to become so self-sufficient that you'll stop needing me."

She shook her head. "That will never happen. I'll always need you in my life . . . but in a different way than I did two years ago. Needs come in different shapes, you know."

"But at least tonight you've given me hope . . . maybe even a brief glimpse of the future."

"That's another lesson I've learned lately: take it one day at a time because fate has a way of thwarting one's plans for the future. And don't forget your parents. It's going to be a tough battle convincing them about us."

"I'm prepared for it. For you, I'm willing to fight a hundred battles." He smiled and raised her hand to his lips, making her heart twist painfully. She couldn't help but gaze at him in adoration.

"If you keep looking at me like that, I'm going to have to take you to the nearest hotel," he said with a shaky laugh and tore his gaze away from hers. A second later, perhaps to get both of them back on an even keel, he changed the subject. "I'm looking forward to reading your articles. I'll probably go out and get a dozen copies of *The Daily Herald*."

"You better! I won't forgive you if you don't," she threatened him. "When will you visit me again?"

"I'd like to next weekend, but I better not. After today you're even more dangerous to be around. And I don't want to interrupt either your studies or your writing. I'll send e-mails instead," he said, before stepping out of the car and coming around to open her door.

They both stood beside the car, reluctant to say goodbye. Instead they absently observed the small group of young women sitting on the steps, carrying on a heated discussion about something while stealing glances at the two of them. Megha wondered if they'd witnessed the kiss. She doubted it since the car's windows were heavily tinted and it was dark outside.

"I'm counting on your lucky pen to perform its magic," she said finally, breaking the silence.

"It won't let you down," he promised. "Good luck in your exams."

"Thanks, Kiran. I'm going to need it. Goodnight." She turned on her heel and started walking towards the building.

Stepping into her room, Megha turned on the light and ran to look outside the window. Kiran was still out there, leaning against the car, waiting for her light to come on. It was such a gallant and endearing habit of his, making sure she got to her room safely before he took off.

She waved at him. Watching him get behind the wheel and drive away was painful—especially today. She was still shaking from the kiss a few minutes ago. Another minute more and she would have begged him to tear her clothes off and have his way with her. The expression in his eyes had told her that's exactly what he had in mind, too.

He seemed anxious to marry her, brand her as his own. It felt wonderful to know that. It was also satisfying to learn that he was somewhat unsure of himself where she was concerned. She'd never again be taken for granted. Of course, she wanted all that he'd mentioned earlier—marriage, children and a cozy home with him by her side. But when she made a commitment to Kiran, she wanted it to be on equal terms.

Besides, it wasn't a good idea to jump instantly from one marriage into another, sort of on the rebound. For a little while longer, she wanted to savor her hard-earned independence, build a career for herself, and enjoy the choices other young women seemed to take for granted. Meanwhile, she had plenty of work to do.

She watched the tail-lights on Kiran's car disappearing into the distance. "See you in three weeks," she whispered and started to change into something more comfortable before she could settle down for a long night of cramming for her exams.

A Special Chat with Shobhan Bantwal

Until I left my native India and came to live in the U.S. in 1974, I didn't realize that my simple life may actually appear interesting to others. I arrived as a young and naive bride in an arranged marriage—naive because I was raised in a strict and sheltered Hindu Brahmin family. Surprisingly though, I was a tomboy, the one hellion among five sisters. But once I got past adolescence, I mellowed and settled down, much to my anxious parents' relief.

Over the years, my American friends, neighbors and coworkers have asked me curious questions about the way I was married. I had tied the knot with a stranger and thought nothing of it. To me it was the most normal way to get hitched. My parents did some serious research, found a suitable young man from a similar caste and class, compared and matched his horoscope against mine through a couple of astrologers and then introduced us to each other. The rest is history. I'm still happily married to the same guy and very much in love with him.

When I decided to take up creative writing, rather late in life I might add, it was only natural for me to weave my stories around my Indian heritage: arranged marriage, the decadent but still prevalent practice of dowry, Hindu religion, spicy curries, colorful silk saris and exotic gold jewelry. They say you should write what you know, so I've stuck to what I know. Also, I'm proud of my rich culture and heritage and there's so much fodder in it to feed the imagination.

Was I a dowry bride myself? No. My parents didn't pay any dowry for me or my four sisters. And thank goodness for that!

With five girls to marry off, the poor dears would have been in perpetual debt after paying those fat dowries.

I'm often asked why I picked the dark subject of dowry deaths for my book. I have certain reasons: First of all, the subject has always fascinated me to no end. While growing up, I often read news items about young Indian brides burned to death or killed by other means, or simply abused because they had failed to produce the expected dowry. I was horrified by these stories, especially because I was lucky enough to be born in a community called the Saraswat Brahmin caste, a forward-thinking, educated bunch of people who don't believe in the dowry practice. I wondered what could possess otherwise normal and sane individuals among certain social groups to kill someone for money, especially an innocent young woman whose only fault was to come into this world as a female. My second reason was to enable folks outside India to get a rare peek into an element of Indian culture that's rarely written about in fiction. I needed to tell the world about it in my own fashion: a story of one young woman trapped in an arranged marriage and the dowry system and her extraordinary journey to freedom. The third is because few Indian authors write mainstream books. Most of them write literary novels that are beautiful but don't always reach large segments of the reading public. I'm talking about the readership that wants to learn about other cultures, but wants to be entertained at the same time, with stories that have romance, mystery, sadness and humor. I wanted to give those readers something to sink their teeth into. So for all those reasons, THE DOWRY BRIDE became a project that I felt compelled to write. I was probably destined to write it. I firmly believe in destiny, fate, karma, whatever its name is. And I also have tremendous faith in astrology and horoscopes.

Although the term dowry and its practice have been around for centuries, very few modern Americans and Europeans know much about it. It's the custom of paying a certain sum of cash and/or gifts to the groom by the parents of the bride. The system existed in Asia and many other parts of the world. Regency and Victorian eras were notorious for peers of the realm giving huge sums of money and real estate to marry off their daughters. But Europe abandoned the system ages ago, whereas India still has the unfortunate custom in many communities. In fact, to a large degree, it has escalated, despite laws to ban it.

THE DOWRY BRIDE started out as a short story, my class project for the one and only brief course I took in creative writing at the local community college. When I read the story in my class, my classmates were fascinated by its cultural elements. My instructor thought I had enough characters and material to make it into a book. That's all the encouragement I needed to make Megha's story a full-length manuscript. I never imagined how much I would enjoy writing this story, how much of my heart and soul I would pour into creating my protagonist and crafting her adventures.

The town of Palgaum, where my story is set, is entirely fictitious. But although a product of my imagination, many of the descriptions are based on the small southwestern town of Belgaum, where I was born and raised. As I wrote about Megha's town, its streets, its shops, its people, and Megha's home, I always had a vivid picture of my hometown firmly planted in my subconscious, all the way down to its landscape, colors, textures and scents.

Coming to my hero, Kiran, I truly wanted Megha to have a caring yet passionate man to save her from ruin, nurture her and heal her heart after what she'd been through. I needed him to be a true hero. I'm a hopeless romantic and have a tendency to fall a little bit in love with my heroes. And Kiran is no exception. I totally adore my heroes' virtues, foibles, long noses, thick eyebrows and all. They may not always be macho men, but their hearts are made of gold. To that end, they display many of my own husband's characteristics.

I've been asked why I've denigrated the practice of dowry throughout my book and yet I've decided to call my contest prizes "Dowry Bags." That's because I have a wry sense of humor and calling my raffle and contest giveaways by that name is just my idea of injecting some fun in introducing the book to my readers. Doesn't everyone like to open a mystery goody bag and find out what's in it?

Some of my friends who read the manuscript before publication were curious as to why I hadn't fleshed out Megha's sisters. Why were they not shown interacting with Megha? Honestly, I didn't think they would have added a lot to the story. I wanted them to be shadows in her background and her back story. Also, with their stable and comfortable middle-class lives, they would provide a perfect foil to Megha's own miserable marriage. Consequently, it makes Megha's life that much more interesting by contrast and that much more compelling for my readers.

Amma's character is loosely based on someone I used to know when I was a child. The woman was a bit insane and used to scare the dickens out of me whenever she visited our home. To this day I get the chills when I think of her. So when I needed a woman who could be a suitable, evil mother-in-law for Megha, I immediately visualized a person similar to that woman from my childhood. Appaji, Suresh and Shanti were just characters that popped into my fertile imagination. There is no resemblance to anyone I know.

With my second manuscript, once again I plan to use Palgaum as my background. Another interesting Indian topic that's been swirling around in my mind will be the theme of the next book. Palgaum has a tremendous attraction for me and I want to base other stories there as well. I hope you will read each and every one of them and share them with your family and friends.

Now that I've given you a small taste of my culture, my characters and their respective stories in *The Dowry Bride,* I hope you'll read my short fiction and nonfiction works as well. My web site, at www.shobhanbantwal.com, has my award-winning short stories and freelance articles, also lots of photographs from India and some of my favorite recipes.

I love to hear from my readers, so please write to me with feedback and ideas, and suggestions for future books at shobhan @shobhanbantwal.com.

Thanks for being such a wonderful audience.

Warm regards,

Shobhan